FEB 0 6   ≡

BRUSH COUNTRY

BRUSH COUNTRY

Two Texas Novels

ELMER KELTON

A Tom Doherty Associates Book
New York

BRUSH COUNTRY: TWO TEXAS NOVELS

This is an omnibus edition comprising the novels *Barbed Wire,* copyright © 1957 by Elmer Kelton; renewal copyright © 1985 by Elmer Kelton; and *Llano River,* copyright © 1966, 1991 by Elmer Kelton; renewal copyright © 1994 by Elmer Kelton.

Barbed Wire was previously published in 1957 by Ballantine Books.
Llano River was previously published in 1966 by Bantam Books.

Book design by Jane Adele Regina

A Forge Book
Published by Tom Doherty Associates, LLC
175 Fifth Avenue
New York, NY 10010

www.tor.com

Forge® is a registered trademark of Tom Doherty Associates, LLC.

Library of Congress Cataloging-in-Publication Data

Kelton, Elmer.
    [Llano River]
    Brush country : two Texas novels / Elmer Kelton.—1st ed.
       p. cm.
    "A Tom Doherty Associates book."
    Contents: Llano River—Barbed wire.
    ISBN 13: 978-0-765-31019-4
    ISBN 10: 0-765-31019-8
       1. Texas Hill Country (Tex.)—Fiction. 2. Texas—Fiction. I. Kelton, Elmer. Barbed wire. II. Title.

PS3561.E3975L58 2006

           2005053665

First Edition: February 2006

Printed in the United States of America

0 9 8 7 6 5 4 3 2 1

CONTENTS

BARBED WIRE

I

It was a sorry way for a cowboy to make a living, Doug Monahan thought disgustedly. Bending his back over a rocky posthole, he plunged the heavy iron crowbar downward, hearing its angry ring and feeling the violent jar of it bruising the stubborn rock bottom. He rubbed sweat from his forehead onto his sleeve and straightened his sore back, pausing to rest a moment and look around.

Across the broad sweep of the gray-grass valley, up the brush-dotted hill and down again on the gentle far slope, new cedar posts stood erect like a long row of silent soldiers. And stretched taut down the length of the line, four strands of red barbed wire gleamed brightly in the late-winter Texas sun.

Doug Monahan had the look of the cowboy about him, the easy, rolling gait, the slack yet somehow right way of wearing his clothes that stamped him as a man of the saddle. But he wasn't riding now, and he hadn't for quite a spell. Sweat darkened his hickory shirt under the arms and down the back, the spots rimmed with white salt and caked with dirt. The knees of his denim pants were worn through and frazzled out. His brush-scarred boots were run over at the heels from a long time of working afoot.

He gripped the crowbar with big, leather-gloved hands, lifting it and driving it down into the narrow posthole. Each strike chipped off rock and caliche. Sulfurous sparks flew angrily against his dusty boots. The rocky ground was fighting him every foot of the way.

At length he went down on his knees with a bent can to scoop dirt and chipped rock out of the hole. Wiping sweat from his stubbled face, he stood up and stretched. His gritty hands pressed against the small of his back, trying to ease the ache that was there. His gaze drifted in satisfaction back down the fenceline, where two other men also were digging postholes. Past them, a dozen cedar posts leaned at crazy angles in unfilled holes an even rod apart. Beyond these stretched the unfinished fence, stout heart-cedar posts hauled up from the river and tamped solid in holes nearly three feet deep.

And on them, the heavy No. 9 wire gleamed with its bright red coat of factory-dipped paint and its wickedly sharp barbs.

The pleasant tang of mesquite smoke drifted to him on the crisp breeze. Monahan looked down toward his chuckwagon. By the sun, which with retreating winter still stood a little to the south, it was almost noon. Paco Sanchez would have dinner ready directly.

Monahan frowned a little, watching his wagon. Gordon Finch sat there with three of his men, sipping coffee. Sat there like a lazy pot hound.

He had a right to, Monahan supposed, for after all, this was Finch's ranch. But nothing ever graveled Monahan quite so much as to have someone sitting around idly on his fat haunches and watching him work.

The easy breeze carried with it a sharp breath from the Panhandle to the north. Monahan shivered as the chill touched him. He picked up the crowbar and began chipping again. Hard muscles swelled tight within the rolled-up sleeves as the bar battered its way downward.

This was a real comedown for Monahan. Once he'd had a ranch of his own down in the South Texas brush country, and there had been a time when he might have been too proud to do this kind of work. But a long, hard drought can make a man do things he never thought he would.

Doug Monahan was young yet, with a glint of red in his hair and whiskers to go with the Irish name. He had blue eyes that could laugh easily, or could strike quick sparks, like the strong iron bar that bruised its way into the resisting earth.

Finishing the hole, measuring it by a ring he had painted thirty inches up on the bar, he walked to a small stack of cedar posts. He picked one and dropped it into the hole. He stood it straight, sighting across its axe-hewn top to hard-set posts which stretched out of view up over the hill. He glanced the other way, where stakes driven in a string-straight line marked the one-rod intervals for more postholes, as far as his eyes could see.

He watched rangy Longhorn cattle plod along in single file down a hoof-worn rut that had had its beginning with the buffalo. Headed for water, they followed an ancient trail that tomorrow would be blocked forever by these shining red strands of wire.

"Company coming yonder, Doug."

Stub Bailey was pointing to four riders who topped the hill and came down in an easy trot, following the new fence. Stub was a short, thickset happy-eyed man Doug had picked up over in Twin Wells and as good a hand as he had ever run across.

Monahan's glance touched the rifle that leaned against the pile of new-cut posts. He hesitated, then moved toward it.

"Reckon it's that trouble Finch hinted about?" Bailey frowned.

"I hope not."

"It's Finch's worry, ain't it?" Bailey asked. "That's what he come for."

Monahan grunted. His own idea was that Finch had come out to feed his men—and himself—at someone else's wagon.

He slipped off the work-stiffened gloves that were worn almost black. Shoving them into a hip pocket, he picked up the rifle and moved unhurriedly toward the wagon.

"May not be trouble atall," he said. "And I sure don't want Finch starting any."

Monahan was sure of only one thing about Gordon Finch, that he didn't like him. He wasn't even sure why. Maybe it wasn't for Monahan to ask questions or pass any judgment. After all, this wasn't his land. He had come here a stranger and contracted to build a fence for Finch—nothing more.

Finch had spotted the riders by the time Monahan reached the wagon. He stood up lazily, squinting, trying to see clearer. He kept sipping the coffee. Monahan suspected he had laced it from a bottle in his coat pocket.

"Couple of my boys," Finch said in a gravelly voice that had a perpetual belligerence about it. He had a way of always sounding angry. "Bringing somebody in."

Finch's shoulders were a little stooped, and a soft paunch was beginning to push out over his belt. He had the florid face of the man who drinks too much and doesn't work enough to stay healthy. He could talk loud and make strong promises, as he had when Monahan agreed to take the fencing job. So far, he hadn't so much as paid for wire and posts, though he knew Monahan was working on a shoestring. He hadn't even furnished grub to the fencing crew.

He had come here yesterday, telling of a rumor that there might be trouble at the fencing camp. Not everybody liked this barbed wire.

"You just go right on putting up fence," Finch had said. "We're here to protect you."

Finch's men had done some scouting around, but all Finch himself had done so far was protect the chuckwagon.

Monahan saw worry in old Paco Sanchez's black eyes. Paco dropped a hot Dutch oven lid back over browning biscuits and wiped his dark, rheumatic hands on a flour-sack apron. His troubled gaze dwelt on the approaching riders.

"Go on with the cooking, Paco," Monahan said quietly. "Stick close to the wagon."

The aging Mexican nodded and eased toward the chuckbox. His eyes, bright as black buttons, flicked from Monahan's rifle to the four riders, then back again. Paco had lived many a long year within gunshot distance of the Rio Grande. He had seen much of violence. Now he was gentled by age, old and weary and dreading.

Monahan sometimes wished he could have left Paco in South Texas, for the old man deserved an easier life than this in his declining years. But nothing had remained to leave him with. The Bar M ranch was lost, and the cattle with it.

Stub Bailey eased and shook his head. "Won't be no trouble out of them two, Doug. That's just old man Noah Wheeler."

"Who's Noah Wheeler?"

Finch growled an answer before Bailey could reply. "A grubby old nester that got hold of four good sections of land that ought to be in somebody's ranch. Raises hay and sells it to some of them two-bit cowmen. He's got chickens, ducks, even some hogs. Rest of the nesters around here went and settled along Oak Crick, but not him. He had to go out and grab ahold of good rangeland. Somebody ought to've run him back with the rest of the dirt farmers a long time ago."

Monahan glanced at Stub Bailey. Stub had been around Twin Wells long enough to know a little about most people here, and Monahan could tell that Bailey disagreed with Finch.

He could see that the old farmer was eyeing the red wire closely as he rode in. Noah Wheeler was a blocky man, solid as a rock fence. He sat his horse firmly, without the cowboy's easy, even lazy way of riding. His battered black hat fit squarely, its brim flat for shade and not for show. He wore a plain woolen coat, frayed with signs of hard work and long use. His heavy mustache, once brown, was now salted with gray.

The rider beside him was a girl. Long skirts all but covered the sidesaddle she rode. She was slender, the man's coat she wore fitting her rather like a collapsed tent. She seemed dwarfed by a wide-brimmed cowboy hat, evidently lined with paper to keep it on tight.

"Morning, Noah," Bailey said pleasantly. "How's the world serving you?"

Wheeler smiled, a pleasant, eye-crinkling smile that held nothing back. "I can't complain about the world, but I sure wish this rheumatism would leave me alone."

Finch glared at the pair. His questioning eyes cut to one of the riders who flanked the old man and the girl.

"Found 'em comin' down the fence," the rider told him. "Noah said he was just lookin' for a way through, and I don't expect he meant any harm. But you said bring anybody we found, so we brung him."

If for no better reason than the contempt he saw in Finch's face, Monahan felt an instinctive liking for the farmer. It rubbed him against the grain when Finch said, "All right, Wheeler, move along."

Firmly Monahan said, "This is my camp. I'll say who goes." He told Wheeler, "Sorry to've bothered you. We been expecting a little trouble. You-all light and rest yourselves. Paco's got chuck about ready."

Wheeler's eyes lighted, and he forced down a smile as Finch sharply turned away. He stepped down from his old high-horned saddle and stamped his heavy boots, trying to restore the circulation in his cold feet. "Thank you, friend. We got food in the saddlebags. We didn't expect to run into anybody."

"Hot meal's a sight better," Monahan replied. He moved toward the girl, hands outstretched, and lifted her down from the saddle. For just a second their eyes met. She gave him a quick smile, then shyly looked away. By her blue eyes, he took her to be Wheeler's daughter. Wheeler confirmed it.

"My name's Noah Wheeler. This is my daughter, Trudy."

Wheeler's giant hand was rough as dried leather and crushing-strong. He had spent his life at hard work.

Monahan bowed toward the girl in the old cowboy manner. She

took off her big hat. He saw a fine-featured face, almost a pretty face, and honey-colored hair done up in long braids tied at the back of her neck. Again there was that shy smile. Country girl, right enough.

By way of conversation, Monahan said, "If I'd known we were fixing to have such company, I'd've cleaned up a little. I imagine I look like a prairie dog."

The girl made no reply, only smiled again. Wheeler said, "A working man ought never to apologize for his looks." He eyed the camp curiously. "We been hunting a few head of our stock. We try to keep them at home, but there's always some of these long-legged Texas cattle coming in and leading them off."

He studied the stacks of cedar posts that had been brought in by wagon. He bent over the red spools of barbed wire. He stooped stiffly and picked up a short curl of wire that had been snipped from a spool. He fingered it as if afraid it might bite.

"Bobwire," he said wonderingly. "Heard a right smart about it, but this is the first I ever seen." He touched a thumb to one of the barbs. "Sharp. These things could really rip up an animal."

"They learn in a hurry," Monahan told him. "You can't hardly get one to hit it a second time."

Wheeler smiled indulgently. "You look like a man who'd know horses. Pretty intelligent, a horse is. But about a few things he hasn't got the sense of a jackrabbit. If there's anything in ten miles that'll hurt him, he'll find it. Especially if he's the best horse you got."

He shook his head and dropped the wire. "The stuffs all right, I guess . . . just hate to think what it'd do to a horse."

Monahan washed his face and hands in a basin of cold water. He dug coffee cups out of the chuckbox and poured them full. He handed one to the girl and felt pleasure at her half-concealed smile. She hadn't yet said a word.

He watched for and caught the pleasant surprise in the girl's blue eyes as she first tasted the coffee. Paco Sanchez had the Mexican way of boiling sugar right in with the coffee. It was sweeter that way than if you just spooned sugar into the cup and stirred it.

Monahan handed a second cup to Wheeler and poured one for himself. "Most people think that way about barbed wire, the first time they see it. I did, too. But it isn't like that. I'll admit, it might cut a few at first, but you'd be surprised how fast they learn. They're using a lot of it down in South Texas. It's the answer for the stock men, Mr. Wheeler. Especially a fellow like you, farming and running cattle both. Country's too dry to grow hedges, and it'd bust the back end out of a bank to build a wood fence around a big pasture. But barbed wire is cheap. Most anybody can afford it. A couple of the farmers over on Oak Creek are interested. Soon's I finish this job, I'm going to do a little fencing there."

Wheeler shrugged, deep in thought. "Maybe you're right, but lots of people don't like bobwire. I've heard some bad things."

Monahan frowned into his coffee. "They just don't know. Anything new like this, it takes time."

Paco Sanchez walked up with pothook in hand. He lifted the coal-covered lid off the biscuits and set it down with a clatter, leaning it against the edge of the Dutch oven. In another oven, hanging on a hook suspended from the crossbar over the fire, steaks sizzled in deep grease. Paco poked at them with a long fork. Satisfied, he took the pothook and hoisted them away from the heat.

"'Stá listo, Doug."

Doug bowed and motioned the girl toward the chuckbox. Paco Sanchez stood beaming as she filled her plate from his ovens. Paco's skin was like fine brown leather, with just a trace of a shine across his high cheekbones, at the upper edge of his coarse gray whiskers. He had come up from the ranchos south of the Rio Grande, way yonder ago, up to the South Texas brush. For more years than Paco could count, he had worked as a vaquero, a brushpopper, his tough skin seared by the sun, scarred by clawing thorns. He had worked cattle for Monahan's father, and he had helped bring up Doug Monahan, had taught him the way of the vaquero.

Now crushed bones and his many years were piling up on him. The old Mexican was finishing out his time over the cookfires. No pensioner, Paco. He wanted only to work—to stay with the Monahans. The aging chuckbox with a Bar M burned deeply into each side was all that was left to show for the ranch. And Doug was the only Monahan.

Eating, Doug found himself watching the girl. These farmer girls were taught to be wary of strangers. Especially a stranger who looked like a cowboy. She and her father ate silently and hungrily. Monahan could tell they had had a long ride. He felt a touch of pity for the girl. Pretty thing, she was, like a wild flower growing up in the middle of nowhere. A girl like this was meant to be seen.

Noah Wheeler pushed to his feet. He took his daughter's empty plate and cup and dropped them into the wreck pan along with his own. "Fine dinner," he said to Paco. "We sure did enjoy it."

"*Grácias,*" smiled Paco, warming to the compliment. "The camp is yours."

Wheeler turned to Monahan. "We'd best get along if we're going to find our cattle. No telling where those Longhorns have led them to."

He looked once again at the barbed wire fence which was edging slowly out across the range. "Going to be a big change. Always been open country. How far do you figure on going with it?"

Monahan replied, "I've contracted to build it all the way around Gordon Finch's range."

Wheeler's thick eyebrows lifted a little. "Finch's range?" He gave the rancher a sharp, questioning glance. "You got more ambition than I thought you had, Mr. Finch."

Finch's eyes flashed anger.

Wheeler walked to his horse and swung heavily into the old

saddle. Monahan gave the girl a boost up. She smiled at him, and in a quiet voice she spoke the first words he had heard from her. "Thank you, Mr. Monahan. Maybe someday we can return the favor."

He watched them ride away, his eyes mostly on the girl.

Firing up a fresh cigar, Finch muttered contemptuously, "About time they left. They got the smell of hogs about them."

Flaring, Monahan turned to answer him, then thought better of it. He hadn't been paid yet. But someday someone was going to make Finch eat that cigar, raw, and maybe with the fire still on it.

Monahan knew it was trouble, as soon as he saw the horsemen. He was using a shovel handle to tamp fresh dirt tightly while Stub Bailey held a post straight. Looking up, Bailey stiffened.

"Uh-oh. Look yonder coming."

Doug let the shovel rest against his broad shoulder. He rubbed a sleeve across his forehead and blinked at the burn of sweat that worked into his eyes.

"*That* ain't Noah Wheeler," Bailey said with tightness in his voice. He suddenly looked as if he needed a drink. "Must be thirty-forty of 'em."

Monahan squinted. Fifteen or twenty, more like it; but that was enough. The riders were moving along the fenceline. As they moved, men stepped down from their saddles, stopping to snip the wire.

"They mean business, looks like," said Bailey. "Cuttin' it between every post."

Down at the chuckwagon, Gordon Finch stood frozen, watching and not making a move. Anger sweeping him like a sudden blaze in dry grass, Monahan dropped the shovel, grabbed his rifle and sprinted down to the wagon.

"Finch," he exploded, "where's that protection? You've sat around here filling your belly and getting in the way! Now what're you going to do?"

Finch's face had paled. "My men," he rasped helplessly, pointing. "They've rounded up all my men and got them along. There ain't a thing I *can* do."

Monahan's small fencing crew gathered and stood tensely beside the wagon, where Paco Sanchez's cookfire had burned down to a few glowing coals which he was keeping alive for supper.

"You want us to fight, Doug?" asked Stub Bailey, spinning the cylinder of a six-shooter.

"Put it up," Doug said. "We don't have a chance, and there's no use getting somebody killed." He set down his rifle and stood there waiting.

II

The riders came on leisurely, knowing they had the upper hand. They didn't leave behind them a single piece of wire more than twenty feet long.

"We're in for it," Bailey muttered. "That's the old he-coon hisself in the lead yonder, ridin' the gray horse. Captain Andrew Rinehart. He don't answer to nobody, not even to God."

A chill worked down Doug Monahan's back. He knew that this was going to be nasty. But this was Finch's land. He ought to have the right to do what he wanted to with it. . . .

The horsemen crowded in close, forming a semicircle around the small fencing crew. Some of the horses fidgeted, slinging their heads. Gordon Finch held back, sliding behind the chuckbox.

The captain edged forward on his big gray, as fine a horse as a man would ever see. Captain Andrew Rinehart was a man of strong will and fierce pride. He was an aging cowman with clipped gray beard and piercing eyes that stabbed from under heavy gray brows. Despite the weight of years, his back was rigid. Not a young cowboy with him sat straighter in the saddle.

He was one of those real old patriarchs, Monahan knew, one of the kind who had whipped and carved this state into being. You still found a few like him down in South Texas. Monahan knew the breed, for his father had been one. Most of them were gone now.

Those commanding eyes searched the fencing crew, then lit on Monahan. "You're in charge here." It was a statement, rather than a question.

Monahan took a step forward. "It's my camp. I'm Doug Monahan."

Rinehart studied him intently, squinting as if to see him better. "Monahan, you're trespassing."

Monahan felt the stretch of tension within him. He had heard about Captain Rinehart. This old man controlled the R Cross, which sprawled haphazardly over a big part of Kiowa County, its boundaries ragged and loose—and uncontested. Once a Texas Ranger, and later an officer in the Confederate army, he had been the first man to move into this county and stay. He had pushed the Indians out. In the years that followed, no one had ever seriously challenged him.

Kiowa County, it said on the map. Around here they called it Rinehart County more often than not.

"Well now," Monahan said. "We have a contract from Gordon Finch to fence his ranch, so I don't see how we could be trespassing."

Rinehart's gaze searched over the men on the ground. "Where is Gordon Finch? Finch, step out here."

Finch moved hesitantly. He came out from behind the chuck-box and stood beside Monahan. His mouth opened, and in his face was a fleeting intention to speak up to this stern old cowman. Then his eyes fell, and his mouth closed.

Rinehart's voice was as hard as flint rock. "I never would've thought you had the nerve, Finch. Now you're through around here. Catch up your horse and git."

Without lifting his eyes to those of the men around him, Gordon Finch walked out to where his horse stood hitched to a stunty mesquite behind the woodpile. He swung into the saddle, shoulders sagging.

"Sell out and leave," Rinehart said to him. The old man didn't speak loudly, but his voice carried the crack of a whip. "I don't want to see you around here again."

Just like that. *Sell out and leave.* And Monahan knew Finch would do it.

Finch rode off without a glance at Monahan. His cowboys followed after him, all but one whose name Monahan remembered was Dundee. Dundee held back a moment, his eyes touching Monahan's and making a silent apology. Dundee's holster was empty. Some R Cross cowboy had gotten himself a six-shooter mighty cheap.

Rinehart's gaze cut back to Monahan. "This isn't Finch's range. It's *mine*. It always was."

Monahan clenched his rough fist. He ought to have guessed, but he hadn't. Finch had tried to run a sandy, and he hadn't had the nerve it took to go through with it.

Monahan said, "He told me it was his, and I had no reason to doubt him."

Rinehart's eyes were cold. He thought Monahan was lying. The captain glanced at a man who sat beside him on a black-legged dun. "All right, Archer!"

Men stepped down from the horses and started throwing loose cedar posts up into a pile. They heaved the red spools of wire up atop the posts. Someone took Paco Sanchez's big coaloil can and started pouring kerosene.

"Rinehart," Monahan protested, "I tell you I didn't know! Finch lied to me. Everything I've got is tied up here. Finch hasn't paid me a cent."

If Rinehart heard him, he gave no sign of it. He just sat there stiffly on the big gray horse, watching.

"Burn it," he said, looking at the rider he had called Archer.

This was a tall, angular man of about thirty-five, a stiff-backed man who might have been the captain's son, he was so much like him. He had the same aristocratic bearing, the same strong face, the same driving will. He struck a match on the sole of his boot and flipped it onto the posts near the bottom of the pile. The flames licked upward, spreading hungrily, seeking out the kerosene.

Monahan took an angry step forward, then stopped as he felt a gunbarrel poke him in the back. Rinehart's men pitched his crew's bedding and camp gear into the flames.

The one called Archer stood watching the fire, his face grimly silent. It was then that Monahan noticed the man's eyes.

They were black, compelling eyes, framed in heavy, dark brows and long black lashes, eyes that burned with a ruthlessness that seemed even greater than the captain's.

Monahan remembered then. He had heard of this man, too. Archer Spann, his name was. Foreman of the R Cross, and the captain all over again except younger. The captain had never had a son, they said, but he had found Archer Spann, and Spann was as much like him as a son could ever be.

Spann picked up the kerosene can and climbed up into the chuckwagon. He poured the rest of the contents out over the chuckbox and into the wagonbed. Paco Sanchez had held still through all that had happened. Suddenly now he broke loose as he realized that the old Bar M chuckwagon was about to be destroyed.

"No, no," he cried, "don't you burn my wagon!"

He grabbed at Spann's long legs, trying to pull him down. Spann lifted the heavy can and swung it at Paco's head. Stunned, Paco went down on hands and knees.

Spann pitched a match into the kerosene. As the flames spread, he dropped down from the wagon.

Near Paco's hands the water basin had fallen to the ground. He grabbed it, scooped up sand and threw it on the flames. Spann jerked the pan from his twisted hands. It went spinning away. One of the horses, nervous already because of the fire, broke into pitching. In a moment of wild confusion, the riders pulled one way and another, trying to stop the bucking horse.

Raging now at the destruction of his wagon, Paco found his fallen pothook.

"No, Paco!" Monahan shouted and jumped to stop him.

Spann stepped back in sudden alarm as the pothook swung at him. It missed, and Paco never had a chance to swing it again. Spann's gun came up. It roared. Paco jerked under the impact, falling against the burning wagon.

"Paco!" Monahan rushed to the old Mexican, grabbing him and dragging him back from the flames. In desperation he ripped away the cook's heavy black shirt. The old man caught a sharp, sobbing breath. For a moment he struggled to speak, but no words came. His tough old fingers closed on Monahan's hand, telling in their own way what Paco wanted to say. Then they relaxed, and the scarred, twisted hand fell away.

Monahan was on his knees, stunned, just holding Paco's body and not knowing what to do. Then, gently, he eased him down to earth and stood up, trembling in fury.

Spann was watching him, his own face taut. He held the smoking gun, its barrel leveled at Monahan.

Captain Rinehart said, "Put the gun away, Archer."

Monahan leaped at the man. He saw the gunbarrel tilt upward. He grabbed Spann's wrist, forced the gun aside as it roared again. He reached for Spann's throat.

Spann wrenched loose. There was a quick swish, and the gunbarrel struck Monahan behind the ear. He fell solidly, the ground smashing against his face. He lay there tasting sand. He pushed onto his knees, trying to clear his head and find Spann again, but the horsemen seemed to swirl around him. He was conscious of the flames, the crackling heat, the stench of smoke. But he could not see. There was sand in his eyes, and a blinding pain-flash of red.

Rinehart's riders held their nervous horses as still as they could, gripped in sudden shock by the quick explosion of violence, the death of the old Mexican. It had not been part of the plan. Rinehart's riders waited uncertainly, and Monahan waited, too, half expecting the gun to roar again.

"I said put it up," Rinehart spoke in a quiet but commanding voice.

Spann dropped the six-shooter back into its holster.

Cold reason returned to Monahan then. He blinked hard, shaking his head, trying to clear his sight. He couldn't fight them now. But he wouldn't forget. He'd bide his time and take whatever else they dealt him, for there would be another day. . . .

The bed of the blazing wagon broke. Camp goods spilled through the charring bottom. The heavy chuckbox lurched sideways, hung a moment in the balance, then slid to the ground with a crash of tin plates and cups and cutlery and a shower of hot sparks.

Horses danced excitedly away from the flames. Captain Rinehart held his big gray with a strong, steady hand.

"We didn't come to kill anybody, Monahan," he said evenly. "I didn't mean it to happen. But it doesn't change anything. This is open range. It was that way when I came here, and it will remain so. Now move out, Monahan. Don't stop for anything. Move out, and don't come back!"

He turned his gray horse about then, and pulled away without a backward glance. His cowboys drew aside to let him pass. Then they fell in behind him. Some of them looked back at the blazing ruin of the camp, but Captain Rinehart never did.

Doug Monahan dragged himself to the old Mexican. He gripped the corded brown hand, closing his eyes against the sudden rush of hot tears. Stub Bailey came and laid his hand on Monahan's shoulder.

Monahan said tightly, "I can't remember a time when Paco Sanchez wasn't somewhere around. As far back as I can remember, he's been with me."

Paco had taught him, had guided him, had occasionally used the double of a rope on him when Doug's own father wasn't there and the job needed doing.

"Time has a way of going on, Doug," Stub said quietly. "It takes away the old things we been used to. We can't hold them forever."

Bailey and the others of the fencing crew threw sand on the fires, snuffing them out. Doug couldn't stand up to it, and right now he didn't care.

Presently he looked up to find the fires out. Bailey was digging around under a flat rock just outside of camp. He came back carrying a bottle, wiping the dirt off onto his shirt. He held the bottle out to Doug.

"Take a good stiff one. You need it."

Monahan managed two long swallows and choked. It was cheap, raw whisky. Bailey took the bottle and turned it up for himself.

"One thing they didn't burn up," he commented, wiping his mouth on his sleeve, his blue eyes watering from the sting. "Bet you didn't even know I had this."

"I knew you had it," Monahan replied. "I just didn't know where."

Bad as the whisky was, it made Monahan feel better. Stub knelt uncomfortably beside him, looking at Paco. One of the men dragged a half-burned blanket out of the fire and covered the body with it.

"We saved some of the stuff," Bailey said. "Cedar ain't easy burned, so most of the posts are still good. Them wooden spools burned quick, though, and the wire's tangled up into an awful mess. Lost the temper, too, I expect. I don't reckon it'll be to where we can salvage much of it."

Monahan stood up painfully to look over the shambles. "Thanks, Stub."

Bailey said, "You better let me fix that place where they hit you. It don't look good."

"It'll be all right." Doug's voice was hollow.

Bailey shrugged. The boss was old enough to take care of himself. "What do we do now?"

"First thing, we better see if we can find a shovel that isn't burned up."

They had to bury Paco without so much as the Scripture, for the only Bible had been in the chuckbox. It hadn't been used much. Sometime, Monahan thought, he would try to find a priest and bring him out here. Right now, a short prayer had to do.

They had just finished filling the grave when Noah Wheeler and his daughter came back, driving three plodding Durham cows. The cows warily skirted the camp, but the two riders came straight in. Their eyes were grim as they read the meaning in the burned-out camp, the cut fence, the new mound of earth where a fire-blackened piece of the chuckbox lid stood as a temporary headboard.

The old farmer solemnly looked over the faces of the men in camp, mentally tallying up. He glanced at the grave and said, "The cook?"

Monahan nodded stiffly. Wheeler slowly climbed out of the saddle. The girl also got down. Her soft voice was tight. "Who did it?"

"Rinehart," Monahan said bitterly.

"The captain?" Noah Wheeler shook his head incredulously. "He's a hard man on occasion, but he's never killed without the need for it."

Monahan said, "Archer Spann did the shooting."

The old farmer nodded grimly. "Cold as ice. He's the man they say will own the R Cross someday." With sorrow, Wheeler said, "I reckon it's my fault. I should have told you it was Rinehart's range, but I figured it was none of my business."

"Wouldn't have mattered," Monahan replied. "It was already too late."

Trudy Wheeler carefully touched the wound on Monahan's head. "That looks bad."

"It'll heal."

Noah Wheeler frowned. "You-all better come with us for tonight. We got plenty of room at home, and plenty to eat."

Monahan shook his head. "The captain's down on us. You take
us in, he's liable to bear down on you, too."

"No," said Wheeler, "we've never had any trouble with the captain." He smiled then, but behind the smile was a dead seriousness.
"I'm just an old dirt farmer. Nobody bothers me. Now you come
along with us and get some rest."

Trudy Wheeler reached far into the overturned water barrel on
the ground beside the blackened wagon, and found a little water
there. She soaked a handkerchief in it and returned to Monahan.
"We're going to clean that wound."

She paid no attention to his objections. Her fingers were
quick and sure and gentle. Watching her closely, keenly aware of
the nearness of her, Monahan realized that Trudy Wheeler was
less a girl than she was a woman, that there was much of beauty
and maturity about her that a man might miss the first time he
looked.

"Too bad we have nothing to put on this," she said as she finished.
A bottle of iodoform had been smashed when the chuckbox fell.

Bailey brought out his bottle again, gazed regretfully at the little
bit still in the bottom of it, and handed it to her. "Here."

It burned worse outside than it had inside.

"You-all catch up your horses," Trudy Wheeler said. "You're
going over to our place."

Monahan was a little surprised at the firmness of her voice. He
had first reckoned her as quiet and meek. Now he had a feeling that
there was nothing meek about her.

He gave in because the men had to sleep somewhere, and there
was nothing left of the camp. "Just for tonight, then. Tomorrow
we'll leave."

★   ★   ★

Doug Monahan half expected to see the usual next-to-starvation look he had found in so many dugout and brush-corral nester outfits, including some of the farms over on Oak Creek. He was surprised. Hard work and careful planning had gone into Noah Wheeler's place, and it showed.

"Got four sections here," Wheeler said proudly. "That is, I'm sort of partners with a bank in Fort Worth, you might say. Most of it's still grazing land. I've got sixty or seventy acres broken out, about all I can farm by myself."

Four sections. If you went by deeded land, that probably made Noah Wheeler about as big an actual landowner as there was in this part of the country right now. That was more than twenty-five hundred acres, if you figured land that way. This wasn't the high-rainfall land of East Texas. Here it took more land to produce as much, and most people figured it in sections instead of by acres.

Monahan wondered if Captain Rinehart owned title to as much as four sections. He probably did; most of the cowmen hereabouts had bought the land where they built their headquarters, and where they could, they bought that around their best water. Control of the water gave control of the land, even though the most of it still belonged to the state, or to schools, or to the railroads which had received it as a grant in earlier times. The ranchers ran their cattle on this land without let because so far there had been little other claims on it. They might own only one section in fee, yet control twenty.

There were some who owned no land at all but simply let their cattle run loose on the open range. By unwritten rule, such land could be used by the first man who claimed it, and any other man who tried to usurp it had better throw a mighty big shadow. Gordon Finch had tried, and he hadn't made it. This unwritten title was so well established by custom that a man might sell his ranch to another without actually owning the land.

Fifteen or twenty good Durham cows were grazing in a green winter oat patch. Monahan noted that there was no fence around it. Wheeler proudly waved his hand toward the cattle.

"That's going to be the end of the Longhorn. I'm building me a nice little herd of Durhams. You won't find any better in a hundred miles. I've already got a few cowmen buying bulls from me, and I'll sell a lot more as my herd grows. A few years from now, they'll have the Longhorn blood pretty well bred out of the country."

The three cows the Wheelers had brought back trotted out into the field toward the others, pausing here and there to grab a bite of green oats.

Monahan frowned. "This is wide-open country. How can you hold your strain pure if you can't keep the native bulls out of here?"

Wheeler said, "That's the biggest trouble we got. We just have to ride our country good every day or two and run the Longhorns out. It's the best we can do. A Longhorn calf shows up from one of our cows, we just have to figure on making beef of it. We can't keep it in the herd."

They skirted past the oatfield. Next to it, lying fallow through the winter, was Wheeler's hay land, plowed clean and neat, the furrows arrow-straight. This field was circled by two strands of slick wire put up on crooked mesquite posts.

"Will that fence turn a cow back?" Monahan asked.

Wheeler shook his head. "Not if she wants in very bad. And when the field is green, they want in."

A Durham bull and two cows came plodding back from water.

"There's my bull," Wheeler said. "He's got a pedigree and a name as long as your arm, but I just call him Sancho because he's such a pet."

He was a big roan bull, not so leggy as the Longhorns but deeper-bodied, with flanks coming down farther and a wide, full rump that would carve out a lot of beef.

"The only trouble with him," Wheeler commented, "he can't outfight these native bulls. I almost had to shoot one of Fuller Quinn's the other day to keep him from killing Sancho. But one way of looking at it, old Sancho will win out in the long run. His progeny'll still be around when the Longhorns are gone."

Pride glowed in Wheeler's voice. "It's nice to be able to count your cattle in the thousands like Captain Rinehart, but I'll settle for having better quality."

A scattering of chickens scratched all about the place. Ducks swam leisurely in a large earthen tank. A few hogs rooted around in damp ground in a pen back a healthy distance east of the house.

Noah Wheeler's solid frame house stood near a spring that bubbled a strong, clear stream of water, the beginnings of a small creek which wound down past the fields and out across the grazing land. Both the house and the barn behind it were painted a bright red. Red barn paint was cheap and not hard to get.

"Built that house myself," said Wheeler. "Hauled the lumber down from the railroad right after they built into Stringtown."

It was a good house, a pleasant-looking house, though not a big one. Monahan wondered where the old stockfarmer intended to bed them down.

"There's a lean-to out in the barn," Wheeler said. "Built it for my son, Vern. If we can't find enough bedding for you fellers, we got plenty of hay out there to help stretch it."

"What about your son?" Monahan asked. "Won't we be crowding him?"

Wheeler shook his head. "Farming got too slow for Vern. He's over at the R Cross, working for the captain." His voice held a touch of regret. "Vern's not cut out for a plow, I guess. There's work aplenty here for both of us, but he'd rather cowboy and be on his own. We don't see him much anymore."

Trudy Wheeler smiled. "There's a girl in town, and he's saving every dime he can. He's afraid if he gets off of that ranch he'll spend some money."

Noah Wheeler rode past the barn and stood up in the stirrups, looking over into a corral. "Wonder if old Roany's had her calf yet?"

Monahan saw a fine Durham cow that was springing heavy, and had made a bag. It was easy to see that the calf was due any day now.

"Roany's my pet," Wheeler said. "Best cow I ever owned, or ever saw, for that matter. She's fixing to have a calf by Sancho, and it'll be the best one in the country when it gets here, I'd bet my boots on that."

Trudy Wheeler smiled. "Dad's been like a kid at Christmas, waiting for that calf."

Noah Wheeler dismounted and opened a corral gate. "Bring your horses on in. We got plenty of feed for them. While you get unsaddled, Trudy and the missus will rustle you up something to eat."

Doug found Mrs. Wheeler a strong, clear-eyed farm woman who talked with her husband's warm enthusiasm for their place and for the country in general. She ran the house in a quiet fashion but with a firm hand. Doug thought he could see where Trudy Wheeler had gotten her deceptively shy manner.

Suddenly Monahan was glad he had come. Sitting here in the front room of their little house, enjoying the company of these good people, he had forgotten his own trouble for a time.

Noah Wheeler said, "You haven't got any business moving out till you get yourself rested a little. Why don't you stay with us a day or two?"

"Just tonight. We'll leave in the morning."

"What do you figure on doing?"

Monahan's face darkened. "I'm not real sure what I'll do later. But first thing, I've got a bill to collect from Gordon Finch."

III

Finch's headquarters lay near the bottom of a long slope, with a big shallow natural lake just below it, lying lazy in the late-winter sun. Spotted cattle of every color watered at its edge, which already was beginning to shrink away from the rank growth of weeds and grass that had sprung up after last summer's rains and now lay dead and brown from the winter frost.

Doug Monahan skirted the lake, Stub Bailey riding beside him. He had sent the rest of the men directly to town to wait for him. In a quick splash of water, cattle scattered as the two horsemen approached. After running a short way, they would turn and look back, ready to run again if it appeared the riders were coming after them.

"Natural location for a ranch headquarters," Stub observed. "Old man named Jenks settled it first. They say Finch cheated him out of it someway or other."

Sitting high on the slope was a big rock house that would be Gordon Finch's. Riding in, Monahan saw corrals that had loose or broken planks and needed repair. A gate sagged and was half patched with wire. An old broken-down wagon stood right where the axle had snapped. No one had bothered to fix it or move it out of the way. Weeds had grown up through the rotting wagonbed.

Monahan rode up to the house, dismounted and strode up the steps. This had been built out of rock hauled in from a breaky stretch of hills a mile or so off yonder up the creek, and Doug was reasonably sure it had been built by Finch's predecessor. It was too good for Finch.

He walked across the lumber-built gallery and knocked on the door. A dog trotted around the corner and began barking at him, but there was no answer from within. Monahan knocked again, trying to see through the unclean oval glass. There was a good chance Finch was inside, avoiding him, but pushing in might give Finch an excuse to put the sheriff on him. Monahan turned and walked back down to the horses. The dog followed him partway, still barking.

Down across the yard was a long frame building with smoke curling out of a tin chimney.

"We'll try the cookshack," Monahan told Bailey. "One thing we know for sure, he likes to eat."

A man stood in the cookstack door, blocking Monahan's way. Monahan sensed that he had come to the right place.

"Mr. Finch ain't here," growled the ranchhand. He was one of those who had been supposed to help guard the fencing camp.

Monahan eyed him closely. "You sure?"

"I *said* he ain't."

"I heard you," Monahan replied, and made a move toward the door.

The cowboy reached behind him and brought up a shotgun. "Stay where you're at, Monahan."

Monahan heard footsteps behind him. He turned quickly, not wanting to be caught between two of Finch's men. He saw the cowboy named Dundee, who had been with Finch at the fencing camp.

"Don't pay him no mind, Monahan," Dundee said, humor flickering in his brown eyes. "He won't use that shotgun. And Finch is in there, all right, a-hiding from you. Been lookin' back over his shoulder ever since we rode away from your camp."

Monahan stared curiously at Dundee, then back to the cowboy at the door. "Well," he asked flatly, "what about it?"

The cowboy slowly lowered the shotgun and stood back. Monahan stepped through the door and blinked in the dim light. There behind the bare dinner table sat Finch, a cup of coffee and a whisky bottle in front of him. He scowled, but in his eyes Monahan could see the sick touch of fear.

"What you want, Monahan?"

"I want my pay."

"You didn't finish that fence. I don't owe you nothing."

Monahan stiffened. "Paco Sanchez was worth more to me than all the land and cattle you'll ever own, and you got him killed. But I'll settle for payment for two miles of fence, completed. Twenty-one spools of barbed wire, burned. All the posts I can't salvage. And two wagons. I got that figured down to twenty-four hundred dollars, even money. I'll take a check, right now."

Finch shoved his chair back. "I ain't paying you nothing, Monahan. You took that job, and you didn't finish it."

"Finch, you used me to try to run a bluff you didn't have the guts for yourself. You ran off like a scalded dog and left me and my men to take the whipping for you. You're going to pay me for that."

Finch turned to the man at the door. "Put him out of here, Haskell. If he won't go, use that shotgun."

The man raised the gun but hesitated to move further. Dundee stepped through the door and placed a firm hand on Haskell's arm. "If he wants Monahan run off, let him do it hisself."

Finch reddened. "Dundee, you're fired."

Dundee shrugged. "I was fixin' to leave anyhow. This outfit's washed up."

Bailey appeared in the doorway, prepared to help Monahan if Dundee threw in with Finch. But that wasn't going to happen. Monahan looked at the cowboy, thanking him with his eyes. Then he turned back to Finch. "If you haven't got a blank check, *I* have."

He pulled one out of his shirt pocket and dropped it on the table. "I got it filled out. All you got to do is sign it."

Finch blustered. "You can't get away with this. It's robbery."

Monahan shook his head. "It's payment for a Job. Legal. And I got a witness." He glanced at Dundee, and was caught off guard when Finch lunged, fist catching Monahan on the nose and flinging him backward against a cabinet. Tin plates and cups clattered to the floor. A bottle rolled down and smashed.

Then anger gushed through Monahan. He surged back at Finch. His fist caught Finch's jaw a hard blow that jerked the man's head back. Finch staggered a step or two. Fear flickered in his eyes as he stared wildly at Monahan. He had triggered this fight out of desperation, and now suddenly he was afraid, not knowing how to stop it.

Hatred burned in Monahan, but he checked himself. Finch would not fight back now. Do what he might, Monahan later would be ashamed of himself. He gripped Finch's collar and jerked him up close. He heaved him backward into a chair.

"Sign that check, Finch."

Finch signed it while Monahan tried to stop his nosebleed.

Dundee moved a step inside the door. "Just as well write me one too. I got a month's pay comin'."

Never looking up, Finch dug a blank check from his wallet and wrote it out. He turned away then, staring out the greasy cookshack window, sagging in defeat.

Bailey still stood at the door, hand on his gun, ready in case the trouble got bigger than Monahan was.

"Let's go to town, Stub."

Dundee followed them out. "Be all right with you if I tag along? Looks like my business around here is all wound up."

Monahan shrugged. "Suit yourself."

"I got a warbag and a roll over at the bunkhouse and a horse in the corral," Dundee said. "I got no good-byes to say."

Directly he rode back, thin bedroll secured behind the saddle, a warbag of clothing and personal belongings hanging from the saddlehorn atop his rope. He rode a long-legged bay horse that had a strong showing of Thoroughbred. Monahan looked questioningly at the bay.

"Don't worry, he's mine," Dundee said. "Owned him when I came here, and I've had to pay Finch for all the feed he's et."

They edged around the lake, scattering cattle again. Monahan showed some uncertainty about the trail to town, and Dundee pointed it out.

"What'll you do now, Dundee?" Monahan asked after a while.

Dundee shrugged and rolled himself a cigarette. "Never gone hungry yet. What about you?"

"Buy me a new outfit and start over again, more than likely."

Dundee's eyebrows went up. "You mean build more fence?"

"It's a living."

"You're on Rinehart's list now. You build another fence around here and the captain's liable to wrap that bobwire around your neck."

Monahan's voice was grim. "He won't find it easy to do."

It was midafternoon when they reached town. Stub Bailey was looking toward the saloon and licking his lips. But Monahan had his eyes on the bank.

"First thing I got to do is deposit this check before Finch sends in here to stop payment."

Dundee said, "I reckon I can use my money, too."

Bailey pulled his horse aside. "Go ahead, then. You-all know where I'll be at," and he turned in and dismounted at the nearest saloon.

The teller was a small, middle-aged man, bald and friendly looking. He glanced at Monahan's check, and his forehead wrinkled in surprise.

"What's the matter?" Monahan asked, suddenly worried.

The teller shook his head. "Nothing wrong, Mr. Monahan. Just endorse it, will you?"

While Doug scrawled his name across the check with a scratchy bank pen, another man stepped out of a back office. He was a huge old gentleman, weighing perhaps three hundred pounds. Grinning, the teller said, "Albert, come over here, will you? Mr. Monahan, I want you to meet Albert Brown, president of the bank. Albert, you've lost a bet."

Pulling his glasses down from his forehead to his nose, the portly banker read Finch's check and the endorsement. "Well, well," he mused with humor, "I wouldn't have believed it."

The teller explained. "You see, Mr. Monahan, when you first came here, Albert bet me ten dollars Gordon Finch would weasel out of paying you for any fence you might build. After I heard what happened yesterday, I was ready to forfeit to him."

The old banker was smiling. "It was worth losing the bet. I just wish we could collect what Finch owes *us*." He glanced at Monahan's right hand. Doug was suddenly conscious of the skinned knuckles. Brown chuckled. "Perhaps we could, if we were a little younger and had your method."

The teller grinned. "You could always sit on him, Albert."

"One of these days I'm going to sit on *you*," Brown grunted.

Monahan took out enough cash to pay off his men. Then he waited on the boardwalk outside while Dundee cashed his check.

Twin Wells was pretty much an average for a West Texas cowtown, he thought. It had the essentials. From the bank's front walk he could count two mercantile stores, five saloons, a church and a school. Scattered around haphazardly were one good hotel, one cheap one, a big livery barn at the head of the street, and a smaller one at the far end to keep the big one honest. There was a blacksmith shop and a little chili joint.

Dominating the town was the courthouse, an imposing two-story rock building squarely in the center of a large block of fenced-in ground that probably was as big as the rest of the business section put together. In the summertime, cowboys would ride into town and tie their horses along this stake fence in the shade of the big live oaks instead of in the sun at the hitchracks that stood in front of most of the business houses. Behind the courthouse stood a smaller structure, built of the same stone, looking very much like the courthouse except that its windows were barred.

When Dundee came out, Monahan told him, "I'm going over and talk to the sheriff."

"I'll string along with you, if it's all the same. I'm curious what Luke McKelvie's goin' to say."

"It's up to you."

They strode across the hoof-scarred street, pausing to let a cowboy ride past them and a loaded wagon roll by. The live oaks had held their leaves all winter, and now they were a muddy green, almost ready to fall and give way to the fresh leaves that spring would bring. A thick mulch of old leaves and acorns crunched beneath the men's feet as they passed under the big trees and through the open gate toward the jail.

The sheriff sat at his desk, frowning over a fresh batch of reward dodgers. Luke McKelvie was fifty or so. He had a lawman look about him but somewhere back yonder he'd been a cowboy before he strayed off into the devious trails of politics, Doug Monahan judged. He still retained a little of the cowboy, but years in town, with easy work and not much heavy riding had left him a shade soft around the middle, a little broad across the hips.

"I'm Doug Monahan."

The sheriff looked up with tired gray eyes. He stood and extended his hand. "Evening. Figured you'd be in, sooner or later. Sit down. You too, Dundee."

The two men dragged cane-bottomed chairs away from the bare wall.

"You've heard about yesterday?" Monahan asked.

McKelvie nodded. "The captain was in with Spann. They told me."

"You could've come out and investigated."

The sheriff's eyes were steady. "I did. Rode all the way out there, and all I could find was a grave."

Monahan felt a touch of guilt for the way he had spoken. He had taken it for granted that the sheriff had done nothing.

McKelvie said, "You should've waited for me. Not just buried the old man and rid off like that."

"Didn't seem to be much else we could do. We had no food left, or bedding or anything."

The sheriff shrugged. "I don't reckon it matters now anyway."

"One thing matters to me. What're you going to do?"

McKelvie frowned. "What *should* I do?"

"A man was killed out there. We all know who killed him. You do anything about murder around here?"

The sheriff pointed his finger at Monahan. "About murder, yes, but was it murder? Look at it the way I have to. In the first place, you were trespassing. You had no business out there."

"I took the job in good faith. I didn't know I was trespassing."

"Whether you knew it or not, you were. Take it to court and they'd find the captain was only protecting his property. In the second place, your man had a pothook in his hand, and he could've brained Archer Spann with it. I'll grant you Spann maybe didn't have to kill him. But he did it, and I expect any jury would acquit him on the grounds of self-defense.

"We got to look at it for what it is, Monahan. Whatever he was to you, to folks around here he was just an old Mexican that nobody knew, in a place where he shouldn't have been."

"Is that the way you feel, McKelvie?"

McKelvie's eyes sharpened as Monahan's pent-up anger reached across to him. "No, it isn't. I hate to see any man die. But I've got to be practical. There's no use putting the county to the expense of arrest and trial of a man the jury's bound to turn loose anyhow. There's nothing you or me can do. You'd just best forget it."

Monahan's hands were tight on the edge of the chair. "Just like that! They kill the old man who brought me up and I'm supposed to forget it."

McKelvie leaned forward, his eyes level and serious. "That and a little more. I'm advising you to gather up whatever loose ends you got around here and leave, Monahan. It's my job to keep the peace, and I got an uneasy feeling it won't be peaceful as long as you stay."

"Is that an order, McKelvie?"

The sheriff shook his head. "Just good advice."

Monahan stood up stiffly. "I'm not ready to go yet. Maybe, like you say, there's nothing I can do about the men who killed Paco. But I'll guarantee you this, I'm not leaving till I try." He turned to go.

"Wait a minute, Monahan," the sheriff said. Monahan looked back at him and saw a coldness in McKelvie's face. "I don't blame you for the way you feel. But I'm not going to let you stir up a lot of trouble. First time you step over the line, I'll bring you in."

"We'll see," Monahan replied thinly.

IV

Walking back across the dusty street, Doug Monahan managed to get a tight rein on his anger. He asked Dundee, "What about the sheriff?"

Dundee shrugged. "He didn't say anything that wasn't the truth. McKelvie's a pretty good kind of a man. Punched cattle for the captain a long time ago, till the captain got him made sheriff. It was about like staying on the R Cross payroll. But things have changed here lately. New people comin' in, people that don't figure Rinehart's got any claim on them. Been tough on McKelvie sometimes, I expect, bein' sheriff for them and the captain, too. He wants to be fair, and he's havin' a hard time figuring out what fair is."

They stepped up onto the plank sidewalk that fronted the little saloon where Stub Bailey had gone. The small sign said, TEXAS TOWN, CHRISTOPHER HADLEY, PROP. Two men sat on the edge of the porch, whittling and spitting and soaking up the fleeting sunshine. They stared curiously at Monahan. Doug knew the story had gone all over town, probably all over the county.

It was a shotgun-shaped saloon, narrow in front but somehow longer than it had looked outside. Stub Bailey sat at a table toward the back. The rest of the fencing crew was there with him. The proprietor brought two fresh glasses. Bailey poured the two full from a bottle he had sitting in front of him. He hurriedly drank what was left in his own glass and refilled it too.

"I always like an even start with the crowd," he said.

Monahan took a quick swallow of the whisky and grimaced at its fiery passage. He hadn't really wanted it.

For Bailey, it went down smoother. His glass was half empty

when he set it back on the table. "You're all the talk around here to-day, Doug. Some of the captain's cowboys was in here talking about you when I came in. They finally recognized me and shut up. They were betting on how quick you'd be out of the country."

Doug said dryly, "You ought to've taken a little of their money."

The proprietor had been watching Monahan until he figured out for sure who he was. Now he came back smiling, bringing a bottle.

"Welcome, Mr. Monahan," he said. "My name's Chris Hadley. This is my place." He picked up the bottle Stub had been using and put the other one down in its place. "This is on the house. It's a plea-sure to serve someone that's had the nerve to stomp the captain's toes."

Monahan eyed him noncommittally. "I'm afraid you got it backwards, friend. He did all the stomping."

"You're still in town, aren't you?" Hadley replied. He was a shortish man, growing heavy now in his late forties, his hair receding to a light stand far back on his head. There was something about him that made him a little out of place as a saloonkeeper. He bore him-self with a dignity which hinted of a better background than this.

Presently Doug heard a stir out in front of the saloon. A couple of cowboys pushed through the door and stood looking over the thin scattering of customers. The pair wore woolen coats, unbut-toned now because the day was not unpleasant. They had on chaps and spurs, and one wore leather gloves. They spotted Monahan and moved toward him.

Monahan stiffened, an angry red ridge running along his cheek-bone. The tall one in the lead was Archer Spann.

Spann stopped and stared at Monahan, a vague contempt in his black eyes. "Monahan," he said sharply, "the captain's outside. He wants to see you."

Monahan stood up angrily, changed his mind and sat down again. "Tell him if he wants to see me, he knows where I'm at."

Spann said, "When the captain says come, you come."

"*I* don't." Monahan sat there with a deep anger smoldering in him. He was hoping this grim man would make a move toward him, hoping for an excuse to lay his gunbarrel against that hard jaw and watch those black eyes roll back.

Spann shifted his weight uncertainly from one foot to the other. It was plain enough he wasn't used to running up against a situation like this. But he could not miss the dangerous smoulder in the fence-builder's eyes. Suddenly, he turned and walked out again.

The proprietor moved to the front window and looked outside. "It's Captain Rinehart, all right. He's out front there on that big gray horse of his."

Chris Hadley nervously wiped his dry hands on his apron. "Four years I've had this place, and the captain's never set foot in it. Folks used to ask him permission to do this or do that. I never did. I put this place up, and I never asked him anything. Couple of years, no R Cross cowboy ever came in, either. But they've been starting to drift in. The old man's word doesn't carry as strongly as it used to."

Spann came in first and held the door open. Captain Andrew Rinehart strode in with stiff dignity. He paused a moment, letting his eyes accustom themselves to the room light.

"He's back here, Captain," Spann spoke, waving his hand toward Monahan.

It took the captain a moment to pick Monahan out. Monahan stood up slowly and pushed his chair back. The captain stopped a full pace in front of the table.

"I thought you'd be gone," the old man said.

Monahan's voice was calmly defiant. "I'm still here."

The cowman's piercing eyes had a way of seeing right through a man without revealing much of what went on behind them. "Maybe you're broke," he said. "I understand you've got some barbed wire stored over at Tracey's Mercantile. I'll buy it from you. That'll give you enough money to be on your way."

Monahan said, "I'm not broke. The point is, I'm not running. I'll leave when I get ready, and I'm not ready."

A sharp edge worked into the captain's voice. "I'm trying to be fair about this, Monahan."

"Like you were yesterday?"

"What happened yesterday wasn't all planned. Sometimes things just happen that weren't figured on atall. You'd better forget it."

Forget it. Twice now Monahan had heard that.

"You burned up my wagons, destroyed my supplies and killed a harmless old man. How do you think I could forget that?"

"Sometimes it's best for a man to make himself forget, Monahan."

"I'll bet *you* never did, Captain. I'll bet you never in your life let a man get away with anything."

A tinge of red worked up the old rancher's ears "Monahan, I was in this country when you were just a little boy. I came out here when everybody else was afraid to. There were Indians here, but I took the country, and I held it." His beard quivered with emotion. "Other people have come in, sure, but only because I let them. It's still my country. It goes by my rules. They've been fair rules, and one way or another, I've seen that they've been kept.

"People may say I've been a hard man. Well, it took a hard man to run the Indians out. It took a hard man to get rid of the cow thieves. Even yet, there's all kinds of land grabbers and leeches, waiting to move in here the minute I soften up. They'd love to see Kiowa County split apart. And you know how barbed wire can split people apart. It's done it other places, and it would do it here. I'll not allow you to come in and stir up dissension. I've told you to leave. I'll not tell you again!"

Doug Monahan had been standing out of his habitual deference

for men older than himself. He realized suddenly what he was doing, and he sat down. He said nothing, but the defiance in his eyes
gave his answer. The captain stood there stiff-backed, his old fists
doubled.

Spann moved up to the captain's side. "I'll take care of this for
you, sir."

"No," said the captain, "no saloon brawl." He had too much
pride for that. "You're feeling ringy, Monahan, because one of your
men was killed. I'll take that into account for now, but don't crowd
your luck." He turned on his heel and strode stiffly out the door.

Spann hung back, watching Monahan. "You won't find me as
easy to talk down as the old man."

Monahan replied tightly, "And you won't find me as easy to kill
as a poor old Mexican with a pothook in his hand."

The saloonkeeper, Chris Hadley, stood at the window, wiping his
hands on his apron as he watched the riders pull away. He came
back, a little of nervousness still hanging on him.

"Well, Monahan," he said, "you've made the history books. But
what are you going to do now?"

"Build fence, if I can. I'm not running away."

Chris Hadley was more than just a barkeeper. He was a man
given to quiet contemplation. He said, "Maybe you're the one,
Monahan, I don't know. For a long time we've needed somebody to
wake people up and make them stand for their rights. The captain
was a great man for his time. He came here when it was a raw, wild
land. He tamed it and he built it up. But he got it to a point where
it suits him, and now he wants it to stay there. In the old countries,
he's what you'd call a benevolent despot."

Monahan said, "What's benevolent about him?"

Hadley shrugged. "There are some good things about him, believe it or not. But he's still a despot, and we've outgrown that kind

of man, Monahan. We've outgrown him, but were too weak to do anything about it."

Presently two men came in and walked up to the bar. "Hey, Chris," one said, "wasn't that the captain we saw walking out of here?"

Hadley nodded, and the man whistled softly. "We must be comin' to the end of the world."

The other man said, "I saw the captain ridin' out of town like he was on his way to a lynching. A big bunch of R Cross cowboys was with him. I guess they all left."

"All but one," the first man corrected him. "That Wheeler boy stayed in town."

"Wheeler? Vern Wheeler?" Worry crept into Chris Hadley's voice. "Where did he go?"

"Last I seen he was headed in the direction of your house," the man said, grinning slyly.

Chris Hadley lost interest in his customers. He absently wiped the bar, his troubled gaze pinned on the side window of the saloon. His house lay in that direction.

Vern Wheeler lacked three months of turning twenty-one. He was a large young man, as husky as his father, old Noah Wheeler. He had a squarish, handsome face with bold, honest features, a picture of what his father must have been thirty years before.

He carried a brashness and a recklessness, though, that were strictly his own. He walked right up to the Hadley house and knocked on the door, standing there on the front porch for all to see him.

Paula Hadley opened the door. Her brown eyes lighted with joy at the sight of him. "Vern Wheeler! What are you doing here?"

"What do you think? I came to see you. You going to make me stand out here in the chill all day?"

She hesitated. "Vern, you know Papa. . . ." Then she opened the door wide. "I guess you might as well come on in. They'll all talk, either way."

He walked in and she closed the door, leaning back against it. She studied him with a happy glow in her brown eyes. Paula Hadley was a slender, small girl who looked even tinier beside big Vern Wheeler. She dressed plainly because her father disapproved of anything else. As a saloonkeeper's daughter, austerity was a penalty she had to suffer to keep her beyond suspicion. But nothing could hide the quiet beauty of her face, a beauty enhanced by her happiness now as she looked at Vern Wheeler.

"Gosh, Vern, it's been a long time. Can't you come around more often?"

"You know I'm working, Paula. Captain Rinehart's got me and another feller staked out in a line shack way over on the north end of the ranch."

"You weren't in that incident at that fencing camp, were you?"

"No, I didn't even know about it till it was over."

That brought her relief. "Gosh, Vern," she said again, "it's been a long time. Two months."

"Costs money to come to town, Paula. I'm saving mine. You know why."

She nodded. "I know why. Vern, who's with you in the line camp?"

"Fellow named Lefty Jones. I don't expect you know him."

She shook her head. "I'm glad it's not that redheaded Rooster Preech you used to run around with. I was afraid he'd get you in trouble someday."

"The captain wouldn't give Rooster a job."

"And you know why."

Vern Wheeler smiled. "Rooster's all right. Folks just don't understand him, is all."

"*I* understand him. He's too shiftless to do honest work."

Vern Wheeler moved toward her, grinning. "Honey, I didn't come here to talk about him."

He held his hands out, and she reached forward, taking them. At arm's length they looked at each other.

"Gosh, Paula," he said admiringly, "you sure look pretty." He took her into his arms. "Paula," he said, "why don't we just go and tell your dad about us? Tell him we want to get married."

"Vern, you know how Papa feels about things. He's got his heart dead set on sending me off to school. He scrimped and saved for years. It would just about kill him."

"He's bound to know about us, Paula."

"I guess he does, a little. He just doesn't realize how serious it is between us. But give me time, and I'll find some way to tell him."

"Tell him about the money I'm saving. It won't be like you were just marrying some saddle bum. They're still holding more than a year's wages for me out at the R Cross. I haven't taken a thing out of them except a little tobacco money and a few dollars for clothes.

"I got my eye on a piece of land back yonder in the hills. It's got a good spring on it, and good grass. A little longer, Paula, and I'll be able to buy it, and the stock to go on it. You tell your dad you'll be marrying a man who knows how to work and save and make his money count. We'll amount to something one of these days."

"I know we will, Vern. Don't you worry about Papa. Now you'd better go, before the gossips all get started."

"All right, Paula," he said. "But one of these times I'll take you with me."

He kissed her and walked out. She stood on the porch and blew him a kiss as he swung onto his nervous-eyed sorrel bronc. Showing off a little, he jabbed his thumbs into the bronc's neck. The sorrel went pitching off down the street, Vern Wheeler laughing and waving back at Paula.

Chris Hadley came walking up as Vern's bronc eased down into a trot, its back still humped. Hadley stood at his front gate, frowning, watching the young cowboy disappear.

"You're home early, Papa," Paula said in surprise as he walked into the small house. "I don't have supper ready yet."

"Business wasn't much, and I wasn't feeling very good anyway," he replied. He watched the girl worriedly as she put on an apron and moved into the kitchen. He followed her, leaning against the kitchen door.

"Vern Wheeler was here, wasn't he?" he asked.

"He came by to see me."

"You let him in the house?"

She paused. "Papa, we wouldn't do anything we shouldn't. You know that."

"I know, Paula, but some of the neighbors around here don't. You've got to remember, you're a saloonkeeper's daughter. With some people it doesn't matter whether you did anything wrong or not. The only thing they see is that you *could* have."

He walked over to the stove and checked the coffee pot. "Paula, I'm going to send you back where you can be with good people, like your mother's folks were."

Impatience came into her voice. "I can remember them. When I was just a little girl, after Mother died, you took me back to see them. They wouldn't have anything to do with us, not you or me either. They were too good for us, remember, Papa? Your family had lost its money, so we weren't good enough."

"It wasn't you they didn't like, Paula, it was me. They didn't want me to marry your mother. We ran off and got married anyway, and it turned out just the way they said it would. We drifted around from one sorry place to another. I dragged your mother down, just like they said."

"Did she ever complain, Papa?"

"She wasn't the kind who would. But I ruined her life. Now I want to make it up. I want you to have the things she never could have."

"Maybe they're not the things I want."

Chris Hadley studied his daughter intently. "Paula, I know how it is when you're young, but I want you to listen to me. Vern's a good boy, I'll grant you that, but look at him. Look at any of these people. Look at those women over on Oak Creek. Do you think I want you to wind up like them someday, washed out, worn out, all their hope and spirit gone? I'm not going to let it happen." He shook his head. "Paula, I don't want you to see him again, ever."

V

The Oak Creek section had always been considered some of the sorriest rangeland in Postoak County. Its grass was stemmy and lacking in strength. The country had a tendency to go to scrub brush, which didn't leave a lot of room for grass in the first place. In the days when no one had ranged this country but Captain Rinehart, most of his cattle had kept out of the Oak Creek section of their own will. Only a few scattering cows of the bunch-quitter type stayed down there much. There were cattle like that, just as there were that kind of men.

But the section had one thing in its favor, the creek itself. Water was always a big consideration in West Texas, where rainfall came only when it got good and ready and could never be depended upon.

So when the farmers began to move in, they started locating on Oak Creek. At first there was resistance on the part of some of the cowmen. A few of the earliest farmers took the hint and moved out again. But as time went on, it became obvious that the farmers couldn't be squeezed out forever.

Captain Andrew Rinehart circulated the word, and the farmers were allowed to settle along Oak Creek. If there had to be farmers, then it was better that they be concentrated in one place than to have them bringing in the Texas Rangers and scattering all over the county, breaking up the rangeland, the captain said. Besides, there were some advantages to having a few farmers around. Cowmen could buy hay from them, and vegetables and butter and the like. When the farm work wasn't pressing too hard, the ranchers could hire the farmers to do the menial jobs that most of their cowhands scorned doing.

Only one farmer had broken the pattern. Without a word to anybody, without even a tip of the hat to Captain Rinehart, Noah Wheeler had bought land scrip for four sections right in the middle of the best rangeland and moved his family out from East Texas.

There had been some bitter talk about it. Fuller Quinn, angry-faced ranchman on Wagonrim Creek, was in favor of riding over there in force and burning the farmer out before he could get himself fairly settled. "Let that nester squat there and he'll attract others. They'll crowd us right off the grass!"

Actually, Quinn was doing more crowding than anybody. He had built up his herd of Longhorns until it was too big for the range he controlled. He let them spill over into his neighbors' country, let them trample across the planted fields along Oak Creek. The one thing about which he was careful was that his line riders keep them turned well back from Captain Rinehart's country.

Unexpectedly, and without any explanation, Captain Rinehart had vetoed action against Noah Wheeler. "If any other farmers start looking over his way, we can quietly discourage them," he said. "But Wheeler will stay where he is."

So they'd left Wheeler alone, and some of the cowmen had come to like him. Wheeler was no ordinary squatter. He had a far-reaching way of looking beyond things as they were now and seeing how they could be. He had turned some of the cowmen into good customers for the feed he raised. A stockman himself, he had sold many of them on the idea of improving their beef by using better breeds of bulls.

But one thing hadn't changed. The other farmers had stayed on Oak Creek. There, more or less congregated, they could turn back most of the stray cattle which worked in from the open ranges around them. True, when the crops were good, some of Fuller Quinn's cattle always seemed to find their way into the best fields. Nobody ever caught Quinn or his men drifting them in there, and there probably wasn't much a farmer could have done about it if he had. Still, it was a constant source of irritation that a good stand of corn might be ruined in a hurry if the farmer was not eternally vigilant.

So it was that Doug Monahan had received expressions of interest from several Oak Creek farmers even before he had started the ill-fated fencing job for Gordon Finch.

"Slick wire and brush enclosures just won't turn them cattle when they're hungry," complained Foster Lodge. "It's got so I have to chase three or four Quinn heifers out of my oat patch every mornin'. I'd like to try a little of that there bobwire, if the price was right."

"I'll make it right," Monahan had promised. "Just as soon as I finish this job for Finch, I'll be over."

The Finch job had finished abruptly. Now, this sharply cool winter morning, Doug Monahan was on his way a-horseback toward Oak Creek. Short, burly Stub Bailey rode beside him to point the way.

"That yonder's Lodge's place," Bailey said finally as they splashed their horses across cold Oak Creek. "I expect Lodge is about the best farmer there is along the crick here. But he don't hold a candle to Noah Wheeler, even at that."

Lodge's place was smaller but neat and well kept, even as Noah Wheeler's had been. Grubbed-up brush ringed his fields, giving the whole thing some appearance of a bird's nest. Doug thought that was where the word nester came from. Lodge had a good set of pens for his work and milk stock. It struck Monahan that these pens were patterned after those of Noah Wheeler.

"They all copy Wheeler, don't they?" he said.

"You see a man doing the right kind of a job, you're foolish if you don't model after him some."

Foster Lodge still lived in the original dugout he had carved back into a hillside. A sign of improving times was that he now had a tin covering over the original sod roof. It would turn the water, where the sod never did. There was a fairly new lean-to, built of lumber, probably raised for propriety when the children began to grow up.

Lodge heard the barking of his dogs and met Doug and Stub at the door. "Come in, come in. Too cool to stand around outside. Did all my chores and hustled myself back in here where it's warm."

A castiron cook stove threw welcome heat. Dry mesquite stumps and roots were piled in a box behind the stove, along with axe-cut dry mesquite limbs.

Mrs. Lodge, a thin, morose woman who acted as if she resented the company, came out and poured them some coffee. Lodge avoided the sharp cut of her eyes. Doug figured she had him buffaloed. Like too many others, she probably had resented leaving security and the small comforts somewhere farther east to try to build something better out here in a raw new land. He was glad when she retreated into the lean-to room and closed the door.

Doug said, "I came to see if you're still interested in having some fence built. We're not busy now. We could start any time."

Lodge made no sign that he knew what had happened to the Finch job. He hadn't been to town, Doug guessed.

"Well, yes I am," Lodge said. "I've talked with some of my neighbors. We been thinkin' we might all have some fence built and share the cost where we can share a fence."

"It would sure save you a lot of damage from stray cattle."

Lodge frowned. "Right there's the only hitch, Monahan. All of us own a little livestock, too—milk cows, work horses and mules, a few beef critters. Some of the boys don't quite trust this bobwire. If it cuts up some of Fuller Quinn's strays, so much the better. But they're afraid it might cut up our own stock, too."

"It won't," Doug assured him, "not after they get used to it."

"I don't know," Lodge commented doubtfully. "It's mean-lookin' stuff. They're goin' to have to see proof, I'm afraid, before they'll go through with it."

Monahan chewed his lip, thinking darkly. How could he show them proof when there wasn't a barbed wire fence anywhere around? Then he remembered an exhibition he had seen in San Antonio.

"I believe I can prove it to where it'll satisfy all of you," he said. "Would you be willing to gamble a few head of cattle on it?"

Lodge frowned. "Gamble? Well now, I'm not a rich man. I ain't got enough livestock to go gamblin' with them."

"Then *I'll* do the gambling," Doug said. "I'll guarantee to pay you for any cattle that get crippled or cut up bad."

"What do you figure on doing?"

"I'll pick out a spot someplace on the creek here, where everybody can see it. I'll put up a good-sized barbed wire corral and turn cattle into it. You'll see how quick they learn what the wire's there for." He studied Foster Lodge. "If it proves out all right, and you men are satisfied that it won't hurt your stock, will you contract with me to build the fence?"

Lodge thoughtfully rubbed his jaw. "Personally, I'd go along with it. I think I can speak for the others. You give the boys a good show and you've got yourself a job, Monahan."

Captain Andrew Rinehart swung stiffly down from his big gray horse and stood a moment holding on to the horn, steadying himself. He was bone-tired after a full day in the saddle. This weariness made him angry at himself, for he used to ride all day and half the night without tiring so.

"Need some help, Captain?" Archer Spann had walked up behind him, leading his own horse.

"No, thank you," Rinehart said firmly.

"You're tired. I can unsaddle for you."

With a flare of impatience the captain replied, "I've always saddled and unsaddled my own horses. I see no need to change that now."

He loosened the girth and slid the saddle and blanket off the gray's back, letting them ease to the ground. He patted the horse on the neck. The captain had always loved horses. Especially gray horses. That was all he rode anymore. There was something about a gray horse that gave a man stature.

He pulled the bridle off and watched the horse turn away. The gray walked across the broad corral, nose to the ground. When he found a place that suited him, he dropped down, hind legs first, and rolled in the dust. This was a sight that had always been restful to the captain. Out of ancient habit he counted the rolls. One, two, three. A horse is worth a hundred dollars for every time he rolls over, the old saying went. Three hundred dollars.

I couldn't roll over once anymore, he thought. *I'm not worth much.*

"Anything else that needs doing tonight?" Archer Spann asked.

"Nothing, thank you," the captain said, jerked back to reality. He hoisted his saddle up onto a wooden rack, placing the blanket on top of it to dry the sweat out. He watched Spann walking away from the barn, and he felt a momentary regret for having spoken so sharply to his foreman.

Spann was quiet and coldly efficient. There was nothing in the way of ranch work that he couldn't do, and do better than anyone else on the payroll. He would get it done quickly and well, with little lost motion, or emotion. Just as the captain himself had done in his younger days. With others, Spann was sometimes harsh, even overbearing. He had little patience with other men's errors, and he seldom made one of his own.

He had an inner, relentless drive that the captain had seen in few men. Occasionally, without warning, Spann could burst into sudden violence, as he had done that day at Monahan's fencing camp.

The captain had instantly regretted that killing. If anybody had needed killing, it had been Gordon Finch, a land-hungry coward who had tried to use someone else to take for him what he lacked the guts to take for himself. Doug Monahan, the captain was convinced now, had been no more than a victim of circumstance. There had been a time, the next day, when the captain would have been willing to make restitution, if it could have been done quietly and honorably.

Now it had gone too far. However innocently Monahan had wandered into this situation, he had now set himself up against Rinehart. From now on, he could only be regarded as an enemy.

Darkness was drawing down over Rinehart's ranch headquarters, and with it came the sharp chill of the late-winter night. Rinehart drew his coat tightly around him. Even the cold bothered him more than it used to. Rheumatism had set up a dull ache in his shoulder, where he had stopped an arrow in a fight with the Comanches way back yonder, while he was a Ranger.

Rinehart wearily climbed the wooden steps to his high front porch. His boots clumped heavily, the spurs jingling sharply in the cold night air. He pushed open the door of the big rock house, and he heard Sarah call, "Is that you, Andrew?"

She always asked that, every time he came in. It had been the same for forty years. With Sarah, it was a manner of greeting rather than an actual question. She had never failed to greet him at the door in the good young years.

Now she was ailing and often had to remain in her bed. Age was catching up with Sarah, too. But she was never too sick to call out to him as he came in. He dreaded the day he would walk into this big old house and not hear that voice.

Automatically he removed his hat. The ranch might be the captain's, but the house was his wife's. He walked into the bedroom and saw her lying there in the gloom.

"You're awfully late, Andrew," she scolded, but her voice was soft with affection.

"It's so dark in here," he said. "Why didn't you have Josefa light the lamp?" He struck a match and lighted the wick, clamping the shining glass chimney back into place.

"Dusk," she said. "It's restful to tired eyes."

She reached out and touched his hand. The captain sat down on the edge of the bed, looking at her. It angered him somehow that he could do nothing for her. He had always been a strong man. All his life, what he had wanted to do, he did. What he wanted to have, he took. When he spoke, men moved. His power had been great.

Yet now he had no power to help this woman he loved. Sometimes she was up and about for two or three weeks at a time. Then she would be down again, weak and helpless as a child. Lately he had begun to consider how life would be without her. It was an empty and terrible thing to contemplate.

"Doctor been out today?" he asked.

She nodded. "He just left some more of those awful pills. I think he uses them to keep his patients sick, so he'll have a steady income."

He was grateful for the good humor he could see in her eyes. Sarah had always been his refuge. When things went wrong, Sarah always seemed to be able to muster a smile from somewhere and make misfortune easier to take.

"I sent for Luke McKelvie," he said. "Has he been here?"

"He came in about sundown. He went down to the cookshack to eat."

Rinehart stood up. "I'll go on down there, then. I need to talk to him."

Sarah reached out and caught his sleeve. "Andrew, I want to ask you about Charley Globe."

"What about Charley?"

"He came up here today and told me he's quitting. Andrew,

Charley's been with us ever since we came up to this country. He's one of the few real old-timers."

The captain frowned. "What's eating Charley?"

"It's Archer Spann. Archer's too abrupt with him. Charley feels he's entitled to some extra consideration around here occasionally because he's been with us so long. He's getting old, and he can't always keep up. He doesn't like to be browbeaten by some younger man. And what happened over at that fencing camp the other day didn't set well with Charley, either. Andrew, you've got to do something about Archer Spann."

Rinehart said defensively, "Archer's a good man, Sarah, the best man we ever had. Sure, he's hard. But it takes a hard man, sometimes."

"But you'll talk to him, won't you? And to Charley?"

"I'll talk to him. And I won't let Charley quit."

The cookshack and bunkhouse were combined in one long L-shaped frame building. Captain Rinehart walked up the steps and onto the porch where the washbasins were. He found Luke Mc-Kelvie sitting there in the near-darkness, smoking a cigarette.

"Evening, Captain," the sheriff said, standing up.

"Evening." They shook hands.

McKelvie said pleasantly, "The place never changes, Captain. It's just the same as it was when I worked here. Even after all these years, this is the only place that seems like home to me."

"No," the captain agreed, "it doesn't change. As long as things suit us, there's no reason why they should ever change, is there?"

McKelvie shook his head. "I reckon not." Then he said, "Cook's got a good supper fixed in there. You ought to eat a bite."

Damn it, the captain thought, *they're all trying to take care of me like an old man.* "Supper'll wait. I've got something more important. Have you heard what that fellow Monahan is up to?"

The sheriff nodded. "A little."

"You know he's been keeping some wire down at Tracey's Mercantile. He's taken some of it out, and he's hauled several loads of cedar posts out to Oak Creek. He's putting up some sort of a barbed wire corral."

McKelvie said, "I know. I was out there. He's going to run a bunch of stock into it to show the farmers that bobwire won't kill their animals."

"You know what he's fixing to do, don't you, Luke? He's trying to get those farmers to let him fence their land for them."

"I understand he's already got them sold, if he can show them that the stock won't be hurt."

Already sold! That jarred the captain a little.

"Luke, you've got to stop it."

"Stop it?" McKelvie dropped his cigarette and ground it under his boot. "How?"

"I don't care how. Throw him in jail. Run him out of town. Why should I have to tell you how?"

"Look, Captain, I can't just jail a man or run him out of town because I don't like him, or don't like what he's doing. As long as he's not breaking the law, I can't touch him."

"Luke, you know what that wire can do to this country! It's always been an open range. It's been *our* range. Once a few of the farmers start, some of the ranchers will. In a couple of years they'll have the range cut up into a hundred pieces. We'll be fenced off from half of our water. The cattle won't be able to graze free with the rain and the grass. When the dry spells come, they won't be able to move the way they used to. They'll stay right there and graze it and tromp it into the dust, and there won't be anything left."

McKelvie sat down again. "I don't know how we can stop it. If it's a man's own land, it's his land, and that's all there is to it. There's no legal way."

The captain's voice grew heated. "If we can't stop it legally, then we'll stop it some other way. But stop it we will!"

"If we find a legal way, fine. Otherwise, Captain, you'll have to count me out."

"Luke, are you forgetting who put you in there as sheriff? Are you forgetting who you're working for?"

"I'm not forgetting anything. Sure, you got me put in office a long time ago. You've kept me in, and I'm grateful for it. You've been like a father to me, Captain. Over the years, I've admired you more than any man I ever knew. But there are other people in the county now. I'm working for them, too. Don't make it any harder for me than it already is."

"I counted on you to stand by me, Luke. Sometimes it seems like I haven't got many friends I can rely on anymore."

"I'm your friend, Captain. And as your friend, I'm telling you to not do anything rash. The old days are gone."

McKelvie stood up again and extended his hand. "Good night, Captain."

Curtly Rinehart said, "Good night," and turned away.

The old days are gone, McKelvie had said. Not yet they weren't!

Old age may be beginning to slow me, but it hasn't got me down, the captain thought angrily. *I'm not going to quit while there's any fight left in me. There was a time when nobody ever questioned me. I knew what was good for this country, and I saw that it got done. People recognized that I was right.*

Now I'm slowing down. I can't get around like I used to. My eyesight's getting bad. I can't see all that's going on around me. But I can see enough to know that they're beginning to point their fingers at me and talk. They're coming in all the time now, these new ones, looking enviously on what I have and plotting to steal it away from me.

Damn them, if it hadn't been for me there wouldn't be anything here! I fought for this range, and bled for it and sweated for it. Now they think because I'm getting old that they can take it away from me! But I've still got friends. I've still got men with the old spirit. They'll find out the R Cross is as strong as it ever was. . . .

Archer Spann walked out of the cookshack.

A hard man, some said about Spann. But he was a man you could depend on when you needed something done.

"Archer," the captain said, "come walk out to the barn with me. We've got some talking to do."

VI

The fencing job went off smoothly enough. The ground near Oak Creek was not rocky, so the digging was not too hard work. By themselves Doug Monahan and Stub Bailey set the posts and strung up the red barbed wire. It was a square corral about a hundred feet long on each side, with a wire gate in one corner and short wings just off the gate to help in penning cattle.

Because it was a temporary job, just for exhibition, they hadn't dug the holes as deep as usual, nor done as tight a job of stringing wire. But it was sufficient for the purpose.

"There she is," Doug told Foster Lodge. "Ready to go. The more people we can get out, the better."

He looked toward Lodge's milk pen. "Folks'll always come out if you offer to feed 'em. You got a fat calf we might butcher?"

Lodge frowned. "Well, there's one out there, but I'm not a rich man, Monahan, and I got a family. You know, I can't . . ."

"I figured on buying it from you, Mr. Lodge. *I'll* give the barbecue."

Lodge brightened. "In that case, now, I reckon maybe I could. . . ."

When they got off to one side, Stub Bailey worriedly caught Monahan's arm. "You sure you know what you're doing? That's a wicked-lookin' corral. One bad break and you'll own a bunch of cut-up cattle."

Monahan said, "I don't think so. We'll let them ease in there and get a smell at the fence. Once they know the wire will stick them, they're not apt to hit it very hard."

"I hope you're right. But you're sure givin' a cow-brute credit for an awful lot of sense."

It looked for a while as if the milk-pen calf wasn't going to be enough. Even Foster Lodge was amazed at the size of the crowd which turned out for the exhibition. Every farmer on Oak Creek was there, along with his family. The kids played up and down the creek and among the trees. They hadn't been there long until one of them fell in the icy water, and a farmer had to grab him up and rush him to the Lodges' dugout, where the women gathered to exchange gossip. Mrs. Lodge was an unwilling hostess, but she managed to cover it up fairly well when the rest of the women began arriving.

Even though Doug had hired a couple of out-of-work ranch cooks to prepare the dinner, many of the women had brought along cakes and pies anyway. It was a good thing, because most wagon cooks couldn't have baked a cake, even if they'd wanted to.

A good many people from Twin Wells were on hand, too, for a look at this new curiosity. Albert Brown, the portly old banker, had left the lending institution in the able care of his teller and was at the barbecue. He was shaking hands and exchanging pleasantries with everybody he could get around to. He seemed to be laughing all the time. One banker who could refuse you a loan and make you feel good about it, Monahan thought.

Three or four of the smaller ranchers from up at the head of Oak Creek were there, too, rubbing shoulders with the farmers and townspeople. These were likable men, and Monahan spent what extra time he could find visiting with them. They were like the neighbors he had known in South Texas, before the drought.

Most of the men spent their time down around the corral, feeling of the wire, testing its strength. More than one of them tore his shirt.

"A taste of this," Doug heard one of them say, "oughta ruin the appetite of them Fuller Quinn cows."

"If Quinn had to pay me for all the feed his stock has ruined, he'd be out twistin' rabbits, he'd be so broke," another said.

Sheriff Luke McKelvie rode out about mid-morning. He didn't have much to say, just stood around and watched, and listened. Once he walked up to look the fence over. He shook his head distastefully as he fingered the sharp barbs.

Still siding with the captain, Doug Monahan thought. He wondered if McKelvie had something up his sleeve.

"Monahan," the sheriff asked, "what do you figure on getting out of all this?"

"A living, Sheriff. You make yours keeping the peace. I make mine putting up fences."

McKelvie grinned dryly, and there wasn't much humor in him. "You're making it darned hard for me to keep the peace. There's lots of people around here who don't like your bobwire."

"But there are lots who *do* like it and need it."

McKelvie frowned. "It's your right to build it, I reckon, and I can't stop you. But I'll tell you frankly, Monahan, I don't like the stuff. It's been a pretty good country, just the way it was. Maybe I'm just old-fashioned, but I don't want to see it changed."

"Change is the only thing you can be sure of in this world."

McKelvie hunkered down and watched the farmers examining the corral. "Look at it like a cowman—that's where your main opposition is going to come from. Bobwire, once it gets started, will cut him off from a lot of watering places, and a lot of free range he's always used. It'll cut him off from the trails he's accustomed to following to market.

"Then there's the extra cattle you always find on the open range. They don't belong there, but you got to figure on 'em. Maybe the barber or the saloonkeeper or the mercantile man have twenty or thirty head apiece. A lot of cowboys, too, have a handful of cattle in their own brand. They just turn 'em loose and let 'em run on the free range.

"As the country closes up, those people will find themselves crowded off first one place, then another. They'll double up wherever the range isn't fenced yet, and make it hard on the ranchers who hold out to the last before they give in and fence too. Eventually it'll freeze the free-grass man plumb out.

"Then, look at it the way the cowboy will. It takes a lot of cowboys to keep a cow outfit running, the country wide open like it is. But you cut this land up into little pieces, it won't take near as many men to work it. A lot of those boys'll be out of a job, and they're smart enough to see that already."

Monahan nodded soberly. "You've got some good points there, Sheriff, but look at it from the other side. As long as the range is wide open, how can a man develop his own land, other people's cattle crowding into his water and onto his grass? A range hog like this Fuller Quinn keeps throwing more cattle on the range all the time and squeezing the other outfits. The rancher can't breed up his own herd much because so many stray bulls are running around loose. Cow thieves can latch onto a man's cattle and carry them off, and he'll never miss 'em till branding time.

"But you put a fence around him, now, and he can do what he pleases. He can build up the best cattle in the country if he's a mind to. He can fence the range hogs out. He can put a crimp in the cow thief because it won't be easy to put stolen cattle across half a dozen fences and not get caught somewhere.

"What I'm getting at, I guess, is that with the fence the country will finally be permanent. It'll produce more and make a living for more people. There'll be more towns, and they'll be bigger ones. Sure, barbed wire is going to hurt some people. But it'll help a lot more of them than it hurts."

McKelvie had rolled a cigarette. He licked the edge of the brown paper and stuck it down, then sat there with it in his fingers. He eyed Monahan keenly.

"We're both putting up some pretty talk, Monahan. Now let's just break down and get honest with each other. I meant all I said, but I reckon the main reason I'm against your wire is because it's going to hurt the captain. You can't understand this, maybe, but he's been a great man in his day.

"And when we come right down to it, you're not really much interested in the people of Kiowa County, or whether they get their land fenced or not. If it hadn't been for what happened in your camp the other day, you'd've probably left here and everything would've been peaceful. But now you're mad, and you got a hate worked up for the captain. You're determined to stomp on him, and nothing else matters much to you."

Monahan shifted uncomfortably. "I'm going through with it, McKelvie. It's too far gone to pull back now, even if I wanted to."

McKelvie nodded. "I knew you would. But I wanted you to know how I stand." He stood up stiffly and started to move away. He paused a moment and turned back around. "There must be an awful emptiness in a man, Monahan, when all that matters to him is revenge."

The barbecue was about done, and Monahan was getting ready to call the crowd to dinner when a young cowboy rode up looking for McKelvie.

"Sheriff," he said when he found him, "there's been a fight down at the T Bars. They sent me to get you."

McKelvie studied the boy, debating whether he ought to go. "What kind of a fight? Anybody hurt?"

"I don't know, Sheriff. I wasn't there. They just sent me to get you."

McKelvie cast a worried glance at the barbed wire corral, then at Monahan. "All right, son," he said then, "let's go."

Monahan ladled out red beans to the crowd. Stub Bailey stood beside him, forking barbecue onto tin plates as the people came by in single file.

"When that banker Brown comes up," Monahan said, "be sure you give him plenty. He's liable to be lending the money for a lot of fence."

After a while the crowd had finished eating.

"They sure didn't leave much of that calf," Bailey remarked ruefully. He had been one of the last to get to eat, and he hadn't found much that was to his liking.

"So much the better," Doug said. "The more there are, the more fence we may get to build."

Once fed, the crowd was getting restless, wanting to see something.

"All right, Stub," Doug said, "it's time to give 'em the show."

The cattle they wanted were scattered in a green oat patch behind Lodge's barn. The two horsemen circled them slowly and eased them down toward the creek. Some were gentle milk stock, but a few showed a strong mixture of wild Longhorn blood. These part-Longhorns were quick to take the lead, stepping long and high and holding their heads up, looking for a booger.

They didn't have much trouble finding it. With women's billowing skirts and the shouting of playing youngsters, the cattle kept shying away from the crowd. Not until the third try did Monahan and Bailey manage to get them to the wings and push them into the corral. Monahan rode through the gate, stepping down to close it from inside.

The cattle pushed on to the far side of the corral and stopped there, nervously smelling of the barbed wire. This was something new to them, and they distrusted it, especially the high-headed Longhorns. Some of them jerked their heads back and pulled away when they touched their noses to the sharp barbs. A couple of the gentler cows licked at the wire until they hit a barb.

Monahan allowed the cattle a few minutes to get used to the en-
closure. Then he rode in behind them, slapping his rope against his
leg to get them milling. They circled around and around the fence,
looking vainly for a way out, but never did they let themselves brush
against the wire.

The crowd had worked down to the corral now.

"By George," a farmer exclaimed, "that's not half as bad as it
looks. They got onto it in a hurry." He pulled back from the fence
and ripped a hole in his coat.

"They learn faster than *you* do," his wife commented.

Deciding the crowd had seen enough to convince them, Monahan stepped down and led his horse through the gate. He left the
cattle inside.

Walking up to Foster Lodge and a dozen others who had gathered around him, Monahan asked, "Well, what do you think now?"

Lodge replied with satisfaction, "I reckon you proved what you
set out to. And you don't owe for any cattle. We're ready to talk
business."

"There'll never be a better time."

Monahan had been so intent in watching the reactions of the
bystanders that he hadn't seen anything else. Now he heard a mur-
mur of alarm move through the crowd. He saw a woman point excitedly, and he turned quickly to see what the trouble was.

A group of cowboys, maybe twenty in number, had ridden up
to the opposite side of the creek. Now they came spurring across,
splashing the cold water high. Gaining the bank, they spread out in a
line and moved into a lope, yelling and swinging ropes. A few fired
guns into the air.

Women screamed and grabbed up their children. Bigger boys
and girls lit out for the protection of the oak timber. Men pulled
back in a hard trot away from the corral.

Caught by surprise, not carrying a gun, Monahan only stood

and watched the cowboys coming, the dust boiling up behind their horses. The line split. The riders circled around his corral. Ropes snaked out and tightened over fence posts loosely tamped in the dry dirt. Riders spurred away, their horses straining as they began pulling the fence down.

The cattle inside were running wildly from one end of the pen to the other. Now, seeing the fence go down, they made a panicked break for the opening. Some cleared the wire, but others jumped into it, hanging their legs and threshing desperately as cowboys yelled and pushed them on. Most of them watched as the cowboys finished destruction of the corral badly. Two steers were hopelessly enmeshed, legs tangled in the vicious wire. They lay there, fighting in terror.

Archer Spann rode up, gun drawn. He stared coldly at Monahan and leaned over, firing twice. The steers stopped threshing.

Most of the crowd had retreated to the oak timber and watched as the cowboys finished destruction of the corral. Monahan stood in helpless rage, knowing there was nothing he could do to stop it.

In a few minutes it was over. The corral was down, a hopeless tangle of wire and posts. The cowboys gathered on either side of Archer Spann. One who somehow had fallen into the wire had his woolen shirt ripped half away, and he was holding one arm that appeared to be badly cut. A couple of the others were looking it over. Spann turned his horse so that he faced the crowd in the trees.

"You folks listen to this," he said loudly, "and you'd better remember. The captain says tell you there'll not be any bobwire fences!"

He turned away from the crowd and faced Monahan, who stood alone out there in the open. "As for you, Monahan," he said evenly, "this means you pull out of the country and stay out. The next time, you'll *eat* that wire!"

Monahan's fists were clenched, and his face darkened. "I swear to you, Spann," he said bitterly, "I'll even up with you if it takes me twenty years."

Sheriff Luke McKelvie solemnly looked over the tangled wire and pulled-up posts and the two dead cattle. "I got back out here as quick as I could. I thought there was something suspicious, that boy being sent to fetch me. It was a trick, all right, to get me out of the way."

Monahan shrugged angrily, not knowing whether to believe the sheriff or not. It could have been a put-up job.

"Not much we can do about it now, Sheriff, unless you're willing to arrest the men that did it."

McKelvie caught the doubting edge in Monahan's voice, and it irked him. "I can and I will, if you'll sign the complaints. But even if you get them in jail, there's not much you can do. Under Texas law it's nothing more than a misdemeanor to cut or tear down another man's fence. If I throw them in jail, the captain will bail them out, and the judge will give them the lightest fine he can because he's in debt to the captain."

"Wouldn't hardly pay me then, would it, McKelvie?" Monahan asked with bitterness.

McKelvie shook his head. "Not hardly."

Monahan and Stub Bailey rode back to town with the sheriff.

Monahan said, "I thought of one thing I could get Spann for. It's a felony to shoot a man's cattle, isn't it?"

The sheriff said, "Yes, but they were Foster Lodge's cattle at the time they were shot. Do you think Lodge would prefer charges?"

Monahan grudgingly answered, "No, I don't reckon he would." Disappointment was still heavy on his shoulders. He had come so close to selling those farmers. Then, suddenly, the whole thing had blown up in his face. They had backed away from the project as they would from a loaded shotgun.

"You saw them, Monahan," Foster Lodge had said excitedly, his face half white. "The captain's men and some of Fuller Quinn's, too. We can't fight those big outfits. We don't aim to try."

The sheriff pulled up as they passed the big rock courthouse. "Whatever you decide, let me know. But I think you should forget it and leave town."

"Thanks for the advice," Monahan said angrily, not even looking back at him. He headed across the street for Hadley's saloon. If there had ever been a time he needed a drink, this was it.

Oscar Tracey, the mercantile man, saw him from the front porch of his store and hailed him. Monahan hesitated, not knowing whether he wanted to talk to anybody right now or not. But he reined his horse over to Tracey's.

Tracey, a tall, sickly-thin old man, came down off the porch steps in great agitation. "Come around back with me, Mr. Monahan. I've got something to show you."

Monahan and Stub Bailey followed the old storekeeper around the side of the building and out the back. There, in a smouldering pile of ashes and snarled black wire, lay all that was left of the many spools of barbed wire Doug had stored in the shed back of the mercantile.

"They came in here a while before dinnertime," Tracey said. "They took out your wire and piled it on a bunch of old lumber scraps that was lying there. They poured kerosene on the whole mess and set it afire. They said if I ever had another roll of barbed wire in my place, they'd burn the whole store down."

The storekeeper's voice was high-pitched with apprehension. "I'm sorry, Mr. Monahan. I'd like to do anything I could to help you, but you can see what I'm up against. I'm too old to start over again. I've got to protect what I have. You see that, don't you?"

Monahan nodded gravely. "I see it, all right. I'm obliged for all you've done, and I won't ask you to take any chances for me. Looks like I'm out of the fence-building business around here anyway."

Shoulders slumped, he pulled his horse around and headed across to Hadley's saloon. Bailey caught up with him.

"You mean you're giving in, Doug? You're leaving?"

Doug Monahan shrugged. "I don't see what else I can do." His jaw tightened. "But on my way out, I'm going to hunt down Archer Spann and beat him half to death!"

They walked into Chris Hadley's place and moved toward the back. Hadley brought a bottle and a couple of glasses. In his eyes was a quiet sympathy. The news already had reached town.

"Tough day," he said.

Monahan nodded sourly and took a stiff drink.

Hadley said, "So Captain Rinehart's still the big man on the gray horse." He shook his head regretfully. "It could be a good country for a lot of people, but it'll never amount to much as long as the captain's sitting up there like God, holding it back with his fist. For a little while I thought maybe this would be the time. I thought we'd fight our way out from under."

Noah Wheeler moved through the front door, closing it behind him. He sighted Doug Monahan and came walking back, his big frame blocking off much of the light from the front window.

"Been looking for you, Mr. Monahan."

Monahan stood up and shook the old farmer's hand. "Nice to see you again, Mr. Wheeler." He motioned with his hand, and Wheeler sat down.

"Have a drink with us?"

Wheeler said hesitantly, "Well, I'm not much of a drinking man. . . ."

"Neither am I," Monahan replied morosely, "but this seems to be an occasion for it." Trying to shake his dark mood, he asked, "How is everybody?"

"Fine. Just fine."

"Did your cow ever have that calf you were looking for?"

Instantly he saw that he had touched a nerve. Wheeler's lips tightened. "She had the calf." He fingered the glass, frowning. "Best cow I ever had, old Roany. And Sancho, there's not a better bull in all of West Texas. For months I've waited, wanting to see what that calf was going to turn out like. Well, it got here, all right."

He turned his glass up and finished it. "It wasn't from Sancho atall. It was from one of Fuller Quinn's scrub bulls. Big, long-legged calf, spotted with every color in the rainbow. Just a pure-dee scrub."

The old farmer turned his eyes to Monahan, and Monahan could see keen disappointment in them. "I want to have a good herd, and the only way I can build it is with good calves out of cows like Roany. I'll never get the job done as long as any old stray bull can come across my land. So I want one of your fences, Mr. Monahan!"

Monahan almost choked on his drink. He got it down. "Are you sure you know what you're saying?"

Wheeler nodded. "I'm sure. Three days now I've thought it over. I want you to build me a fence."

"Haven't you heard what happened today out on Oak Creek?"

"I heard."

"And you still want to go on?"

"It's *my* land," Wheeler said stubbornly.

Deep inside, conscience was telling Doug Monahan not to agree. Angered because of that scrub calf, the old man might not fully realize what he was letting himself in for. Conscience said to turn him down.

But Doug Monahan paid no attention to his conscience. Suddenly he felt a wild elation, a soaring of spirit. Out of defeat had come his chance.

"Then, come hell or high water," he declared, "we'll build you that fence!"

VII

Doug Monahan walked up to the town's smaller livery stable and found the owner out front, patiently hitching a skittish young sorrel to a two-wheeled horse-breaking gig, a light buggy with long shafts that would keep the animal from kicking it to pieces. Doug watched with interest while the man tied a rope on one of the pony's forefeet, then drew it up through the ring on the hames.

"He starts to run," the liveryman volunteered, "I'll just pick up that forefoot. He can't make much speed on three legs."

Cautiously the man climbed up on the rig, and it looked as if the horse was going to break and run. "Whoa now, be gentle," the man said in a soothing voice.

"You seen Dundee?" Doug asked quickly, for it looked as if the horse was going to run anyway. "They told me he was here."

The liveryman pointed with his chin and took a tight hold on the reins. "Out back yonder, shoeing his horse." The sorrel moved forward, quickly stretching into a long-reaching trot, looking back nervously at the rig which wheeled along behind. The liveryman had him under full control.

Doug glanced up and grinned at a sign over the door: COWBOY, SPIT ON YOUR MATCH OR EAT IT. A livery stable fire was a thing to dread.

Passing through the dark interior and its musty smell of hay, he found Dundee behind the barn, shoeing his good bay horse in the shade. This was one of those mildly warm Texas winter afternoons when an idle man enjoyed leaning back in a rawhide chair and soak-

ing in the fleeting sunshine, while a man working came to appreciate the shade.

Dundee had shod the hind feet first. Now he lifted the horse's
left forefoot and ran his thumb over his preliminary hoof-trimming
job. He straddled the foot and held it between his legs, rasping the
trim job down to a smooth finish. The horse began to lean on him,
and Dundee heaved against him. "Get your weight off of me, you
lazy ox."

He glanced up at Doug Monahan. "Gettin' him in shape to
travel. Looks like we got to, if we're both goin' to eat much longer.
The captain's got the word out he don't want any ranch around here
hirin' men who worked for Gordon Finch."

"Got any plans?"

Dundee shrugged and carefully felt of the hoof, noting an uneven place in it. "Never had a plan in my life. I get tired of a place, I
just move on and hunt me somethin' else. I'd purt near used this
place up anyhow."

Doug squatted on his heels and examined the shoe Dundee was
going to put on the horse's hoof. "How'd you like to work for me?"

Dundee stopped the rasp. "Doing what?"

"Building fence."

Dundee smiled indulgently. "You still on that? Somebody'd
have to hire you before you could hire me. And who's goin' to, after
what happened out there on Oak Crick?"

"Somebody already has."

Dundee straightened. "Who?"

"Noah Wheeler. Nobody knows it yet, and I want it quiet as
long as we can keep it that way."

"I won't say anythin'."

"What do you think about that job?"

Dundee dropped the horse's foot and wiped his half-rolled

sleeve against his forehead, leaving a streak of sweat-soaked dirt. He dropped the rasp into a box. "I never could get a shovel handle or a crowbar to fit these hands of mine," he said, holding out his right hand and bending the fingers.

"Fit a gun all right, though, don't they?"

Dundee smiled. "They always considered me a fair to middlin' good shot."

"Maybe I'll need that gun hand more than the shovel-handle hand. I never was any great shot, myself."

"It'd take more than just me. You'd have to have several good men, Monahan, if you was to really make it stick."

"That's where you come in, Dundee. I need a good crew. Most of mine left the country. I figured you might know some good men who can work hard and at the same time could handle a fight if one came at them."

A strong flicker of interest was in Dundee's eyes. "I think maybe I could rustle up a few."

Relieved, Monahan said, "It's a deal, then? I've got Stub Bailey left, and maybe one or two more. If you can find me as many as six or seven more, I can use them. What're cowboy wages around here?"

"Vary with the man. Average about thirty dollars a month, and found."

"I'll pay forty. And a little bonus if we get the job done without too much cut wire or other damage from the R Cross."

Dundee grinned with admiration. "You get your mind set on somethin', you just don't quit, do you? I thought they'd quit makin' that kind anymore." He turned back and patted the bay horse on the neck. "Well, old hoss, looks like we may stick around a while and watch the show."

★   ★   ★

It was a fifty-mile ride to the cedar-cutters' camp, down on the river and out of Kiowa County. That was a long way to haul posts in a wagon. It would have been easier to use mesquite or live oak, but Doug was convinced that cedar would make better, longer-lasting posts.

He reached the camp in time for supper. The night chill was moving in with a raw south wind, and he was glad for the sight of the big side-boarded tent the Blessingame men used for a home. They would set it up in the heart of a cedar thicket and proceed to cut the cedar down from around it. When the posts were all cut and sold, they would simply hunt another thicket.

In the edge of camp, amid a tinder-dry litter of trimmed-off limbs and browning dead cedar leaves, Monahan saw dozens of stacks of cedar posts, some of them no more than three inches across the top, and some of the longest ones a foot or more, stout enough to build an elephant pen.

He could hear a clatter of pots and pans. The noise stopped, and huge old Foley Blessingame ducked through the tent flap, looking to see who was riding up. His big voice boomed, "Git down, Doug, and come on in here. We'll have a bite to eat directly."

Foley Blessingame was crowding sixty, Doug knew for a fact. If he hadn't known, he wouldn't have been able to guess within twenty years. Foley stood six feet four, and his powerful shoulders were axe handle–broad as he stood there, his tangled red beard lifting and falling in the cold wind. The man had arms as thick and hard as the cedar posts he cut for a living.

"You ain't going to like the supper," Foley said, "but it won't be any worse on you than it is on the rest of us. Mules spooked the other day and run over me with a wagonload of posts. Bunged up my chopping arm. I got to do the cooking now till I kin handle an axe ag'in. The kids are out yonder workin'."

From somewhere in the brush echoed the ring of steel axes biting deep into heart-cedar.

"Just bunged up your arm?" Doug asked wonderingly. "Is that
all the damage it did?"

"Well, it like to've tore up an awful good wagon." Blessingame
motioned at Doug's horse. "Just skin the saddle off and turn him
loose. He'll find our bunch and stay with them. The kids'll put out a
little grain directly."

Doug unsaddled and followed the old man through the tent flap.
A big woodstove had it much warmer inside, but the place reeked of
scorched grease and burned bread.

"Never did care much for cookin'," Blessingame complained.
"I'd rather cut fifty trees with a dull ax than stick my hands in a keg
of sourdough. I always leave this chore up to the kids. Ain't no job
for a growed man anyhow."

"Let me take a turn at it," Doug offered, and the old man
stepped aside. "I'd be much obliged."

Paco Sanchez had taught Doug a deal about camp cooking.
There wasn't much he could do about old Foley's sourdough now. It
was too late for a new batch to rise before supper, so he'd just have
to use this. He sliced thick venison steaks off a tarp-wrapped hind
quarter hanging from a tree outside. He salted them and flopped
them down, one by one, into a keg of flour, until they were well
coated. The Blessingames made their living cutting cedar, but Monahan noted with relief that the fuel in the woodbox was all dry
mesquite. It was better for cooking.

Old Foley sat on the edge of a cot, grinning. "You missed your
callin', boy. You ought to been a wagon cook."

That brought up a memory of Paco Sanchez, and Doug Monahan's face went tight. Blessingame was quick to sense the change.

"One of the kids was in town day or two ago and heard a rumor," he said. "Heard you lost that good old cook you had."

Doug nodded, dipping lard out of a big bucket and dropping it into a skillet. News sure could get around. He told Blessingame the whole story.

The old man nodded gravely. "Looks like a good country for a smart man to stay out of. There's plenty other country needin' fences anyway."

"I'm not staying out of it," Doug told him.

Blessingame's bearded face showed a little of a grin. "I figured that. I said a *smart* man."

When the supper was about done, Blessingame walked outside and gave a great roar. His voice was as strong as his bull shoulders. That yell should have reached to Kiowa County.

In a moment he returned. "Here come the kids."

The "kids" were four huge, brawny men with red hair and red whiskers. The youngest was in his mid–twenties, the oldest probably thirty-five. Every one of them showed the gross stamp of old Foley Blessingame in the breadth of shoulder, the deep boom of voice. Doug had made a point to have flour and dough on his fingers so he wouldn't have to shake hands with them as they came in. Those great ham–sized hands would crush his own like an egg. Even as it was, they pounded him on the back till his breath was gone.

Here was a family known all the way back to East Texas, old Foley Blessingame and his four "kids," Foy, Koy, Ethan and John. Nearly three-quarters of a ton of hard muscle among them, and not an ounce of it fat. Most of the time they stayed out in the country and never bothered anybody. But when they came to town for a little unwinding every two or three months, townspeople took up the sidewalk, locked their doors and hid their daughters.

Widowed fifteen years, old Foley never let his boys outpace him. "Snow on the roof ain't no sign the fire's out inside," he often said.

When the hangovers were done, he always went back to town alone and sober, remorsefully paying for the breakage. "Bunch o' growin' boys," he would explain; "a man can't always hold them down."

None of the boys had married yet. The sight of them, Doug imagined, was enough to stampede a girl anyway. Even if one ever got interested, she was bound to reason, and correctly so, that she would immediately find herself burdened with cooking and washing and scrubbing up after the rest of the family as well as the one she took on.

There wasn't much extra room in the tent, what with five cots and a cookstove. Doug left supper in the pans he had cooked it in, letting the five men file by and take what they wanted. They took plenty.

"Doug's havin' a little trouble convincin' some of the boys over in Kiowa County that he likes his fences to stay up," old Foley told his sons. "I think mebbe we ought to some of us step over there and give the folks a little lecture."

Doug fidgeted uneasily. "Well, that's not exactly what I came over here for. Mainly I need a big order of posts."

"We got 'em," Foley said. "We been choppin' more than we been sellin' here lately."

"I noticed that," Doug replied, "and I've been thinking. Maybe you ought to quit chopping awhile and let the demand catch up with the supply."

"Got to eat someway," said Foley.

"You could work for me, building fence."

Foley frowned. "Sounds like hard work. That's the main reason I quit farmin' back in East Texas, wanted to git away from that hard work."

Doug grinned. There wasn't any harder work in the world than cedar-cutting, and Foley Blessingame knew it better than anyone.

"The way I see it, Foley, you and your boys could have a hundred yards of fence built while most people were still gouging out that first posthole. And when the folks over in Kiowa County see the size of the Blessingame bunch, they're going to study awhile before they do anything to sour your temper."

"Well," Foley conceded, "I've noticed folks gin'rally let us have our way about things. Not that any of my kids ever loses their temper. We're easy to get along with."

"I'll pay you good."

Foley nodded. "I know you would. But I ain't sure about it. Never did cotton to working for the other feller. Always liked to be my own boss, you know what I mean? Never any argument thataway. I worked for a man once when I was jest a button, twenty-five or -six years old. He got to sassin' me one day, and I let my temper git the best of my good judgment. Always did feel sorry for that feller afterwards. I just rode off and never even let him pay me the wages I had comin', I felt so bad about it."

He frowned. "Course, I would've had to wait a week to git it. He was that long comin' to."

Foley got up and began gathering the boys' tin plates, dumping them into a tub. "Say, Doug," he asked pleasantly, "you like to play poker?"

Doug shrugged. "Used to, a little."

Foley commented, "I'd rather play poker than eat, only I can't get these shiftless kids of mine to play anymore."

Doug didn't feel like playing, and he caught the friendly warning in the eyes of the Blessingame boys. But he wanted to keep on Foley's warm side. "I'll play you a game or two, if we don't put much money in it."

"Penny ante's fine. Ethan, you go fetch us some matches to use."

In two hours Foley seldom lost a hand. He had a pile of matches in front of him that could burn off all the grass in three counties. Doug never had seen anybody with such a phenomenal streak of luck. Even at penny ante, he had lost more than he wanted to.

"Bedtime," Foley yawned at last, raking up the matches and starting to count them out. "Unless you want to keep on and try to win it back."

Doug shook his head. "I can't beat your kind of luck."

Foley walked outside a few minutes, and Ethan Blessingame whispered, "We tried to give you the high sign. It ain't all luck. He cheats!"

Next morning Doug got up and cooked the breakfast. He started a pot of red beans and mixed up a new batch of dough before he left the Blessingame camp. Foley watched admiringly as Doug put the dough together.

"You ought to been a woman," he said. "But on second thought, if you was, you wouldn't be out here. I reckon we'd best leave well-enough alone."

Doug said, "Made up your mind yet about working for me?"

Foley nodded. "Full stomach always weakens my judgment, Doug. We decided we'd take you up on that proposition. Jest one condition."

"What's that?"

"Make sure there's somebody in your outfit can play poker. You play a mighty poor hand, yourself."

From the Blessingame camp Doug rode on to Stringtown, the nearest point on the railroad from Twin Wells. He struck the rails several miles out and followed them in. They still had a little of the new shine to them, and the ties hadn't weathered out badly yet. It hadn't been more than a couple of years since the line had come through.

Stringtown wasn't fancy to look at, but it was all new. The original paint coat still stuck to those frame buildings which had been painted at all. Springtown had sprung up because of the railroad.

Doug's first stop was the railroad depot, where the telegrapher was tapping out code on the key. "Can you take a message to Fort Worth?" Doug asked.

"If you can write it to where I can read it," the little man said and nodded at some sheets of yellow paper weighted down by a small gear wheel from a locomotive.

Doug wrote the address of a Fort Worth hardware company and asked the price of a hundred spools of No. 9 barbed wire, including freight to Stringtown. He handed the message to the telegrapher. "I'll be back around directly for the answer," he said.

He walked out of the depot building, thinking he might cross over to a saloon and while away the time where it was warmer. On the platform, he heard the whistle of an approaching train, and he leaned back against the yellow-painted wall to watch it.

It was an eastbound passenger train. It whistled again, coming into town, and began slowing down. A conductor hung precariously off the side of one car as the train's momentum slowed, and he jumped down to the ground, his shoes sliding on the grime-blackened gravel. A Negro porter stepped down and set a wooden platform in place.

Suddenly Doug wished he wasn't standing out in the open this way, for he saw Sheriff Luke McKelvie of Twin Wells, walking up to the train. A sullen young man was handcuffed to him. A tall man in a dark suit stepped off the train, looked around, then moved directly toward the pair. McKelvie shook hands and motioned toward his prisoner, saying something. Taking a key from his pocket, he removed the handcuffs. The other man immediately brought out his own cuffs and locked himself to his new prisoner. The engine whistled a warning. The two boarded the train and disappeared inside.

McKelvie watched until satisfied. Then he turned and walked toward Doug Monahan, dropping the cuffs in his coat pocket. "Hello, Monahan. Saw you as I came up, but I was too busy to say howdy. Had to transfer a prisoner."

Monahan shook hands with him, wishing he hadn't had the misfortune to run into the Kiowa County sheriff.

"Got my job done, and now I can relax," McKelvie said. "Care to have a drink with me?"

Monahan declined as gracefully as he could. "I got some business to attend to, thanks." He didn't care to have McKelvie pumping him, and he had a notion the sheriff could worm a lot of information out of a man without really seeming to.

"Well," replied McKelvie, "that's too bad. But I think you're showing good judgment, getting out of Twin Wells."

A sharp thrust of stubbornness brought a reply from Monahan before he could stop himself. "I haven't left there for good. I'll be back soon enough."

The sheriff's easy smile faded. "I'm sorry, Monahan." Regret clouded his gray eyes.

Monahan watched the sheriff walk down the street, and he felt like kicking himself. Whatever secret there might have been was out now. McKelvie would probably poke around until he knew just what Monahan was up to, and the report wouldn't be long in getting to Captain Rinehart.

Well, that was the way it went. A man got mad and said things he didn't mean to. There wasn't much he could do about it now except go right on as he had planned. He didn't go across to the saloon, though. Instead, he went back into the depot and sat down on a hard wooden bench, leaning back against the wall and waiting for the answer to his wire. When it came, he sent another message constituting an order for wire and staples to be shipped to him at Stringtown. He promised to send a check immediately. Mailed here, it would be in Fort Worth before they got the order ready to ship.

Handing it to the telegrapher, he asked, "Who's a good freighter around here? I'll want him to haul this shipment out for me."

The telegrapher said, "Try Slim Torrance over at the livery barn. He's got new wagons, and he's a good man. Besides, he's my brother-in-law."

"Reason enough for a recommendation," Doug said.

The livery barn bore the name Spangler & Torrance, and it smelled strongly of dry hay and liniment and oil, horse sweat and manure. A practical combination, Monahan thought, livery barn and freighting outfit. He found Slim Torrance in the rear of the barn, rubbing some evil-smelling concoction on the leg of a lame mule.

"I got a shipment of barbed wire due from Fort Worth in a few days," Doug told the chunky, red-faced freighter. "I'd be much obliged if you'd haul it over into Kiowa County for me."

Torrance nodded. "Freightin's my business. You jest tell me where you want it, and I'll git it over there."

Monahan gave him instructions as to the trail. He added, "It wouldn't be a bad idea if you skirted around town. Folks don't have to know about it for awhile. Wouldn't hurt to cover the load with a tarp, too, so it won't stand out if somebody happens to pass you on the trail."

Torrance frowned. "Wait a minute now. If it's one of them kind of deals, I don't know . . ."

"I'll pay you half of it in advance."

Torrance wrestled with himself a minute, and the money won. "All right, I'll do it."

Writing out the check, Monahan said, "It'll be better for all of us if nothing's said about this till the shipment's delivered. No use setting out bait to catch trouble."

"No use atall," Torrance agreed, carefully folding the check and shoving it deep into the pocket of his denim pants.

"By the way," Monahan said, "I sure could use a wagon cook. Know anybody around here who can cook and needs the job?"

Torrance said, "Got jest the man for you. Come on back in here."

Later, riding out, Monahan saw McKelvie's horse tied down by the depot.

In there now pumping the telegrapher, he thought, more angry at himself than at McKelvie. *He won't leave town till he knows.*

VIII

R iding in abreast of the Blessingames' three post-laden wagons, Doug found that Stub Bailey and Noah Wheeler had been busy while he was gone.

"Watch out for those stakes yonder," he called back to old Foley Blessingame, on the lead wagon. "They mark where the posts are to be set."

Foley saw them and swung his mules a little to the right so the heavy wheels would pass between two stakes, set a rod apart.

Stub Bailey rode out grinning to meet the wagons. He shook Doug's hand and motioned toward the line of stakes. "Half afraid you wasn't comin' back, Doug. I sure would've hated to drive all them stakes for nothin'." His gaze roved over the Blessingames' wagons, and especially over the Blessingames themselves. "Man alive," he breathed, "they all come out of one family?"

Monahan nodded, and Bailey shook his head. "I'd sure hate to be the woman who had to give birth to that bunch."

Monahan grinned. "Well, they came one at a time, I reckon. They'll haul in all the posts we need, then stay and help us build the fence."

Bailey approved of that. "I'll bet they can make a pick and shovel sing Dixie."

"The first Rinehart man who gets himself crossways with them may sing a little, too," Doug said.

Big old Noah Wheeler was standing in front of his barn waiting as the three heavy wagons rolled up, their iron rims grinding deep tracks into the shower-dampened earth, crushing the cured brown grass. "Howdy, Doug," he said. "Looks like you've brought the makings."

Doug stepped off his horse and shook the farmer's rough hand. "Ought to be enough posts to get us started. Plenty more where these came from. Wire ought to be here by the time we get enough posts up to commence stringing it."

He hadn't realized how tired the long ride had made him until he sat down a moment on the barn's front step. He was glad to be back here. He felt himself drawn to this pleasant place with its good corrals, its scattering of Durham cattle, its ducks swimming out there on the surface tank, and its chickens scratching around in the yard. He liked the Wheelers' little red frame house with the front porch that would be so good for sitting and rocking in the late summer evenings.

Without wanting to show it, he looked around for Trudy Wheeler and felt vaguely disappointed that he didn't see her anywhere.

"How's the family, Noah?"

"Fine, getting along fine." Wheeler looked toward the house. "Halfway thought they'd come out to look, but I reckon not." He frowned. "Doug, in case they say anything, don't worry yourself too much about it."

"What do you mean?"

"They're not as much in favor of this fence as I thought they'd be. Fact of the matter, they're against it. You know how women are. Or do you? You're not married, are you?"

"No, sir."

"Time you get married, you'll know what I mean. A man ought to go ahead and do what he wants to and not let the women bother him, I guess. Ought to let them know he's the boss. But when the time comes, you hate to do it. A man who's got womenfolks has just got to put up with a certain amount of that, I reckon."

Doug had an uneasy moment, afraid Noah Wheeler was leading up to calling the whole thing off. He thought of Captain Rinehart, and of his foreman, Archer Spann, and he felt his heart quicken. Wheeler *couldn't* call it off now, and cheat Monahan out of the satisfaction he'd get from humbling them.

Wheeler put an end to his anxiety. "I thought maybe we'd start down on the southwest corner and work up. That's where the most of the strays come in from, and we'll cut them off first."

There was the immediate problem of getting settled. Best thing to do with the posts was to unload them right where they would be needed.

"Where'll you be putting up, Doug?" Foley Blessingame asked. When Doug showed him the barn, the old cedar cutter said, "If it's all the same to you, we'll just put up our tent when we bring that last load of posts. Me and the kids is used to it, and the barn won't be none too roomy anyhow with this crew you got." Dundee had brought out four men.

Out at the side of the barn, Doug rigged up three posts and stretched a tarp to them from the edge of the roof. This cover would help protect the cook in bad weather. They could set up a stationary chuckbox out here under the tarp. The cook could have his fire just beyond it, where the smoke would lift clear and not drift back underneath.

The cook was Simon Getty, the grunting, red-faced man Doug had picked up in Torrance's livery barn. Monahan had borrowed a horse from Torrance so the cook could ride with him. Torrance was to pick up the animal when he brought the wire. But the cook had barely managed to stay on him to the Blessingames' camp. From there, he had ridden the last wagon.

"Looks like what he needs is a good sweat bath," Foley had commented dryly. "Sweat the alcohol out of his system. Man ain't got no use drinkin' if he can't hold his liquor."

"Looks to me like he's holding too much of it," Monahan had replied.

Getty was a shortish man with a puffed face and a soft paunch. And, it had developed, a short temper. He hadn't been in condition to do the cooking the first night at the Blessingames', but he had done it since. He put up a pretty decent meal, too, if a man didn't mind listening to him complain.

"Damn these outfits that don't give a man decent pots to cook in," he said ten times with every meal. "I've cooked for a hundred of 'em, and there ain't a one ever give me anythin' I'd cook for a dog in."

Doug took it with a grain of salt, for he had seen few wagon cooks who didn't gripe a little. It put a little extra flavoring in the food, like salt. And, as long as it didn't get to rankling anybody, it gave the rest of the crew something to snicker about—when they got out of earshot.

Stub Bailey came around, and Doug asked him, "Did you go over and see what cooking equipment you could salvage from Paco's camp?"

"I went over, but there wasn't anything left. Somebody beat us to it. Stole ever' Dutch oven, beanpot, knife, fork and spoon there was. Even a couple of wagon wheels that the spokes hadn't burned out of."

Monahan swore under his breath. "I was counting on that stuff. Been borrowing from the Blessingames, and I didn't want to keep on doing it. Took everything we had, did they?"

"One of them poverty nester outfits over on Oak Crick, I figured. Took everything but the posts and burned-up wire. I don't reckon there's anybody fool enough to want that." Bailey added as an afterthought, "By the way, there's plenty of good posts over there, in the ground. They ain't set so hard yet but what we could take a good team of mules and yank them out of the ground one at a time."

Monahan shook his head. "They're Gordon Finch's posts. He paid me cash for them. He can take them up himself, if he wants to."

Out of the corner of his eye, Doug kept watching for Trudy Wheeler to show herself. But so far as he could tell while they were setting up camp, she never did. She was staying in the house.

Late in the afternoon everything was in its place. The Blessingames' wagons had been unloaded and made ready for a return trip after more posts tomorrow. The cook had a fire going just beyond the tarp on the side of the barn, and pots and pans were rattling. It would be a while before supper.

Doug walked to the Wheelers' house, up onto the porch and knocked on the door. He could hear a stirring inside, and presently Mrs. Wheeler opened the door. Doug took off his hat. This tall, strong, graying woman looked at him with no unfriendliness but with no special welcome.

"Good evening, Mrs. Wheeler."

"Good evening, Mr. Monahan."

"We've gotten everything in order, and I thought I'd come over and pay my respects."

"That's nice of you."

He tried to see around her, but he couldn't spot Trudy Wheeler. He could tell that Wheeler had been right about the women. They weren't strong at all on this fencing business. It showed on Mrs. Wheeler, in her withdrawal from her inborn hospitality. She was vastly different from the last time he had been here.

When it became evident that she wasn't going to invite him in, he said awkwardly, "Well, I guess I better be getting back. Horses got to be fed." A shading of disappointment crept into his voice. "I'll be seeing you again, Mrs. Wheeler."

"Yes," she replied, and he thought her voice softened a little, for she must have caught his disappointment. "I'm sure we'll see each other, Mr. Monahan."

He put his hat back on and walked off the porch, discontent gnawing at him. He hadn't considered this, the opposition from the women. He was at a loss to put a reason to it. Well, what difference did it make to him, anyway? Main thing was to get the fence up.

After all, they weren't *his* women.

The Blessingames were up before daylight. By the time the sun broke over the low hills to the east, they had their horses hitched to the three wagons and were ready to go. Doug Monahan stood there watching the breath of the horses rise as steam in the sharp morning air.

"Going to be cold up there on those wagons seats, till the sun gets up high enough to take the chill off," he told Foley.

The huge old man tolerantly shook his head. "Like a spring day. You South Texas boys don't know what cold weather is. Prob'ly never saw a frost in your life till you come up here."

Doug shivered and smiled. "Well, I know what it is now." He went serious then. "Be careful, Foley. It'd be better if nobody saw you. If anybody asks you, don't tell them where the posts are going. I'd like to get all the wire and posts in before any trouble starts. After that, they can do what they please, and we'll be ready."

Foley flipped the reins and led off with his wagon. From a hundred yards away he turned and yelled back in a voice that would have scared a Longhorn bull out over the corral gate: "Don't you worry none about me and the kids. We'll be as quiet's a mouse!"

The wagons rolled away with a groan of wheels and clanking of chains. Horses snorted in the cold. Doug watched until they were well on their way. Turning then, he saw Trudy Wheeler walking toward the spring, carrying a wooden bucket in each hand.

It was the first time he had seen her since he had returned, except for a glimpse or two of her at a distance as she stepped out on the porch a moment. He stood watching her, admiring her slenderness, her easy way of moving. Then he followed after her.

Entering the rock spring house, she filled the buckets one at a time from the water which bubbled up to flow through the milkcooling trough and on out into the creek. As she straightened, Doug said, "I'll carry them for you."

Startled, she whirled to face him. "Oh, it's you." Her breath came fast for a moment. "Why don't you make a little noise when you come up behind somebody that way?"

"I was afraid you might walk away and leave me."

She fixed a half-hostile gaze on him, and her voice was cool. "I might have, at that."

He picked up the buckets. "Where to?"

"The washpot. We're fixing to put out a washing today."

He walked along beside her, trying to think of something to say which might offset her coolness, but nothing came to him. She contributed nothing, either, until they reached the big blackened pot behind the house.

"Just pour a little water in there and let me sweep out the pot," she said.

He did, and she swept the water around inside the pot with an old wornout broom, washing away the settled dust. When she swept the last of the water out she said, "I'll handle it from here on, thank you."

He shook his head. "It'll take a lot of water. I'll do it."

He kept toting water until the pot was filled. While he was doing that, Trudy was piling dry mesquite wood underneath and around the pot. She poured a little kerosene around it from a five-gallon can, struck a match and flipped it under the pot. The flame spread slowly, timidly, at first, then grew stronger and bolder with the taste of the wood. In a few minutes it was a crackling blaze.

The warmth of the fire felt good in this chill. But watching it, Doug could not help thinking about another fire a few days ago, and a restless spirit moved in him. "I've been wanting to talk to you ever since I got back. Why've you been avoiding me?"

"Don't you know?"

"No, I don't, except your dad says you don't like the fence."

"The fence itself is all right. It's what we may have to go through because of it that I don't like."

"If there's a fight, I'll be here to handle it."

Her eyes were suddenly flinty. "That's just it, you know there'll be a fight. That's why you're here in the first place. You don't really care whether we have a fence or not. You're just looking for a fight with Captain Rinehart, and by building us a fence you figure on provoking it."

He opened his mouth but she cut him off before he had a chance to reply. A mounting anger colored her face. "There's one thing you can say about the captain—he's no hyprocrite. He tells you what he wants and doesn't want, and no mistake about it.

"We all felt sorry for you that first day, Mr. Monahan. We brought you here because you'd been done an awful wrong. I can't say I blame you, even yet, for wanting to get even. But when you take an old man like Dad and talk him into building a fence so you can provoke trouble and have a chance at getting revenge, you're doing him an awful wrong, too. You're just using Dad and us for bait!"

"Now, that's not the way it is. . . ."

"Isn't it?" Her eyes sparkled. "Then maybe you can tell me what way it is. No, I don't want you telling me anything! I just want you to leave me alone."

She turned her back on him, and he knew there was no use trying to talk any further with her, not today. He could feel the red color warm in his cheeks. Something between anger and hurt swelled in him. He left her and walked back toward the barn.

Stub Bailey came out the barn door and saw Monahan's face. He looked past Doug to the girl, who was cutting up blocks of homemade soap and stirring it in the heating water with a wooden paddle, agitating it a lot more than she needed to.

"Got the lecture, did you?" Stub said. "I could've told you."

Monahan felt like snapping at Stub to shut up, but he managed to withhold that. Still, he couldn't look Bailey in the face.

"I got a little of the same, but I expect she saved the big load for you because you're the boss," Stub said. He paused and gazed seriously at Monahan. "Maybe you ought to take a good look at yourself and do some thinkin' on what she said. She could be ninety percent right."

IX

Captain Andrew Rinehart sat in the heavy oak swivel chair at his big roll-top desk, cavernous eyes blinking in disbelief at his foreman Archer Spann.

"Noah Wheeler building a fence? You must be mistaken, Archer."

"No mistake, Captain. Shorty Willis and Jim was scouting that south prairie when they came up on three wagons loaded with fence posts, moving northwest on that old freighter trail. There was a big old man driving the lead wagon, and four others coming along on the other two wagons. Whole bunch was redheaded and looked like a set of giants, Shorty said. Shorty stopped and asked them where they was taking the posts. The old man told him, 'To hell, Sonny, and we'll take you with us if you don't go on about your business.' "

The captain shook his gray head. "Redheaded giants. Sounds like Shorty's been drinking. I've warned those boys. . . ."

Spann protested, "He wasn't drinking, Captain. Jim backed him up. They left the wagons but circled back and trailed them. They went straight to Noah Wheeler's place."

"Did the boys look around any? What did they see?"

"They saw men digging postholes and setting posts. They didn't see any wire, but there were posts scattered along Wheeler's boundary, up next to Fuller Quinn's country."

The captain took a long breath and let it out slowly. Regret sharpened his wind-bitten face. "Noah Wheeler. He's the last one I'd ever have thought would do it."

"The last one?" Spann asked sharply, then softened the edge in his voice. "He was the first one to move into this country and break up land away from Oak Crick. He's never asked you about anything or told you what he was going to do. He's got a head of his own, that nester has, and it's time somebody bumped it for him."

The captain studied Archer Spann silently, his eyes unreadable.

Spann said, "I tried to get you to let me do something about him when he first moved out there and took up land that you'd been using. It would've been easy to chase him back to the crick. Clear out of the country would've been even better." Spann's dark eyebrows knitted, and his black eyes took on an eager light. "It's not too late. When we get through with him, he'll pack up and leave, and he won't look back."

"What would you do, Archer?"

"Burn him out. Tear up whatever fence he's got built. Run cattle into his fields. Show him he's nothing but a farmer after all, no better than the rest of those Oak Crick nesters."

The captain slowly shook his head. "He's more than just a nester, Archer, a great deal more. There won't be any burning him out. And there won't be any R Cross cattle on his fields, either. We'll just ride over there and talk to him."

Spann swallowed hard. "Talk to him?"

The captain nodded. "He'll see our way."

Disappointed, Spann said, "It's a mistake, sir." The captain eyed him sharply, and Spann backed down a little. "I mean, sure, we'll talk to him first, if you'd rather. We can do something else later, if we have to. When do you want to go?"

"In the morning will be all right."

"I'll get a bunch of the boys ready."

The captain sounded impatient. "We don't need a bunch of men! Just you and me. We're going to talk to him, that's all. He'll listen."

Spann nodded in resignation. "I hope so, sir. I hope so."

He walked out, softly closing the captain's office door behind him. Out of the old man's sight, he let the welling anger run its course. He struck his right fist sharply into the palm of his left hand.

He half hoped Wheeler wouldn't listen. Then perhaps Archer Spann could give that contrary old farmer what he'd been asking for ever since he had been out here.

Sarah Rinehart made her way into the captain's office and sat down, breathing a little harder for the effort. She had done better these last few days. She had been walking some outside, and she seemed to be regaining much of her strength. There was color in her face that the captain hadn't seen in months.

Seeing her like this had given him a lift he hadn't felt in a long time. Every cowboy at the headquarters had noticed how much better the captain's spirit had been. At times he would even soften up and laugh with them. It had been a long time since the captain's stern manner had eased so.

"What was the matter with Archer Spann?" Sarah asked. "He walked out of here looking awfully mad."

"Mad?" The captain sounded surprised. "He didn't act mad. A little disappointed, maybe."

"Looked mad to me. What happened?"

Briefly Rinehart told her. Worriedly Sarah asked, "What are you going to do, Andrew?"

"Nothing much. Just go over and talk to Noah."

"And if that doesn't change his mind? What then?"

The captain frowned darkly. That possibility evidently hadn't entered his mind. "It will, Sarah. Don't you worry yourself over it."

Sarah said, "Perhaps if it were just you, I wouldn't worry about it. But Archer Spann worries me. And lately he seems to have a lot of influence over you."

Rinehart stiffened. "I always do what *I* want to, Sarah. No man ever tells me what I ought to do."

"No man ever used to," she said resolutely.

*   *   *

Archer Spann pulled up his horse and pointed out across the rolling gray prairie. "Yonder it is, captain, just like Shorty said."

Andrew Rinehart felt a sharp stab of disappointment, seeing the line of firmly set fence posts stretching several hundred feet along Noah Wheeler's boundary line. All the way out from the ranch headquarters the captain had tried to maintain a hope that the boys had been wrong. He had known all the time that it was a vain wish. Yet, seeing the proof now brought a painful letdown.

"Looks like I owe Shorty Willis an apology," the captain conceded quietly. From the corner of his eye he caught the fleeting smile of self-satisfaction that crossed Spann's face before the foreman could suppress it.

It brought a touch of anger to him, for the captain was still a man of pride, a man who hated to be found wrong in any degree, who hated most of all to give another man the satisfaction of having been right.

"I'll do the talking, Archer," the captain said curtly. Spann had the good judgment to nod agreement. "Yes, sir."

From behind them somewhere a horse nickered. Turning in the saddle, the captain saw a rider trailing along at a respectful distance, saddlegun cradled in his arm. Rinehart realized that they probably had been under surveillance for some time. He clenched his fist and had a sudden feeling of being squeezed into a tight corner.

"Not a friendly outfit," Spann observed.

The captain squinted but could not make the man out. "Who is he?"

"Name's Dundee. Used to work for Finch."

"I passed the word around I didn't want anybody hiring any of Finch's hands."

"It looks like he's working *here*," Spann said pointedly.

Grinding out a harsh word under his breath, the captain

touched spurs to his big gray horse, moving across the thick mat of cured grass toward the fencing crew. The men who had been digging holes and tamping in posts dropped their tools and drifted together. The captain could see they were all armed. It was different from the way it had been at Monahan's fencing camp.

He saw a thin wisp of smoke rising, and the sight of a campfire reminded him how cold he was. Riding in closer, he kept watching for Noah Wheeler. His fading eyesight made it hard for him to see faces, but he finally recognized the big farmer's tall frame, moving toward him from a pile of cedar posts.

"Hello, Andrew," Wheeler said.

Spann glanced sharply at the captain, surprised at this farmer's casual use of Rinehart's first name. He had never heard anyone but Mrs. Rinehart herself call the old cowman Andrew.

"Hello, Noah." The captain held back a moment, then reached down and took the big hand that Wheeler offered.

Wheeler said, "Pot of coffee on the fire. Get down, Andrew, and have a cup with me."

The captain waited, and Wheeler said, "You must be cold. A little hot coffee would do you good."

The captain caught the pleasant aroma of the simmering coffee, and he felt a strong yearning for it. He was a-quiver from the morning cold which had worked through to his bones.

He felt the eyes of the men upon him, however, and he hesitated. He had not allowed himself much familiarity with anyone these last years. Men watched him in awe, and part of the reason was that he somehow stood apart from the others, apart from and a little above them. With familiarity, some of this awe would surely vanish. Many a lonely time he would have given half of what he owned to be able to mix with men and be one of them again, the way it had been forty years ago. But with his strict self-discipline he had managed to remain aloof—aloof and alone. Noah Wheeler held out a cup of hot coffee. "Come on, Andrew, for old times' sake."

And Captain Andrew Rinehart stepped down from his big gray horse and took the farmer's cup. "Thank you, Noah."

Archer Spann watched in wonderment.

The two men stood staring at each other, sipping their coffee. "Been a long time, Andrew," Wheeler said presently, "since we stood around like this and drank coffee together."

The captain nodded gravely. "A long time and a long way off. Things were different then, Noah, and so were we."

Wheeler thoughtfully shook his head. "Not so much. We're a right smart older, but I doubt that we've really changed so much."

"I guess you know why I've come, Noah," said the captain.

Wheeler nodded. "The fence."

"I thought you knew how I felt about fences. I thought everybody knew."

Wheeler nodded. "I know."

"Then why are you doing this?" the captain said sharply.

Wheeler frowned into his cup, studying hard for the right words. "Because I have to, Andrew. I've done a lot with this land in the years I've had it, but I've gone about as far as I can go with it open the way it is. I've got to close it in; then whatever I build can stay."

"Fences will ruin this country, Noah."

"You're wrong, Andrew. They'll change it, but they won't ruin it. You watch, they'll be the making of the country."

"I like it the way it is."

"Andrew, you were one of the first white men to come to this country and stay. You could see the possibilities in it, but you had to make a lot of changes first. Now other people are coming in, and there are a lot of changes *they've* got to make.

"I've got a dream for my place here, Andrew. I know what I want to do and how I've got to do it. But right now I can't raise good crops for stray cattle coming into my fields. I can't breed better cattle as long as scrub bulls keep getting with my cows. If I can't do these things, then from here on out I'm standing still. That's why I've got to have the fence, Andrew."

The captain said, "I can send some of the boys by every two or three days and keep the cattle thrown back, Noah."

Wheeler shook his gray head. "It wouldn't work. Every two or three days wouldn't be enough, and besides, your men have more things to do than help me to farm. If I want to make anything, I'll have to make it for myself."

The captain saw a rider coming up in an easy lope. He squinted, trying to recognize him. The horseman was less than a hundred feet from him before he recognized Doug Monahan.

The captain said, "I should have suspected, Noah. That the man who's building your fence?"

Wheeler nodded and faced around as Monahan reined up beside him. Monahan's eyes were cold. "Any trouble, Noah?"

"No trouble, Doug. We were just talking."

Doug looked at the captain, his face grim. "If you've come threatening, Captain, you'd just as well go home. We're ready for you this time. This fence is going up, and it'll stay up."

The captain stared hard at Monahan, and he felt the young man's eyes hating him. It disturbed him somehow. The captain had never tried to be a popular man. He moved in his own way, in his own time, caring little what anyone else thought. He was becoming increasingly aware of the talk that went on behind his back, but much of it came from people who wore a pleasant smile when they faced him. Not in years had anyone boldly shown him such unmasked enmity as he saw in Doug Monahan's blue eyes.

It brought an immediate response in kind. The captain said, "Monahan, I've given you more chances than I'd give most men."

"I'll make my own chances, Captain, and I'll take them."

Spann, who had not dismounted, edged his horse a little closer. "Say the word, Captain, and I'll put him in his place."

Noah Wheeler took a step forward, placing himself in front of Monahan's horse. "This is my place, Andrew. Doug Monahan is here because I want him here."

The captain's face colored. "He thinks he has a private war with me, Noah. Don't let him drag you into it."

Wheeler replied, "I'm not in any war and I don't want any part of one. I'm just trying to fence my land so I can build this place into what I want it to be, that's all."

Restlessly the captain moved his cup around and around in a circle, sending the remains of the coffee to spinning.

"If it was only you, Noah, I wouldn't care. But if you build a fence, others will. Out of respect for old times, I'm asking you not to do it."

Wheeler solemnly shook his head. "Out of respect for old times, Andrew, I'm asking you to understand why I *have* to do it."

The captain looked at him with sorrow. "That's your answer?"

Wheeler nodded.

The captain flipped the rest of his coffee out and dropped the cup into the brittle grass. He stepped stiffly back into the saddle. His spurs tinkled as he reined the big gray horse around and headed out again the way he had come. He never looked back.

Archer Spann rode silently beside him, watching the old cowman's face twist with the bitter conflicts that went on in his mind. When at last it seemed that the captain had made his decision, Spann asked, "What was there between you and Noah Wheeler, years ago?"

The captain made no answer, and Spann said, "Whatever it was, he seems to've forgotten about it. He's declared war on you, Captain. When do we hit him?"

The captain frowned, his mind still dwelling on something else, perhaps something far back in time. "Hit him? What do you mean, hit him?"

"Burn him out."

The captain pulled his horse to a stop, and Spann reined up, turned back to face him. He had seldom seen the captain's face clouded so.

"Whatever else we have to do," Rinehart declared, "I don't want to hurt Noah Wheeler. Doug Monahan's the one behind this. He's the one we want to hit. Cut his fences, burn his posts, run off his men. Do what you have to to stop Monahan. But leave Noah Wheeler alone!"

Spann rode along silently a while after that, keeping his thoughts to himself. Finally he asked, "What about Wheeler's boy?"

"Wheeler's boy?"

"Vern Wheeler, the kid we've got with Lefty Jones over in that north line shack."

The captain nodded then. "I'd almost forgotten. Better let him go, Archer. If he's any account he'll want to side with his father. And if he's not any account, we don't want him anyway."

Archer Spann smiled a little then, and the pleasure of anticipation shone in his dark eyes. He doubled his fist.

"I'll go over there as quick as I can."

He was waiting in the line shack when Vern Wheeler and Lefty Jones rode in from the morning's work to cook themselves some dinner. He had been there an hour, resting in the warm comfort of the little bachelor stove, and had made no move to fix anything to eat. He would let them do that.

Husky young Vern Wheeler shook hands with him, showing him the deference of a well-brought-up youngster to the older man he works for. Lefty Jones, fifteen years older than Vern, nodded and gave Spann a civil howdy but didn't shake his hand. It was plain enough that he didn't think much of the foreman, yet he wouldn't go so far as to be insubordinate. Jones' glance flicked to the stove, then to the coffee pot which still sat cold and empty on the cabinet top. Range etiquette demanded that Spann fix coffee for the chilled incoming riders, if he didn't do anything else.

Jones went about the business of fixing dinner, saying nothing. The way he saw it, if there was any talking to be done, it was Spann's part to do it. Vern Wheeler, younger and more eager, tried to be polite by drawing Spann out, asking him questions about the rest of the ranch. Spann gave him short answers, when he answered at all. He waited until dinner was over before he sprang it.

"I came over to tell you you're through here, kid. Your dad double-crossed the captain."

Vern Wheeler stiffened, almost dropping the dirty dishes he was carrying to the cabinet. In a strained voice he demanded, "What're you talking about?"

"He's putting up a fence, a bobwire fence. And after the captain all but begged him not to."

Lefty Jones snickered at the thought of the captain begging anything.

Shaken, Vern put the dishes down on the cabinet and turned back to face Spann. "My dad wouldn't do anything he didn't have the right to."

"In this country the captain tells people what they've got a right to do. He said no bobwire fences. Your old man's building one anyway."

"And you're firing me for it?"

"You're his son. If we can't trust him, we can't trust you."

Face darkening, Vern Wheeler took a threatening step toward Archer Spann. "Watch what you say about my dad!"

Spann stood up, bracing himself. "Noah Wheeler's nothing but another dirt farmer who's let himself step over the line, kid, and before we're through, he'll know it."

Lightning flashed in Vern Wheeler's eyes, but the youngster held himself down.

Spann pulled a small roll of green bills out of his pocket. "It's been three weeks since last payday. I've got you twenty-one dollars counted out here. Take it and git."

Vern Wheeler stared incredulously at the money. "Twenty-one dollars?" He hurled the bills to the floor. "I've got a year's wages coming to me! You've been holding them."

"Back wages? You're crazy, kid. This is all we owe you."

Vern's face drained. "You're a liar, Spann. You've got it. You've been holding it, saving it for me so I could get married. Now I want my money, Spann."

Spann's hand dropped to the butt of the six-gun on his hip. "I told you, boy, you've got all that's coming to you. Now pack up and git!"

Vern's voice rippled with fury. "Not without my money, Spann. You give me my money."

He lunged at the foreman. Spann's hand came up, the gun in it. Lefty Jones grabbed Spann's arm and wrenched. A blast rocked the line shack, and sugar spilled in a white stream from a can on a raw-pine shelf. Spann swung his arm back. The gun struck Jones in the face and sent him sprawling.

Vern Wheeler got hold of Spann's arm, trying to twist it, to get his hand on the gun. Spann strained, cursing as he attempted to throw off the heavy weight of this husky farm boy. He wrenched savagely and tore his arm free. He swung, hard. The gun glanced off Vern Wheeler's head, staggering him.

Spann saw his chance then. He lifted his knee to the boy's groin. Wheeler gasped and stiffened. Spann lifted the gun and brought it down again. Vern Wheeler dropped like a sack of grain, a red welt rising angrily on the side of his head.

The boy struggled to regain his feet. Spann stood heaving, trying for breath. When Vern had almost managed to steady himself, Spann swung the gun again. This time Vern Wheeler wouldn't get up, not for a while.

Lefty Jones sat on the floor, rubbing his hand across his bleeding mouth, still half dazed.

"You pack up too, Lefty," Spann said. "You're done. You had no business poking in there. It was between me and the kid."

Jones was coming around. He blinked a few times, finally managing to focus his gaze on Spann. "That boy wasn't lyin'. You owe him that money, and you're stealin' it from him."

"I owe him nothing, Lefty."

"Three hundred dollars. It's all he talks about. The captain wouldn't steal it from him. That leaves you."

Archer Spann grabbed Lefty Jones by the collar and jerked him to his feet. Jones stood awkwardly off balance, his hand moving to take Spann's fist from his collar. Then he stopped, feeling the fury that rippled in Spann's face, seeing murder in Spann's eyes.

Jones swallowed and looked down. Fear touched him with a death-cold hand.

"All right, Spann, mebbe I was wrong."

"Ride, Lefty." Spann's voice crackled. "Don't even go by town. Don't stop riding for a week." The voice dropped almost to a whisper, but it stung. "If I ever see you again, I'll kill you!"

He gave Jones a shove, and the man fell back against a table, turning it over with a crash. The cowboy got up, silently gathered his scattered belongings and rolled them in his blankets. With a quick glance down at Vern Wheeler, then up at Spann, he walked out the door and off the porch.

Spann already had heard the hoofbeats trailing away before Vern Wheeler began to stir. Spann gathered up the remaining clothes and personal effects he found around the line shack. He rolled them in Vern Wheeler's bed. As Vern pushed himself to his knees, Spann

pitched the roll at him. He drew the gun again and stood there holding it, letting Vern get a good look at it.

"I could kill you and swear you made me do it, Wheeler, but I
won't. You just go on and keep your mouth shut about that money.
Mark it up to experience and your old man's fence."

Vern Wheeler got shakily to his feet. He touched a hand to his
face and felt the stickiness of blood. He stared blankly at his hand,
and the red smear that was on it. His eyes lifted to Spann. They were
glazed by pain, but they held a writhing hatred.

"I'll go, but don't you forget me. I'll be back, and one way or
another, I'll get my money."

Spann watched him go, then reached in his pocket and touched
the roll of greenbacks there. He felt like cursing himself, now that it
was over. He had brought the money with the intention of paying
young Wheeler. He didn't know what had changed his mind. Some
grasping impulse had driven him into a spur-of-the-moment decision, and once it was made, he could not back down. He realized
now that it probably had been a mistake. He pulled his hand away
from the money as if it had been hot. What was three hundred dollars to the man who might someday control the R Cross?

Archer Spann had been on his own most of his life. As a boy he
had known much of hunger and desperation, and it hadn't been
many years since a dollar bill looked as big as a saddle blanket to him.
The memory of those grim times still haunted him, still put a cold
touch of fear in the pit of his stomach when he thought of them.

That, he realized, was what had prompted him to keep the
money. In a man who yearned to be big, this was a deeply ingrained
streak of littleness that he despised but could not purge from his soul.

X

The bitter anger grew in Vern Wheeler as he started the long ride home. At nightfall he stopped and made a dry and hungry camp beneath a wind-breaking cutbank, no food or coffee to warm him. He wrapped in his blanket and kept a small fire going through the night, more miserable here than he would be in the saddle. But a thin blanket of clouds hid the stars from sight. He knew he might get lost in the darkness and ride many unnecessary miles.

Before daybreak he was up and traveling again, the cold having driven through to the bone. His head throbbed dully from the pistol-whipping. His stomach was tight and painful from hunger. The bitterness grew rather than subsided. He rode in a swirling, blinding anger.

Sight of the fencing crew at work slowed him but little. He paused for just a moment, making note of the fact that there was one, just as Spann had said. He felt a sharp resentment of the fence. This was what had brought his trouble.

Unseen, a rider came up on his left side, saddlegun across his lap. "Who're you?" the man demanded.

Vern Wheeler glared at him. "None of your damned business!"

He started to ride on, but the man touched spurs to his horse and pulled up directly in front of him. The saddlegun lifted now, not quite pointing at Vern but resting in a position from which it could instantly come into play.

The man eyed him levelly. "I don't mean to be rough, kid. I just asked you who you are. I'll even go halfway with you and tell you my name. It's Dundee. Now, what's yours?" The voice was pleasant but firm. That gun wasn't to be argued with.

"I'm Vern Wheeler." It was a grudging answer.

The saddlegun lowered. Dundee said, "I ought to've seen that for myself. But it would've saved us both some trouble if you'd just said so to start with."

"To hell with you!" Vern said angrily and rode past him.

The encounter served to fan his anger. By the time he reached the farmhouse his hand was a-tremble on the reins.

Trudy Wheeler saw him and set down the basket of dry laundry she was carrying in from the clothesline. She moved toward him in an easy walk at first, then quickened her pace as she got close enough to see his face.

"Vern, what's happened to you?"

Vern Wheeler swung down from the horse and stood weakly for a moment, holding onto the saddle, for the strength had been worn out of him.

Trudy caught hold of his shoulders. "Who beat you?"

"Archer Spann. He pistol-whipped me. Robbed me of the pay I had coming. And all because of that infernal fence out yonder. What's the matter with Dad, anyway?"

Trudy Wheeler bit her lip. "Tie the horse and come on into the house, Vern. You're cold, and I expect you're hungry."

She took him in the warm house, got the heavy coat off of him and sat him down in front of the big wood stove. She poured coffee into a big tin cup and placed it in his hands. He held it there, enjoying the warmth until it worked through the cold skin and became burning hot.

Vern started to sip it but found it scalding. He blew it gently, watching his sister. "I asked you about the fence." His black mood showed in the way he moved, the way he looked at her.

Just then their mother came in, and the answer was delayed. He had to repeat the whole story for Mrs. Wheeler. The retelling of it did little to cool his anger. Trudy already had some biscuits pressed out and rising.

When Vern once more asked about the fence, Mrs. Wheeler parried the question. "He's hungry, Trudy. Put those biscuits in the oven. Let's fry him some beef."

Vern ate hungrily, letting the question ride while he satisfied the insistent grumbling of his stomach. But when he was finished, he pressed for an answer.

"Vern," said Mrs. Wheeler, "you need to go and rest. Forget about it all for a while."

Vern looked at Trudy, and she said, "Have you heard of a man named Doug Monahan?"

"The fellow who was building a fence for Gordon Finch? Yeah, I heard about him. I wasn't in on any of it, though. I was off in a line camp."

Trudy said, "Well, he's the one building the fence."

"Is he out of his head? He knows what happened the first time. It'll happen to him again."

Trudy shook her head. "Not to *him,* Vern. To *us.*"

Face clouding, Vern Wheeler set down his coffee. He rubbed his head, feeling the painful swelling where the pistol had struck him. "It started with me."

Trudy said with bitter feeling, "He's looking for a way to get even with the R Cross. He caught Dad on his weak side and talked him into letting him fence the place. He knows Captain Rinehart won't let it go by without trying to stop it. He's set us up like a target, and he's got rough men hired out there, waiting for a fight. He doesn't care what happens to us, just so he gets his chance at the captain."

Mrs. Wheeler said sharply, "Hush, Trudy. You're making it worse than it really is."

"I'm not. It couldn't *be* worse."

Vern clenched his fist. "And for this Monahan I lose my job, and all the money I've saved for a solid year. I lose the place I aimed to buy, and I might even lose my girl. I'd like to see this Monahan. I'd like him to get a taste of what I got yesterday."

Trudy Wheeler was looking out the window. "You won't have to wait long. He's riding up with Dad."

"Trudy!" Mrs. Wheeler cried.

Vern Wheeler stood up, shoving his chair back abruptly. He moved to the window for a good look at Doug Monahan.

"No better time to do it than right now," he said.

Mrs. Wheeler said, "Wait a minute, Vern. There's no call for trouble, and you're not in any condition . . ."

She was talking to empty space, for Vern Wheeler had gone out the door.

She turned back on Trudy, her eyes flashing anger. "Don't you know what you've done? You sent him out there spoiling for a fight, and he'll be beaten again. In his condition, that's all that can happen. You've done to Vern what you're blaming Doug Monahan for doing to us."

Trudy flushed guiltily as her mother's words went home to her. She moved to the door, wishing for some way to stop what she had started, and knowing there was nothing she could do.

Doug Monahan and Noah Wheeler rode up to the house together and stepped out of their saddles. The old farmer's gaze swept to the porch and caught his son, standing there.

"Vern! Dundee said he ran into you. What're you doing home?"

Vern's gaze was not on his father but on Doug instead. "Ask Monahan."

Doug stopped short, seeing fire in the young man's eyes and at a loss to understand it.

"Because of you, Monahan," Vern Wheeler said, "I was beaten up and robbed of my wages and thrown off of my job. You've put my family in line for even worse than that. But I'm going to stop you."

He stepped down off the porch, his fists tight, his angry eyes on Doug. He towered tall above Monahan.

Noah Wheeler said, "Hold on, Vern."

"Stay out of this, Dad."

Monahan took a step backward. "Wait a minute, Vern. I don't understand what this is all about, but we can work it out someway."

He could see the swollen red streaks where the gun had struck. He could see the exhaustion in Vern Wheeler's face. But Vern kept coming. He looped a hard swing. Monahan leaned and caught the jar of it on his shoulder.

"You wanted a fight," Vern shouted. "Now you got one."

"Vern, I don't want to fight you." The boy went on swinging. Doug put up his hands to ward off the blows. "Vern, listen to me. . . ."

He had to keep backing up. Vern hit him a hard blow on the side of the face and it jarred him, set his ears to ringing. He caught a right fist with his arm, then felt half the breath gust out of him as Vern's left came in under his ribs.

"Fight!" Vern shouted. "Come on and fight!"

Doug kept his arms in close to his body, trying to anticipate where Vern would hit him. "Vern, I'm not going to fight you!"

Vern was breathing hard, exhaustion catching up with him. He kept swinging until the strength was all gone from him, until he could barely stand. His father stepped in and grabbed his arms.

"Vern, stop it!" He shook his son. "Vern, I don't know what touched you off, but you're wrong, dead wrong. Now go back in that house and sit down. You've got nothing to blame Doug Monahan for. You ought to be thankful he didn't knock your head off. He could have."

Breathing heavily, Vern pointed his finger at Monahan. "Another time. I'll do it another time."

"Come on," Noah Wheeler said curtly, turning Vern around and leading him back toward the house. Mrs. Wheeler came down the steps and helped.

Trudy Wheeler stood on the porch, her stricken gaze following her brother first, then drifting back to Monahan.

Noah Wheeler paused at the door. "Trudy, come on in the house. I got something to say, and I want you to hear it."

There was a bench out in the yard. Doug Monahan slumped on it, his hand over his ribs where Vern had struck him hard. He struggled to regain the breath that had been knocked out of him. A thin trickle of blood worked down from a small cut above his eye. His battered hat lay on the ground. Either he or Vern had stepped on it.

Hesitantly Trudy Wheeler came down off the porch and moved out beside Monahan. He watched her silently, pain in his eyes.

"I'm sorry," she said haltingly. "I'm afraid I caused this. I wanted it awhile ago, but now I'm ashamed."

"It's all right. I expect I know why you did it."

"You could have hurt him bad, if you'd wanted to."

"It looked like he'd been hurt enough already."

"Thanks," she said softly, "for not hurting him anymore."

Noah Wheeler called her again. Trudy glanced once more at Monahan, then went into the house.

Paula Hadley took it better than Vern Wheeler had hoped.

Soberly staring at his big hands, trying to keep down the lump of disappointment in his throat, he said, "I reckon we'll have to put off getting married. I can't buy that land till I find some way to get my money."

They sat together on the sofa in the front room of the Hadley house. Paula took his big hand in her little one. She lifted it to her lips and kissed the bruised knuckles. Tears glistened in her brown eyes.

"I don't care about the land, Vern. You're all that matters."

"I'm not going to marry you broke, Paula. When we get married, I want it to be open and proud, and your dad approving of it."

She gripped his hand tightly. "It isn't fair, one stubborn old man like the captain, ruining things for us this way. We're just little people, we couldn't hurt him. What does he want to hurt us for?"

"I don't know."

"Keeping your money that way—three hundred dollars can't mean much to him."

"Maybe that's it. It don't mean much to him, and he can't realize how much it means to somebody else."

Paula said, "Or he doesn't care. He's too used to running everything to suit himself. Somebody needs to show him that we don't belong to him. Nobody belongs to him."

Vern's face was troubled. "Maybe that's it. I was so mad, I didn't realize it at first. I've watched the R Cross push other people ever since I've been here. None of it ever touched me but now I've had a dose of it myself, and I can see it for what it is."

Understanding came into his face. "They pushed Monahan, and he's fighting them back the only way he can. He's about the first one that ever did."

"What about your father, Vern? Doesn't he realize what he's getting into?"

Vern nodded soberly. "He sits still most of the time and don't say much, but he sees everything. Maybe he just figured it was time folks declared their independence."

Paula leaned her head against Vern's broad shoulder. "That doesn't make it any easier on us."

"Maybe it wasn't meant to be easy. The things that count don't always come easy, Paula."

"What're you going to do, Vern?"

"Go help them, I guess. I'll find some way to get my money

back, maybe. And even if I don't, maybe I can help whittle that bunch down to size."

Heading down the track-ribboned dirt street for the road out of town, Vern heard a youthful voice call his name. "Vern Wheeler, hold up there!"

He pulled his horse around and spotted his old friend Rooster Preech stepping off the boardwalk in front of a saloon and striding out into the sun to meet him. A broad grin cut across Rooster's red, freckled face. He always had looked as friendly as a collie dog. Uncut red hair bristled out over his ears and curled into a tangled mess on the back of his neck, just above the collar. A short, uneven thicket of rusty whiskers covered his face, too, some of them still soft and fine, some stiffening with the arrival of manhood.

"Don't be in such an all-fired hurry, Vern. Come on, let's have us a drink together."

Vern glanced toward the saloon, his eyebrows raised. "You reckon they'd let us have it?"

"Sure, I got the barkeep thinkin' I'm twenty-five."

Vern doubted that. He figured the barkeep just didn't care. He swung down from the horse and slapped Rooster on the shoulder. "With all that cover on your face, he couldn't tell but what you was sixty. You been out in the brush lately?"

Rooster waited while Vern tied his horse, then held the door open for Vern to get in ahead of him. "I was. Cattle been keeping me busy."

"Who you working for?"

Rooster was a moment in answering that. "Well, myself, I guess you'd say."

"You haven't got any cattle."

Rooster laughed. "I stay busy."

The bartender looked questioningly at Vern Wheeler. Self-consciously, Vern said, "I'll take whatever Rooster does."

"Bourbon," said Rooster. The bartender left them a quarter-filled bottle and two glasses, and Rooster watched over his shoulder till the man was gone out of hearing. "I happened to run into Lefty Jones yesterday. He was leavin' the country in kind of a hurry."

Vern's interest quickened. "I been wondering about him. He sure got away from that line camp fast. I never even saw him leave."

"From what he told me, Archer Spann didn't give him much choice."

Vern frowned darkly. "That figures."

"Lefty told me what happened to you. Pretty raw deal about your money, son." Rooster had a habit of calling Vern "son," even though they were the same age. It was his way of showing he'd been around more and knew more of the world and its ways.

An eagerness was in Rooster's voice as he leaned forward. "You want to get even with 'em, don't you?"

When Vern did not reply, Rooster said, "Sure, you do! And you'd like to git your money back while you're at it, wouldn't you?"

Vern looked up sharply. "What're you driving at, Rooster?"

Rooster nodded at Vern's glass. "Drink up." Vern cautiously tasted it and flinched. Little as Vern knew about whisky, he could classify this in a hurry. "I like my women and my whisky cheap and plentiful," Rooster used to say, even when he was too young to have much savvy about either one.

Vern set the glass down still nearly full. "Get to the point, Rooster."

Rooster grinned like a fisherman seeing a fish well on the hook. "Workin' that line camp, you oughta know that country up on the north end of the R Cross mighty well."

"Like the back of my hand."

"You know where the best grazin' is and where the cattle is gen'rally at. You could find 'em in the dark, and you'd know the best way to push 'em outa there in a hurry."

Sensing the rest of it, Vern drew back, a vague disappointment bringing pain to him. But he knew there was no reason for surprise. He'd known Rooster Preech a long time, had liked him and ridden with him. But he had always sensed that Rooster would wind up riding the back trails with a fast horse and a quick loop, worth more money in jail than out.

"Rooster, I'm not going to steal any R Cross cattle."

"Nobody said anything about stealin'! But if you was to decide to take enough cattle to get your three hundred dollars back, I know where there's a man who'll take 'em off your hands and not ever worry hisself about the brand on 'em. It wouldn't really be stealin'. It'd jest be gittin' back what they stole from you."

For a moment Vern was tempted. Why shouldn't he do it? They had taken his money with no compunctions at all.

"It's dangerous, Rooster. There's been men got their necks stretched out real long for getting caught with R Cross cattle."

"They got caught. We won't. You know that country to where we'd always have a way of gittin' out."

Vern studied him speculatively. "Rooster, what would you be getting out of this, if we just took three hundred dollars' worth of cattle?"

Rooster smiled and looked back over his shoulder to make sure the barkeep was still out of earshot. "Now, you wouldn't want them to git off scot-free, would you? I thought we might jest take along a few extry head. Sort of exemplary payment, they call it in court. Enough to justify me and another feller or two I know for helpin' you. You wouldn't have to have them extry cattle on your conscience. As far as you're concerned, you'd only be takin' enough for your three hundred dollars. The rest'd be jest between me and them other fellers."

Vern stood up, shaking his head. "Thanks for the drink, Rooster." Most of it remained in the glass. "But I reckon not. I want to fight the R Cross, but that's not how I figure on doing it."

Rooster shrugged, disappointed but still smiling. "Well, you can't say I didn't try, son. It's still a good offer, and any time you change your mind, jest holler."

Chris Hadley closed his saloon at dusk and walked home, content to let the other places have the night business. A man with a teenage daughter couldn't leave her alone all the time. He moved along with head down, barely nodding to the people he met on the street, for his mind was on other things.

He hung up his hat and coat and stood before the wood heater, warming in its pleasant glow. His daughter said, "Good evening, Papa. I'll have supper ready in a little."

Worry creasing his high forehead, Chris Hadley said, "Paula, come here and sit down. I want to talk to you."

She came, but she didn't sit, for she had supper cooking on the stove.

Hadley said, "Vern Wheeler was in town today. He came here, didn't he?"

"Yes, Papa, he did."

A grimness came to Chris Hadley's face. "What for?"

Paula was a moment in answering. Her face tightened with decision. "I guess you know, Papa, without having to ask, but I'll tell you. He asked me to wait for him. And I told him I would."

Chris Hadley sat down wearily and exhaled a long breath.

He rubbed his hand over his face without looking up at Paula. "I knew we'd stayed here too long. I ought to've sold out and moved a year ago. Paula, I'll not let you do it."

"I love him, Papa. I'm going to marry him."

Hadley said, "Paula, for years I've saved so I could send you back where you belong, give you the kind of life you were born for. I'm not going to let you throw it away on Vern Wheeler or anybody like him."

"I don't know anything about any other kind of life, and I don't care. I just know I love Vern Wheeler, and I'm going to marry him."

Angered, he said, "Paula, you never gave me any trouble when you were growing up. No man could have had a better daughter. I never thought you'd ever defy me this way."

Her lips trembled, but her brown eyes were firm. "I never thought I'd have to."

"I'll remind you, Paula, you're under age! I can stop you from marrying. I'll send you away somewhere to school until you forget this foolishness."

She brought her hands up over her breasts and clenched a small fist over the locket her mother had left her. "It's your right, Papa, but I'll tell you this: I won't forget. As soon as I'm of age, I'll come back, and I'll marry Vern Wheeler!"

XI

Doug Monahan was worried. The barbed wire hadn't arrived. The work had gone on without trouble. Occasionally a rider would show up on the high rise out yonder and sit awhile in the gray grass, watching. Eventually Dundee would drift his way, and the man would get back on his horse and fade out of sight.

The line of set posts was a long one now, stretching well over a mile already and waiting for the wire.

"Stub," Monahan said, "something's wrong. That wire ought to've been here a week ago. I wish you'd take a horse and ride over to Stringtown. See what's the matter."

Stub returned bringing the kind of report Doug had expected.

"That wire's sittin' over there in the depot gatherin' dust. They won't anybody haul it."

Angrily Doug said, "What about that freighter, Slim Torrance? I paid him half of the freight in advance."

Stub Bailey dug a wrinkled, sweat-stained check out of his shirt pocket. "He sent it back to you. Here."

Doug swore under his breath while Stub explained. "Sheriff McKelvie seen you over there that day and knew there was somethin' up. He hung around till he found out what it was, and he went to see this Torrance. Now, it seems like Torrance did something or other over here one time that wasn't strictly according to the statutes. He never did say just what. Anyhow, the sheriff told him if he brought a spool of that wire into this county, or even had it sent, he'd yank him up by the scruff of the neck and throw him in the jailhouse over at Twin Wells."

Stub added, "So that's the reason we ain't had any wire. And not apt to get any unless we go fetch it ourselves."

Doug Monahan drew his lips in tight and smashed his fist into his hand. "Then we'll go get it ourselves. And we'll haul it right through the main street of Twin Wells!"

Stub frowned. "That's askin' for trouble."

Angrily Doug replied, "We already got trouble. That's just telling them we can take care of it."

He left Stub Bailey to oversee the post-setting job, Dundee to continue his watch. He took the five Blessingames and three wagons. And, because he wanted to go, Vern Wheeler.

Vern had come back from town with his anger at last expired. He had apologized and asked to be allowed to help. A husky boy, he had made a good hand ever since, digging holes, tamping posts, throwing in where the hottest and the hardest work was. Some deep-seated determination seemed to be driving him. He was setting a strong pace for the rest of the men to follow.

They left as soon as darkness had lifted enough that they could see the wagon trail. Doug and Vern rode horseback, the Blessingames on the wagons. The morning was uneventful, but about midafternoon a rider broke over a hilltop and spotted them. He sat there a while, watching, then pulled back and disappeared over the hill.

By the time the wagons groaned into Stringtown the second day, Monahan was positive they were being followed. Several times he had glimpsed a rider far behind them. The man never got any closer or dropped any farther back. Now, as they loaded their wagons at the depot, he saw a man sitting his horse across the dusty street, watching. When the rider turned away, Monahan caught a glimpse of the R Cross on its hip, stamped with the small horse iron. He looked questioningly at Vern Wheeler.

"Name's Bodie," Vern said. "Kind of a strawboss for Archer

Spann sometimes. If Spann has got any friends atall, I reckon Bodie's one of them."

Starting back, Doug knew within reason that they would find a reception committee somewhere on the trail. He wished they had Dundee and the other men with them. But he couldn't afford to leave the Wheeler place without protection.

"We'll just have to face up to it ourselves," he told the men. "Seven of us, and burdened down with loaded wagons."

Foley Blessingame spat disdainfully, leaving a string of brown tobacco juice in the dust. "Don't you worry none, Doug. You got *thirteen* men, the way I see it. Them four kids of mine will count for two men apiece, and I'll count for three."

"Thirteen's an unlucky number, Foley," Doug pointed out.

"For whoever tries to tamper with us."

They rode watchfully, guns never far from reach, but nothing happened the first day. In camp that night, two men were on guard all the time, and others were never deeply asleep.

Nothing came that night, and home was not too far away. As they broke camp, Vern Wheeler pulled up beside Monahan.

"Doug, I been thinking where I'd go to stop a string of wagons, if I was Archer Spann and wanted to. It just occurred to me that Drinkman's Gap would be the best place on the whole trail to do it."

Doug remembered the gap, although he hadn't known what it was called. It was a place where the trail passed through a line of small rocky hills too rough to go around in a wagon. It was nothing like a mountain pass, but it did provide a place where a few men, well-positioned in the mouth of the gap, might halt a string of wagons. Horses could move freely enough up the hillsides, but a loaded wagon could move only through the pass.

"If they're of a mind to stop us," Vern said darkly, "I reckon they could do it. We couldn't move these wagons off the road, and they'll likely block it with men."

"Then," replied Doug, "if we can't get the wagons off the road, we'll just have to get the men off of it."

The gap came into sight at mid-morning. Doug rode out in front of the wagons for a look-see. Sure enough, men waited down there, sitting on the ground, smoking, holding their horses. He counted nine, perhaps ten. At sight of him they stood up. Most of them swung leisurely into their saddles.

They didn't move after him. They plainly preferred to meet him on their own ground. They couldn't have chosen a better place.

Doug rode back to the wagons. He saw Vern Wheeler checking his six-shooter. "I don't want you using that, Vern. Not to shoot anybody, anyway."

"They're blocking the trail. How else we going to get through?"

"We'll get through, and we shouldn't have to shoot anybody."

He dismounted by Foley's wagon. He lifted down a heavy spool of wire and eased it to the grass. "Hand me that pair of wire cutters in there, Foley."

This wire was a different brand from the one he had used before. This one did not have the coat of red paint. Pulling up one end of the wire, Doug held it out to Vern. "Here, take ahold." Then he pushed the spool along on the ground, unrolling a piece which he judged to be about twice as long as the gap was wide. He snipped the wire off, then doubled it back. While Vern held the two cut ends, Doug twisted the wire.

"Double thickness," he said, "will be strong and a lot easier to handle than just one strand."

He coiled the doubled wire, lifted the rest of the spool back into the wagon and remounted his horse. "All right, let's go. We'll take it slow at first. Let them think they're going to stop us. Then, when I give the signal, let those mules have everything you've got."

He motioned Vern to ride beside him. They moved out twenty

or thirty paces ahead of the wagons. They held their horses in a walk, so the wagons could keep up with them. Slowly they drew closer to the gap, where the R Cross waited. Most of the men were a-horseback, but a couple stood afoot, holding their horses.

"That's Spann, isn't it?" he asked Vern.

Vern nodded, and his blue eyes were hard. "That's him." His fingers flexed, and Doug knew the boy itched to get his hands on Spann.

"Take it easy," Doug said. "We're not aiming to kill anybody, no matter how bad he may need it."

They rode closer. The men in the gap were at ease, confident that all they had to do was wait, and the wagons would fall into their laps like ripe apples out of a tree.

"It's time now," Doug said. He handed Vern one end of the doubled wire. "Take a wrap on your saddlehorn and pull yonderway with it. Then spur for all you're worth."

Vern nodded, face taut. He comprehended for the first time what Doug Monahan planned to do.

When they had the wire stretched out tightly between them, Doug looked back over his shoulder and gave Foley Blessingame the nod. Then he yelled and spurred his horse. He heard old Foley's voice rise behind him like the angry squall of a panther. He heard the rattle of chains, the sudden clatter of the mules' hoofs on the hard ground as the lead wagon jerked forward.

For a few seconds there was confusion among the riders at the gap. They stared in consternation. Then they saw the barbed wire, stretched between the two horsemen, coming straight at them.

There is something about barbed wire that strikes dread in those who know it. A man stretching fence always has his nerves keened by realization that the wire may snap and lash at him with its sharp and wicked barbs. A man running a horse alongside a fence, chasing down a runaway cow, knows the fear of falling, of hurtling helplessly into the ripping wire.

These men saw the wire coming, and it loosed a sudden panic among them that guns might not have done. They spurred up the hillsides, out of the way.

Archer Spann stood afoot in the middle of the gap, shouting at them, cursing, so angry he did not realize his own situation. Seeing it then, he tried to swing into the saddle and run. But the excitement had carried to his horse. The animal reared, jerking the reins from his hands. It loped up the gap, head high in panic. It stepped on one of the dragging reins and nearly threw itself to the ground. The horse turned aside from the trail then and started up the hill.

Spann stood rooted to the spot, watching helplessly as the wire flashed toward him between Monahan and Vern Wheeler, the wagons hurtling along behind. He started to run, saw he couldn't make it, then dropped to the ground as the wire sang over his head. Heart pounding, he heard the hammering of the mules' hoofs and the rumble of the heavy-laden wheels. Desperately he rolled over in the dust, got to his knees and scrambled out of the way.

The wagons rolled past him, leaving him choking in the cloud of dust that the heavy iron rims had raised from the hard ground. He got to his feet and watched the wagons pulling away. He ripped off his hat and hurled it to the ground, cursing and stomping.

Slowly his men worked back down from the hillsides and gathered around him.

"Washerwomen!" he shouted. "I ought to fire every blessed one of you!"

"Archer," offered the one called Bodie, "we could still catch them."

"And do what?" Spann demanded. "You had them right here, the best place on the whole road, and you scattered like a bunch of quail."

The men sat red-faced, smarting under the tongue-lashing he gave them.

Bodie finally put in, "You don't know what that bobwire can do, Archer."

"I know what it'll do to this country if they ever put it up," he exploded. "About half of you hombres'll be riding the chuckline."

One of the men left the group—gladly—and caught Spann's horse. By the time he brought him back, Spann had cooled a little.

"The R Cross has always meant something in this country," Spann said, calmer now. "It's not something that people laugh at. But they'll laugh when they know what happened here."

His face twisted as he looked down the gap to the dust of the wagons. His knuckles went white, the way he clenched the leather reins. More than anything else, more even than the idea of Noah Wheeler's fence, he hated the thought of ridicule.

"They won't laugh long," he gritted. "Not very long."

Doug Monahan moved out to one side to drop the twisted wire out of the way, then eased up, letting the wagons go past him. He loped along behind them, looking over his shoulder for reassurance. Then he touched spurs to the horse again and pulled up beside the wagons, one by one.

"Slow them down now. They're not coming after us."

The Blessingames sawed on the lines, gradually bringing the heavy wagons to a stop. The ground was softer here, and dustier. Doug pinched his eyes shut as the dust from the wheels drifted past him. He sneezed once and turned his face away.

Foley Blessingame was laughing and slapping his knee with a hand as big as a Percheron's hoof. "Did you see that feller's face jest before he hit the ground? You never saw a madder man in your whole life!"

"That," Doug told him, "was Archer Spann."

Foley's eyebrows lifted. "So that was him. Well, we give him a nice remembrance, I do believe."

Vern Wheeler was grinning, but it was a bitter, vengeful sort of grin. "I wish we could've rimfired him with that wire. It wouldn't have been any more than he deserved."

"It would have killed him," Doug pointed out.

Vern said flatly, "There's not much wrong with that."

The Blessingame boys were off, patting their mules, talking gently to them and calming them down.

Foley Blessingame said, "Well, Doug, you still aim to take these wagons right through town?"

Doug's jaw had a firm set to it. "Right through the big middle!"

Their arrival in Twin Wells could not have attracted more attention if they had brought a brass band. People came out and stood in front of houses and stores to watch them pass. Dogs trotted along, barking at the mules, and kids ran beside the heavy wagons. Some people smiled, some frowned with disapproval. Many just watched silently, withholding judgment, or if they had made it, hiding it.

Paula Hadley stood in front of her picket fence. Vern Wheeler pulled his horse over toward her. He reached down and gripped her hand a moment, and the look that passed between them said all there was to say.

Doug Monahan caught this, and he smiled. He had heard a little, and he knew now that there was even more to it than he had heard.

Sheriff Luke McKelvie strode out from under the heavy old live oaks in the courthouse square. There was something of resignation in his crow-tracked eyes as Doug Monahan pulled over beside him.

"Still not taking any advice, are you, Monahan?"

Doug shook his head. "Not yours, McKelvie."

"I was afraid you wouldn't. But I thought a little discouragement or two along the line might make you listen to it, anyway."

Resentfully Doug said, "We wouldn't have had to go after this wire if you hadn't thrown a scare into my freighter. Why did you do it?"

"Like I said, I hoped a little discouragement would slow you down till you had time to do some thinking."

"I'm not breaking any law, McKelvie. What business is it of yours?"

"I'm a peace officer, Monahan. It's been a peaceful country, in the main. I do what I can to keep it that way."

"The only thing I can't understand is why the captain didn't send somebody over to destroy the wire in the Stringtown depot."

McKelvie shrugged. "Mainly, I guess, because he didn't know it was there."

Surprised, Monahan demanded, "You didn't tell him?"

McKelvie shook his head. "Like I said, keeping the peace is my job."

XII

With the wire on hand, the fencing job began to show some real progress. Doug and his crew started by burying a big rock "dead-man" anchor for the corner posts, then bound the wire securely around these posts and started stringing it from the corner. The wooden spools were built with a hollow center. Two men would shove a crowbar through it. Then, one on either end of the bar, they would walk up the fence-line, the wire unrolling itself as they went.

They had no regular fence-stretching equipment. Instead, they would block up the axle of a wagon, secure the wire to a stick wedged between the spokes, and turn the wheel by hand, drawing the wire taut against the posts. They drove sharp staples into the hard cedar posts, fastening the wire solidly in place.

This was a faster job than setting the posts, so Monahan left most of the crew on the digging and tamping job, trying to keep ahead of the wire stringers. With the winter lull in his own field chores, Noah Wheeler spent most of his time with Monahan's crew, helping at the work and joying in the strong fence that shaped in his hands.

The crew worked well together, broken in to the hard labor now. Foley Blessingame and his four sons kept the men in good humor with rowdy jokes and rough horseplay that stopped only a fraction short of broken arms and legs. Old Foley was an everlasting wonder to Doug—how any man that old could do so much hard work. He would wear a young man into the ground and then do the work for both of them.

Then at night, under lanternlight in the barn, he would play poker with anyone who still had the courage to sit in against him. Almost everybody in the crew except Stub Bailey had tried him, and to a man they had lost.

Every once in a while Foley would make a try for Stub: "Why'n't you come on and play me a game? You can git your fun and eddication at the same time."

But Stub always turned him down with a grin. "I never was much of a hand at poker. You better stick to the experts."

Some of the crew who had considered themselves as experts were reappraising themselves after a set-to with old Foley. That he cheated was common knowledge. Just how he did it was a mystery. At penny ante it wasn't too expensive, and the men started choosing up to see who would play against him each night while the others watched, trying to catch him in a trick. They never did.

The only misfit in the bunch was Simon Getty, the cook. His cooking was decent enough the first few days, but he finally got the "rings," as the cowboys called it. He grumbled and carried on about everything and everybody. Foley Blessingame and those "kids" of his ate more than ten men decently ought to. That Dundee thought he could ride into camp any old time he felt like it and eat. Didn't he know that dinner was ready at twelve o'clock, and not at one or two or three? That saddlegun he toted around didn't make him any privileged character.

And those men Dundee had brought out—some of them didn't know enough to wash their hands before they shoved them into a man's Dutch ovens. That Stub Bailey, sneaking a bottle out of his bedroll these cold mornings and lacing his coffee on the quiet. Doug figured the cook's main objection here was that Stub hadn't offered him any of it.

And Doug Monahan himself—why couldn't he buy a man something decent to cook in? A man couldn't cook for a pack of pot hounds with the equipment this outfit furnished him.

Doug took it quietly. He knew a cowcamp cook's temper served to keep the rest of the crew in its proper place. But sometimes a man could overdo a thing, even if he was right.

Simon Getty made his big mistake one cold morning as the Blessingames came up under the tarp for breakfast. Faces flushed from the raw chill, they approached the chuckbox with a raging hunger. They found Simon Getty ringier than usual. He must have been cold too.

"Damn you, Foley Blessingame, stop kicking sand into the ovens. Lift up them big feet before I take a singletree to you."

Normally Foley would have retreated, for few men ever tampered with the cook. His revenge would be certain and hard to swallow. But this time Foley stood his ground, his mouth setting in a hard line. The cook had jumped him just one time too many.

Getty growled, "Five growed men without no better manners than a heathen Comanche Indian! The whole bunch of you swarm around them ovens like a passel of razorback hogs. Pity you don't fall in that crick and drown."

Foley's bearded face changed color a couple of times. He said abruptly, "Speaking' of fallin' in the creek, I don't recollect as I've seen you take a bath since you been out here. Right now would be as good a time as I know of."

Before Getty could draw away, Foley had him by the shoulders, his huge hands holding the cook as helpless as a baby calf. A couple of Foley's sons grabbed the cook's legs, and they packed him down to the creekbank like a sack of bran. Without ceremony, they heaved him in.

The first two times the cook crawled out cursing. They pitched him back. The third time he got out on the opposite side, so busy shivering and moaning and coughing up water that he couldn't say much. Presently Getty circled clear around the spring and came back on the other side, blue with cold. He went directly into the barn, took off his wet clothes and crawled into his blankets. He lay there sulling like a possum.

The news brought no cheer to Doug Monahan, even though it didn't surprise him much. "Well, Foley," he said, "since you ran off the cook, it's up to you to finish the breakfast."

He knew he would have to send Getty back to Stringtown. What would he do for a cook now?

Trudy Wheeler gave him the answer. "What were you paying him?"

"Forty dollars a month."

"And furnishing the food?"

"Yes."

"Pay me that and I'll take the job."

Doug didn't know if she was serious or not. "Thought you didn't like this fencing project."

She shrugged. "You're not going to stop it, and men have to eat. If you're paying, I'd just as well get some of that money as see someone else take it."

Doug was pleased. A woman's cooking would go over a lot better with these men than that of a camp cook, no matter how good he was.

"You wouldn't like cooking out in the open like this," he pointed out.

"I'd cook in the house, on the big woodstove."

Doug felt relief. Trudy Wheeler was softening. He had thought he saw it after Vern Wheeler had come home fighting. Now he was sure.

"Then you're hired," Doug said. He extended his hand, and she took it. "You can start right now, and fix dinner."

Captain Andrew Rinehart paced the scarred pine floor of his office with the slowed step of an old man. An uneasiness creased his weathered face as he looked at Sheriff Luke McKelvie.

"What else is new in town?"

It wasn't the question he wanted to ask, McKelvie knew that. The captain would bide his time, but he would get around to that question eventually if the answer didn't come of its own accord.

"Not a great deal," the sheriff said, dropping cigarette ashes into a chip-edged old saucer. The captain never had ash trays around. Too strong-willed to indulge himself in life's smaller pleasures, the captain made no allowances for those who did.

McKelvie said, "Gordon Finch has left. Dumped the ranch, livestock and all, right into the bank's lap. Just rode off and left it."

The captain nodded in satisfaction. "It's what I told him to do."

"Albert Brown's wringing his hands. He says he's a banker, not a rancher. He don't know what to do about it."

The captain frowned. "Funny he hasn't come to me. I'd buy it, he ought to know that."

McKelvie stared reflectively at the captain. A thought came to him, but he kept silent about it.

The captain evidently sensed McKelvie's thought anyway. His frown deepened. "You think maybe he don't want to sell to me?"

The sheriff shrugged, not wanting to make a definite answer. "I wouldn't know, Captain. I haven't talked to him about it myself."

The captain paced some more, pausing to look out the window. "They're talking in town, aren't they?"

McKelvie said, "They're talking."

The captain shoved his hands deeply into his pockets. His voice was defiant. "Let them talk, then. It's *my* town. I built it. I don't care what they say."

But by the dark worry in the old man's face, the way the gray head was bowed, McKelvie could tell that Rinehart *did* care. He had been the patriarch, the bell-wether, much too long to stop caring now.

McKelvie said, "It was just a little place in the old days, Captain. Everybody in town worked for you or owed you something. But it's not that little anymore. There are lots of people in it who don't believe they owe you a thing. They think they can get along without you."

Rinehart gave him an angry, raking glance. "Who are you working for, Luke, them or me?"

Not attempting to answer, McKelvie switched his gaze to Archer Spann, standing gravely by the door, out of the path of the captain's restless pacing.

"They're talking about you, too, Archer," the sheriff said. He caught the quick resentment in Spann's narrowed eyes.

"What're they saying?" Spann demanded.

"Laughing, mostly, about that incident over at Drinkman's Gap."

Spann colored. Mouth hardening, he sat down stiffly in a straight chair covered with a stretched, dried steer hide, the red hair still on it. Spann seemed to submerge in his own dark thoughts, losing himself from the other two men. It was almost as if he had left the room.

The captain said, "The ranchers are all with us, that's what counts."

"Are they?" asked McKelvie. "I heard Archer made the rounds, trying to work up all the opposition he could against the fence. I heard some of them turned away from him."

Stubbornly the captain said, "They'll come in with us when they realize what this fence will do to the country."

McKelvie considered awhile before he made any comment. "I've spent a lot of time asking myself what that fence means to the country. It could bring some good things, Captain."

Captain Rinehart stared incredulously. "Luke," and there was shock in his voice, "are *you* turning against me?"

The sheriff looked at Rinehart. "I'm not against you, Captain. I'll never fight you," he said in a hurt voice.

The captain walked back to the window and stared out awhile, a growing tension in the ceaseless flexing of his nervous, rope-scarred hands. "What's that story they're telling about the Wheeler boy, and three hundred dollars?"

McKelvie replied, "All I know is what I hear. You better ask Archer."

Spann glanced up sharply at mention of his name. "It's a lie. It's just something they made up to swing people against us. You know I took the cash out to that boy. You counted it off to me yourself, Captain."

The captain said, "He's right, Luke. I counted it out. The R Cross doesn't steal from its men."

McKelvie kept his eyes on Archer Spann. "No, the R Cross wouldn't."

Tiring, the captain sat down at his desk. He was silent awhile, his mind running back to other times and other places. He opened a drawer and took out a small object. He gazed at it a moment, then extended it to McKelvie.

"Ever see that, Luke?"

"Arrowhead, isn't it?"

The captain nodded. "I caught it on the Pecos, a long time ago. Packed it around in my shoulder twelve or fifteen years. Maybe I was still carrying it when you were on the ranch here, I don't remember. It finally worked close to the surface, and I had it taken out at Fort Worth."

There was a strange gentleness to the captain's voice as he talked of the olden times.

"Quite a souvenir," McKelvie commented.

The captain took it back and gazed at it with something akin to reverence. For a while, then, he forgot the worry of the present. He talked of things that had happened in those early days, of a time when he was in his element. Of a time of open range and freedom and plenty of opportunity for the man who had guts enough to try the impossible and make it work. A time when he had youth and vitality and a driving ambition.

It had been years since McKelvie had heard the captain talk like this, and he knew it for what it was. Sensing that time was inevitably closing in upon him, sensing the trouble that already had begun and could no longer be stopped until it had run its course, the old cowman was taking momentary refuge in the past.

"Those were the real times, Luke," the captain said. "They're gone now. There's a new breed of men in the country, men that don't know what we went through in the old days. They want to tear down all we built. Can you blame me, Luke, for wanting to keep it the way it used to be?"

McKelvie shook his head. "I can't blame you, Captain. But I will tell you this: you can't stop them. You'd just as well go out there and try to stop the river. You may slow the thing down, you may destroy some people. But in the end, Captain, they'll get you. They'll destroy *you*."

The captain stared unbelievingly, his face drained a shade lighter. Finally he pushed wearily to his feet, as if he carried a huge weight on his shoulders. His heavy-browed eyes were more sad than angry. His voice was pinched with hurt.

"I reckon you'd better go, Luke. If that's the way you feel, I don't want you around here anymore."

Luke McKelvie blinked back a burning in his eyes. The old cowman had been like a father to him. Now McKelvie yearned to go to him and put his arm around the old man's shoulders and help him see it through. But he realized that the way was hopelessly blocked, that it had been blocked from the beginning by stubborn pride and an old man's deep-etched memories of a time when he had been king.

"Captain," McKelvie said, "think hard before you do anything."

"Go, Luke. Just go."

Luke McKelvie picked up his hat and walked out of the room without looking back. He moved with his head down, the hatbrim crushed in his strong, unfeeling hand.

Sarah Rinehart was waiting for him at the front door. Seeing the look in his eyes, she knew. "You quarreled?"

McKelvie nodded. "I'm sorry, Sarah, I did the best I could. I knew it was going to happen, though, sooner or later."

"I know," she said. She brought a handkerchief out of her old lace sleeve. "What're we going to do with him, Luke?"

"I don't know, Sarah. He's getting set for a big fall. About all we can do is wait and try to help him up again."

Sarah said, "A lot of it's Archer Spann. Oh, I know Andrew barks at him sometimes, to remind him who's boss. But he's getting old, and he thinks he sees something of himself in Archer. He lets Archer influence him more than any man ever has before."

Luke McKelvie took Sarah Rinehart's thin hand. He could feel more strength in the old fingers than had been there in a long time. "I'm glad to see you looking better, Sarah. You've got to take care of yourself for his sake. One day soon, he's going to need you. You've got to be here."

She said, "I'll be here, Luke."

In the office Archer Spann stood at the window, watching Luke McKelvie mount his horse. "They've bought him off, Captain. He's sold out."

Captain Rinehart sat heavily in his big office chair, his hands hanging limply. Weariness settled in his eyes, and he closed them. He rubbed a hand over his forehead, wondering why Providence had chosen to set Luke McKelvie against him. He knew his friends were dwindling in number day by day, but Luke McKelvie was one he had counted on.

He knew Spann was wrong about McKelvie. Luke would never

sell out. He just looked at the thing differently, that was all. But whatever the reason, he was in the enemy's camp now. And that camp was growing.

Spann said, "Time's getting short, Captain. The farther they go with that fence, the harder it's going to be to stop them."

Rinehart was only half listening. He was thinking of other days, of happier days when Luke McKelvie had been an R Cross cowboy, one of the best the captain had ever known. Losing him now was almost like losing a son.

Times like this, Rinehart wished he *had* had a son. Everything else he had wanted in life had been provided him. But this he had always been denied. Once Luke McKelvie had come close to filling the need. Of late, it was Archer Spann.

"What about it, Captain?" Spann pressed with a trace of impatience.

"I've told you, you can do whatever you want to about that fence and about Monahan."

"We need to go farther than that. You don't stop a snake by cutting its tail off. We need to hit Noah Wheeler, too. Hit him with all we've got, and we'll stop this thing for good."

The captain shook his head. "No, Archer, I've told you that, too. We're leaving Noah Wheeler alone."

Spann rubbed his hands nervously behind his back as he looked out the window again. "Do you mind telling me, Captain, what it is about Noah Wheeler that makes him so special? What's the hold he's got over you?"

The captain frowned and stared at his rough old hands. "It goes back a long, long way. We were in the war together, Archer. Maybe you don't see him as much except a quiet old farmer, but I know differently. I can remember.

"We were both in Hood's Texas Brigade. I had a commission— still got it put away in an old trunk somewhere—and Noah Wheeler was one of my sergeants. We went through some hard times together—Gaines Mill, Second Manassas." He smiled faintly, calling up memories. "We had a marching song then, called 'The Old Gray Mare Came Tearing Out of the Wilderness.' I'll never forget Noah singing that song as the men went marching down the road.

"Then we came to Antietam. You never saw a hungrier, dirtier bunch of men in your life. They put us up against Hooker and his federals, and it was murder. It looked like the Yanks had us whipped when Hood ordered us to charge. Up through the cornfield we went. It was the nearest thing to hell there'll ever be on earth, the bullets whistling like hornets, the shells screaming in. But we kept on going.

"I caught a bullet in my leg and went down right under a Yankee gun. They had me. I was looking death in the face, and there wasn't any way out. But Noah Wheeler came and stood over me and put that gun out of service while the bullets ripped by him like hail. Noah Wheeler brought me out of that battle alive, Archer.

"That's why I'm not going to hit him. I owe him my life."

XIII

Dundee was getting impatient. "I'm beginnin' to think I never will be able to get in a lick," he complained to Doug Monahan as they sat on the edge of the Wheeler porch, eating supper. "Two miles of fence already strung up and they're not makin' a move against it. All I do is wear out my saddle lookin' at the scenery."

Doug gulped a big swallow of black coffee. "We ought to take that as a blessing. Or maybe you just like fighting a lot more than I do."

Dundee shrugged. "I wouldn't exactly say I like it. It's only that I seem to thrive on trouble. Always did, even when I was a kid. Others could go fishin'. Me, I always had to go get in a fight. Things got too quiet, I got restless, started looking for something to muddy up the waters a little bit. I generally managed to find it."

Doug said, "Maybe you were born a few years too late. You ought to've been in the army, fighting Indians."

Dundee shook his head, smiling. "About the time the fightin' started, I'd've been in the guardhouse for hittin' an officer. I never did cotton to takin' orders."

"You've taken them from me."

"If I hadn't liked 'em, I wouldn't have took 'em."

They were the last ones to eat. Since Trudy had taken over the cooking job, the men came up to the house for their meals, filling their plates from food piled high on the kitchen table. They usually sat on the porch outside to eat it, for the house would be uncomfortably cramped with that many men sitting around on the floor.

Stub Bailey was finishing up, rubbing his stomach in satisfaction.

He had been back to the table the second time. Watching Stub, Dundee said, "That girl's cookin's goin' to cost you a heap extra, Doug. One thing about Simon Getty, he wouldn't make a man over-stuff himself." He smiled then. "Of course, I reckon there's more to it than just the cookin'. Most of 'em go back the second time just to take another look at that girl."

Dundee's eyes touched Doug Monahan's for a moment with a hint of shared secrets. Doug knew Dundee was including him, too. Dundee had a way of standing off and shrewdly sizing people up, and he wasn't often wrong.

Funny the way it was with Trudy. After all she had said earlier about the fence, she had loosened up and become friendly and easy-mannered to the men of the fencing crew. There wasn't one of them now who wouldn't have charged hell with a bucket of water if she had asked him to. Maybe she had belatedly caught some of her father's enthusiasm about the fence.

Dundee finished first and walked off toward the barn. Doug sat on the porch, eating the last of a big slice of gingerbread. Trudy walked out onto the porch with a large pan in her hands. Leaning over Doug, she dropped another piece of gingerbread into his plate.

"Whoa now," he said, "I've had enough."

"There's too much to throw away and not enough to keep," she told him firmly. "Eat it." She ran her kitchen in the ironclad manner of a wagon cook, and she made the men like it.

Doug smiled, remembering how wrong his first impression of her had been. That day she had ridden into his fencing camp with her father, he had her figured as a quiet, shy little country girl who would never speak above a whisper. He had missed by about a mile and a half. There was something of steel about Trudy Wheeler. It might be hidden most of the time, but stress would bring it out.

Doug knew he was thinking too much about her. It wasn't that he wanted to. But whenever she was anywhere in view, he found himself watching her, hoping she didn't notice.

Doug Monahan had never been in love in his life, and he didn't want to be in love now. There was too much else to worry about.

He couldn't tell for sure what was wrong that night. An uneasiness came over him as darkness settled down, a prescience he had felt at other times, one he had learned to respect. He watched the men crawl into their blankets in the barn, but he didn't go to bed himself.

"What's the matter, Doug?" Stub Bailey asked.

"I don't rightly know. Just got a queer feeling."

"So've I, but it was just that third slice of gingerbread. It'll be all right in the morning."

Doug went outside and walked restlessly in front of the barn. He smoked half a cigarette, then flipped it away. It didn't taste right.

It was dark outside, except for the brittle winter starlight. He didn't like it, and he wished the moon would rise. Then he remembered it was time for the new moon.

Restlessness still needling him, he saddled his horse and rode down the steadily lengthening fenceline. His horse nickered, and another answered from nearby in the darkness. Doug kept his hand on his gun until he assured himself that the other horseman was one of the two guards he had constantly riding the fence.

"Who is it?" a stern voice demanded. Doug heard a hammer click.

"Me, Doug." He rode up slowly. He had to get close before the man could be sure of him in the darkness. The rider relaxed then and slipped the gun back into its holster.

"Just checking up, Milt," Doug said. "See or hear anything?"

"Nope, quiet as a church. Just like it's been every night."

"How long since you've seen Wallace?"

"Passed him ten minutes ago. He was ridin' along on the other side. He'll make a *vuelta* and be back directly. Somethin' wrong?"

"Nothing I can put my finger on. Just a feeling."

He found the other guard presently and got the same sort of answers. Doug was almost ready to concede that it *was* too much gingerbread and go back to the barn. But, to satisfy himself, he decided to make a short swing of a mile or so out in the direction of the R Cross headquarters.

The horse picked them up first. How a horse could unerringly find others of its kind in pitch darkness had always been something of a mystery to Doug. His mount perked up its ears and turned its head a little. Doug stood in the stirrups, looking and listening. He could hear and see nothing. He swung out of the saddle to get away from the constant creak of leather and stood off at the reins' full length from the horse.

He began to hear it then, the muffled thud of hoofs in the dry grass, a fragile tinkle of spurs and bit-chains in the crisp night air.

They were coming.

He swung back into the saddle and spurred into a long trot, hoping the sound would not carry to the oncoming riders as their own had come to him. The sharp breeze was in his favor. He hurriedly found his two guards.

"Riders on their way," he said. "Wallace, you ride back to the barn and pick up the rest of the crew. Milt, you and I'll go down to the end of the fence."

They struck an easy lope down the fenceline. Doug wished for good moonlight, but he knew there would be little of it. They wouldn't see their enemy until the men got close. But that worked both ways. The fencing crew wouldn't be easily seen, either.

He wondered why he hadn't thought of the new moon before. The R Cross probably had checked the almanac to be sure of coming in the dark of the moon. With a little thought, Monahan would have known they'd come on a night like this, if they were coming at all.

At the end of the fence were stacked the spools of wire and most of the cedar posts which hadn't been used yet. Down here the R Cross riders could do more damage in ten minutes than they could elsewhere in half the night, laboriously snipping away at the finished fence.

Saddlegun in his lap, Doug sat his horse quietly and waited, the blood pounding in his temples. Maybe Dundee would get his satisfaction tonight.

He heard a faint hum in the fence. Somewhere above, someone had cut a strand and eased the tension of the wire.

Doug's hand tightened on the gun. All that hard work, and they were setting in to destroy it! Listening hard, hearing the sharp gnash of cutting edge against cutting edge as the steel cutters bit through the wire, he felt growing in him the same anger that he had known the day Paco Sanchez had died.

But this time there was a difference. This time he was not helpless.

The horses were coming down the fence. Doug stepped out of the saddle, squatting low in the brittle grass so he could see the riders against the skyline. The sky was almost as black as the ground, and he could make out only the blurry outlines of the men as they reached the corner posts. He tied the ends of his split reins together and looped them over his arm.

"Here's the end of it," a man said in a low voice. "Them spools have got to be here someplace. Fetch up them kerosene cans." There were three riders, maybe four; it was hard to tell. That others were still busy up-fence, Doug was certain.

He lifted the muzzle of the saddlegun just enough so the slug would clear the men's heads, and squeezed off the shot.

His horse jerked back, almost throwing Doug to the ground. A couple of the raiders' horses squealed in panic. The wire stretched and sang as a horse hit the fence. Doug flinched at the sound. He heard the solid clank of a small kerosene can hitting the ground as some rider turned loose of everything and concentrated on staying in the saddle.

Doug moved so the men could not pinpoint him by the flash of the gun. For a moment or so there was confusion among the riders. Their horses danced excitedly, and Doug thought he heard a man hit the ground. Hoofs clattered as a horse broke in terror out across the prairie. One man afoot, Doug thought.

Somebody fired in Doug's direction, but it was a wild shot, more an angry gesture than an earnest attempt to hit him. The riders backed off.

He could hear men cutting the fence farther up. And there was a louder noise. The top strand of wire sang loudly. Staples sprang out of the posts.

"What're they doin' up there?" Milt asked worriedly.

"Tied on with a rope, I think. Trying to jerk down as much wire as they can in a hurry."

"Shouldn't we go stop 'em?"

"No," Doug replied, "we got to guard these stacks till the rest of the bunch gets here."

He fired again in the direction of the fence cutters. Someone shouted. He knew he was hitting close to home.

Then came the sharp rattle of gunfire farther up the fence. His own crew was coming now. They were shooting wild, trying to scare the raiders back from the fence. The guns moved nearer as the fencing crew strung out. Doug and Milt joined in, firing into the blackness until their gunbarrels were too hot to touch.

"Doug," a voice shouted, "where you at?" It was Dundee's.

"Here, at the corner."

He heard the roll of hoofbeats from across the fence. The raiders were retreating in hasty confusion. The wild, indiscriminate fire from the strong fencing crew was hard to face. There was no cover anywhere along the fenceline, no protection from the bullets that came whining by in the black.

The R Cross men were not gunfighters, and they were not getting gunfighter pay. They were drawing wages as cowboys, twenty-five to thirty-five dollars a month, depending on what they were worth for solid cow work, done a-horseback. No frills, no fancy stuff. They might be good men, top cowhands, but most of them probably had never been shot at in their lives, and they found this first time hard to take. So they were leaving.

It was the smart thing to do, Doug conceded. In their place, he would have done it himself.

Dundee came loping up. The fencing crew was strung out behind him. "We got 'em on the run," he shouted. "We could maybe catch up and give 'em somethin' to really remember us by."

"No," Doug said, "it's too dark. They'll remember us, all right."

Dundee was shaking with the excitement of a high-strung Thoroughbred horse which has just finished its race and still wants to run. For a moment he acted as if he'd go along anyway. "I say we ought to go after 'em!"

"No," Doug replied firmly, "if we push it any farther, somebody's liable to get killed. We ran them off, that's all I aimed to do."

Dundee accepted the decision with reluctance and shoved his gun back into the holster. "They've done us some damage. We oughtn't to just let it go like that. They get the idea we're an easy mark, they'll be slippin' back in here every night, cuttin' wire and makin' a nuisance."

"We're not just letting it go by," Doug told him, although he wasn't sure yet just what he was going to do about it.

Then Foley Blessingame brought him his answer. "Lookee here what me and the kids found," he said jubilantly. He pushed in close enough so Doug could see a man afoot at the end of a rope. "Feller lost his horse out yonder," Foley explained.

"Who are you?" Doug demanded.

The cowboy gave him a go-to-hell look.

Young Vern Wheeler came to see who it was. "Howdy, Shorty," he said. The R Cross man softened a little at the sight of Vern. "Howdy, Vern."

Vern said, "He's Shorty Willis. We worked together some while I was on the R Cross. Let's go easy on him. He's a pretty good feller."

"We don't aim to hurt him, Vern," Doug promised, "unless he gives us a reason to. Right now I'd just like to get a little information out of him."

"I got nothin' to tell you," Shorty said.

Doug glanced quizzically at Foley Blessingame. "Reckon he'd change his mind if you dunked him in that icy creek?"

Foley grinned. "You mean like we done that grouchy cook? I expect it'd loosen up his tongue a little. It sure made the cook talk."

The cowboy looked pleadingly at Vern Wheeler. Vern said, "You better tell 'em what they want to know, Shorty. They'll make you talk sooner or later. You'd just as well do it now and save yourself a soaking. That's mighty cold water."

Shorty Willis shrugged. "I ain't paid to do no swimmin'. What do you want to know?"

"Who-all was on the raid, and how many?" Doug asked.

"Big part of the R Cross cowboys, all that Archer Spann could round up without havin' to drag 'em in from the line camps. He got some of Fuller Quinn's bunch in on it, too. Quinn's been itchin' to do somethin' about this fence, only he ain't had the nerve to try it by hisself."

"Were Quinn and Spann both out here?"

"Yep. Spann was givin' the orders, though. He allus does. It's a funny thing to me, Quinn bein' a ranch owner and all. When Spann's around, Quinn lets him give all the orders, and Spann don't even own a good horse, much less a ranch. Somethin' about him that naturally makes a man sit up and take notice, I reckon."

"What was his plan?"

"He figured on cuttin' and rippin' out all the wire you'd strung. We was goin' to burn all the posts and wire you had stacked up out here. Cripple you good, he said, and you'd quit."

Doug said, "It didn't get very far, though, did it?"

Willis shook his head. "The dark had us boogered some to begin with. Spann said there'd be nothin' to it, that you'd fold up like a wet rag. But it's a creepy feelin', movin' into somethin' like this and not bein' able to see what's ahead. You-all could've been settin' up an ambush for all we knew. And when the guns opened up and them slugs started whinin' around, it was too much. A few of the boys started pullin' back, and then all of us was scatterin' like a bunch of quail. Archer Spann was fit to tie, but he couldn't stop it."

The cowboy rubbed his hip. It evidently was sore. "One of them wild bullets got my horse. Spilled him right on top of me. I hollered for somebody to pick me up, but everybody was so excited I guess they didn't hear me. Nobody except"—he nodded his head at the Blessingames—"them big oxes there."

Foley Blessingame grinned. "I always taughts my boys to give a man his money's worth."

Doug asked Willis, "Were you going to meet again somewhere after the job was through?"

Willis nodded. "Spann didn't seem to have any doubt we'd do the job up right. He said if we got scattered to meet at the Lodd line camp. He left some whisky there and said when we got back ever'-body could celebrate." Willis grimaced. "Some celebration!"

Vern said, "I thought it was against R Cross rules to have whisky on the place."

"What the old man don't find out about won't hurt him any." Willis shook his head. "Funny about Spann. Never touches a drop hisself. He's as straitlaced as the old man. But he'll buy it for some-body else if it suits his purpose, and that's somethin' the captain never would do."

It would be a different kind of a whisky party than Spann had anticipated, Doug figured. They'd be drinking to quiet their nerves and drown the ignominy of the rout.

"Let's mount up," Doug told the men. "We're going to drop over to that line camp and join the party."

XIV

The fencing crew sat their horses in a live oak motte above the line camp and looked down through darkness at the dim outline of a little frame house. This had been built as some small rancher's home, before the captain had bought him out. Or run him out.

"I don't hear any celebratin'," Stub Bailey commented dryly. "I thought they were really goin' to hang one on." There was no light in the window.

Doug Monahan smiled, but it was a grim one. "Wasn't much to celebrate. I imagine they tanked up and hit their soogans. How many horses down there in the corral, Dundee?"

Dundee had just come back from a short exploration afoot. "Ten, maybe twelve. I don't figure the men all stayed. Some of 'em likely just wanted to go home and hide their heads."

Doug nodded in satisfaction. Ten or twelve men would be all he wanted to try to handle anyway.

"Cold up here," he said evenly. "Let's go down where the fire is."

They moved down out of the motte and across the open stretch of tromped-out ground in front of the corrals. Doug's ears were keened for any noise down there which would indicate they had been seen. But he doubted there would be any. Whoever was in that house now would likely be too groggy to see or hear anything.

Nearing the house, he made a motion with his arm, and the men fanned out into a line. He could barely see the men on the ends, it was so dark. He stepped out of the saddle and motioned Dundee and Stub Bailey and Foley Blessingame to come with him. Vern Wheeler dismounted and held their horses. Doug drew his gun and moved carefully to the creaky front porch.

Quietly he pushed the door open and stepped inside, quick to get out of the doorway. Dundee and Bailey followed suit. Foley Blessingame was a little slow, standing there and blocking the door until Doug caught his arm and gave a gentle tug.

The place smelled like a distillery.

Doug gripped the gun tightly, listening and watching for movement. Someone turned over and groaned beneath blankets on the wooden floor. Doug leveled the gun on him and held it there until the man began to snore.

His eyes adjusted to the darkness, and he made out a kitchen table in a far end of the room. On it sat a lamp. "Cover me," he whispered, and moved slowly toward the table, careful not to step on any of the sleeping men. Lifting the glass chimney, he struck a match on his boot and lighted the wick. He slipped the chimney back in place.

Someone halfway across the room rose up on one elbow and rubbed his eyes. "Put out that damned light," he said irritably, blinking. He stiffened then as it penetrated his brain that the man at the lamp didn't belong here.

The lamp was smoking. Gun in his right hand, Doug trimmed the wick with his left. "Just take it easy," he said. "Keep your hands where I can see them."

The light and the sound of the voices stirred some of the other men. But Doug's fencing crew was coming in the door. As each man woke up, his sleepy eyes beheld someone standing in front of him, holding a gun in his face.

"You boys just get up quiet and peaceful," Doug said evenly.

Dundee and Vern Wheeler made a round of the room, picking up guns wherever they found them.

It took a while for the full meaning to soak in on some of the men, and it wasn't hard to tell why. Several empty whisky bottles lay scattered about the room. One sat overturned on the table, a big stain around it where the whisky had spilled out unnoticed.

"Looks like you boys were having you a little party," Doug said. "Well, I kind of like parties myself. I got another one planned for you." He motioned with the gun. "Get your clothes on, all of you."

The men fumbled around, trying to pull on their clothes. Two cowboys got their boots mixed up, and each of them wound up wearing one of the other man's, along with one of his own.

To the one that looked the clearest-headed, Doug said, "Where's Archer Spann? Thought he'd be here with you."

The cowboy started to shake his head but stopped abruptly. It hurt. "He was so mad he didn't even stop. Just kept on ridin'."

Doug turned to Vern Wheeler. "They all R Cross?"

Vern nodded. "Most of them. Those four aren't. They're some of Fuller Quinn's bunch." He squinted, looking in a corner. "By George, that's Fuller Quinn himself."

It was indeed Fuller Quinn the range hog, the man who was always crowding his cattle onto somebody else's grass. He glared belligerently, his red-veined eyes glassy with drunkenness. He reminded Doug of Gordon Finch.

Doug had hoped for Archer Spann, but he would take Fuller Quinn as a substitute. He had always disliked range hogs. Today, Doug thought, he'd make Quinn put out sweat for the free pasturage he had stolen from Noah Wheeler in the past.

Dundee was poking around, looking over the R Cross guns. Suddenly he spoke up happily, "Well now, look what I found." He held up a .45 and rubbed his hand over it fondly. "Looks just exactly like one somebody took off of me that day the R Cross raided Monahan's fencin' camp. Same scratches, same feel. Even got the same initials carved on it."

His eyes sharply searched over the men. "Anybody claim it?"

Nobody answered. Nobody would have dared to. At length Dundee said, "Well, if it don't belong to anybody, I reckon I'll just keep it," and triumphantly shoved it into his waistband.

A remnant of warm coals still smouldered in the woodstove. Doug punched them up and put in a little kindling to rebuild the blaze. Slowly he fed dry mesquite into this until he had a good fire going. He set the coffee pot on, then turned to see what he could cook. He was hungry from the long, busy night, and he was sure the rest of the men were, too. Finding a side of bacon, he sliced it. He found a keg of sourdough and filled a big biscuit pan.

When breakfast was ready, he let the R Cross and Quinn men eat right along with his own crew. "You boys that were on those bottles so hard last night better take a little extra of this coffee," he said. "You got a catawampus of a day coming up."

A pink promise of dawn had begun to streak the eastern sky when he herded the men out of the house and made them saddle their horses. Made frisky by the chill, one bronc pitched out of the corral. Stub Bailey had to help the rider up off of the ground. Back across the dry prairie they rode, toward the Noah Wheeler place.

For some of them, it became torture. Two or three had to stop. Doug held up the ride until they finished being sick. Some of the rest were whitefaced and not far from the stopping point themselves, but Doug kept pushing them.

For a long time Fuller Quinn could do little more than groan. He was halfway to the Wheeler place before he finally found his voice. "This is kidnappin'! I'll have you throwed in jail and left there till you rot!"

Doug said caustically, "Why, it's just the good old cow country institution of neighbor help. You came over and helped us last night, and now you're going to help us again today."

In the dark, Doug hadn't been able to see how bad the damage was. Now, riding up to it in the full light of morning, he felt the anger build again. They had wrecked about a mile of fence. In places the wire was pulled down but could be put up again. In others it was cut in so many places as to be useless.

"Made a pretty bad mess of it, didn't they?" Stub Bailey said.

Nodding grimly, Doug turned back to the sobered R Cross and Quinn cowboys. "You fellers can get down now and unsaddle. You're so good at cutting fence, we'll see how you are at patching it up again."

Vern Wheeler took the horses and turned them loose in the grain patch. Doug scattered the raiders, delegating his crew to supervise them. The first thing they had to do was pull down all the short pieces of cut wire for discard. The longer stretches that could be salvaged were spliced together.

By noon they had the splicing done and a good part of the wire restrung. Up and down the fenceline lay scattered pieces of wicked wire, cut too short to be worth anything. Left lying on the ground, they would always be a hazard to livestock.

Fuller Quinn groaned and complained, cursed and threatened all morning. So did a tall, sour-faced cowboy named Sparks, who was with him. After dinner Doug handed Quinn a shovel and Sparks a pick.

"You two are going to bury all that wasted wire. I want a hole four feet deep, big enough to take care of the job. Get after it."

Quinn swore and shook his fists, but in the end there was nothing for him to do but take the shovel and go. Doug left the rest of the men on the wire-stringing job. It was much easier, but most of them were suffering from the night before. They sweated and groaned, and occasionally one fell sick.

Doug no longer pushed them. When he saw a man who seemed to be getting too much of it, he called him out and had him sit down. These weren't bad men. Most of them were cowboys, men of his own kind. What they had done here was not so much out of malice as from the fact that they had been ordered to do it. True, they probably had not registered much objection. They might have enjoyed the idea of ripping out the fence, but they would not have attempted it except under orders. Doug doubted that they would enjoy it so much the next time.

By supper most of the damage was patched up. Even most of the R Cross cowboys seemed to take some interest as the job went along and they saw a good tight fence shaping under their own blistered hands. Once they gave up the idea of rebellion, they pitched in and worked hard. They labored and sweated the whisky out of their systems.

A while before sundown, Doug sent Vern after the men's horses. He signaled the men in. "That's enough. You've done more than I ever thought you would." He smiled now, for the anger was gone. Weariness lay heavy on his shoulders.

"Before you start back, Trudy Wheeler's got you a good hot supper fixed. I don't believe in working a man and not feeding him."

Some of the cowboys grinned. Fuller Quinn didn't. He was swelled up like a toad. So was Sparks, the tall rider who had helped him bury the wire. Doug had made them dig the hole big enough to bury an elephant in. He had made them throw all the wasted wire in the bottom and cover the hole up again.

The way Trudy Wheeler treated the men, a casual visitor would never have suspected that they had come to destroy. Like Monahan, she seemed to feel that they had served their sentence. She smiled and talked and saw that their plates were full. The cowboys watched her covertly, admiring her.

"Vern," said weary Shorty Willis, "if I'd knowed you had a sister like that, I'd've been over here workin' for your old man instead of over yonder with the captain."

After supper, Doug stood on the porch with Noah Wheeler and watched the cowboys ride away.

"Well," he said, "I don't expect I made any friends in that crowd. But Trudy did."

Tired, sleepy, Doug was glad the day was over. Another hour and he wouldn't have made it. All the way out to the barn, he thought of old Foley Blessingame, crowding sixty. This was hard enough on a young man. Pity touched him. The old man was probably already in his blankets, asleep.

Pushing the door open, Doug heard a loud voice. It was Foley's. The cedar-cutter had a small table pushed out in the middle of the dirt floor and sat there shuffling the cards. He was bright-eyed and r'arin' to go.

"How about it, Bailey? You worked up the nerve yet to try me a game?"

Archer Spann stood in the back of the Twin Wells mercantile, watching distrustfully while storekeeper Oscar Tracey stacked the goods listed on the R Cross bill. He kept glancing at the duplicate list, making sure Tracey didn't cheat on the count. He never had, as far as Spann knew, but the foreman believed it didn't pay to trust anybody.

Up in the front of the cluttered store, a couple of women customers were stealing glances at Spann, and he knew they were whispering about him. He tightened his fist and tried to keep from looking at them. He had felt that whispering ever since he had been in town. More than that, he had sensed people laughing. They kept a solemn face when they were near him, but he could see the laughter hidden in their eyes.

It was the Wheeler fencing job that had done it. Never before had people laughed at Archer Spann. Some hadn't liked him—some had even hated him—but that hadn't bothered Spann. Let them hate him, for all he cared.

But not laugh at him.

First it had been that fiasco at Drinkman's Gap, and now it was the rout over on Wheeler's fenceline. Twice Archer Spann had tried to stop Doug Monahan, and each time the whole thing had blown up in his face. He didn't know what he would do next. But *this* he knew, next time it would have a different ending.

He felt needles pricking him as a man walked through the front door and closed it against the cold. Noah Wheeler!

For a moment Spann considered going out the back way so he wouldn't have to face Wheeler. He had developed a gnawing hatred for the old farmer. He didn't even want to look at him. But Spann knew that to walk out the back would be taken for a retreat. There had been too many retreats already.

Steeling himself, he shoved the duplicate supply list in his pocket and started to the front. He heard Wheeler say, "I got a list of goods here I need to take back to the farm today, Oscar."

Tracey replied, "Be with you directly, Noah."

Wheeler turned and Archer Spann walked toward him. The R Cross foreman stopped and glared at the farmer. He felt his hatred well up like something indigestible. Here was the real root of the trouble, he thought darkly. Monahan was the most obvious cause, but had it not been for Wheeler, Monahan would not have been able to stay. Even yet, were Wheeler to fold, Monahan could go no farther.

The captain could believe what he wanted to and say what he wanted to about Noah Wheeler, but to Archer Spann he was nothing but a plain dirt farmer too big for his britches.

Spann turned angrily on Oscar Tracey. "Oscar," he said, "the R Cross has bought a lot of supplies from you in the past. If you want to keep getting that trade, you better stop selling to its enemies."

To his surprise, Oscar Tracey never wavered. "It's your right, Mr. Spann, to buy from whoever you please. And it's mine to sell to whoever I please."

Spann rocked back on his heels. A month ago, there wasn't a man in town who would have said that. And Oscar Tracey, this thin, gray old storekeeper who looked ready to blow away if a strong wind hit him, was the last man Spann would ever have expected it from.

Spann stamped out the front door and into the raw chill of the open street. He stopped then and wondered where to go to kill time. He didn't drink because whisky too often got in a man's way, and he didn't like to idle in saloons where men sat around lazily instead of going out to hustle, to make money. There was nothing about this rough little prairie town that he liked. He had always hated it. He hated it even more now that he could feel its laughter.

Someday, he thought grimly, I'll be running the R Cross, and then I'll snub them up short of the post. There won't be any old man going soft and saying hold off. They'll do what *I* tell them, by God!

He half turned and glanced at the window of the store. Spann doubled his fist. Here Wheeler was, right in his grasp, and there wasn't a thing he could do about it. Captain Rinehart had tied his hands. If only . . .

Spann felt a sudden elation. Why hadn't he thought of it already? Sure, the captain had tied his hands, but he had no say-so over anybody else. Not over Fuller Quinn, for instance. And Spann had seen Quinn ride up to the Eagle Saloon down the street an hour ago.

Spann pushed the saloon door shut behind him and stood looking. He spotted Quinn slouched in a chair at a back table. With him was a tall, hook-nosed cowboy—Sparks, his name was. They had emptied the better part of a bottle of whisky just since they had been sitting there.

The bartender stared in surprise at Archer Spann. The R Cross foreman was seldom seen in a place like this. "What could I get you, Mr. Spann?"

"Nothing," Spann said curtly. Then, because he was cold, he said, "If you got coffee, I'll take that."

He walked back to Quinn's table. Quinn looked up at him belligerently, for some harsh recriminations had passed between them after that affair out at Wheeler's place. Finally Quinn said, "Sit down, if it suits yuh."

Spann nodded toward the bottle. "Hitting that pretty hard, aren't you?"

"Don't see it's any of your business," Quinn responded sharply. As if in defiance, he looked Spann straight in the eye and poured his glass full again.

Spann could see that Quinn was already far gone. He got a look at the palm of the man's hand, lying slack on the table. It was blistered and sore. "That hand looks bad."

"Yours'd be too if you'd spent the whole day with Monahan's gun pokin' you in the face, and you workin' with a pick and shovel like me and Sparks done."

Sparks sat sullenly, feeding on some deep anger and paying little attention to anybody. The barman brought Spann's coffee. Spann sat and blew it awhile, then sipped it as he sized up Fuller Quinn. Quinn might just be mad enough and drunk enough to do it.

"Why don't you do something about it?" Spann asked.

"Like what?"

"Noah Wheeler's over at Tracey's mercantile. Was I you, I'd take it out of his hide."

Quinn glared suspiciously. "The R Cross got a worse dose of it than we got. Why don't *you* do it?"

"The captain says no. Seems he and Wheeler were friends once a long time ago, and he won't let me touch the old devil."

"And you want me to do it?"

Spann shrugged. "It don't make any difference to me. All I said was, you got a good chance, if you're a mind to."

Quinn took another long drink. His eyes watered, and he blinked hard to clear his sight. With one eye squinted almost shut, he rasped, "Tryin' to get somebody else to do the dirty work for yuh!"

Spann said, "It wasn't me that had to dig that hole and bury all that wire. If you got the guts to, you can give Wheeler what he deserves. If you're scared, you can let him go. It don't matter a damn to me."

Fuller Quinn straightened, his face getting redder. "I'm not scared of you or Wheeler or Monahan or anybody else, Spann! I'll do as I please, and you can go to hell for all I care!"

Spann forced himself to keep a tight rein. He had planted the seed, and maybe the whisky would germinate it. There would be plenty of time to make Fuller Quinn eat those words. Spann would not forget them. He stood up and shoved his chair back under the table.

"Take care of those hands, Fuller. I'll see you around."

After Spann's wagon was loaded, he stalled a while and watched for Noah Wheeler to leave the store. Wheeler's wagon rolled off down the street and out onto the trail that led toward his farm. Presently Fuller Quinn and Sparks swayed out of the saloon. With some difficulty they managed to get on their horses. Quinn pointed, and the two headed out in the same direction Noah Wheeler had taken.

Nodding in satisfaction, Spann said to the cowboy who had come with him to drive the team, "Roll 'em. I've seen all I want to."

It was dark when Sheriff Luke McKelvie came in driving Noah Wheeler's wagon. Noah was slumped on the spring seat beside him, and McKelvie's horse was tied on behind. Men who had been sitting on the porch, eating supper, put their plates down and hurried out to the wagon.

"Easy with him," McKelvie cautioned as Doug Monahan reached for the old farmer. "He's pretty bad beat up."

Noah Wheeler's square face was swollen and bruised and angry red in places where rough knuckles had broken the skin. A white bandage was bound around his head. His clothes were dirt-streaked and torn.

"Easy, Noah," Doug breathed, "just relax and let your weight come on me."

Stub Bailey was helping him, and Foley Blessingame and a couple of the Blessingame boys. The others were crowding around anxiously, ready to make a grab if Wheeler should start to fall.

The commotion caught the attention of the two women in the house. They came running as Wheeler got his feet to the ground. The men moved aside for them. Mrs. Wheeler's face went white, and she swayed for just a moment. Then she was in complete control.

"Bring him into the house," she said. "Whatever's to be done, we can do it better in there."

Luke McKelvie climbed down from the wagon and followed them toward the porch. "Mostly what he needs now is rest, Mrs. Wheeler. The doctor said no bones are broke."

Noah Wheeler protested weakly that he was all right, but they carried him to his bed, pulled off his boots and laid him across it anyway.

Doug turned to the sheriff. "What happened?"

"He left town with the goods he bought at Stacey's. About a mile or so out, Fuller Quinn and that cowboy they call Sparks caught up with him. They were drunk and mad. They roped him off of the wagon and drug him around some, then beat him up."

Doug Monahan felt ice in his stomach.

The sheriff went on, "A kid was out hunting a stray horse and happened up on them. They cussed him out and rode off. The kid got him back up in the wagon and brought him to town."

Doug sat down heavily. He hadn't expected revenge to come this way, not against a helpless old man.

"It's my fault," he said dully. "They were mad at me because I drug them over here and made them work all day. They couldn't get to me, so they took it out on him."

McKelvie said, "It's a wonder they didn't kill him. Drunk like they were, and dragging him around on a rope, they could've done it easy enough, even if they didn't mean to."

Doug sat there dumbly, head bowed, cold chills running up and down his body as he considered what might have happened. He put his head in his hand while Mrs. Wheeler and Trudy got the torn clothes off of Noah Wheeler and pulled the covers up over him.

He only half heard McKelvie saying, "If you don't mind, I'll stay here tonight. Then I'll go over to Quinn's tomorrow and arrest him. He's going to pay for this."

Trudy was saying, "Of course, we'll be glad to put you up, Sheriff."

Suddenly Doug arose. "Noah," he said bluntly, "I'm going to quit!"

All activity stopped. Everybody turned to stare at him. "I'm going to quit," he repeated. "All this is my fault. I brought it on you. I kept telling myself it wouldn't happen this way, that we could protect you, but I know now we can't. We can't watch every minute, every day. I never would've thought they'd waylay you away from home like this, or I'd have sent somebody with you. If it happened once, it can happen again."

He had never seen Noah Wheeler actually angry before, but now he did. Lying in the bed, his face bruised and beaten, the old farmer said loudly, "Doug, I'm not going to let you quit. I was the one that wanted this fence."

Doug shook his head. "No, it was me. I wanted to build a fence somewhere—anywhere—and rub the captain's nose in it. Trudy was right, all I was interested in was revenge. I didn't consider the trouble I'd be getting other people in. I didn't let myself consider it."

Noah Wheeler said, "If you'll just remember, you didn't come to me about building that fence. I was the one that went to you. I suggested it, you didn't."

"But I knew what was bound to come. Deep down, I knew it, and I should've told you."

"Do you think I'm a fool, Doug? Don't you think I knew it,

too? I did, and I thought about it a heap, and I was still willing to take the risk."

He motioned with his hand. "Doug, come here and sit down." Doug sat on the edge of the bed. Wheeler said, "I got to thinking about that fence the day the captain raided you. I commenced to seeing how much this country needed fences like that, the little men especially. It was the only real hope they had of staying, of building something good. I'd thought I'd let some of the others start first, and I'd see how they looked. But the captain stopped them.

"I've always thought a lot of the captain. Away back yonder we . . . but that's another story, and I'll tell you someday. The point is, as much as I thought of the captain, I knew he was wrong. I knew that no man has got a right to stand in the middle of the road and block everybody else. Somebody had to stand up to the captain and show him that, and I figured it was up to me to be the one."

Monahan had always admired this forthright old farmer, but never so much as now. Wheeler had been thinking beyond his beloved Durham cows—old Roany and Sancho and the rest—and the crops in the fields. Those had been his avowed purposes, but he had been thinking way beyond them.

Trudy Wheeler said sternly, "I was opposed to that fence when it started, but now I'm going to stand by my father. If he wants that fence, he's going to get it. And if you try to ride away from here, Doug Monahan, I'll—I'll shoot you, that's what!"

The heavy weight of conscience lifted from Doug's shoulders. He managed a thin smile. "I reckon you can leave that shotgun in the corner. I'm not going anywhere."

Much relieved, he walked out onto the porch. It was dark now, and the first stars were beginning to wink. Luke McKelvie followed him out. The men of the fencing crew were standing around, waiting.

"Noah's all right," Doug told them. "About all they did was make him good and mad."

The men relaxed, but they still just stood there. Finally it was Stub Bailey who broke it up.

"Foley Blessingame," he said, "ever since you been here you been trying to get me into a poker game. All right then, tonight I'll take you on."

The rest of the crew followed along to watch. Doug shook his head sadly. "Stub's fixing to get himself trimmed," he told the sheriff.

They sat a while on the porch, smoking. Presently Doug said, "You remember one day, Sheriff, you told me there must be an awful emptiness in a man when all that matters to him is revenge?"

McKelvie nodded. Doug said, "You were right. It came home to me when you brought Noah in. I was ready to shuck the whole business. Revenge is a bitter thing when it's your friends who have to pay the price for it."

Young Vern Wheeler came out onto the porch behind them and stood leaning on a post, his face tight with anger.

Doug said, "I'm just glad it wasn't the R Cross that was responsible for this today."

McKelvie frowned and looked back at the boy. "I hate to tell you this, but you'll hear it anyway, sooner or later. Archer Spann was in the Eagle, talking to Quinn and Sparks a while before they went out and followed Noah. The whole town knows it now. They figure Spann egged them on."

Doug Monahan's jaw tightened. "What do *you* think, McKelvie?"

McKelvie took a long, worried drag at his cigarette. "I know Archer Spann. I reckon they're right."

Fury rippled in Vern Wheeler's face. "Archer Spann." Abruptly he said, "Doug, I've got to quit you."

Surprised, Doug said, "What're you going to do?"

"I can't tell you that."

"Vern, you're feeling mad. Don't let it make you do something rash."

"It's nothing rash. I've been thinking about it for quite a while. Only now I'm going to do it." Vern turned and walked back into the house.

When McKelvie was gone, Trudy came out onto the porch. "Let's go for a walk, Doug. I want to talk to you."

They walked along in the moonlight, out to the springhouse and down the creek. The cold began to touch them both. Trudy put her arm in Doug's and walked close beside him.

"Doug," she said, "I didn't mean all I said while ago. I wouldn't have shot you."

He nodded, smiling. "I guess I wouldn't really have left, either. It would be hard for me to leave here anymore."

"Why?"

"Don't you know why, Trudy?"

He stopped and turned her to face him. She said nothing, but the look in her eyes told him she knew.

He said, "I didn't mean it to happen. I've told myself I couldn't afford to get interested in a woman until I had something of my own again, till I had something I could offer her. But these things happen to a man, and I guess there's nothing he can do about it."

She whispered, "Nothing at all." She tipped her chin up, and her fingers tightened on his arm.

Then he pulled her into his arms and kissed her. . . .

When he walked into the barn, he heard the rattle of wooden matches on the small table. Stub Bailey had a big pile of them, and he was raking them in to count them. Stub held his mouth straight, but his eyes were laughing.

"Sure you won't try another hand, Foley?"

The whole crew stood around grinning. Old Foley Blessingame sat bleakly staring at the matches. Disbelief was in his red-bearded face. "What for? You done got it all."

Foley stood up, a shaken man, and walked out the door. He beckoned Doug to follow him. For a while Foley just stood there silently in the cold night air, trying to regain his wits. Finally he said:

"Doug, I know how much you like Stub Bailey, and it hurts me to say anything against a friend of yours. But you know what? I do believe that boy cheats!"

XV

Captain Rinehart was angrier than Archer Spann had seen him in a long time. He paced the floor of his office, cursing as the captain was seldom heard to do, and through it all he laced the name of Fuller Quinn.

"That fool," Rinehart thundered, "that pig-headed fool! I'm sorry for the day I ever told him he could stay up there on Wagonrim Creek."

He turned on Spann and Spann hoped the captain could not see the sweat breaking out in his face.

"You know what they're saying in town, Archer? They're saying the R Cross was responsible for it. They're saying you promoted it."

"They're after us now, Captain. They'll say anything."

"You were in town that morning. Did you see Quinn?"

"Yes, sir, I saw him. I tried to talk to him, but I found him drunk, and I left."

"You didn't say anything to him about Noah Wheeler?"

Spann felt the sweat trickle down his face. A little of it stung his eyes, but he dared not even blink while this fiery old man studied him so closely. "No, sir, I did not."

A worry was digging at him. He thought he knew Fuller Quinn. He thought Quinn would sull and say nothing. But he could be wrong, Quinn might start talking. What then? What if Quinn said Spann had browbeaten him into going after Wheeler?

Spann cared little what anyone else thought, but he had to keep the captain's confidence. It would be his word against Quinn's. He had always managed to make the captain believe him in the past.

Could he do it again? For the first time, Spann was really beginning to worry.

Cautiously Spann asked, "What else do you hear, Captain? What're they doing out at Wheeler's?"

"They're going on with the fence."

Spann sagged a little. He had hoped the beating might stop the fencing project. He decided to take a gamble. "Captain, I'd like to say something. I know how you feel about Noah Wheeler, and I can understand why. But maybe Quinn had the right idea, in a way."

He knew he was on thin ice by the way the captain's eyes narrowed. The old man's eyes seemed to be boring into Spann. "How so?" the captain demanded.

"Monahan won't scare, we've found that out. The only way to stop him will be to cripple or kill him. But if we can stop Wheeler, we don't have to worry about Monahan."

"Noah Wheeler doesn't scare, either. I've known that since the war days. I just told you he's going ahead with his fence."

"He'd stop quick enough if we hit him the way I've said all along. Burn him out. Run off his cattle. You don't kill a snake by cutting its tail off. One quick, hard thrust, right to the head. That's how we can stop this fence."

The captain turned away. He wasn't even considering it, Spann saw. "Look, Captain, that war was a long time ago. Things are different now. He's fighting you, and you don't owe him anything. He's not your friend anymore, he's made that as plain as he can. You let him by and you'd just as well take down the sign."

Captain Rinehart sat down with his brow furrowed. For a while he just sat there with his eyes closed and tugged at his gray beard, the way he always did when he was worrying out a dark problem.

Spann felt the warming of sudden encouragement. Maybe

Rinehart was beginning to see it his way. Maybe now he would cut this rope that had kept one of Spann's hands tied behind his back.

But finally Rinehart shook his head. "Not yet, Archer, not yet. Maybe we'll have to do it in the end, but . . ." his face was thin-drawn and brooding ". . . I want to wait a little longer—see what's going to happen."

Impatience prodding him, Spann tromped down to the barn to see how Charley Globe was coming along with his horse. He wasn't worth much anymore except in shoeing a horse occasionally or in raking the yard. If it were up to Spann, he would have put Charley off the place. No use having an old relic like him hanging around long after his usefulness was done.

Charley was putting the last shoe on Spann's dun. He could tell somehow that Charley knew he'd had a hard conference with the captain.

"Well," Charley said, "what's the captain say? We going to run Noah Wheeler out the country?"

It was none of Charley's business, but Spann said, "We decided to wait a while."

Charley snickered. "*We* did? I'd like to've heard that."

Spann felt color squeezing into his face.

Charley Globe said, "What'd he say about you eggin' that Fuller Quinn on to beat up a helpless old farmer?"

Spann's hand shot out and grabbed Globe's frazzled collar. He jerked Charley so hard that the old man dropped the hammer. "That's a lie!"

The old cowboy was shaken, but he wasn't scared. "If I was younger, Spann, I'd'a knocked you in the head with that hammer. But I'm old enough now to have better sense. I know you ain't worth it. I'll still be here when you're gone."

Spann let go of Globe's collar and stepped back. "You better shut up, Charley, or I'll forget how old you are."

Charley Globe leaned against Spann's dun horse. He was angry now. "You know, Spann, I've spent a lot of time tryin' to figure you out, and I reckon I got you pegged. By rights you ought to be a big man. You don't drink or gamble or waste time with the women, like most men do. You never make a mistake when it comes to cow work. There was a time I thought you ought to be as big a man someday as the captain is. But you never will, Spann, and you know why?

"You got a mean, selfish streak in you a mile wide, Spann. Inside you, you're rotten. You're tryin' to pattern yourself after the captain, but you'll never fit the cloth. There's nothin' big about you. Deep down you're little and greedy, like when you took that Wheeler boy's money. No, don't deny it. I know you done it, and most other people know it, too. You're little and greedy and mean."

Archer Spann stood stiffly, wondering why he took this. He could break this old man in two with his bare hands. But what was the use?

Angrily he replied, "You say I'm mean; well, maybe I am. I never had anything in my life I didn't fight for, even when I was a kid. Maybe you'd be mean too if you had a drunken bum of a father that beat you and made you work, then took what you earned and drank it up and left you with an empty belly. I lived for just one thing, and that was to get big enough to whip him. One night I did it. I beat him with my fists till he went down, and then I took a club to him. I found out later that I hadn't killed him, but I always wished I had.

"I swore I'd amount to something someday, and by God I will! I learned a long time ago that a man's got to watch out for himself, that nobody else cares. The captain's got no son to leave all this to. I'm taking the place of that son, Charley, and some day all this will be mine. It's a mean world, and you got to be mean to get anything out of it. No dirt farmer like Noah Wheeler and no grubby fence builder like Doug Monahan is ever going to stop me!"

Charley Globe said solemnly, "Then you got some fightin' to do, Spann. And you know somethin'? I don't think you'll make it. I think when the showdown comes and you're up agin the taw line, you'll fold. Alongside that meanness, you got a yellow streak in you, Spann. And some day the captain's goin' to see it."

Vern Wheeler slapped his coiled rope against his leather chaps and yelled hoarsely at the cattle strung out before him. Dust burned his eyes and grated at his throat. Far ahead of him he saw a tough, sun-darkened rider turn in the saddle and wave impatiently at him. He couldn't hear the words. The bawling of the cattle wiped away all other sound like the roar of springtime thunder. But Vern could see the whisker-fringed mouth, and he knew well enough what the man was shouting.

"Hurry up! Bring up them drags!"

It had been a fast, hard drive, risky as walking the edge of a sharp-hewn cliff, and there was plenty more of it ahead.

Young calves in the bunch had dropped back to the drags. They shambled along with heads down, tongues protruding.

"*Hyah*, babies!" Vern shouted at them, slapping his chaps. The sharp noise picked some of them up a moment or two, but not for long. They were hopelessly worn out.

The big rider spurred back in a long trot. He was a begrimed, bewhiskered man in a greasy black hat and filthy blue wool coat. "Button," he shouted in a coarse voice, "how many times I got to tell you? Let them calves drop out if they can't keep up."

"They'll starve back there," Vern protested.

"It's none of our lookout," the man said, and jerked his horse around again. "Keep them cattle moving."

Vern nodded angrily and pulled around a couple of limping baby calves. He knew what would happen to them without their mothers. They would dogie, and most of them would die. Those

few which learned to rustle for themselves on the dry grass would
be forever stunted by the ordeal.

Still, Vern knew the dusty, harsh-voiced old cow thief was right.
They must keep moving, and moving fast, for these bawling cows
bore the R Cross brand on their left hips, the R Cross swallowfork
in their right ears. And they were still on R Cross range.

Restlessly Vern's eyes searched the skyline for sign of riders.
He'd had a bad feeling about this thing ever since it had started.
Rooster had agreed to help him take and sell enough cattle to make
up the three hundred dollars he had coming. Vern had sworn he
would buy his little piece of land and put up a fence around it and
kill the first man who touched a hand to one strand of the wire.

But Rooster had brought three hardened old cow thieves along
with him. And instead of taking a small bunch, they cut deep and
greedily took out several hundred head. Now they were driving fast
for the nearest boundary of the R Cross range, driving for the brush
country that would swallow up this herd in a maze of mesquite and
catclaw and whitebrush. Vern had wanted to pull out of it, but it had
been too late.

The one called Bronc had drawn his six-shooter and leveled it
carelessly at Vern's heart. "It's gonna take all five of us to push these
cattle outa here. Don't you git any idees 'bout quittin' us, boy."

Rooster Preech was helping Vern bring up the drags. He
worked his horse over beside Vern's. Dust lay like powder on his
face. "Don't you pay much mind to Bronc. He talks mean, but he's a
pretty good old boy."

Vern scowled. He knew better than that. The time he'd spent with
Rooster's three outlaws had convinced him of one thing: there was
mighty little good about any of them. They were greedy and dirty and
coarse and mean. Not one of them had any inclination to try to make
an honest living. Vern was convinced that any one of them, and Bronc
especially, would shoot his own brother if there was a good profit in it.

Vern had known at the outset that he was making a mistake. He didn't belong here. It had looked like a good idea at first, but he wished now he had never hunted up Rooster, that he had never heard of Bronc and these other two.

Rooster said, "You're sure makin' a bust, Vern, not takin' but three hundred dollars. Your share of this bunch oughta be worth two or three times that much."

Stubbornly Vern shook his head. "The R Cross owes me three hundred dollars. That's all I set out to get, and it's all I'm going to take."

Rooster shrugged. "Suit yourself, it's just that much more for the rest of us. Sure beats diggin' postholes, don't it?"

Vern glanced sharply at Rooster. They'd been friends for years, but Vern could see that Rooster was getting to be just like these three cow thieves who rode swing and point. Though still a brash kid, he was talking like them, acting like them. He was picking up their cautious habits, their free and easy way of looking at the law and at the rights of other people. When the three old rustlers bragged of slick thefts and fast deals they had pulled in the past, Rooster had one or two of his own to tell about. Granted that they were mostly lies, there was enough of truth in them to prove one thing. Rooster belonged to the back-trail bunch now.

Vern could see now that it had been in the cards all the time. He hadn't recognized the signs because they had been boyhood friends, and he hadn't realized things would ever change. Rooster's mother was dead, and his father paid little attention to him.

Rooster had swept out saloons sometimes to get something to eat. A time or two he was caught taking money out of the drawer behind the bar, and the barkeep had peeled the hide off of him. Later, it was bigger things. Luke McKelvie had tried to talk to him, but by the time it came to that, Rooster had little use for anyone who wore a badge.

He had been left to his own devices. When at last he came to that big fork in the road, lacking any sound guidance, he took the wrong one. It was as simple as that. Watching him now, Vern doubted that there would ever be any turning back for Rooster. He had already gone too far down that road.

Now Vern Wheeler was on the same road, and he wondered what he would do if he found himself trapped on it, unable to turn back.

He was going to try hard not to be. When they finished this drive, he was going to take his three hundred dollars and run like a scared rabbit. Never again in his life would he lay a hand on an animal that didn't belong to him, not even if, as he had told himself over and over, he was only taking that which was due him anyway.

Once more Bronc came riding back. "You two think we got a tea party here? Spread out and drive these cattle, or I'll take and pistol-whip the both of you when we git where we're goin'."

Rooster jerked his horse away and started yelling at the cattle. Vern let a couple more tired calves drop out. He wondered how many had fallen back since they had started. Thirty or forty. That many calves left to die or go dogied.

An old cow kept turning, bawling for one of the calves that had stayed behind. The calf tried hard to follow, but his tired, spindly legs barely carried him anymore. Twice Vern choused the cow back into the bunch. The third time she tried to break out, he made sure Bronc wasn't watching, and let her go.

One calf saved, anyway.

He looked back with a glow of self-satisfaction to see the cow smelling of the calf in the worried way that only a cow can, and the tired calf butting its head against her bag, getting the milk that meant life to it.

Then it was that he saw the riders. Two of them broke out over a rise and hauled up, watching the cattle. Vern jerked his horse to a stop and sat frozen. They were so close to him that he could have hit them with a rock. He recognized them both. They were R Cross men he had worked with. And he knew they recognized him.

Bronc saw them, too. He came riding back fast, leaning down to pull a saddlegun out of its scabbard. The R Cross cowboys saw him coming. One of them started to pull away, but the other held his ground. Pulling out his six-shooter, he fired a long shot that kicked up dust thirty feet from Bronc. The cowboy swung the gun back on Vern. Vern sat stiffly, paralyzed with horror as he realized the cowboy was going to shoot him.

He saw the flame, and he felt the sudden jar that struck his shoulder with the weight of a sledge. It carried him halfway around and lifted him far out of the saddle. For a second or two he tried desperately to regain his balance. Then he saw the ground coming up. He hit it hard and tasted dirt.

He was only half conscious of his horse plunging in terror, its hoofs barely missing him, and he realized dully that he had somehow held onto the reins. He let go. The horse jerked free and ran.

In sudden terror the cattle in the drag turned back and ran, too. The clatter of their hoofs broke past Vern. He lay helpless, waiting to be trampled, and somehow he cared little if it happened. The wounded shoulder had him twisting in agony.

But he wasn't trampled. In a moment Rooster rode up, bringing Vern's horse. He jumped down and knelt beside Vern.

Somewhere over the rise, the shooting continued.

"You all right, boy?" Rooster asked. "Think you can ride?"

Clenching his teeth against the pain, Vern said, "I don't know. . . ."

"You got to, boy. The fat's really in the fire now."

Rooster helped Vern to sit up. Vern's head reeled. He brought his right hand up to the left shoulder and felt the wound warm and sticky to the touch. The very bone seemed to be afire.

Vern fell over on his face and was sick. Rooster stuck by him, holding him. Presently Bronc and the other two outlaws came back over the rise.

"They got away," Bronc declared, cursing. "Hell of a help you two was." He jerked his head angrily toward the scattering cattle. "Git out there and git them cattle throwed together. We really got to push 'em now."

Rooster hesitated. "Vern's hit. He can't take no fast pace."

"Then he'll hafta stay here. He oughtn't to've got hisself shot."

When Rooster still held back, Bronc drew his gun. "I said move."

Rooster glanced apologetically at Vern. "Sorry, boy," he said, and mounted his horse.

For a while Vern sat there unable to move. The other riders drifted away from him and he was alone, sitting in a patch of brittle grass miles and miles from help. He looked up at his horse, which stood calmly now. If he could only get on him . . . But he knew he lacked the strength. He felt the blood still flowing slowly out between his fingers. Holding his handkerchief over the wound, he had gotten the blood clotted and stopped most of the flow. But a little of it still trickled, slowly draining the life and the hope from him.

He didn't know how long it was before Rooster came. His friend rode up in an easy lope, slowing down before he got there so he wouldn't cause Vern's horse to jerk away. Rooster jumped to the ground and looked back over his shoulder.

"Whether you think you can do it or not, boy, you got to get on that horse. Old Bronc'll be along lookin' for us directly, and we better not be here."

With Rooster's help, Vern managed to get into the saddle. He would have fallen off again if Rooster hadn't been there to hold him on.

Rooster said, "Bronc'll be back huntin' me soon's he finds out I slipped away. But there's a crick down yonder a ways, and plenty of brush. Maybe we can hide in there. He can't spend much time lookin'."

Rooster holding him, they rode to the creek. Rooster took time to dip up water in his hat and let Vern gulp it down. Then they made their way into a thick tangle of mesquite and catclaw. Vern stayed in the saddle, slumped low over the horn. Rooster stepped to the ground and kept watch. Presently he saw Bronc top out over the hill. Rooster drew the horses deeper into the brush and stood holding his hands over their noses so they wouldn't nicker to Bronc's horse. For a little while they could hear Bronc riding up and down the creek, cursing and calling Rooster's name. Bronc knew they were in there somewhere. Then, because of the urgency of moving the cattle, he gave up and disappeared out over the hill.

Rooster led the horses into the open. He took another look at Vern's wound. "You're fixin' to get in a bad way, boy, if we don't get you some help. Hang on, I'm takin' you home."

Painfully Vern shook his head. "No, not home, Rooster. I don't want to bring the R Cross down on them."

"You've probably done that anyhow. But have it the way you want it. I think I know another place we can go."

Vern nodded dully. "Let's get started, then."

XVI

Captain Andrew Rinehart stopped his gray horse in the thick dust left by the running cattle. Somewhere above him he could hear gunshots, and he knew his cowboys had run down the two thieves who had tried to break out over the hill. The third thief lay here on the ground, facedown, his fingers frozen with the last convulsive movement that had made them dig into the dry earth. A greasy black hat lay on the grass, and drying blood was edged out from under the blue wool coat.

A cowboy stood over him, gun in his hand. The cowboy's face was white, his hands a-tremble.

"Take it easy, Shorty," the captain said calmly. "It's always hard, the first time."

Shorty Willis tried twice and the third time managed to get his gun back into the holster. He licked his dry lips and wiped the cold sweat from his forehead onto his sleeve. "It happened so fast," he said. "All of a sudden there he was shootin' at me, and I shot back. Just once."

"Don't let it start eating at you, Shorty, or you'll carry it with you a long time," the captain said. "Just remember this, he was a cow thief and he was trying to kill you. You did right."

The captain motioned with his chin. "Looks like he's got a real good gun, Shorty. It's yours by rights, if you want it."

Shorty drew back, shaking his head. He mounted his horse and turned away from the body which lay there in the dry grass.

The rest of the cowboys came riding over the hill. The captain nodded in satisfaction as he saw that they had the other two thieves with them, hands tied to the swells of their saddles. They were foolish, he thought, to have kept trying to get away with the cattle after being discovered. Too greedy to let go, apparently.

"Good work, Archer," the captain said to Archer Spann.

Spann explained, "They ran off down there a ways and decided to give up. That one yonder"—he indicated the dead man—"was the only tough one."

He looked speculatively at the pair. "There's a creek over that hill. And some cottonwood trees."

The captain said, "No, I think this time we'll take them in, Archer."

"You wouldn't have in the old days."

"The old days are gone," the captain replied. Then he was suddenly uncomfortable, for he realized that this was the same thing McKelvie had said to him, and Monahan.

"How about Vern Wheeler?" Spann demanded.

The captain frowned. He turned to one of the cowboys. "Mixon, are you sure it was the Wheeler kid?"

Mixon nodded confidently. "I was as close as from here to that bush yonder. It was him all right. And I winged him. I saw him fall. That redheaded Preech kid was along, too. There was five of them, and we only got three here."

The captain said, more to himself than to anyone, "I wonder where they could've gone."

"We all know where they went," Spann declared. "They high-tailed it back to the Wheeler place. Don't you see it, Captain? All the time you've been thinking Noah Wheeler was your friend, he's been stealing from us. Why do you think he sent the kid over to work on the R Cross? It wasn't any case of a hungry nester butchering one stray steer. They were moving them out wholesale. No telling how many they got while that kid was at the north line camp."

The captain said, "Archer, Noah Wheeler wouldn't steal from me," but his voice was beginning to lack conviction.

Spann argued, "You're remembering how he used to be in the war, Captain. But that's been a long time ago, and men change. He's used your friendship and dealt you a bad hand all along. I've tried to tell you, and now you can see it for yourself."

The captain's head was bowed. He was tugging at his gray beard, and a tinge of red showed along his cheekbone. Spann could tell that he was wavering.

"Now," Spann said, "maybe you'll let us do what I've been trying to get you to do all along. We can put a stop to Noah Wheeler and that fence once and for all, if you'll just give me the go-ahead."

Rinehart still hesitated.

Spann said, "Captain, it's your choice, but you've got to make it now. It's either you or Wheeler. Which one is it going to be?"

Captain Rinehart closed his eyes a moment. Then he stiffened. He raised his chin, and he was the same iron-hard old soldier he had always been. He had made his decision.

"We'll do it your way, Archer."

Sarah Rinehart was horrified. She stood stiffly in the doorway, watching the captain strap his old cartridge belt around his waist and fill it with shiny brass cartridges that winked with the light.

"Andrew, you're making a terrible mistake!"

He never looked up at her. "The mistake I made was in waiting."

She folded her thin arms. A strength showed in her determined face that hadn't been there in a long time. "If it hadn't been for Noah Wheeler, you wouldn't be here today. He's been your friend. Are you forgetting that?"

"He's forgotten it, I haven't."

"Perhaps Mixon was right about the Wheeler boy. It doesn't prove that his father had anything to do with it."

"Everything adds up, Sarah." Impatience grew in his voice.

"Archer Spann has told you it does. To me, it doesn't. I don't believe it. I won't ever believe it unless I hear it from Noah Wheeler himself."

"You can stop arguing with me, Sarah. My mind's made up."

There was ice in her voice. "Then so is mine, Andrew. You're making a mistake today that's going to wreck you. If I can't stop you, then I don't want to be here to see it."

Rinehart stopped and stared incredulously at her. "What do you mean?"

"This isn't the place it used to be, Andrew. Once it was a happy place, and I loved it. But it's changed. *You've* changed. And do you know when it started? When Archer Spann came. You think you run this ranch, Andrew, but you don't, not anymore. Spann does. He makes you think they're all your ideas, but he plants them and sees that they grow.

"He's ruining you, Andrew. In fighting Wheeler and those small men with their fence, you're riding a dead horse. If you raid Noah Wheeler, the whole world will fall in around you because you're wrong—dead wrong!

"I've thought a lot lately about leaving. I've thought I might go to Fort Worth, where I wouldn't have to hear about Archer Spann, and wouldn't have to watch you wreck the R Cross because of him."

The captain's voice was dull with shock. "Sarah, the trip would be too much for you. You might never make it."

Firmly she said, "I can try. If you leave here today, I'll get Charley Globe to drive me to town. When I've rested up, I'll take the stage to Stringtown and catch the train. It's up to you, Andrew."

For a long time he stood there staring at her, not knowing whether to believe her or not. He could hear the thud of hoofs outside as the men gathered from the line camps. Spann had even sent for Fuller Quinn's men.

The captain motioned toward the window. "You see all that,

Sarah? It's too late now for me to stop it, even if I wanted to. And I don't want to. We're going through with it."

Sarah Rinehart's lips tightened. For a moment her eyes misted, then she drew herself up and blinked them clear. "Very well, Andrew."

She stood stiffly, listening to him stamp out of the house. When he was gone, the stiffness went out of her. She sat wearily in her favorite rocking chair and listened to the sound of horses and men in the big yard below.

As the horsemen left, she called to the Mexican woman who cared for her. "Josefa," she said, "go see if Charley Globe went with them. If he didn't, tell him I want to see him."

Not far from the Wheeler place, Spann raised his hand and drew up. He turned and looked back over his men. Sixteen of them. It wasn't as many as he had figured on. He'd been sure of Fuller Quinn, and Quinn had let him down.

Scowling darkly, Quinn had said, "The first time you suckered me in, I spent all the next day with a shovel in my hands. The second time, they threwed my tail in the hoosegow. This time you can go to hell."

Nor was Quinn his only disappointment. Something was chewing on the captain. Spann had been able to see that ever since they had left the headquarters ranch. Something between the captain and his wife, Spann knew. The captain had been visibly shaken as he had walked out of the house.

Spann wondered why a strong man like the captain ever let a woman influence him as Sarah Rinehart did. That was the trouble with women, as Spann saw it. They were always interfering in man's business, trying to run things that were better left up to a man.

"Bodie," Spann said, "I want you to take four men and hit that fence. Don't get close enough to get hurt. Hunt out some cover and snipe at them. Draw them all away from the house and the barns. When it's clear there, the rest of us will charge down from the other end and set everything afire."

"What about the fence?" Bodie asked. "We'll never be able to touch it if we draw that bunch down on us."

"You won't have to. If we can stop Noah Wheeler—burn him out—we'll automatically stop the fence."

Bodie nodded, satisfied. Spann pulled a watch out of his pocket. "You got a watch?" he asked. When Bodie said yes, Spann told him, "Give us an hour to make a wide circle. Then go on in." He told off the four men who were to go with Bodie. "Don't get close enough to get hurt," he warned them again. "If you have to retreat some, fine. Main thing is to draw them away from the headquarters till we've had time to do our job."

He pulled away then, and his men started their circle.

They reached their point in a little less than an hour and drew up there to wait. Most of the men smoked quietly. They were nervous, and he could tell that some of them didn't like it.

Shorty Willis was the main one. "We're makin' a mistake, Spann. Them's good people down there."

"If you don't want to go with us, Shorty, then ride out. But you're through in this country. You'll never get another job anywhere around here."

Shorty ignored Spann. He pulled his horse up beside the captain, who had been riding along silently on his big gray, his gaunt old face creased with worries of his own. "Captain, you know this is wrong. Even if Vern *was* helpin' steal them cattle, he mebbe thought he had a good reason."

The captain peered intently at Shorty. "What do you mean?"

"You've heard the story about that three hundred dollars, ain't you? Spann says it's a lie, but Vern told me about it that day Monahan had us fixin' the fence. He talked like a man tellin' the truth."

Spann felt a momentary surge of panic. The captain was listening to Shorty. Damn that boy and his three hundred dollars! They'd brought Spann nothing but trouble.

"Shorty," Spann blurted, "there's no truth in it! You're fired!"

The captain raised his hand. "I'll do the firing. Just what was it the Wheeler boy said?"

Shorty started telling it, and Spann felt his mouth go dry. He could see that the captain was wavering. The old man didn't want to go through with this thing, that was apparent. Now he was looking desperately for some reason to call it off.

The shooting started. The crisp crackle of guns rolled in from the distance. Spann shouted, "Everybody in the saddle!"

The tension went out of him with a long sigh. Shorty Willis wouldn't get a chance to finish that story now. With luck, maybe he never would.

Spann put his horse up over the top of the hill, so he could see the farmhouse and the barn and the yard, the fields and the grazing cattle. The gunfire was coming clearer and sharper now. More guns had entered into it. His riders gathering around him, Spann watched two men spur away from the barn down below and lope out along the fenceline. He watched and saw no more activity at the house.

The captain said, "Archer, just a minute . . ."

He was going to call it off, Spann realized. "Let's go!" he shouted, and spurred down the hill.

Trudy Wheeler stood on the front porch, squinting her blue eyes and wishing she could see what was going on down there where the shooting was. Her father and one of the Blessingame boys had been at the barn repairing a wagon when the shooting started. Although still stiff and sore from the beating, Noah Wheeler had thrown a saddle on a horse and loped down to make a hand. That left no one here but Trudy and her mother.

Some new noise made her spin around. She saw the horsemen loping down the long slope toward the house. Instantly she comprehended the R Cross strategy.

"Mother," she cried, "they're raiding us!"

Mrs. Wheeler ran to the front door and looked out. For one short moment she stood with hands pressed against her paling cheeks. Then she shouted, "The shotgun. We've still got the shotgun in the house." She whirled and ran back for it. She brought it out, and with it a handful of shells.

Trudy took the gun from her hands. "Here. I always was the best shot."

Chickens flew away squawking, and ducks waddled hurriedly across the tankdam and out into the water as the riders reached the haystacks. They milled around, some of the men getting down. In a moment thin smoke began to curl. Red flames burst out of the stacks, and smoke suddenly swelled thick and gray.

Her heart drumming with excitement, her face heating with anger, Trudy had to fight against the temptation to run out and try to stop them. She knew it would be useless. She could not save the haystacks. She could not save the barn, if they decided to set it afire. All she could do was stay here and try to keep them away from the house.

Sure enough, the next move was the barn. Trudy spotted Archer Spann, and she leveled the shotgun at him. The heavy recoil jarred her shoulder. The range was too great for strong effect, but through the angry wreath of powder smoke she saw Spann's horse kick up. The well-spent pellets had stung him.

Spann rode his horse right through the open barn door, and a couple of men followed him. Hay was stacked inside the barn too. In a moment smoke was rolling out the door and squeezing between the red planks in the siding. From the barn, Spann pulled over to the nearby chicken house. Not even that was he going to spare.

A couple of Monahan's horses ran crazily about in a pen next to the barn, panicked by the fire and the choking smoke. One of the R Cross cowboys mercifully opened the gate and let them out. Spann raised his six-shooter and leveled it as they came by. He fired twice, and both horses went down, threshing.

Trudy felt rage swell helplessly within her, forcing hot tears to her eyes. She saw the R Cross cowboy who had opened the gate staring in disbelief. Then the cowboy shouted something at Spann and shook his fist. Spann paid him no heed. The R Cross foreman turned back to other pens where some of Noah Wheeler's good Durham cattle had been eating hay. He stopped at the fence and fired over it.

Trudy cried, "Oh, no, he's killing the cattle!"

Horror-stricken, she realized that she had seen her father's favorite, old Roany, walk into that pen with her half-longhorn calf not twenty minutes ago.

Most of the R Cross cowboys had stopped and were watching Spann in shocked fascination. Turned loose to destroy at will, he was suddenly a man burning in fury, loosing all the pent-up hatred he had nursed for a world which had once treated him harshly, releasing that pressure of bitterness in an unreasoning spasm of destruction.

Old Roany made a break through the gate, her long-legged calf well in the lead. Spann was delayed a moment, reloading. Then he jerked his horse around and came spurring.

Trudy gripped the shotgun and jumped off the porch. She ran to meet Spann, screaming at him as she ran. He was paying little heed. She saw him level the six-shooter at the cow, and she pulled off a quick shot at him. She realized instantly that she had missed.

The thunder of the big gun brought Spann up short. Black with fury, he reined his horse at Trudy. She stood in the middle of the yard, struggling to get another shell into the shotgun. He leveled the pistol at her, but some remnant of reason made him lift it again. He spurred harder. In her haste Trudy got the shell jammed halfway in the chamber. She looked up, her eyes widening in alarm as she saw that Spann was going to run her down.

She tried to step aside, and the horse tried to miss her. But Spann held the animal with an iron hand and spurred him savagely. The horse's shoulder struck Trudy a blow that sent her spinning. Then the panicked horse was over her, trying desperately to miss her with his hoofs. But one foot struck Trudy in the small of the back. The breath gusted out of her. A blinding pain knifed through her. Another hoof struck her before Spann's horse got away.

She lay helpless, fighting for breath. A sickening darkness reached for her, trying to pull her down. She was conscious of Archer Spann stepping off beside her. She groped for the shotgun, got it in her hands.

Spann slapped her and grabbed the shotgun, smashing it on the ground. She tried to push to her knees, and he slapped her once more.

"Touch her again and I'll kill you, Spann!"

Spann jerked his head up in surprise. Shorty Willis stood in front of him, a gun in his hand and death in his eyes. Spann took a step forward, then stopped abruptly. He saw that Shorty meant it.

Cursing him, Spann whirled and remounted his horse. He took a few seconds to look around him. The haystacks were alive with fire. Smoke billowed from the blazing barn, flames licking up through the shingled roof. He swung his hand in an arc and shouted at the other R Cross men.

"Come on. There's more to be done!"

To his astonishment they all stared at him as if he were some wild animal. He shouted again, and they made no move. He looked around sharply and saw Shorty Willis kneeling beside the Wheeler girl.

Realization struck like a mule kicking him in the belly. They had rebelled. It had not been without warning. He could remember the hesitancy, the reluctance many of the men had shown. He could remember how some like Shorty Willis had tried to argue with him.

He cursed them, and they sat on their horses and stared at him. He jerked around and spurred toward the Wheeler house. From down the fenceline he could see dust rising. Monahan was coming with his crew. This had to be finished in a hurry.

Mrs. Wheeler was running across the yard toward her daughter. Spann jumped off his horse and ran into the house. Just inside the kitchen he spotted a kerosene lamp. He smashed it against the wall, splashing kerosene over the wallpaper and spilling it down onto the floor. He hurried into the next room, found another lamp and hurled it down. He struck a match, dropping it. As the flames crackled and spread, he retreated into the kitchen and tossed another match.

Outside the house again, Spann saw the dust moving closer. They would never make it in time now, he thought with a thrill of triumph. Try what they would, there would be nothing left here but ashes. Smoke drifted all around the place, panicking the horses, choking the men. Spann swung onto his head fighting mount. He saw the roan Durham cow and her leggy calf, the ones he had tried to shoot when that crazy woman opened up on him with the shotgun. He loped after them, fired once and saw the cow go down. The calf was running like a jackrabbit. Spann started to follow, then decided to let it go.

He looked back. To his amazement, many of the R Cross men remained in the Wheeler yard. Some of them were running afoot toward the house.

He blinked hard, not believing what he saw. *They were going to put the fire out.*

He sat there numbly watching, realizing that the rebellion had been complete. Victory had been in his grasp, and suddenly his own men were snatching it out of his hands.

Soberness slowly came to him then. His heart still hammered from excitement. His mouth was so dry his tongue stuck to the roof of it. He watched most of the R Cross men start drifting back toward the hill where the captain had waited and watched the whole thing.

Spann turned and moved that way too. As he approached the men, he felt them watching. He looked, and he saw no loyalty in their eyes—only fear or contempt, and in some of them, hatred.

He glanced at the captain. For a fleeting moment he saw bitter disillusionment and heartbreak in that gaunt old face. Then the captain turned away from him, his shoulders slumped. The captain touched spurs gently to his big horse and moved down the other side of the hill.

In that moment, Archer Spann knew he was done.

Trudy was not the only one needing a doctor. One of the fencing crew had been wounded in the skirmish with Bodie's decoy force. One of Bodie's men had taken a bullet in the leg and had been left there by the others. So Stub Bailey headed for town.

When the smoke had been cleared from the house, Monahan gently picked up Trudy and carried her in. He winced at the sharp odor of charred wood. He placed her on her bed and stood beside her, holding her hand, not knowing what else to do.

Shorty Willis of the R Cross had stayed with the girl. "I think she's got some broken ribs," he said quietly. "Spann ran his horse over her."

Mrs. Wheeler pointed to the door. "You men get on out of here. This is a woman's job."

Doug moved out of the room, Willis with him. He stood with hands shoved deep into his pockets. He stared blankly at the blackened wall. R Cross men had beaten out the flames before they could spread far or eat deeply. New wallpaper would hide the black. As to the floor, fresh paint and some kind of rug would cover the damage.

Noah Wheeler found old Roany lying on her side, kicking in agony, a bullet in her stomach.

He reached out to Dundee, and Dundee silently handed him a pistol. Wheeler raised it, held it a moment, then let it down, shaking his head. "Here, Dundee. You do it." He handed the pistol back.

Dundee waited until Wheeler had walked away. Noah Wheeler flinched at the shot.

In the house, Doug clenched his fists and blinked at the burning in his eyes. To Noah Wheeler he said, "I should've known it would come to this. I ought never to've started that fence."

Noah Wheeler rubbed his hand across his smoke-blackened face. "I told you before, Doug, it's not your fault. I wanted the fence. It's my fault this happened." His face was grave. "But it's not going to whip us. We'll build it back better than it ever was."

Shorty Willis said, "It's Spann's fault. It would've happened sooner or later, fence or no fence. Spann kept pushin' the captain. I think he believed the captain would leave the R Cross to him someday. He always did want to drive you farmers out, and he had his eye on some of the little cow outfits, too. The fence was just a startin' place. Gave him an excuse he hadn't had before. Then, when your son got caught with them R Cross cattle . . ."

Noah Wheeler's head jerked. "Vern? What cattle?"

Willis frowned. "You didn't know?" He stared at Noah Wheeler, satisfying himself that the old man really didn't know. Then he told it.

Noah was pale and shaken. "How bad was he wounded?"

Willis shook his head. "I wasn't there. All I know is, they said it knocked him outa the saddle."

Noah Wheeler stood up shakily and walked out of the house, head down. Willis looked after him worriedly. "Monahan, is there anything we can do for him?"

Doug said grimly, "Not unless you know where we can find that boy."

The doctor came just before dark. He stayed a long time in the room with Trudy. When he came out he said, "She'll be all right, but it'll take a while. She's got some cracked ribs and some very bad bruises. I don't think she'll stir out of that bed for a good many days."

Shorty Willis sighed in relief. "She's a brave little woman."

Doug Monahan walked into her room. Mrs. Wheeler smiled at him and left, closing the door behind her. Doug stood by Trudy's bed. Trudy raised her hand, and Doug took it.

"Doctor says you'll be all right, Trudy."

Pale, she nodded. Doug said, "I've been waiting outside there the whole time. I couldn't make myself leave the house."

Trudy smiled weakly. "I knew you were there, Doug, and I liked it. I want you to keep on staying there. I want to know that you're somewhere close around."

"I'll be around, Trudy, I promise you that. Only one thing. I'll be gone awhile tomorrow. But I'll get back as soon as I can."

He saw the worry cloud up in her eyes. "The R Cross?"

He nodded, and she said, "I wish you wouldn't. It was foolish, me running out after Spann that way. I don't want you to do something just as foolish because of me."

Doug didn't want to argue with her. He said simply, "I'll get back soon as I can." Impulsively he leaned over and kissed her. He started to straighten, but she reached up and caught him and pulled him down to her again. He felt the wetness of her tears against her cheek.

"Go then, if you have to," she whispered. "Only be careful, and come back to me."

XVII

Doug hadn't intended to take anyone with him, but the whole fencing crew was up in the darkness long before dawn. The fire in the barn had destroyed all their bedding and personal belongings, so they had slept on the floor in the house, the wood heater aglow to keep them warm.

"It's my fight," Doug had said with stubbornness.

"It's ours," Dundee replied solemnly. "No use arguin', we're goin' too."

Doug had given in reluctantly. "All right, you can go along to make sure it stays fair. But otherwise, keep out of it."

As he rode in the raw chill, his mind dwelt on Trudy. Again and again he pictured Spann forcing his horse to run over her. A throbbing anger built in him.

He had never been to the R Cross before, but he headed instinctively for the long L-shaped bunkhouse. Seeing no movement, he reined up and shouted. "Spann, come out here!" Steam rose from his lips in the frosty air as the words came.

He could hear movement in the building, a clinking of tin, a scuffle of boots.

"Spann, come on out here or I'll go in there and drag you out!"

An R Cross cowboy came out the door, a crooked grin on his face. He gave Monahan a careful appraisal, then said, "He'll be out directly."

Up at the big house on the slope, Captain Rinehart walked out onto his high front porch. Seeing the riders in front of the bunkhouse, he moved slowly down the steps and limped stiffly toward the stamping, nose-rolling horses. Other cowboys came out of the bunk-house and stood in front of it, watching the door. Then came Archer Spann, moving slowly, his feet dragging a little. His clothes were rumpled. His face was haggard and unshaven, his eyes red from loss of sleep. Doug Monahan sensed that something had happened here yesterday after the raid, and that Spann had had a hard time of it.

He looked into Spann's sullen eyes, and his own rising anger came to the boiling point. He stepped out of the saddle and handed the reins to Dundee.

Spann demanded, "What do you want, Monahan?" His voice was hoarse.

"I've come to settle with you for what happened at Wheeler's. And I'm going to settle for Paco Sanchez, too."

"I shot the Mexican in self-defense, you know that."

"A court might have to accept that, but I don't. You just wanted to kill somebody. Paco gave you an excuse, and you did it."

Archer Spann's eyes glowed, but he said nothing.

Doug gritted, "It's not just a poor old Mexican with a pothook in his hand, or an old man on a wagon, or a girl standing out in the middle of an open yard. It's me, and I got a gun on my hip. I'm going to kill you with it, Spann."

The men along the bunkhouse wall began spreading out, giving room. The riders moved from behind Doug. Archer Spann stood watching Doug Monahan, his square jaw twitching.

Doug's voice cut like the popper on a bullwhip. "I'll give you a chance, Spann, a chance you never gave Paco Sanchez. You got a gun on. I'll give you first grab. Go on, reach!"

Spann just stood there.

Doug moved a step toward him. "Reach, Spann. Damn you, reach!"

Spann's hand shook, but he made no move toward the gun.

"You're a coward, Spann. You're tough when you got somebody

helpless, but now look at you, standing there shaking like a cur dog. Damn you, reach for that gun!"

Spann's hand inched downward, then jerked away as Doug's own hand darted. Doug stopped his gun halfway out of the holster. Spann would never draw. Doug swallowed the bitter gall of disappointment. In his rage he burned to cut Spann down. But he could see the fear curdling in Spann's reddened eyes. He knew he could not shoot the man in cold blood.

Doug closed the gap. He reached down and grabbed the gun out of Spann's holster. He hurled it away, then slapped Spann's face with the back of his hand as hard as he could swing.

"If you won't shoot it out with me, then I'll beat it out of your hide!"

His right fist came up and sent Spann flying back against the bunkhouse wall. For a moment Spann cowered there. Then his own bitterness and hatred welled up. He waded into Monahan, fists swinging.

They grappled there in the rising dust like two fury-driven stallions, swinging, driving, choking, rolling over and over in the dust and getting back to their feet and driving against one another again. Doug Monahan could taste the salty bite of blood on his lips, and his left eye was afire from an ugly cut above it. His knees were weakening. Each blow of his fists struck a bolt of pain through his bruised and bleeding knuckles. But none of it mattered now. Nothing mattered except this roaring anger that drove him.

For Archer Spann, it was a losing battle almost from the start. He had burned up much of his anger, much of his hatred, in the blazing raid on the Wheeler place yesterday, and there was little left for him to draw on. There had been little sleep for him last night, because he had felt the showdown coming, and he had known somehow that he was going to lose. He had lost the captain already, and the R Cross cowboys.

So Archer Spann fought, but dragging him down was the bitter knowledge that no matter what happened here, he had already lost.

At last Spann went down to stay, but Doug Monahan was not through with him. He dragged the man to his feet and struck him a smashing blow to the ribs. When Spann crashed to the ground, Doug grasped his collar and pulled him up again. This time he drove his fist into Spann's jaw. Spann rolled over against the bunkhouse and lay there in a crumpled heap.

Heaving, Doug took a step toward him and bent down to pull him up a third time. But Dundee gripped Doug's arm.

"That's enough, man! The next one might kill him, and you don't want that on your hands. You've made him pay."

Doug leaned with one hand against the bunkhouse for support. He fought for breath. Sweat rolled down his face, mixed with blood and dirt. His mouth was dry, and his tongue seemed swollen. His lips were puffed, bruised and broken. His hat was gone somewhere. He rubbed his sleeve over his forehead and his face and stood up straight, looking at the solemn faces of the men around him, his own fencing crew and the R Cross alike.

He saw Captain Rinehart standing at the edge of the group. The captain was looking down blankly upon his battered foreman, Archer Spann.

Doug tried once to speak but found his tongue too dry. The second time, he managed it. "Take a look at him now, Captain." His voice was weak, but it crackled with the last embers of his anger. "That's not just Spann lying there, it's you, too. After this, there won't anybody be afraid of you again. You're whipped."

There was no emotion in the captain's face. It was as if he already had been whipped, as if he no longer cared.

Doug Monahan heard the dull thud of hoofs. He turned stiffly and saw Sheriff Luke McKelvie riding up. The sheriff stepped to the ground, walked over to Spann, then glanced up worriedly at Doug.

"He's not dead, is he?"

Doug shook his head. "He's not dead. But he's finished." Mc-Kelvie breathed a long sigh of relief. "For a minute I was afraid . . ." He looked up at the R Cross men. "You better take him inside. He needs some attention, looks like."

Not one of them moved toward Spann. McKelvie nodded then, seeing how it was. Spann stirred a little, and McKelvie knelt beside him. "Archer, can you hear me?"

Spann nodded weakly.

McKelvie said, "I got a warrant here for you. But I'd rather have you out of the country than in my jail. Soon as you're able to get up, you saddle your horse and go. Don't stop anywhere in this county, and you'd be better off if you kept right on riding to New Mexico. I ever catch you here again, I'll lock you up. You hear me?"

Spann nodded again.

McKelvie turned away from him and toward the captain. "I'm sorry, Captain. I've got to put you under arrest."

The captain blinked. "What did you say, Luke?"

"I said I've got to put you under arrest. I've got the warrant here in my pocket."

The captain suddenly looked tired. His gaunt old face was drawn and haggard, and his eyes had lost their luster. Tonelessly he said, "I thought you were never going to fight me, Luke."

McKelvie answered solemnly, "It don't look like there's much fight left, does it, Captain?"

The captain slowly shook his head. "No, Luke, it surely doesn't."

Luke McKelvie placed his hand on the old man's shoulder. "I wish it didn't have to be this way, Captain. I tried to tell you, but . . ." He bit his lip. "Take all the time you want to tell Sarah. I'm not in any hurry."

The captain spoke almost in a whisper. "Sarah's not here. She's gone." He was a broken, spiritless old man. "I've got nothing to go to the house for. Have somebody saddle my horse, and I'll be ready to go."

The Wheeler place was a sad sight to come home to. The outbuildings lay in ashes, charred timbers standing like the ribs of a skeleton. The haystacks that represented a year of work for Noah Wheeler were only piles of black dust, lifting and spreading and falling with each gust of dry wind. Here and there dead cattle lay with stiffened legs in the air. Fine Durhams they had been, Noah Wheeler's pride.

Doug Monahan looked upon these things and felt a sharp pain touch him, for this place had become home to him. But the anger and the hatred were gone now. They had worked out of him in the fight with Archer Spann. He was purged of them, and now there was only the cold sense of regret, the knowledge that it had all been without cause, without reason.

He was surprised at all the people he saw there. Two or three buggies and buckboards and a couple of wagons stood in front of the house. Several saddled horses stood hitched wherever their riders had found something to tie them to.

He realized these were neighbors and townspeople. Some wandered around, looking tight-lipped at the destruction. Several were piling up wreckage, clearing the littered ground. Two men with sleeves rolled up were making temporary repairs to a damaged corral so it would hold livestock. A couple were dragging dead cattle off to get them away from the house. Doug noticed that the two dead horses were gone.

He found the house half full of people, bustling about. Women were peeling charred paper from the wall. Two men were scraping black from the floor. The kitchen was crowded with food the visitors had brought. Women stood stolidly in Mrs. Wheeler's way and cooked while she protested vainly that she was perfectly able to do it for herself.

Banker Albert Brown sat in a corner with Noah Wheeler, figuring up what it was going to cost to rebuild everything. "Don't you worry about the financing, Noah. Folks aren't going to forget that you took the whipping for all of them."

Noah was only half listening, his mind miles away. At sight of Doug Monahan he stood up quickly. "Doug, did you see or hear anything of Vern?"

Reluctantly Doug shook his head. "I'm sorry, Noah."

He peeked in Trudy's room but found her asleep. Quietly he closed the door.

He looked at all the people, and he felt an uplift of spirit. It was real neighbor help, the kind he had known in South Texas. When a man faltered, his neighbors helped pull him to his feet. When one man faced trouble, his neighbors sided in and faced it with him.

Doug could see something more in this: a declaration of independence from the rule of the R Cross. In this show of respect and support for Noah Wheeler, they demonstrated that from here on out they would do as they pleased.

After a while Noah walked out of the house. Big Albert Brown came over and placed his hand on Doug's shoulder. "Would you like to listen to a proposition?"

Doug said, "If it's a good one."

"I'll let you decide that." The banker peered intently at Doug. "I like you, Monahan. I have, right from the first. Fact of the matter, I even went so far as to do some checking on you. Wrote a letter to the bank back where you came from. They said you're a good cowman."

"It's all my family has ever done."

"They said you'd be ranching yet except for drought and low prices both hitting you at the same time. That's a combination nobody can beat."

Doug shook his head. "I know *I* couldn't."

"Well, Gordon Finch left the country. Left his ranch and cattle and everything in our hands. Now, I may not be very smart, but I do know one thing, I need to stick to banking. I'm no cowman. I've been wanting to find somebody who could take over that Finch outfit and get us our money back out of it. Then it would be his, and he could do anything with it that he was big enough to."

Doug's breath left him. "You're offering it to me?"

"You come by the bank and look over the books. See what you'll be up against. Then, if you want it, it's yours."

Trudy waked up. Doug found her sitting up in bed. Her eyes widened in dismay at sight of his battered face. "Doug, you're hurt."

He shook his head. "No, I feel fine, Trudy. After all this, I feel fine."

"What happened over there, Doug?"

Solemnly he said, "I'll tell you sometime. Not now. But I can promise you this, it's over. The R Cross won't fight you again."

She reached out and took his hand. "I'm glad. I only wish now we knew what happened to Vern. He could be dead somewhere, for all we know. We don't even know where to start looking."

Doug touched his hand to her cheek and wiped away a tear that started there. "Maybe something will turn up, Trudy."

It did. Chris Hadley, the saloonkeeper, rode up to the Wheeler place and dismounted. Walking inside, he signaled Noah Wheeler and Doug with a quick jerk of his balding head. "May I see you, right now? It's important."

The three of them walked away from the house, out toward the grim pile of ashes that had been Noah Wheeler's barn. Hadley said, "Noah, it's your son. He's hurt, and my daughter's gone to him. I think you'll want to go, too."

Wheeler caught Chris Hadley's hand. "Is he . . . how bad is he hurt?"

"He'll live. Badly wounded, though. That wild, redheaded

Preech boy came to my house after midnight. He'd taken Vern to an old deserted shack a couple of miles from town. He was afraid to fetch the doctor, so he came to get Paula.

"I'm a pretty good gunshot man. In my trade, I've treated quite a few. We got your boy fixed up all right. I left Paula and Preech with him and came on out here."

He paused, frowning. "The boy's badly disturbed, Noah. He doesn't know whether he ought to run or give up. I think you'd better go to him."

Noah Wheeler was already on his way to catch a horse. He stopped and turned. "Doug, I know you're tired, but I'd like to have you go with me."

Doug wondered how he could make another long ride without sleep, but he said, "Sure, Noah."

As they rode, Chris Hadley told them, "I tried every way I knew to break it up. I told Paula I'd rather be dead than see her go through the kind of life her mother had. I even threatened to send her off to school. But watching her out there, helping take care of that boy, I could tell I was barking into the wind. You can't live your kids' lives for them. They're in love with each other, and there's nothing I can do about it. I'm not going to fight it anymore."

Rooster Preech sat on the front step of the shack, whittling on an old weathered piece of pine. He stood up, dropped his hand to his gun and kept it there until he recognized the men.

"He's inside yonder," Rooster said nervously.

The shack was an old one some small rancher had built and hadn't managed to stay in. The country had whipped him, as it whipped many of those who tried to fight it instead of taking it for what it was and learning to live with it. Now the shack was leaning, its windows broken out. But it stood, and it broke the cold wind.

Noah Wheeler pushed open the front door, which dragged

heavily on the buckling pine floor. His son lay on a blanket-covered cot in the corner. Paula Hadley sat on the cot beside him, holding his hand.

An old wood heater was glowing. Doug thought it was a wonder that its rusting chimney hadn't set the shack afire.

Noah Wheeler stood just inside the door a long moment, looking across the little room. He took three long strides then and knelt by Vern. He placed his big hand on the youngster's arm, and his shoulders began to heave.

About that time something got in Doug's eyes—out of that leaky flue, he thought—and he walked outside for fresh air and a long smoke. But he could hear Vern Wheeler's voice.

"Dad," Vern was saying. "Paula and I have talked it out. There's just one thing we can figure. I'm going to Sheriff McKelvie and give myself up. I don't want to run. If I start it now, I'll be running the rest of my life, and Paula with me. Whatever it is I have to do, I want to do it now and get it over with, so we can have a chance."

Doug glanced in the door. He could see the pretty girl still sitting there, keeping Vern's hand clasped tightly in her own, her soft brown eyes never leaving the young man's face.

Noah Wheeler was nodding gravely. "I'm glad, Son. It's the right thing. Sure, I know it's going to be hard. Time seems mighty precious when you're young, and you hate to give any of it up. But it's the right thing."

Rooster Preech was whittling faster, his freckled face twisting with the run of his thoughts. When Noah Wheeler came out, Rooster looked up at him and Doug.

"You fellers fixin' to go pretty soon?"

Noah nodded. "I expect. It's not too far to town, and I think Vern can make the ride."

Rooster was having a hard time gathering up the words. Nervously he gouged holes in the gray pine siding with the sharp point of his knife. "I know it's the right thing for Vern, but with me it's different. I was wonderin' if you fellers would mind too much me jest saddlin' up and ridin' off. I might get me a few hours' start on the sheriff. That'd be all I need."

Doug thought he could understand. He judged this Rooster Preech to be the kind who would always be in trouble. Likely they'd give him a tougher sentence than Vern Wheeler would get. No matter whether he rode away now or not, he would probably soon be in somebody's jail, somewhere.

Noah Wheeler said, "You're free to do what you want to, Rooster. I just want you to know we appreciate what you did for Vern."

Rooster shrugged. "No more than he would've done for me, and mebbe not near as much. I better step in and say good-bye to him, then. I don't expect I'll ever be back around here ag'in."

And in a few minutes Rooster Preech was gone with a jingle of spurs, a smiling flash of teeth and the wave of a greasy hat above his tangled red hair.

XVIII

Captain Andrew Rinehart sat in the tiny six-by-six cell, staring miserably at the rock wall just as he had stared ever since he had been brought in here. Seated in a cell next to the one occupied by the two cattle rustlers he himself had sent in, he hadn't spoken a word and had hardly moved.

Sheriff Luke McKelvie watched him covertly from his chair at the roll-top desk. What he saw in the captain's desolate face was what he had seen in the eyes of a wild horse that had been caught and thrown and tied, a captive thing waiting with broken heart for death to bring once again the freedom it had lost.

McKelvie stood up and paced restlessly across the floor, pausing to look out the door. He turned away from it, and couldn't remember a thing he had seen out there.

"Captain," he said, and his voice almost pleaded, "isn't there something I can bring you—coffee maybe, or something to eat?"

The captain slowly shook his head, not even looking up. "Nothing, Luke, thank you." McKelvie could hardly hear the voice.

McKelvie said, "If it's cold in there, Captain, you can come out here by the stove."

The captain gave no sign that he had heard. McKelvie turned away, a tightness in his throat.

"Captain," he said, "I'd give anything in the world if—"

He broke off. Blinking rapidly, he looked down at the star pinned to his vest. He studied it awhile. Then, abruptly, he unpinned it and hurled it to the floor.

The captain looked up at him then, and his voice was firm. "Put it back on, Luke."

Luke McKelvie shook his head. "Captain, I've done some hard jobs in my time, but this . . ."

"Put it on, Luke. There's not another man in the county can wear it half as well as you."

McKelvie stared unbelievingly. "How can you say that, after what I've done to you?"

Rinehart shook his head. His voice was soft again. "I did this to myself, Luke."

"Archer Spann was the one who brought it on."

"I didn't have to listen to him, Luke—but I listened. I knew almost from the first that I was wrong about Noah Wheeler. But I'd been mad there for a little while, and I'd told Archer yes. Then I had too much pride to back down. Pride's a treacherous thing. It can be the making of a man, or the breaking of him.

"I guess the main trouble was that I'd lost confidence in myself. You don't know how hard it is to find yourself an old man and lose confidence. You find people aren't listening to you anymore. You can't do the things you used to do, you can't ride like in the old days, you can't even see good. Things you do turn out wrong, and you get to wondering if you ever can do anything right again.

"That's the way it was with me, Luke. Then Archer Spann came along. He was a real hand, never made a mistake. I'd look at him and I'd see myself the way I used to be. I got to leaning on him, letting him make up my mind for me. I guess you could say I was letting him be the captain."

McKelvie said, "Archer Spann never saw the day he was fit to wipe the dust off your boots."

"I shut my eyes to the bad things till it was too late. You tried to tell me, and so did Sarah. But I wouldn't listen because when you spoke against Archer Spann, it was like you were speaking against me."

The captain went silent for a time then. Presently he said, "Luke, there *is* a favor I'd ask of you."

"Anything you want."

"I wish you'd find out if Sarah is still in town. I wish you'd tell her I'd like to see her."

"I'll go after her, Captain."

A woman's voice spoke from the doorway. "Never mind, Luke. I'm here."

Sarah Rinehart walked slowly toward the cell. Luke McKelvie hurried to help her, but she waved him away. She was a tired old woman, but she had the Rinehart pride. "I'm all right." The sheriff stepped to the cell and swung the door open. It never had been locked. Sarah walked inside, and McKelvie dragged a couple of chairs up close to the stove.

"Out here," he said gently. "That cell is no place for a lady."

The captain said, "Hello, Sarah," then dropped his head and stared at the floor. Sarah Rinehart took his hands and led him out of the cell, to the chairs McKelvie had set up. "It's all right, Andrew. I know what you want to say."

"I was wrong, Sarah."

"And so was I, Andrew. I should have known I could never leave here. I never got farther than the hotel. Then I was ready to go back to the ranch where I belong. When this is over, we'll go back together. We'll pick up whatever is left and make it good."

"What can we do, Sarah?" the captain asked miserably. "We're old. Time has gone off and left us."

"Time never goes off and leaves anyone," she replied evenly, "unless he is standing still."

Sight of the captain sitting in the tiny cell, a helpless, bewildered old man, brought tears to the eyes of Noah Wheeler. The big farmer motioned Luke McKelvie to one side.

"Luke, that's no place for a man like the captain."

Luke McKelvie looked surprised. "Noah, you know why it has to be. You're the one who's suffered."

Noah Wheeler shook his head. "Sure, he's made a mistake, Luke, but look at all the big things he's done, too. The country still owes him too much to let him sit here in jail."

Doug Monahan stared at Noah Wheeler, wondering how the old farmer could so readily forgive. But then he looked at Captain Rinehart, and he thought he could understand. He had never believed the captain could be shattered like this, so thoroughly humbled. Looking at him, Doug realized that he no longer hated the captain, either. All the anger, all the bitterness somehow had drained out of him, and now he felt only pity.

Noah Wheeler pleaded, "Let him go, Luke. For me, let him go."

McKelvie's eyes were grateful. "I reckon if that's the way you feel, Noah, there's no use me holding him. If you won't press charges, there's not much case."

"No charges, Luke."

McKelvie walked across the room and opened the cell door. "You hear that, Captain? Noah won't prosecute. You're free to go."

The captain arose stiffly, hardly believing. Noah Wheeler moved forward, meeting him halfway, his hand outstretched. "We used to be friends, Andrew. As far as I'm concerned, we never stopped."

The captain took Noah Wheeler's hand, but he made no reply. He couldn't.

The front door opened. A breath of chill wind came with the shadow that fell across the room. Luke McKelvie stared in surprise at the pale young man with the bandaged shoulder, and the girl who stood beside him.

"I've come to give myself up," Vern said. "For stealing Captain Rinehart's cattle."

The captain swallowed hard, studying the boy and looking at Noah Wheeler. "Son," he said, "I've lost no cattle."

Vern replied, "You would have, if we'd got away with it."

Luke McKelvie put in, "Why did you do it, Vern?"

"To get my three hundred dollars, the money the R Cross owed me."

McKelvie said, "It was Spann that took your money."

The captain frowned. "What were you going to do with the money, Vern, your three hundred dollars?"

"Buy some land with it. A start for me and Paula."

The captain nodded. "I started like you once, and I didn't have three hundred dollars. The R Cross will pay you what it owes you. As for cow theft, I don't know what you're talking about. There weren't but three cow thieves. Two of them are in that cell yonder, and the other is dead."

After that, there wasn't much to be said. They all stood around looking at each other. Paula Hadley was crying into a handkerchief, and Doug Monahan was afraid someone else was going to start.

Luke McKelvie said with studied curtness, "Well, if we got all our business attended to, I wish you-all would clear out of here and let me get my paperwork done. I'm a week behind on the mail."

As they went out, Doug heard the captain say, "Noah, you remember that old marching song we used to sing, 'The Old Gray Mare Came Tearing Out of the Wilderness'?"

Noah nodded, smiling. The captain said, "I've fogotten some of the words. I'd like you to freshen up my memory on them sometime."

"I'd be tickled, Andrew."

Doug Monahan held back as the others left. "McKelvie, I want to apologize for the things I've thought and said about you. You're a pretty good Indian."

McKelvie passed it off with a shrug of his shoulders. "I still don't like your infernal bobwire fences, but I reckon they're here to stay. You're apt to have enough fence-building now to keep you busy a long time. I expect even the captain will come to it by and by, in self-defense."

Monahan nodded. "It's no life's work, Sheriff, but it's a living. Maybe it'll put me back on my feet and into the cow business again."

McKelvie said pointedly, "This is as good a cow country as you're ever apt to find."

Monahan said, "That's the way I see it, Sheriff."

Noah Wheeler got back to the farm long before Monahan did. Doug rode up and found a lot of neighbors still milling around, cleaning up the debris. One of the Oak Creek farmers had even brought a milk cow, a hungry calf trotting along behind it, grabbing a drop or two of milk every time the cow stopped for a moment.

Doug found Trudy sitting up in a big rocking chair in the front room. Her face was swollen, and it had several spots bruised blue. But some of the healthy color had returned. Doug took her chin in his hand.

"How you feeling?"

"Better. How about you?"

"I'm fixing to get me a blanket and crawl up in that corner yonder and sleep for a week."

Trudy said, "Dad's already given us all the good news."

Doug smiled. "Maybe not all of it." He reached in his coat pocket and withdrew a bundle of papers. "I stopped by the bank and had a long talk with Albert Brown about the Gordon Finch place. It's not the Finch place anymore."

Trudy's eyes widened. "You mean you . . ."

Doug nodded, grinning. "I'm going to have to build a many a mile of fence to help pay for it, but it's mine." He gripped her hand. "Or it can be *ours,* Trudy, if you'll have it that way."

"Ours." She tested the word fondly. She reached up and caught his chin and pulled him down to kiss her.

"Yes, Doug, I think I'd like that a lot."

LLANO RIVER

I

Some men seem blessed with a jovial nature, an even humor that lets them take reversal and insult in stride without losing their smile or clenching a fist.

Dundee was not one of these. His temper was like a hammer cocked back over forty grains of black powder. The echo racketed for miles when Old Man Farraday brought a new son-in-law out to the ranch and handed him Dundee's job as foreman. A man with any self-respect couldn't just stand there like a sheep and abjectly accept demotion to cowhand thataway. So after the discussion was over, Dundee painfully rubbed his bruised knuckles and asked for his time.

He had stopped in a ragtag shipping-pen settlement later to wash away the indignities and suffered one more: he lost most of his payoff money over a whisky-splashed card table.

He had no clear idea where he was riding to. In the Texas free-range days of the '80s, a man seeking fresh grass usually drifted in a westerly direction. He might veer a little northward, or southward, but the main direction was always west, for that was where the "new" was, where a man could cut a fresh deck and hope for a new deal all around. Dundee had ridden several days. Now darkness was about to catch him as his half-Thoroughbred bay splashed across a narrow creek toward a dusty little cowtown which the sign said was Titusville. His outlook hadn't improved much as the bay had slowly put the long miles behind him. Dundee was tired, hungry, near broke, and ringy enough to do bare-handed battle with a bobcat.

The two-rut wagon road widened into a many-rutted street. At the head of it Dundee passed a set of horse corrals and a big barn that said "Titus Livery." He thought how much the bay would like a clean stall and a good bait of oats. A little way down the hoof-softened street he saw a thin little man lighting a lantern on the front gallery of a long frame building. The sign by the front door said TITUS HOTEL. Dundee looked with appreciation at the deep, narrow windows and imagined how soft the mattresses were, how pleasant must be the bright colors of the wallpaper. But he jingled the few coins left in his pockets and knew that after a drink and a meal, he'd retrace his steps down to the creekbank, stake the bay on grass and stretch his own frame on a blanket, looking up at stars instead of wallpaper.

Slim pickings, sure enough, but there wasn't any use a man biting himself like a stirred-up rattler. If he was strong he took the hand which was dealt him and played it through, even when it was all jokers. Tomorrow he'd scout around and try to find him a ranch job. Tonight, the hell with it.

He saw the words TITUS MERCANTILE on a big, false-fronted building, and TITUS SALOON on still another. *Ain't there nobody here but Titus?* he asked himself irritably.

Across the street lay a narrow, deep building which he took to be a second saloon, and he angled the bay toward it. On the porch, a lanky man sat rocked back in a rawhide chair, balanced against the clapboard wall. The sign over his head read: TEXAS BAR. Since it didn't say anything about Titus, Dundee decided to give the place a try. *That Titus is already rich enough,* he thought. *No use giving him my business.* He stepped off of the horse and dropped the reins through a ring in a cedar post, taking a hitch to be sure the bay didn't get a fool notion to wander off in search of Titus, whoever the Samhill that was.

Dundee stretched himself. He dusted his felt hat across his leg, raising a small cloud. He glanced at the stubbled old-timer in the chair and found the man sitting motionless, watching him. The man finally spoke: "Evenin'." Saloon bum, Dundee judged him by his look, by the dusty, threadbare clothes he wore, the runover old boots.

If he was figuring on Dundee buying him a drink, he was out of luck. But it didn't cost anything to be civil. "Evenin'."

The tail of his eye caught a movement, and he turned. From around the side of the building three young men came ambling along as if they had all night to do whatever it might be that they had in mind. Cowboys, Dundee figured. Boil them all down and you wouldn't have fifty cents' worth of tallow, or anything else. They paused at the edge of the low porch and eyed Dundee like they were appraising a bronc at a first-Monday horse sale. One of them looked at the bay, finally, and foolishly asked, "That your horse, friend?"

Dundee's voice was sharply impatient. "I ain't had a friend since a year ago last March. And you just try riding him off. You'll find out right quick whose horse he is."

His voice was rougher than he meant it to be. Damn Old Man Farraday and his flat-chested daughter and his ignorant new son-in-law, anyway! He saw a flash of anger in the young man's eyes. *I'm too touchy,* he thought. *I cut him off a little quick. But when a man asks a foolish question, he ought to expect an answer in kind.*

He went into the saloon and leaned his elbows heavily on the dark-stained bar. "A drink," he said. He glanced at his own scowling face in the cracked mirror behind the bar and quickly looked away, for he didn't like what he saw. Even as a baby, he hadn't been called pretty by anybody but his mother, and thirty years hadn't improved the situation. Right now he looked forty, face dusty and be-whiskered, brown eyes hostile, when deep down he knew he didn't have anybody to be mad at, really, except Old Man Farraday, who was a long way behind him.

The heavy-jowled bartender studied him as if trying to decide whether Dundee could pay. "Good whisky or cheap whisky?"

"It better not cost much. I'm almost as broke as I look."

The bartender's heavy moustache tugged with the beginnings of a grin. "That don't leave a man but little choice." He brought up a plain bottle from beneath the bar. "The quality ain't much, but it sure does carry authority."

Dundee choked on the first swallow and cut a hard glance at the bartender. But he couldn't say he'd been lied to. He poured himself a second glass and lifted it. "Here's to truth."

"I *told* you the truth."

"That is purely a fact."

He heard a commotion outside, and a stirring of hoofs. It struck him that that crazy cowboy just might be taking him up on his dare. In three long strides he reached the door and stopped. One cowboy was holding the bay's reins up close to the bit, trying to make the horse stand still. Behind, a second cowboy had hold of the bay's tail, stretching it taut. The third—the one who had asked the question—was using a pocketknife in an attempt to bob the tail off short.

Roaring, Dundee left the porch like a firebrand flung in fury. He barreled into the man who was holding the horse's tail and sent him staggering. The cowboy with the knife stared in disbelief at the speed of Dundee's fist streaking toward his eyes. The cowboy reeled backward and fell in the dust, a believer.

The third man turned loose of the reins and trudged forward, his fists up in a bare-knuckle boxer stance. Dundee didn't know the rules. He just went under and caught him in the belly. The cowboy buckled, gasping for breath. He went to his knees, out of the fight.

The first cowboy charged back into the fray. Dundee turned to meet him, his fists doubled hard as a sledge. Of a sudden this wasn't just any cowboy; he was Old Man Farraday, young enough to hit. Dundee thought the man got in a lick or two, but he didn't feel them. In a moment the cowboy was on the ground, out of it.

Only the pocketknife man was left. His nose was bleeding, his eyes wild, and somehow he looked a little like Old Man Farraday's son-in-law. Dundee gathered the pent-up anger of many days and delivered it into the cowboy's ribs. It was a considerable load. The cow-boy cried out in pain, but he didn't stop coming. He swung fists awk-wardly, trying for any kind of contact he could make. Dundee fetched him a hard lick on the chin, and another in the belly. They hurt; he could tell. But the cowboy stayed. He got his arms around Dundee and wrestled until Dundee lost his footing. Falling, he managed to twist so that the cowboy didn't land on top of him. The instant he hit the dirt he was pushing himself up again. He dropped the cowboy onto his back and straddled him, grabbing at the swinging fists.

"Boy," he gritted, "you better give up. I got you by the short hair."

Raging, the cowboy continued his struggle. Somehow now he didn't look quite so much like Farraday's son-in-law, who hadn't fought this hard. But Dundee thought of the pocketknife and the bay horse's tail, and his conscience didn't twinge as he swung at the jutting jaw. The cowboy stiffened, then went to struggling again. He was game, anyway.

"Boy," Dundee warned, "I tell you, I'm fixing to get out of sorts with you."

The struggling went on, so Dundee fetched him another lick.

The nondescript old man on the porch slowly let his chair away from the wall and pushed himself to his feet. He looked down calmly at the cowboy pinned to the ground. "Son Titus, I believe you've caused this stranger trouble enough. You better let him go."

The cowboy twisted and fought beneath Dundee's weight.

The man on the porch said a little firmer, "Son Titus, you get up and leave that stranger alone."

The cowboy relaxed. "All right, Pa. But I could've whipped him."

The older man snorted. "The day we have six inches of snow here in July, maybe you can whip him. Git up from there and dust yourself off."

Dundee pushed away from the cowboy but kept his fists clenched. That crazy button might decide to try just one more spin of the wheel. Dundee's knuckles were bruised, his breath short. He couldn't rightly remember when he'd had so satisfying a little fight.

The young cowboy's face was red-smeared. From his eyes, Dundee judged he hadn't had quite enough yet. But the older man's voice was strong with authority. "Son Titus, go wash yourself."

Son Titus turned away, looking back over his shoulder at Dundee. The look spoke of things unfinished, and things to come.

The other two cowboys got shakily to their feet, but they didn't seem much inclined to continue what they had started. *Some people,* Dundee thought, *just can't stay interested in one thing very long at a time.*

He turned back to check his horse. Wonder the bay hadn't jerked loose and run off, all that scuffling going on around him. Dundee patted the horse reassuringly. He took hold of the tail, stretching it out to see how much damage the cowboy had done, while at the same time he warily watched the bay's hind feet. It would be just like a horse to kick now that the trouble was over.

He couldn't see they had cut much hair. Dull boy, dull knife.

The man on the porch said, "Stranger, I apologize for my boy. He was just by way of having a little fun."

"It wasn't very funny to my horse."

"Little town like this, there ain't much for a young man to do to entertain himself. So it's natural they turn their hand to mischief when they see a stranger. Hope they didn't spoil the looks of your horse."

"They didn't, but it's no thanks to you. You sat right there and let them do it."

"I was curious to see if I'd judged you right."

"Well, did you?"

"Sized you up when you first come. You did just about what I expected you would. A little quicker, even. Nice job you done on them three buttons."

"If one of them was your son, you take it awful calm."

The man shrugged. "Does a boy good to get himself whipped once in a while. Teaches him humility. Come on back in. I'll stand you to a drink."

The heavy-jawed barkeep with the smiling moustache reached beneath the bar and came up with a bottle that even *looked* better than the one Dundee had tried. He poured two glasses.

The man from the porch said, "I didn't hear your name."

"No, I don't reckon you did."

"It's none of my business, but I got to call you something."

"Dundee will do. I answer to that."

"I doubt that you answer to anybody. I'm John Titus."

Dundee nodded. "I gathered that when the boy called you Pa. You the Titus that owns everything in town?"

"Most of it. Whichaway did you ride in from?"

"Northeast."

"You been on my ranch the last twenty . . . twenty-five miles."

"You don't look like a big rancher."

"Meaning my clothes?" Titus shook his head. "Hell, everybody here knows me. I don't have to impress anybody."

"You dress up different when you go away from home?"

Titus shook his head again. "Why should I? Nobody would know me anyhow."

Dundee mulled that a while and finished his drink. He glanced at the big barkeep and back at Titus. "This saloon ain't got your name on it. How come you're in here buying whisky from the competition?"

"It's better than the kind *I* sell. Anyhow, the people who work in *my* saloon wear the knees out of their britches trying to please me. I get tired of being 'Mistered' all over the place. Badger here, he's so independent that even his mother hates him. I like a man who's a little contrary. Shows he's got character." His eyes narrowed. "*You're* a contrary man, Dundee."

Dundee didn't reply, for this was no news to him. He'd been only about fourteen when his brothers had decided they couldn't stand him anymore. They had ganged up and run him off from home.

Titus picked up the bottle and his glass and carried it to a small round table. Dundee followed suit. Titus said, "You look tired. I hope you're figuring on spending the night in my *ho*tel."

"I expect I'll sleep out on the creekbank."

Titus gazed at him intently. "That's what I thought. Broke, ain't you?"

"What gives you that kind of a notion?"

"The look of you. It's all over you, like dark skin on a Comanche. Anyway, you're a cowboy. Cowboys are stone broke nine-tenths of the time."

"I won't go hungry."

"You don't have to. You need a job, I need a man. I bet we could work up a deal." Titus paused. "I seen a carbine on your saddle. You know how to use it, I expect."

"I generally hit what I aim at."

"How about a pistol?"

"Got one in my saddlebag. Always liked a carbine better."

"Ever hire your guns out?"

Dundee scowled. "You got somebody you want killed, you just go and shoot him yourself. I do honest work."

He thought he saw a flicker of a smile across Titus' face, and a look of satisfaction. "I'm sure you do, Dundee. What I had in mind would be honest. I wouldn't lie to you, though. It's so damned honest it just *could* get you killed."

"How's that?"

"Where I want you to go, honest men are as rare as fresh peaches in January. They're in open season the year around."

"If somebody was to shoot me, I don't see where that money of yours would do me any good."

"I got a notion you can take care of yourself. Anyway, man, think of the challenge."

"I'm not a schoolboy. A challenge don't stir me anymore."

"But I'll bet money does."

Dundee took the bottle and poured himself a fresh drink. "You got the money; I got the time. Long as your whisky holds out, I'll at least listen. What's your problem?"

"Cowthieves. Hideburners. They're after me like heel flies after an old bull. I need them stopped."

"Why don't you just call in the Texas Rangers? That's their line of work."

"It's *my* cattle; I'll pay for my own remedies. Man runs to the government with all his trouble, it's a sign of weakness. When I itch, I scratch for myself."

Or hire somebody to do the scratching for you, Dundee thought. "How come you think I'm the man to do it for you? You don't know me. For all you know, *I* could be a cowthief." He grunted. "For all *I* know, I *could* be one, if the profit looked big enough."

Titus shook his head. "You're not one of that kind. Some people are easy to read, minute you set eyes on them. I got a strong notion you could go down into that den of snakes and bite as hard as *they* do."

"Where is this snake den?"

"You ever been down in the Llano River country, south of here?"

Dundee said he hadn't. Titus said, "It's rough country, lots of brush and timber. A regular outlaw paradise. They even got a town of their own, if you'd *call* it a town . . . a place by the name of 'Runaway.' Ever hear of it?"

Dundee shook his head. "Never even heard of Titusville till I rode in here."

"Runaway's not on any map. It's just down there, like a boil on a man's backside. It's outside of this county. Local sheriff's got no

jurisdiction down there, and what's more, he don't want any. Runaway's a far piece from its own county seat, and they don't even keep
a deputy there. Bad climate, hard on your health."

"Looks like the thing to do is just to hire you a couple or three
dozen gunslingers, go down there and clean house. Be done with it
once and for all."

"I will. But I got to go about it right. Old days, a man could just
go down and throw a nice, big hanging party and burn the damned
place and be shed of it, and no questions asked. But now people have
got awful righteous about things like that. They get upset and call
for investigations and such . . . cause a heap of bother. Anyway, I'm
not a hard man, Dundee. There's some good people down there—a
few, at least—and I don't want to have to hurt them all just to get at
the heel flies. Trouble is, I don't know just who-all's doing the stealing. That'd be one of the things I'd want you to find out. Once I
know the guilty ones, I'll get me some men and go down there and
throw one hell of a good party."

Dundee's opinion of Titus was slowly on the rise. Some cowmen he knew would simply ride down on such a town like a cy-
clone, sweep it clean and tell God they'd all just died.

"Titus, you're a wealthy man. A few cowthieves won't break you."

"No?" Titus clenched a big fist on the table. Dundee could tell
by the rough look of it that it had known a long lifetime of hard
work. "You've heard the old saying: the bigger a man is, the harder
he goes down. I got debts, Dundee, debts that would scare old Jim
Fisk himself. The cattle I'm losing can be the difference between me
hanging on and going under. I got to stop the leaks, and I will. I
want to do it the right way: get the people who are hurting me and
leave the innocent folks alone. But if I wind up with my back to the
wall, I'll take desperate measures. I *will* go down there and wipe the
whole slate clean. When a man comes up to the snubbing post, he's
got to save himself."

"And what about the innocent ones?"

"I expect there was a few good people in Jericho, Dundee. But when Joshua blew that trumpet, they all went down."

Dundee shrugged. It wasn't any skin off of his nose, one way or the other. But he had a feeling he could get to like this Titus, if he stayed around. Dundee liked contrary men, too. "You asked me if I'd ever hired out my guns. I have, but only when I liked the deal."

"I'm not asking you to go down there and kill out all them varmints. I'm not asking you to kill *anybody*, unless there comes a need for it. I just want you to go find out who's running off my stock. I'll handle it from there. I'll pay you more than you could make in two years if you was to try to earn it cowboying."

Dundee thought about Titus' hotel, and the beds in it, and the colored wallpaper. "How much in advance?"

"Say, two hundred dollars. The balance when you get back."

"What if I don't *get* back?"

"Then I save the rest of the money." Titus let a tiny smile flicker, then go out. "I'll be square with you, Dundee. I've sent two men down there already. One of them acted like a broke cow-puncher riding the chuck-line. Figured that would give him a chance to see a lot. They dumped his body in the street here one night, right in front of my *ho*tel. The other one went down there acting like a cattle buyer. I never *did* see him again."

Dundee reached for the bottle, then changed his mind. He could already feel a glow starting. If he was going to dicker on a deal, he didn't want any cobwebs on his brain. "Saying I was to decide to go down there, I don't intend to do it acting like somebody I ain't. Been times in my life I ain't told all there was to the story, but there's never been a time I ever out-and-out lied about anything. I won't make any big point of it, but if anybody asks me, my name is Dundee and I'm working for you. No lies, no playacting."

Titus shrugged. "How you do it is up to you. I just want to be damn sure it gets done."

Son Titus stepped through the door. He had washed the blood from his face and dusted his clothes a little. But around one eye a blue spot the size of a half dollar was beginning to show up. And one cheek was skinned down to the color of calf meat. Dundee nodded in satisfaction. It had always pleasured him to see a job well done.

Son Titus said suspiciously, "Pa, what you talking to this drifter about?"

Titus stirred in annoyance. "Nothing that's any concern of yours. Go find yourself something to do, and this time leave that knife in your pocket."

"There ain't nothing to do, Pa, and you know it. You don't allow no high-stepping women in Titusville, or no high-limit poker games. Anyhow, I wouldn't ask you if I didn't want to know. What you getting mixed up with this stranger for?"

"Hiring him for a little job of work, is all. Go play marbles, or something."

Dundee judged Son Titus to be about twenty-one or -two, somewhat beyond the age for marbles.

Son said, "I heard a little of it from the porch. You're sending him to Runaway, ain't you? You think maybe he's going to catch them cowthieves." The young man answered his own question with a show of contempt. "He won't. He'll take whatever you give him, then go down there and join up with them. That is, if that's not where he come from in the first place. I can tell by the look of him. I bet you a million dollars he's a cowthief himself."

Dundee slowly got to his feet. He clenched a fist, wincing as pain lanced through a battered knuckle. "Boy, if you keep working at it, you're finally going to make me take a disliking to you."

John Titus said, "Son Titus, you get along out of here. You

haven't *got* a million dollars, and you never will. You haven't got much sense sometimes, either."

"I got sense enough to take care of that Runaway job for you, if you'd let me. You don't have to go hiring some drifter."

The father's voice was sharp. "Son Titus, if you don't want to spend all this summer roundup jingling horses and holding the cut, you better do what I tell you."

Son Titus turned and walked out talking to himself. He paused on the porch, looking back, his eyes hot with resentment.

John Titus said, and not without pride, "He's contrary. I reckon that's why I like him."

Only a father could, Dundee thought. *And maybe a mother.* He settled back into his chair. "If I was to take this job, you got any ideas where I ought to start at?"

"I'll give you the names of some people I think are honest. And I'll tell you about a few of the other kind. Main name to begin with, I think, is old Blue Roan."

"What kind of a name is *that*?"

"It's the name of a cowthief, the daddy of them all. Smart as a mustang, mean as a one-eyed polecat. Whatever you find down there, I expect old Roan Hardesty is at the center of it."

"Sounds like you know him."

"I do. Long time ago, down in deep South Texas, him and me used to steal cattle together." Titus paused, seeing surprise in Dundee's eyes. "Hell yes, I used to steal cattle. How else do you think I got my start? We all did, them days. But I reformed. Blue Roan never did."

Titus sat in silence, waiting. "Well, how about it, Dundee? You want to take the job?"

Dundee bit off the end of a cigar and then lighted a match. He drew, getting the tobacco worked up to a glow.

"The beds in that *ho*tel of yours . . . they good and soft?"

II

In the 1880s, much of the Texas Hill country which shed its waters into the Llano River, and down into the Frio and the Nueces, was known far and wide as thieves' territory, for it was a big land of high, rough hills, of rocky ranges, of deep valleys and heavy, protective timber—live oak, Spanish oak, cedar and mesquite—of hundreds of clear-water springs and dozens of creeks and streams—of the Llanos themselves, the North, the South and the main Llano. Here great herds of cattle could be swallowed up and lost. Bold men could make fortunes in the light of the moon by the ambitious use of long ropes and fast horses, fanning out in all directions to take other men's cattle, other men's horses, bringing them here to this favored land of strong grass and abundant water, far from law, far from the harsh hand of retribution.

Riding the bay, leading a packhorse lent him by John Titus, Dundee took his time heading south and west into the Llano River country. Carrying a generous amount of Titus grub in his pack, and *most* of two hundred dollars in his pocket—that hotel had overcharged him—he saw no reason to be in a hurry. He doubted the cowthieves would leave before he got there.

He took a long, leisurely look at the Titus cattle he came across. He decided they weren't different from most other people's. Some places, cowmen had brought in improved bulls such as the imported Shorthorn to start a gradual upgrading. Titus still held on to the pure Longhorn, the native Texas "mustang" breed. The only visible step toward improvement was that he had steered all the male produce except the ones he had selected as best—and the ones he couldn't catch. The latter bequeathed a certain hardihood to their progeny, whatever shortcomings they might have had as beef. Some of the Titus bulls showed strong Mexican blood, and even beyond that, the fighting strains that went back to ancient Spain. Most range cattle fought horsemen only when provoked. Twice Dundee found bulls coming to meet him halfway, pawing their challenge.

He guessed Titus liked his cattle contrary too.

One thing he noted was the form of the Titus T Bar brand, made with three stamps of a straight bar iron, the bar under the T. Every time Dundee sat awhile on the ground, whether to eat, rest the horses or just ease his tired rump, he would take a stick and draw the T Bar in the dirt. Then he would start improvising various ways it could be burned over with a running iron and converted into something else. He was amazed at the many variations. He could join the T to the bar and then cross a line through it and make a Double E. He could run the upright through the top of the T and make a Cross Bar. He could make a Double Cross, a TE, a TF Bar, a Big I, a Rocking R, a JE. There was little limit other than a man's ingenuity, and Dundee had observed that when it came to thievery, many a dull man was transported into genius.

John Titus must surely know his brand was easy to alter. Its lines were too simple. If he would use something complicated, after the Mexican style, he would present the hide-burners a challenge. But this was probably a measure of the man's stubbornness. The brand was *his*. He would hang on to it come hell or high losses.

As he drew the various brands that he could conceive from the T Bar, Dundee catalogued them in his mind. As far as he was concerned, any cattle he came across with such a brand belonged to Titus.

The country became rougher and brushier, the farther he went south. He never was sure when he passed beyond the boundaries of the Titus ranch. Actually, he knew Titus didn't own more than a fraction of the land he used. What he had done—what a great many early Texas cowmen had done when the land showed signs of settling up—was to buy or lease all the land he could get that had natural water on it. The man who controlled the water thus controlled all the land within a cow's practical walking distance of it, for the land was valueless without water. A dry ranch up in the hills wasn't worth the shirt on a man's back. Dundee figured that a map of Titus' deeded land would be little more than a map of springs, creeks and streams. It was legal enough, and ingeniously simple. Dundee didn't begrudge him his holdings. He only regretted that he hadn't gotten here early enough to do the same thing himself.

The breaks of the game, he reasoned. *Them as has, gits.*

He found awesomely twisted gray-green live oaks edging the shell-studded limestone hills, and Mexican cedars growing in dense brakes, single cedars dotting the hills all the way to the rimrocks. There was often a tangly type of underbrush in the valleys, rustling with the wind and with the unseen movement of animals and rodents and Lord knew what. Now and again he would catch a glimpse of a big rack of horns an instant before a whitetail buck deer darted off into the protection of the heavy sumac and Spanish oak. Once in a while he stirred up a few wild turkeys, which sprinted away like racehorses, or flew up explosively like the bobwhite quail. Once the bay snorted and jumped and almost lost him as a long-nosed, thick-plated armadillo scurried out from underfoot.

Good country for wild animals, Dundee thought. *No wonder it appeals to wild men.*

The first scattered bunch of cattle he found in the roughs were standing around a half-dried waterhole in a rocky draw. He rode up on them quietly and with care. He managed to see the brands before the first old cow jerked her head up high, took one good look at him and went clattering off for the thickets. The rest followed close behind her, their tails up, their dignity injured.

Most of them carried what he took to be a Rocker M, or maybe it was meant for a Hat. Either way, it wasn't a conversion from the

T Bar. However, Dundee saw one which looked suspicious. Best he could tell in the second or two he'd had a view, it was a box with a straight line down through it. That one could very easily have been made over from the Titus brand. He took a small tally book from his pocket and sketched the brand as he had seen it. He recorded the Rocker M, too, just for reference. As he went along, tallying every brand, he would begin to find out who claimed each one. There would come a time, someday, for a reckoning.

He spent long days quietly riding out the creeks and streams as he came across them, noting brands, jotting each new one in the book, sketching a rough map. During that time he found at least half a dozen brands which could have been—and most probably were— the illegitimate offspring of the T Bar.

Somewhere he had read about the big fish living off of the little ones. Here it looked more like the little ones living off of the big.

Dundee studiously avoided people. Now and again he would see a picket cabin or a small rock house or even a tent pitched some- where close to water, with perhaps a few brush corrals and a rude barn or two. These he observed at length and committed to map and memory, but he didn't go down for a talk.

He found few cattle carrying the Titus brand. That, he thought, was a little odd. Even with Titus riders patrolling the outer edges of what Titus considered to be his rightful range, it seemed probable that on an outfit so large, some cattle would naturally stray out of bounds. It was to be expected. Seemed like the bigger the ranch, the farther the cattle wandered.

Dundee figured they wandered, all right, and probably a good many were encouraged more than somewhat. Any strays which showed up this far from home likely didn't carry the T Bar very long. It would be converted into something else in no more time than it took somebody to get a fire going and an iron hot.

One morning, moving the bay and the packhorse down a ridge,

he heard cattle bawling. He paused to listen. From the sound of it he knew they were being driven. A cow bawling for a strayed calf sounds one way. Bawling of a cow forcibly separated from a calf under stress sounds another. And the bawling of many cows at one time means a herd being moved. Dundee eased into the protection of a cedar motte and waited patiently, smoking himself a leisurely cigarette.

In due time the cattle came into sight. At a distance he estimated seventy or eighty head. As they gradually came nearer, he counted about fifty cows and twenty-five or thirty calves. Dundee reached into his saddlebag and brought out a small spyglass Titus had lent him. It was too far yet to read the brands and earmarks, so he studied the four riders. Best he could tell, the one in charge was a tall, heavy man in a Mexican sombrero. At least he seemed to be giving orders, what few were being given. These men knew their business without needing much instruction. It occurred to Dundee they were moving the cattle too fast, though. No bigger than this bunch was, if they would let the cows set their own pace, the calves would keep up with their mammies and there wouldn't be all this bawling. A real cowman wouldn't push his own cattle this way except for a short distance. These had been walking a long time. They had a trail-drawn look about them.

The riders were putting the cattle across a nice grassy flat, one of the best Dundee had seen this side of the T Bar. Most of the cattle he had found in this region carried the Rocker M, or the Hat, or whatever it was. A little before sundown yesterday Dundee had scouted what appeared to be the headquarters, on up about three or four miles beside a nice spring. He had sat on the brow of a hill and looked down with the spyglass for an hour or more, studying the layout. A double cabin there, built of logs, was better constructed than most he had seen. Whoever these people were, they had built with every intention of staying. He had seen a picket saddleshed and a set of corrals, part of them built of brush and some of stone, laboriously stacked.

A couple of times he had seen a woman. At the distance he couldn't tell much about her. She was small, and by the ease of her movements he guessed she was young. He hadn't seen any children. About sundown two horsemen had come in from somewhere above, had unsaddled their horses and put the saddles in the shed. One man was a bit heavy and moved with the stiffness of age. The other had the movements of a young man, and the energy. While the older of the two limped slowly to the cabin and flopped beneath a brush arbor to rest, the younger strode to a pile of rocks beside the corral and carried several to the fence he was building, setting them in place. He didn't stop until the woman came out and waved him to supper. About that time Dundee had decided he was hungry too, so he had pulled back a safe distance and made camp.

He had thought about that stone fence some as he sat around his own campfire, chewing venison and sipping boiled coffee. Stone fences and laziness didn't go together.

He noted that none of the riders pushing these cattle sat their horses like the two he had observed yesterday. Eventually the small herd came close enough that with the spyglass he could read the brands. Most of the calves were still slick-eared, but the cows weren't. They belonged to Titus.

Sitting there, Dundee tried again to study out a way the T Bar could be altered into the Rocker M. It couldn't be done.

This don't add up, he thought. *I reckon I'll just follow along.*

As he was fixing to ride out from the motte, he hauled up short. Three riders were coming from the south. Another minute and he would have been in their view. They came upon the trail of the cattle, paused a moment and followed the tracks. Dundee scratched his head, wondering. He decided to stay on the higher ground and see without being seen. Some games, it was better to watch than to play in.

Presently the three riders overtook the cattle. They howdied and shook with the drovers and sat their horses in a circle, taking time to smoke and parley. One man rode off. Before long he came back, pointing.

Across the big flat, from the southwest, a rider pushed along in an easy trot. Dundee dismounted with the spyglass. He could recognize people sometimes by the way they sat their horses. He knew this was the man he had observed yesterday working on the corral.

Three men peeled away from the herd and rode to intercept the rider. Dundee could see angry gestures. At length the heavy man in the Mexican sombrero turned back and spoke to the two who sat a little behind him. The heavy man held a pistol. The two men dismounted slowly, deliberately, and walked to the fence-builder's horse. One reached up and grabbed. The horseman slid out of the saddle, and they sprawled together in the dust. The two set in to beat him with their fists.

The other man abandoned the cattle and spurred up to watch the fight. They formed a semicircle around the sombreroed horseman who had done their initial arguing and had given the orders. The breeze brought Dundee their shouts of encouragement.

Though it was two against one, the lone man put up a good fight of it, for a while. Toting those rocks had put a good set of muscles on him, Dundee reasoned. One of the two who was beating him finally stretched out on the ground and didn't get up. The heavy man ordered fresh blood into the fray.

The unequal contest raised a resentful anger in Dundee, and he considered going down there. But the odds were too long. There were too many guns. He reasoned that if they had intended to kill the man, they would have done it at the start.

Anyway, it wasn't any of his put-in.

The fencebuilder didn't have the chance of a one-legged pullet in a coyote den, but he resisted with all he had. Wearying, he swayed,

staggered, swung without strength. Someone's fist hit him every
time he opened up. He went down, pushed to his feet, went down
again, came up as far as his knees, got struck in the jaw and went
down to stay. The man in the sombrero dismounted and delivered
him a couple of hard kicks in the ribs. Gritting his teeth, Dundee
held the spyglass on that man long enough to decide—he wasn't a
Mexican, despite the hat.

You got something coming to you, hoss, Dundee thought. *I hope I'm
there when it's delivered.*

The leader pointed back to the slowly scattering herd. The
horsemen grudgingly turned away from the downed fighter and
trailed in a ragged line to the cattle. After a bit they drove the cows
and calves by the beaten man, and on beyond him.

Even in the shade, the close heat was oppressive here in the
cedars, where the thin breeze could not move through the dense fo-
liage. Dundee wondered about that man down yonder, sprawled on
the ground in the open sun. *Least they could do was drag him to the
shade.* His impulse was to go on down and help, but he made himself
wait until the cattle passed over a rise and out of view.

The lone man heard him coming. He raised up onto hands and
knees, defiance in his eyes. He reached back to his hip, but they had
thrown his pistol away into the grass.

Dundee raised his hand in the peace sign. "I don't mean you no
harm." The young man tried to push to his feet. Dundee said: "Wait
and I'll help you. Go slow. If they've busted anything, you don't
want to lose the pieces."

The man swayed. His face was bloody and torn, his beribboned
shirt crusted with dust and sweat. His hands were laced and bleeding.

Dundee said, "They done a right smart of a job on you."

The man licked his bleeding lip. "Where'd my horse go?"

"He run off. That's the way with horses." Dundee hunted around
till he found the pistol and returned it. "You gave them a good fight."

A suspicious gaze bore into Dundee. "Who are you?"

"You wouldn't know me. Name's Dundee."

"You saw the fight?"

"Had me a spyglass."

"And you didn't do a thing to help me?"

Dundee shrugged. "I spent a lot of money across a poker table before I learned there's no use going against a stacked deck. Figured your health was lost anyway and I'd keep mine so I could come down here and put the pieces back together." He jerked his thumb toward the bay. "Think you can get on my horse? I'll take you to the creek. You'll feel better once you wash the dirt and blood off."

Dundee had to help him into the saddle, then swung up behind the cantle and sat on the bay's hips. "I'd as soon not have to keep calling you *'You.'* You got a name?"

"McCown. Warren McCown."

McCown. That would fit with the Rocker M brand.

Dundee squatted patiently on his heels and flipped rocks into the creek while McCown stripped off his clothes and waded into the water. He noted that McCown's face, neck and hands were brown, but the rest of his body was white. Most early cowboys buttoned their collars and their sleeves. They believed it was cooler if you kept the sun out, the skin covered.

McCown soaked till the dirt and blood were washed away.

Lord help the fish, Dundee thought.

Now that he could see the cowboy's face plainer, he judged him to be in his late twenties. Presently McCown came out and sat on the gravelly bank to let the wind dry him. "Feel better?" Dundee asked.

McCown only nodded.

"Some of them marks didn't wash off. You'll carry them a spell." McCown still only nodded. Dundee said, "You sore about me not coming down and throwing in with you?"

McCown shrugged. "You didn't know me."

"I still don't."

McCown glanced at him sharply. "And *I* don't know *you*. I do know that packhorse is carrying a T Bar brand on him. You steal him?"

Dundee's eyes narrowed. "Make any difference to you if I did?"

"I got worries enough of my own. Old Titus can watch out for himself."

Dundee reflected a moment. "Who *were* them jolly lads you was entertaining back there?"

McCown stared him straight in the eye. "While ago you didn't want to get involved. You'd better just stay clear of it all around. What you don't know won't cause you no trouble."

McCown put on his hat first, then his long underwear, then his boots, his remnant of a shirt, and his trousers. "Mind letting me ride double with you to my cabin? Ain't far."

"I know where it is."

When McCown showed surprise, Dundee said. "I know more than you think I do. I know you got a log cabin and brush pens and you're building yourself a set of rock corrals. I know you got an old man living with you, and a wife."

McCown's eyes narrowed, but he held his tongue.

Dundee said: "What's more, I know you brand a Rocker M, and that there ain't no way to make a Rocker M out of a T Bar. I already tried."

"Who the hell *are* you?"

"Told you, my name's Dundee."

"A man can change names like he changes shirts. A name don't mean nothing."

"I'm working for John Titus. I come to see what's been doing with his cattle."

"And you been watching me, figuring me for a thief."

"Not necessarily. I thought you *might* be."

"Now you figure I'm not?"

"Not necessarily. Mount up. I'll ride behind again."

"I think I'd as soon walk as ride with a man who thinks I'm a thief."

"I ain't said you are, and I ain't said you're not. I got a wide-open mind. Now, if you want to ride home, you better get up on that horse."

They moved up the creek in an easy trot, McCown silently nursing his resentment, Dundee making no apology and, indeed, not even considering the possibility that he should. To him, apology was a sign either of weakness or of being wrong, and he seldom conceded either.

A mile or so from headquarters, he saw a rider approaching, leading a horse. "Hope this is a friend of yours, McCown."

McCown squinted. "It's Uncle Ollie. He's bringing my horse."

An elderly man slouched gracelessly in the saddle, taking his time. His face furrowed in concern, though worry didn't seem to enhance his speed. "Horse come in without you, Warren. Millie like to've had a fit." He cocked his head over. "Look at you! I been telling you this horse'd throw you off."

"It wasn't the horse, Uncle Ollie. It was . . ." He turned half around to look at Dundee. "I run into some boys back yonder."

"Was old Blue Roan with them?"

Dundee listened intently, remembering what Titus had said about Roan. McCown frowned. "I didn't say it was Roan's bunch."

"They marked you, boy, they surely did. They'll kill you, you don't watch out." The old man turned his squinting attention to Dundee, his eyes light gray, set against a sun-darkened skin wrinkled and dried like neglected leather. "And who might you be?"

McCown answered for Dundee. "You can call him the silent observer."

Dundee said, "The name's Dundee."

The old man reached out, his grip casual. "Mine's Ollie Mc-Cown."

To dismount without Dundee's having to get down first, Mc-Cown threw his right leg over the bay's neck and jumped to the ground. Weaker than he thought, he went to his hands and knees. He straightened. "I do thank you, Dundee, for what help you *have* been. Maybe I'll get to do the same for you sometime . . . if I'm real lucky." There was a touch of malice in it. McCown took the reins from his uncle's hands and swung up onto his own horse. Then a thought struck him. "How come you home when my horse came in, Uncle Ollie? You were supposed to be out rocking up that spring on the south branch."

The old man shrugged like a kid caught at mischief. "I got tired. Anyway, I thought it'd be nice to go down to the creek and catch a nice mess of fish for Millie to fix for supper."

McCown grumbled: "You and that fishing pole! I'd burn it, but you'd just fix another."

Glad I don't work for him, Dundee thought. *All he lacks is a whip.*

Dundee noticed Uncle Ollie looking with concern at the brand on the packhorse. Warren McCown saw, too. "Dundee works for John Titus. He's down here to find out where the Titus cattle are going."

The old man said, "Reckon people might think we're taking sides with him, Warren?"

"Let them."

"They done beat you up. Next time they might kill you!"

"This is my place, and I'll do as I please on it." McCown turned to Dundee. "Since you're this close, you might as well come and have supper. I owe you that much for the ride."

"Much obliged." Dundee decided if he kept his mouth shut and his ears open, he might learn something. And even if he didn't learn anything, he'd get something in his belly besides old bacon and gamy venison and poor coffee and promises. If a man couldn't get rich—and Dundee doubted he ever would—the next best thing was to get fat.

There was nothing elaborate about the McCown place, for this was not a country given to fancy things. Poor for pretty but hell for stout. They passed the incomplete stone corrals, and the piles of wagon-hauled rocks which one day would find their place in the fences. The stones had been selected for size and shape up in the hills, more than likely, through long, hot days of back-breaking toil.

McCown pointed to a finished rock corral in which stood the saddleshed. "You can put your horses in there and feed them. You'll likely want to be a-riding again come morning."

Dundee carried his saddle into the shed and set it across a rack that was simply a smoothed-off log placed atop a pair of posts. He noted that the shed's walls were upright cedar pickets, axe-hewn for a close fit and set well into the ground to hold them solid. The roof was tightly built of live oak timbers, cedar and sod.

Another contrary man, Dundee thought. He'd have to be to drive himself to this kind of work.

Somehow Dundee thought McCown might have oats for his horses, but instead the rancher dug into a barrel and came up with dried mesquite beans. Well, what they lacked in feed value, they made up in convenience. And they didn't cost anything.

McCown paused at the gate and looked toward the unfinished rock fence. "I reckon I'll come back out here after supper and work till dark. Don't lack too much finishing me another pen."

Uncle Ollie said: "After that beating you got? You better go to bed, Warren McCown."

A woman stood in the open dog-run that separated the two sections of the cabin. Moving in that direction, walking to the right of the hobbling Uncle Ollie, Dundee found himself studying her. She was slender; he could tell that at a distance. Nearer, he could see she was younger than he had thought, watching at a distance through the spyglass. Now he could see her long brown hair, strands of it lifting in the wind, strands that when down to full length must reach nearly to her waist. She had a thinnish oval face, not yet sun-hardened but still clean and soft. It was a natural face, one that probably had never known powder or rouge or any form of lip-reddening like the town women sometimes used.

The young woman—she might have been twenty or so—gasped at sight of McCown's face. "Warren . . ."

McCown gestured that it didn't amount to anything. "You about got supper ready? I want to do a little more work before it gets too late."

Uncle Ollie shrugged in futility.

The woman turned to stare at Dundee in curiosity and, perhaps, a touch of fear. Dundee ran his hand over his face and realized his whiskers hadn't felt a razor since he had left Titusville. Moreover, he was dusty and streaked with grime and woodsmoke. To her, he must look like some robber chieftain, some brigand out of employ.

Dundee ventured, "I know I appear fearsome, ma'am, but I got a good heart."

Warren McCown added drily: "And a good appetite, too, I ex-pect. We just as well feed him some of Uncle Ollie's fish."

The woman glanced at Uncle Ollie and began to smile. The old man said to Dundee, "We had it made up that if Warren raised cain about me fishing instead of working on that spring, we'd say it was Millie caught them."

Looked like nobody was going to introduce him, so he would have to do it for himself. "Mrs. McCown, my name is Dundee."

She smiled shyly. Dundee suspected the beard still worried her. "I'm Millie McCown. And it's not Mrs.; it's *Miss.*"

Warren McCown said in a small triumph: "You see, you didn't know everything after all, Dundee. She's my sister, not my wife."

Dundee let it pass. A man was entitled to a small mistake now and again. For no reason he would have admitted to himself, he was somehow pleased to find she was unmarried.

The kitchen was the biggest room in the double cabin. On one wall stood a black Charter Oak stove. At a time when most people in Western Texas still cooked in an open fireplace, this was an uncommon luxury worth a dozen head of cattle or several fair-to-middling horses. A woodbox beside it was heaped full with mesquite and oak wood, chopped to length. The fish was sizzling in a deep iron skillet. Millie McCown had set three chipped plates on a plain wooden table. Now, allowing for Dundee, she set a fourth. Waiting, Dundee looked around at the plain lumber shelves, the homemade rawhide-and-cedar chairs, the two cots that would be Warren's and Uncle Ollie's. The place was built for utility. The stove was the only thing in it that would sell for three pieces of Mexican silver.

On a shelf Dundee saw an old tintype propped against a big family Bible. It pictured two soldiers in what appeared to be Confederate uniforms. One, he realized, was Uncle Ollie. This had been a good many years ago.

Ollie McCown said: "That's me on the left. I was still full of vinegar, them days. I ain't changed much in looks, just the vinegar has about run out." Dundee glanced at the old man. If Ollie didn't think he'd changed, he hadn't stood close to a mirror lately. The old man said: "That other feller, that's my brother George, the daddy of Millie and Warren. He's gone now. We buried him a long ways back."

"I'm sorry," Dundee said, and he meant it.

Dundee approached the fish with some uncertainty. He'd been seeing them in the clear-water streams and wished he could catch some, but he'd never lived in a part of the country where there were creeks to fish in. He didn't know how to start. Even if he had caught any, he wouldn't have known whether to skin them like a beef or eat them with the hide on.

Dundee found himself looking at the girl through supper, cutting his eyes away when she glanced in his direction. He knew she was aware of his staring, for once her face reddened a little. She'd been sheltered, this girl.

After supper, Warren McCown did just what he said he would do; he went out and stacked rock for the fence, despite the soreness, despite his bruises. Dundee thought he owed it to him to help, but McCown shook his head when Dundee picked up the first stone. "Wrong shape, wrong size for the tie I'm making here. I can do it better by myself."

Dundee dropped the rock and left McCown to handle the job all by his lonesome. He walked down to the saddleshed, rubbing his beard and looking back at the cabin. He fished around in the pack for his razor and soap. He shaved in the cold water of the creek, wincing as the razor scraped. Done with it, he asked himself why he had gone to the trouble. He had no intentions to justify it. When a man courted a country girl like this Millie McCown, he had to have one thing in mind: marriage. Anything less would draw immediate rebuff from the girl and very possibly a bellyful of buckshot from an outraged father or brother.

Dundee knew marriage was not for him. His itchy feet hadn't been to the far side of all the hills yet. Temporary female companionship could be had in most any town, if the urge got so strong a man had to give in to it. It could be bought and paid for, then he could turn his back and ride away from her with no regrets, no sense of shirked responsibilities.

He had no thought of despoiling this country girl, even if there were no penalty for it. This was a man's country, good women as scarce as gold and as highly valued, to be treasured and protected from all that was thought dirty and raw and unpleasant. He subscribed to an old cowboy code that put a woman on a pedestal. She didn't leave it unless she deliberately stepped down. Unless a man had marriage in mind, he tipped his hat, as the knights of old tipped their visors, and held himself afar.

Uncle Ollie had stayed long at the table. Now he was stretched on the ground beneath the arbor, belching. The sun had gone down, and there was no longer any need for shade, but habit is a slavemaster. Dundee joined him, sitting on the ground, crossing his legs. Ollie's eyes narrowed as he studied Dundee's shaven face. "Don't expect you'd win no prize, but you look a *little* better. You still got a dab of soap under your left ear."

Dundee wiped it off onto his sleeve. He pointed his chin toward the distant figure of Warren McCown, working in the dusk. "Is he thataway all the time?"

Ollie nodded. "He expects a lot out of a man, but he drives hisself the most of all."

"What's his hurry? Nobody gets out of this world alive."

"Maybe it was seeing his old daddy die without a dollar in his pocket, hardly. This here place is Warren's . . . his and Millie's, anyway. He's worked for it and fought for it. It's like a fever in him. I ain't sure sometimes whether Warren owns the land or the land owns him."

Millie McCown walked out into the dog-run, drying her hands on a cloth. Dundee pushed to his feet and took off his hat, bowing slightly, awkwardly. She smiled, and he sensed she was pleased he had taken time to shave. He noticed she had brushed her long hair. He wanted to pay her a compliment, but he didn't know what to say.

She said: "You don't have to get up for me. Please, be comfortable."

Dundee fetched her a rawhide chair from against the house. Then he stepped back beside Uncle Ollie and once more seated himself upon the ground. Dundee watched the girl until he knew she was nervously aware of his eyes. He looked away.

She said, "It's a nice, cool evening after such a warm day."

Dundee thought a man could hardly argue with a statement like that. "Yes, ma'am."

"Maybe it'll be the same again tomorrow."

"I expect."

"It was like this yesterday."

"Yes, ma'am."

A long silence followed. But Dundee could see Millie Mc-Cown's lips working a little. She was biting them, working up nerve to ask him: "Mister Dundee, I couldn't get Warren to tell me what happened to him, how he got so skinned up and bruised. Will *you* tell me?"

Dundee hesitated. If McCown wanted her to know, he would have told her.

"Please, Mister Dundee?"

The pleading tone of her voice melted him like butter. Mc-Cown *ought* to have told her. "I don't know who the men was, ma'am. They was driving a herd of cattle that sure as he . . . heck didn't belong to them. Your brother rode up, and a fight started."

"Maybe they were our cattle."

"No, ma'am, they was carrying the T Bar, old John Titus' brand." Maybe no one had told her. "I work for John Titus."

She nodded. "Oh. And you were trailing the cattle to see where they were being taken."

"That's about it, ma'am."

"And you helped my brother."

He squirmed. "I ain't fixing to lie to you; I didn't get in the fight. But later I went down and done what I could."

"If I know Warren, he didn't even think to thank you. So *I* thank you, Mister Dundee."

"No trouble, ma'am. I'd of done as much for a broken-legged dog." He rubbed his neck. *That* hadn't come out the way he meant it.

She seemed not to notice. "It was old Blue Roan, or some of his men; I'd bet on that. Warren's had trouble with them. They keep bringing cattle across our land, cattle that don't belong to them."

Uncle Ollie stirred nervously. "Millie . . ."

She went on: "We're minding our own business, or trying to. If Roan Hardesty steals cattle, that's between him and the law, or between him and the people he takes the cattle away from. But he's got no right to drive them across our land and draw us into it. One of these days there'll come a reckoning. We don't want to be caught up in it."

Uncle Ollie's eyes were narrowed. "Millie, you better hush up and not be making loose talk. That'll get us in trouble too."

"I'm just saying what's true."

"You're saying it to a man who represents John Titus. Ain't no use having Roan and his crowd come over here some fine day and shut all of us up for good. They could do it, you know."

She said with confidence, "Warren can take care of us."

The old man grunted. "He ain't but one man. I'm only half a man, and you're no man atall. If it comes a showdown, we won't last long."

Guardedly Dundee suggested: "You wouldn't have to be alone. I think John Titus would help anybody who helps *him*."

She asked, "What kind of help could we give him?"

Dundee brought out his tallybook. "I been jotting down brands. I'd be much obliged if you'd tell me who claims them."

Uncle Ollie said tightly: "Dundee, I was in the big war. I didn't own no slaves; it wasn't none of my business. But I got in it anyway. All I got for it was a hole in my leg and some sense in my head. I learned one thing; take care of your own self and stay out of a fight any way you can. Us McCowns, we're not messing into John Titus' trouble. We don't owe John Titus nothing."

"If I tell him you helped me, he might figure he owes you something."

"So might Blue Roan." The old man gritted, "Dundee, you go riding down into old Roan's backyard and you may not ever *see* John Titus again."

III

Dundee had seen ranches where it didn't take long to spend the night, but this place was extreme. McCown was up and stirring two hours before good daylight. Dundee had spread his blankets outdoors, beneath the arbor. Through the open window he could hear McCown poking a fire into life in the big cookstove and fussing at Uncle Ollie to rouse his lazy bones and get his clothes on so Millie could come in from her side of the cabin and start breakfast. Dundee dressed in the dark, hiding himself beneath the blanket until he had his pants on.

McCown put in an hour of work on the fence before breakfast. Dundee felt he ought to do something to pay for the hospitality, so he jerked an axe loose from the chopping block and cut stovewood until Millie McCown called the men in.

They ate hurriedly, McCown impatient to get on with work. Nobody talked much. Dundee stole glances at the girl by lamplight.

The sun came up. McCown blew out the lamp to save coal oil. "Well, Dundee, Uncle Ollie and I have got work to do, and I expect you're anxious to be on your way."

As a matter of fact, Dundee wasn't, for he kind of liked sitting here looking at the girl. But he knew an invitation to leave when he heard one. "I reckon. I got a right smart of ground to cover."

He was behind the saddleshed, lashing down the pack when he heard horses. He glanced cautiously around the cedar-stake wall. Five riders were nearing the cabin. A heavyset old man with a hunch to his shoulders raised a big hand, and the riders stopped. The old man rode on a couple more yards. His voice was deep and loud and carried well in the cool morning air.

"McCown, I came to parley with you."

Warren McCown stepped out onto the small porch, followed by a cringing Uncle Ollie. Both had six-shooters strapped around their waists. Millie McCown's frightened face appeared in the doorway. Seeing her, the old man took off his floppy old hat. His gray hair sparkled like frost in the early sun. His voice seemed almost pleasant for a moment. "Morning, Miss McCown. I swear, you do get prettier every time I see you."

If she made any reply, Dundee couldn't hear it. As yet unseen, he decided to stay put awhile.

The big old man said: "Little lady, what I got to say to your brother ain't of no concern to you, and if they was any cusswords to be accidentally dropped, I wouldn't want them falling on your ears. Ain't you got some chickens to feed or a cow to milk or something?"

Millie didn't move. The old man said: "I promise you, ma'am, there's not a man here would harm a hair on your head. I'd shoot ary one that tried. Now, why don't you go on off and take care of the chores or something, so me and your brother can have us a talk?"

Warren McCown said, "Go on, Millie."

Millie McCown glanced fearfully at the men, then walked briskly toward the saddleshed. Dundee stepped out of sight, knowing the men's gaze would follow her.

When she came around the shed, Dundee put his finger to his lips. He said quietly, "I reckon that's be Blue Roan?"

She grabbed Dundee's arm. "If there's trouble, will you help my brother?" Her fingers were tight. "I'll take another look at that tallybook. I'll give you the names of all the people I know."

Right then he'd have charged hell with a bucket of water if she'd asked him to. And not for any tallybook.

He stepped to his bay and gingerly slipped the carbine up out of the scabbard. He peered around the wall. The riders had their backs

turned partially to him and all their attention riveted on the Mc-
Cowns. He could hear Roan Hardesty's bull voice.

"McCown, I understand you and some of my boys butted heads
yesterday."

McCown only stared in defiance. Hardesty said: "Now boy, I
thought you and me had come to an understanding. I told you how
things was going to be. Now, they're going to *be* thataway, whether it
suits your pleasure or not."

McCown gritted, "This is my land."

"You got some papers that was signed in Austin, but you're a
long ways from Austin now. I was here before you ever come. I expect to stay here a long time yet. Whether you stay or not depends
on you." He paused. "McCown, you got guts; I'll give you credit for
that. Now, I'm not a mean sort of a man. I don't like to have to go
and get hard with anybody. And killing just ain't my idea of the
right way atall. But, boy, there's an end to my patience."

"You got no right to dictate what goes on in this whole section
of the country. You're just one man," McCown said.

"But I got a lot of men with me. *You're* just one man, McCown.
Your uncle here makes two. You don't have to have no schooling to
figure out that two is an awful little number."

Dundee thought, *And two and one makes three.* He stepped out
from behind the shed, the saddlegun cradled across his left arm, one
finger in the trigger guard. He walked slowly toward the horsemen,
until one of them heard the jingle of his spurs and turned, stiffening.
The others saw him. Big old Roan Hardesty twisted slowly in the
saddle, surprised, squinting for recognition that wouldn't come.

Dundee stopped, the rifle not pointed at anybody in particular
but in a position that it could, quickly.

Hardesty stared. "Boy, I reckon you know how to shoot that
thing?"

Dundee nodded.

Hardesty sighed in resignation. "I got a feeling you do. You some kin of McCown's?"

"Never seen him till yesterday."

"Then how come you're siding him?"

"I owe him for breakfast."

The old man's round face softened a little, for he seemed to find some odd kind of humor here. "It must've been a better breakfast than the one *I* got. Don't it occur to you that you may be paying too high a price? You could be making an awful big mistake."

"I've made a few in my time. One more won't hurt me."

"Don't bet on it." The old man pointed his heavy jaw toward the men who flanked him. "You can count, can't you? And there's plenty more where these come from. There ain't but three of you."

Dundee said evenly: "If trouble starts, I shoot you first. It wouldn't help you none if you had a *hundred* men."

The old man shrugged. "Logic like that, there ain't no use arguing with. I never did think I'd want to die in the cool of the morning; it's too pleasant a time to leave. Boys, let's be moving on. I think McCown has got a pretty good notion what I was meaning to tell him."

The men reined about, but they did it so as to keep Dundee in view. It seemed they knew Dundee was the man to contend with, rather than McCown. Roan Hardesty edged his dappled gray horse up closer to Dundee and halted. Only then did Dundee get a good look at the aging but strong face, the full power of stern gray eyes that fastened on a man like a pair of spikes. And he saw—without being told—why they called him Blue Roan. Across the side of his face, as if flung there by an angry hand, was a scattering of large blotches, like freckles almost, except that they were blue.

"Young fellow," Roan said, "nerve is a nice thing to have, long as you don't abuse it."

"I never was noted for good sense."

"You'd best cultivate it, then, or you may not be noted for long life, either." The old man turned and rode out of the McCown yard.

Warren and Ollie McCown didn't move a toe until Hardesty's men were a good two hundred yards away. Then McCown stepped down from the little porch and slowly walked to Dundee. "You didn't have to come out."

"I owed you."

"They wasn't fixing to do any shooting."

"How do you know?"

"I just know. You could've stayed put, like yesterday. Then *I* wouldn't be left owing *you*."

Dundee frowned, his patience thinning. "Does it bother you, owing somebody?"

"It chews on me like a dog worrying a bone."

"Then forget it. Like I told Hardesty, I just paid for my breakfast."

Dundee turned away sharply and left him standing there. At the saddleshed, Millie McCown waited, her face a shade whiter. She watched as he slipped the saddlegun back into the scabbard.

"Thank you, Mister Dundee."

He turned slowly, facing her. "Thank *you,* ma'am, for saying 'thanks.' You must've learned it from your old daddy. It didn't come from your brother."

"You're a good man, Mister Dundee."

"Some people would argue with that," Dundee said.

"Not with *me* they wouldn't. Now where's that tallybook?"

It turned out she didn't know but a couple of the brands. She didn't get away from this house much. But anything was good for a start. Dundee swung into the saddle, then took off his hat. "Thanks for the good meals, ma'am. They'll be long remembered."

"So will you. Come back again, when you get hungry. I'd be glad to cook some more."

"You can expect me, ma'am." He gave the lead rope a tug to

bring along the packhorse. He didn't put his hat back on until he was out of the gate.

He cut across country and found the trail of the T Bar cattle still almost as plain as yesterday. Wind had begun to smooth the tracks, but he figured a blind man could still follow them, riding backwards. He moved along at a steady trot, his gaze sweeping the cedars and the live oaks, up the valley ahead of him and back down the valley behind him. It wasn't hard to figure why the rustlers chose this route to move cattle. The grass was good and water was plentiful. They didn't have to climb up and down a lot of rocky hills. That would appeal to a lazy man. In Dundee's reckoning, the average rustler was inclined to be basically a lazy man, shunning honest work. He had little sympathy for the breed.

Hard work, he had always figured, was not something to be feared. *Avoided,* if possible, but not feared. And not avoided at the cost of making oneself an outlaw. He had seen some of the running kind through the years, always looking back over their shoulders, always wearing guns loose in their holsters, checking the back door before they trusted the front. That, he had decided long ago, was too high a price to avoid honest work. Most of the long-riders he had ever known had lived in fear, then died broke and hungry and in mortal pain. It was a coyote life . . . and death. Badly as he disliked sweat, sometimes, it was better than blood.

He came to a grassy pecan bottom where the herd evidently had been held a while to settle down and allow the cows and calves to pair. Then the cattle had been split into two bunches. One set had been pushed westward, the other south. Dundee arbitrarily chose the south.

He had to devote closer attention to the trail now, for the ground was rockier. The cattle had been moved into rougher country where limestone hills were more rugged, the postoak and cedar thicker, the grass thinner. Times he could not be sure where the driven cattle's prints stopped and loose range cattle began. He would circle and hunt till he found a horsetrack, and then he knew he was still right.

He was about to concede defeat when he heard the bawling of a calf in pain and fear. He knew the sound. He would bet the calf had been roped, or perhaps it was being branded. Drawing the saddlegun, he walked the horse slowly, watching the ground to avoid loose rocks or fallen timber. He paused every so often to listen. Now and again he heard the bawling of another calf. Each time he could tell he was closer. Afraid to crowd his luck, he finally tied the two horses and moved on afoot, cradling the carbine. He crouched to see under the low timber, and to be able to drop instantly into cover. He picked his footing carefully amid treacherous loose stones and rotted scrub brush. He climbed a hill and tried vainly to see a way down the other side that would keep him under cover. He had to backtrack partway and circle the long way around, staying well below the hill's crest to remain in the brush.

Lying on his belly, he looked down the small valley below him to cattle bunched in one end of a crude brush corral, two men and a horse with them. Every so often one of the men would climb onto the horse, swing a loop and drag a big calf by its heels. The other man would grab the calf's tail and jerk the bawling critter down on its side, then kneel on the neck and hold a foreleg. The horse would hold the rope taut and keep the animal helpless. The rider would step down, walk to a small fire and pick out a long iron. Dundee couldn't tell at the distance, but he would bet a keg of snake-head whisky that this was a running iron, designed to change brands.

He wished for the spyglass he had left in the saddlebag. He wanted to be sure about those brands. Now the only way was to move in closer. Keeping to the brush, he crept downhill toward the corral.

He stopped again, for now he saw a rude log cabin he had overlooked from up on the hill. He studied it a long time, wondering if somebody was in it. He saw no smoke curling out of the chimney. He waited, warily watching for movement. None came.

The man throwing the calves was the big rider who had been in charge of the stolen herd, the one who had seen to it that Warren McCown was beaten to the ground. He still wore that Mexican sombrero.

Dundee didn't intend to show himself. All he wanted was to get close enough to see the brands, and to get a good look at these men's faces. Intent on watching the men, he missed seeing a downed cedar. He went down sliding, sending rocks clattering, the dead cedar limb cracking like the angry strike of buckhorns.

Damn a country where a man busts his ribs on a rock!

The men ran for cover of the heavy brush fence. Almost before Dundee quit sliding, flame lanced from between logs. A bullet ricocheted off of rocks near his face.

Dundee, you've went and spilled the buttermilk again!

He was exposed, and he knew it. What he didn't know was how good a pistol shot old Mexican Hat might be. Dundee swung the saddlegun up, took reckless aim and dropped a bullet at the place he had seen the flash. The moment the woodchips flew, he sprinted for a rock the size of a washtub. A bullet whined by him, striking sparks and scattering small rocks like buckshot. Dundee fired again, taking more time to aim. He heard a howl of pain. From behind the fence he caught a frenzy of movement. At first he thought it was the cattle, stirred into panic by the firing. Then he saw the smaller of the men jump upon the horse and spur hard, shouting. The horse went up over the low brush fence in a long leap, caught his hind feet and almost fell, straightened and went on, the rider spurring him all the way.

Dundee aimed, reconsidered and lowered the muzzle. He had never shot a man in the back, and he didn't want to cultivate any bad habits at this late date. He turned his attention back to the fence.

Well, Mexican Hat, it's your move now. Do something.

He waited, but nothing happened. Impatient, Dundee aimed at the same spot where he had fired before. Once more the chips flew.

He heard a man cry weakly: "Quit your shooting. I already been hit."

"Raise up and drop your arms over this side of the fence where I can see them."

"I'm hit in the leg. I can't get up."

"You can if you want to bad enough. I want to see you before I move."

A hand showed at the top of the fence, then another, then the mashed-in, greasy sombrero, and finally a grimy, stubbled face. The big man painfully dragged himself up onto his legs—or leg, Dundee judged—and hung his arms over the fence where Dundee could see them.

Dundee pushed to his feet, the saddlegun pointed at the man. "Now, you just stand there thataway. Make one move and I'll put a bullet through the third button on that dirty shirt."

"I'm bleeding, I tell you."

"You *could* bleed a lot worse."

Dundee had forgotten the cabin in the excitement. He glanced that way again but saw no one. He cautiously approached the wounded cowthief. The man's face was rapidly draining of color. Just as Dundee reached him, the rustler's good leg gave way, and he slid slowly down on the inside of the fence.

Fearing a trick, Dundee sprinted the last three strides to the fence and shoved the carbine across. The rustler's six-shooter lay on the ground. The man wasn't going to reach for it anyway; he was all but unconscious. Dundee climbed over the fence and set the carbine against a post, where he could reach it in a hurry. He dropped to one knee. He saw a small pool of blood beneath the leg, and a spreading stain on the trousers.

"Looks like I can still shoot a little."

"Damn you," the man muttered, eyes glazing.

"You shot at me first," Dundee pointed out. "Or else your partner did. Great partner he was. Took to the tulies like a boogered rabbit."

"Damn him, too."

Dundee slit the pants leg open. The bottom of it had sealed and was holding blood like a sagging canvas holds rain. Best he could tell, the bullet had gone clean through.

"First thing we got to do is stop this bleeding, or you'll just lie here and drain your life away." He wrapped his neckerchief around the leg, above the wound. He stuck the closed pocketknife inside and used it to twist with. The flow of blood eased to a tiny trickle. "I expect you need a good shot of whisky. You got any in the cabin?" The rustler shook his head. Dundee said: "I got some on my packhorse. I'll go fetch it. Don't you run off noplace."

He saw no guns, other than the rustler's six-shooter. Examing it, he was tempted to keep it. But on reflection he decided some town-raised judge might find him guilty of theft, even though he had taken it off of a cowthief. Courts had a way of doing off-center things like that. He hurled the pistol as far as he could throw it out into the tall grass.

The cattle moved out of a corner as he crowded them a little. He saw one cow lying dead. She had caught a bullet.

It'd be like old John Titus to dock my pay by the price of that cow. What he don't know won't never hurt him.

A horse tied to a tree back of the corral had broken one leather rein in the excitement, but the other rein had held him. Dundee opened the corral gate so the cattle could wander out, then strode to the horse. It rolled its eyes at him, hinting trouble. Warily Dundee swung up and took a tight grip with his knees, expecting the horse to pitch. It humped a little, but that was all. Dundee rode him over the rocky hill, got his own two horses and came back. The rustler still lay in the same spot.

"Nice of you to stay around," Dundee said. He tilted a bottle of Titusville whisky to take a drink himself first, then handed it to the outlaw. "Here, you better have yourself a strong snort. It won't cure anything, but it'll fuzz the edges a little." He loosened the neckerchief and found the blood had almost stopped. "We better clean this wound out or you'll get an infection in it, and somebody'll have a job of digging to do, in these rocks."

He poured whisky into the bullethole.

Dundee had thought the rustler was only half conscious, but the searing of the raw whisky brought him up cursing and fighting. Dundee poured until the bottle was almost empty. Then he held it up and stared ruefully. "See there what you went and made me do? I brought this whisky along to drink, not to pour it down some cowthief. Here, you'd just as well finish what little is left."

Done with the bandage, he leaned on the fence and studied the wounded outlaw. "Your partner may not come back. He left here in an awful hurry."

"Damn him."

"If you just lay here and nobody comes, you'll likely fade away to the Unhappy Hunting Grounds. That leg'll go to gangrene."

"Damn the leg."

"I ought to just leave you, you having a penful of burnt cattle that rightfully belong to another man." Dundee frowned thoughtfully. He had never left a man alone in this kind of shape, not even a cowthief. He knew what he had to do and he regretted it, for he hadn't intended to show himself until he had finished scouting this whole Llano River country. "Seeing as I'm the one that shot you, looks like I'm duty-bound to haul you in to Runaway."

"Damn Runaway!"

In the cabin, Dundee found a lantern and a can of coal oil. He poured the oil on the floor and walls, stepped to the door and flipped a match inside.

The whole shack wasn't worth three dollars Confederate. Burning it was a gesture rather than any real damage to the cowthieves. But a man had to start someplace.

That done, he managed to get the wounded man onto his horse and head in the direction where town ought to be.

IV

The pleasant smell of woodsmoke reached him before he came over the hill, and he knew he was nearing Runaway. Dundee stopped the bay horse at the crest and looked down on the rock and log and picket houses clustered west from the sun-bright limestone face of a bluff, just back from the riverbank. He recalled John Titus' words about Runaway being not so much a town as simply a boil on a man's backside. The description was apt.

Down the valley perhaps three quarters of a mile he saw men lined up a-horseback, waving their hats and cheering. In front of them, two riders spurred and whipped their horses in a tight race, coming to the turnaround point, sliding and then spurring back to the finish line. Dundee had lost track of days, but he figured this was Sunday. Horseracing wasn't decent, except on a Sunday. Other days, a man was supposed to work.

The wounded rustler was slumped in the saddle, tied on so he couldn't slide off if he lapsed into unconsciousness. Dundee considered turning the man's horse loose here and letting it carry him on down into town where somebody would find him. But that was chancy. It would be like a fool horse to stop and graze, or even head home again, so long as the man in the saddle was unable to rein him or spur him any.

If I got it to do, I'd just as well get on with it. He led the horses down off of the hill.

Dundee had seen a few army-camp "Chihuahuas" and "scabtowns" in his time, the sort of makeshift cutthroat communities that followed in the wake of the military like scavenging dogs. This looked like one of those, except there weren't any soldiers.

Studying an aimless scatter of ugly buildings—most of them saloons plain and simple—he remembered what Titus had said about there possibly being a few good people here.

Damn few, if any, Dundee judged.

The first place he came to was a wagonyard, its fence built of cedar pickets sunk into the ground and tied together at the top by strips of green rawhide. Most wagonyards had a good-sized livery barn, but not this one. Where men slept beneath the stars much of the time themselves, nobody thought of putting *horses* under a roof. The barn was nothing more than a big shed. A bewhiskered man slouched out front on an upended barrel. A considerable pile of wood shavings lay in front of him, and he was adding to it right along. He squinted at the horses and said: "It'll be two bits a head. They'll run loose in the corral. You can sleep under the shed for nothing, provided you don't get careless and set fire to the hay. That comes extra."

"I ain't trying to put the horses up. I got a man here with a bad wound in his leg. Is there a doctor in this town?"

The man got up and lazily walked around to Mexican Hat's horse. "Who is he?"

"Can't rightly say. Maybe his name is Damn. That's about the only word I been able to get out of him."

"Who shot him?"

"I did."

The stableman frowned. "Your aim ain't much good, is it?"

"I asked you if there's a doctor here."

"No doctor. Far as I know, there never was. I reckon most people here are straight-enough shots that when a man gets hit he don't need no doctor; he needs a preacher. But there ain't no preacher, neither."

"There ought to be somebody to look after a wounded man."

"You might carry him down to the Llano River Saloon. There's a woman down there pretty good at patching up after other people's sloppy shooting. Ask for Katy Long." The stableman's eyes narrowed. "Stranger here, ain't you?"

Dundee nodded.

"Well, that feller you got there, I recognize him now. He belongs to old Blue Roan. You won't be a stranger here very long." His gaze drifted to the T Bar brand on the packhorse. "I expect you got that one awful cheap."

Dundee shrugged. They'd know soon enough. "I came by him legal. I work for John Titus."

The stableman said quietly, "May you rest in peace."

Dundee took his time, studying the town as he moved along. Most of the buildings, he noted, were devoted to the sale of strong spirits and sundry types of entertainment. They ranged from little picket shacks that reminded him of a chicken crate up to one big, long structure built of stone. That one bore a small painted sign saying "Llano River Salon." They'd left an O out of the last word, but he doubted that many people noticed.

He tied the horses and said to Mexican Hat, "Don't you run off."

"Go to hell," the man mumbled.

Gratitude, Dundee reflected, had gone the way of the buffalo.

A skinny little bartender scowled. From his looks, Dundee judged that he drank vinegar instead of whisky. "What's your pleasure, friend?"

"I don't know as it *is* a pleasure. I'm looking for a woman by the name of Katy Long."

The frown didn't change. "I expect Katy is taking her siesta."

"Wake her up. I can't wait."

The frown deepened. "You been steered wrong about Katy, friend. Anyhow, there's a couple of places down the street where the girls don't ever sleep. Go try one of them."

"I got a man outside bleeding to death. I'm told she's pretty good at patching up things like that."

The bartender sighed. "She won't like it, but she'll come." He walked through a double door and down a hall. Dundee could hear him knock and call for Katy. In a moment he was back. "She'll be here directly. Let's me and you see if we can get your friend in."

A rider came jogging down the street, half asleep from some long celebration, almost bumping into the tied horses. He came awake at sight of the slumped-over man in the sombrero. "Jayce! Jason Karnes! What in hell happened to you?"

Karnes just mumbled. The rider glanced at Dundee and the bartender. "I better go tell Bunch. And Roan." He jerked the horse around and spurred into a lope toward the races.

Dundee said to the bartender: "Well, I've found out who this is. Now, who is Bunch?"

"Bunch Karnes. He's a brother to Jayce."

"Tough?"

"Mixes rattlesnake juice with his whisky."

Physically, there wasn't much strength in the little bartender. He lent moral support but not much else. Dundee supported most of the weight as they carried Karnes, dropping his sombrero in the dust. A young woman came through the double doors at the back of the room, still buttoning a high-necked dress. "Bring him on back. We'll put him on a cot and see what we can do."

She was a good-looking woman, and Dundee figured she ought to be successful in her trade. She held a door open. He brushed against her, not altogether by accident.

The woman said to the bartender: "Cricket, we'll need hot water. You better go start a fire in my cookstove."

Dundee pulled the wounded man's boots off and pitched them under the cot. "I reckon he's yours now, Katy."

She showed resentment at the familiar use of her name. "You can call me Miss Long. You don't know me, and I don't know you."

He started to say, *I know you, even if I never saw you before.* She must have seen it in his eyes. Her dislike of him was instantaneous. "You've got the wrong idea, cowboy. I make enough money selling whisky. I don't have to sell anything else." Curtly she said, "Let's see what we can do for your friend Jayce."

"He's not my friend."

"You brought him in."

"Figured I ought to. I shot him."

"Accident?"

"Not especially."

She carefully unwrapped the cloth Dundee had bound around the leg. Karnes moaned and cursed. The woman said contemptuously: "Why didn't you just go ahead and kill him? Don't you know a dirty bandage can kill a man just as dead as a bullet can?"

"I had to make do with what was there."

"Lucky thing the wound bled some and washed itself clean."

The bartender brought hot water in a pan. Katy Long cleansed the area around the wound with the skill of a trained nurse. Karnes sucked air between his teeth, but she was careful not to hurt him more than she had to.

Dundee decided to give credit where it was due. "You know your business."

"My business is whisky, and nothing else. There's no profit in this." To Karnes she said, "Grit your teeth and hang on." Karnes gripped the cotframe, his knuckles going white. He cursed and raved.

The woman glanced accusingly at Dundee. "I'm glad you had to watch."

Dundee wanted to defend himself, but pride stopped him. He didn't owe any explanation to a saloon woman. Let her think what she damn pleased.

He heard the strike of heavy boots in the hall. A gruff voice shouted: "Jayce! Where you at, Jayce?"

The woman called impatiently: "You don't have to holler. He's here."

A tall figure filled the narrow doorway. Dundee's gaze lifted to a dirty, tobacco-stained beard, to a pair of angry, blood-tinged eyes. The tall man demanded, "Who was it done this to you Jayce?"

Katy Long tried to head him off. "He'll be all right."

Dundee tensed. He knew this would be Bunch Karnes, the brother.

Karnes seemed not to hear the woman. "Jayce!" His voice was more demanding. "I said, who done this to you? I want to know."

Dundee was glad he had strapped on his pistol. He let his hands rest at his hips, handy. He suggested: "Maybe you ought to leave him be."

Hard eyes cut to Dundee's face. "What business is it of yours?"

The wounded man rasped: "He's the one done it, Bunch. He's the one shot me."

Karnes' hand dropped. Dundee brought his pistol up so fast that Karnes froze, blinking. At this range Dundee couldn't miss. Karnes swallowed.

Katy Long watched open-mouthed. For long seconds she held her breath until Karnes slowly raised his hand. Then, the moment of crisis past, she pointed to the door. "Bunch Karnes, this is *my* place, and I'm telling you to clear out. If you two have got to kill each other, do it someplace else. I don't want to clean up the mess."

The gunman's fingers flexed, his flashing eyes watching Dundee's pistol. Dundee didn't let the pistol waver from Karnes' belly. He didn't speak, for at times like this he'd never seen much gain in conversation.

Anger high in her face, the woman said sternly: "Karnes, I told you to *git!* You-all do any shooting in here, one of you is liable to hit your brother. Damn if I want to see all my work wasted."

Karnes sullenly backed toward the door. "When you come out, cowboy, I'll be waiting in the saloon."

His eyes didn't leave Dundee until he was in the hall and out of the line of vision. Dundee listened to the heavy footsteps tromping across the floor. His lungs cried out for air, and only then did he realize he had held his breath the whole time.

Katy stood in silence, her face paled.

Dundee told her, "It's all right now."

Her voice was sharp. "I don't know how you figure that, with him waiting out yonder in the saloon. You don't know this town. You don't know people like Bunch and Jason Karnes."

"I've run into a few."

"Bunch Karnes isn't the smartest man on earth, but he's hard. Minute you step out into that hall, he'll put a bullet in you."

"What difference would that make to you?"

"Blood leaves a dark stain on the floor. It's hard to get out."

"I'll try not to cause you no extra work." Dundee moved to the deep, narrow window. Its frame was set so that the window moved sluggishly to one side. He didn't know that he trusted the woman to keep quiet, but circumstances didn't permit him much choice. He slipped out the window and eased to the ground.

Pistol in hand, Dundee edged up to the one side window of the saloon and peered cautiously with one eye. The bartender saw him but gave no sign. Bunch Karnes sat facing the double doors, pistol lying in front of him on a small square table.

Dundee moved hurriedly past the window and on to the front of the building. He still held the pistol, but in a fight, the carbine would suit him better. He walked up to the bay at the hitching rail, drew the carbine and dropped his pistol back into its holster. He moved quietly up to the door. Inside, he could see Karnes seated, back turned, his attention still fixed on the double doors. The bartender saw Dundee and dropped out of sight behind the bar.

Dundee leveled the carbine. "Karnes, back away from that table. And leave your six-shooter right where it's at."

Karnes went stiff. Dundee said: "I got a gun pointed at you. Give me a reason and I'll blow a hole in you they could run a wagon through."

Karnes slowly stood up. Dundee held his breath, watching the pistol. Karnes' hand was only inches from it. He drew clear of the table and turned, hands empty, face raging.

Dundee said: "Why don't you just quit? I got no wish to kill you."

"But I'm going to kill *you*, cowboy."

"Your brother's alive. Why don't you just let it go at that?"

He wasn't reaching Bunch Karnes and knew it. *I ought to shoot him where he stands,* Dundee thought. *That would be the end of it. There won't be an end to it till I do.*

The man was a thief, and in all likelihood a killer. The world would shed few tears if Dundee cut him down. In fact, it would be a better place. But Dundee knew he couldn't pull the trigger, not this way.

"Step away from that table, and leave the pistol."

"I can get another pistol."

A voice in Dundee kept telling him, *Go on and kill him.*

Boots clomped on the front steps. Dundee stepped backward toward the corner, not letting the carbine waver from Karnes.

A big man blocked off most of the light from the doorway, the same heavy-built old man who had been at McCown's.

This was Blue Roan.

Roan Hardesty paused in the door, as if undecided whether to come in or to step back out into the street. He saw then that Karnes was out of reach of his pistol. He cast a long look at Dundee. "You again. They told me some stranger had brung Jayce Karnes to town with a bullethole in him. I ought to've knowed it'd turn out to be you."

Dundee said, "If you got any influence over this man, you better use it."

Hardesty turned to Karnes. "Well?"

"It was him that shot Jayce. I'm fixing to kill him."

"With your six-shooter lying over there on the table? You're just fixing to get your light blowed out, is all. This cowboy looks like he means business, Bunch."

"So do I."

"I need you alive, Bunch. Anyway, the weather's too hot for a funeral. You git yourself along."

"But I . . ."

"I said git on along. I'll talk to you later."

Karnes stared resentfully at Roan Hardesty, his eyes then drifting to Dundee and spilling their hatred. "I'm going because Roan says to. But don't think it's over, cowboy. I ain't even started yet."

He stomped to the door, down the steps and out into the street, leaving the pistol on the table. Dundee held the carbine, not pointing it directly at Hardesty but not letting the muzzle drop far, either.

Hardesty's voice was deep and gravelly. "You can put away the hardware. I ain't going to do you no harm."

"You can bet your life you're not."

"I promise you. I don't ever break a promise." He turned. "Who the hell is tending bar around here? Where's Cricket?"

The little bartender's head tentatively rose from behind the pine bar, eyes cautiously appraising the situation before he stood up to full height.

Hardesty said, "Whisky, Cricket." He started toward the few small tables. Dundee picked up Karnes' pistol and shoved it into his waistband. Hardesty pulled out a chair. "Set yourself down."

Dundee sat in a corner, where nobody could come up behind him. He watched Hardesty with distrust. The bartender set down a bottle and two glasses. Hardesty pulled the cork and poured the glasses full. "Here's to all the bold and foolish men. And there's a hell of a lot of them." He downed his drink in one swallow. Dundee didn't touch his own. Hardesty noticed. "You don't trust me?"

"I make it a practice not to trust nobody."

"A safe policy. But I gave a promise. Old Blue Roan has broke most of the laws that was ever passed, but he don't break a promise."

Dundee looked at the blue spots on the old man's broad face. "I didn't figure they called you that where you could hear it."

"I'm not ashamed of my face, boy. I bear it like a medal, a thing to be proud of. I got it in the line of duty. I was in the late war, boy, the war between the states. We charged into an artillery emplacement, and the whole thing went up . . . right in my face. I was lucky I kept my eyes. When it was over, I had these marks for life. Sure, I fretted over them awhile, but bye and bye it come to me that they was honest marks. They was like a medal that a man wears all the time and don't even take off with his clothes. They tell the world that Roan Hardesty done his job." He paused to take another drink. "People has said some hard things about me, but there's one thing they can't take away. I done my duty, and I got the marks to prove it." He refilled his glass. "Anyway, I didn't come here to talk about me. I want to find out about *you*. How come you to shoot Jason Karnes?"

"I come up on him and his partner venting the brands on some cattle. He shot at me first."

"Where was this?"

"Back up in the hills, close to a cabin." Dundee pointed his chin.

"How come you fooling around up there, anyway?"

Dundee figured he'd just as well tell it all. "To see what I could find out."

"What *did* you find out?"

"Where some of John Titus' cattle been going."

Roan Hardesty got up from the table. Dundee took a firm grip on the saddlegun. Hardesty walked to the door and looked out at Dundee's horses. "I'm getting old, I guess. Never even noticed the brand on that packhorse when I come in. You working for John Titus?"

Dundee nodded.

Hardesty spat on the floor. "What's old John figure on doing?"

"If I told you that, you'd know as much as *I* do."

Hardesty sat down again, taking another sip out of the glass. "Old Honest John. Bet he never told you he was a pretty good hand with a long rope once. As good a thief as *I* was, pretty near. But he got to letting his conscience talk to him. And then he went and married. Church-going kind, she was. She ruint him; he went honest. Got rich and turned his back on all his old friends."

"Maybe you ought to've done the same."

"No need to. I always had women. Never had to marry one."

"I mean, you should've turned honest."

"The meanest, dullest, most miserable people I know are honest. I like it better where I'm at."

"Somebody may kill you one of these days."

"You, maybe?"

"I hope not." Dundee wouldn't have admitted it, but he found himself drawn to this old reprobate. The old man had the same disarming frankness as John Titus.

"I'd as soon not have to shoot you neither, Dundee. I always had a soft spot for an honest man with guts. Wisht I'd had you with me in the war. A few more like me and you, we'd of whipped them Yankees."

"We might have."

Blue Roan stared at him through narrowed eyes, appraising him like he would judge a horse. "Dundee, I know John Titus. Whatever he's paying you, it ain't enough for the risk. Join up with me and I'll show you where the money's at."

"Venting other people's brands? I reckon not."

"Look at it this way: it's free range, most of it. Biggest part of the land John Titus uses still belongs to the state of Texas. He's taking the use of it free, not paying a dime. And who is the state of Texas? Why, it's me and you and everybody else. John Titus is robbing all us taxpayers. If we run off a few piddling head now and then, it's just our way of making sure he pays something for the grass. We're doing the state of Texas a service, you might say."

The reasoning brought Dundee a smile. He wondered if Roan Hardesty had ever actually paid a dollar of tax to the state of Texas. "I made John Titus a promise. I'll keep it."

The outlaw regretfully accepted Dundee's judgment. "I like a man who keeps a promise. But I can't guarantee you your safety. I can't be responsible for people like Bunch Karnes who think slow but shoot fast."

"I've always took care of myself."

"Keep on doing it. I'd sooner not have you on my conscience." Hardesty stood up to leave, then turned again. "What connection you got with the McCowns?"

"Like I told you, I stopped there and they fed me."

"That's all?"

Worry started building in Dundee. He hadn't intended to get the McCowns any deeper in trouble than they already were. "That's all, and I'll swear to it. I never saw them before."

Hardesty paused in the doorway. "You're worried because you think this is going to cause me to bear down on them. Don't fret yourself. Them and me, we had our trouble before you ever come here." A faint smile tugged at his big mouth. "That girl is the one you're really thinking about, ain't she? You know, she reminds me of the one old John Titus married. Pass her by, Dundee. She's not for you, all that honeysuckle and home cooking. She'd hogtie you like a slick-eared yearling."

When the old man was gone, Katy Long came back. "I heard most of that. You really come from John Titus?"

"Yep."

"And you tell anybody who asks you?"

"I never been one to lie."

"There's a time and a place for everything. In your place, I'd lie."

"Way I heard it, a couple of other fellers come into this country and lied. They got killed. Me, I just come to find out who's been taking John Titus' cattle, and where they're going with them, that's all. Maybe you'd like to tell me, and save me some trouble."

"You're *already* in trouble. I'm keeping clear of it."

Through the front door Dundee could see the corner of a small mercantile building across the rutted road that passed for a street. He saw a shadow move. He stood up, the carbine in his hands.

Katy Long caught the tension. "What is it?"

"You said you didn't want no trouble. Just stay put." Keeping within the darkness of the room, he moved to a point where he had a better view of the mercantile. He watched a few minutes, waiting for more movement. He saw a hat brim edge out, and then part of Bunch Karnes' face as the tall man peeked around the corner. He saw a little of a gunbarrel.

Well, Dundee thought regretfully, *I tried. I could as well have shot him while ago.*

He maneuvered toward the door, staying close to the wall. He paused a moment, his shoulder to the wall, gauging where the horses were tied. He didn't want a stray shot to kill his bay or the pack animal. He glanced at the wide-eyed bartender, at the silent woman. He took a deep breath, leaped out the door and lit running.

He took Karnes by surprise. Dundee made three long strides before Karnes stepped out into the open, the pistol extended almost to arm's length in front of him, swinging to try to bring it in line with the running target. Dundee threw himself to the ground. He saw the flash as he brought the carbine up. He aimed at Karnes' chest and squeezed the trigger.

Karnes was flung back grabbing at his shirt in open-mouthed bewilderment, the pistol falling from his hand. He crumpled in a heap.

Cautiously Dundee moved forward, trying to watch Karnes and at the same time looking up and down the street for trouble. He kicked the pistol away, then knelt. He touched Karnes and drew his hand back. Karnes shuddered once, then lay still.

Dundee arose, turned and walked back to the saloon, the carbine smoking in his hands. In the front door stood Katy Long and the little bartender.

A bitter taste in his mouth, Dundee said, "Well, at least we didn't leak blood on your floor."

She didn't back away from him. "Don't take it out on me. When you came here for John Titus, you knew you might kill somebody, or maybe get killed yourself."

He nodded darkly, watching a small crowd begin to gather around the body.

"Then don't blame me. All I do is operate a saloon."

"In an outlaw town."

"Look, cowboy, nobody's taken care of me since I was fourteen. I've minded my own business and left everybody else's alone. I just sell whisky. And you're shooting my customers."

From down the hall Jason Karnes' voice called weakly: "What's happened out there? Somebody tell me what's happened!" In a moment, when no one went to him, he shouted again, anxiety rising: "Bunch! Bunch! Where you at, Bunch? What's happened out there? Bunch!"

Katy Long's handsome face twisted with regret. "I suppose now it's up to me to tell him. Cowboy, I wish to hell you'd ride out of here."

"I was just fixing to leave."

V

Dundee had had a bellyful of Runaway. The hour or so he had whiled away in its contentious clime would do him till hell froze over. As far as he was concerned, they could burn the place to the ground. He even studied a bit about dropping a match in the dry grass, but the wind was blowing in the wrong direction.

Bunch Karnes' blood drying in the sand was not the first Dundee had ever seen, or even the first he'd ever spilled. But this was one experience not improved by repetition. It was a thing that curdled a man's stomach, made him want to get off someplace and face up to his own private demons alone, with no eyes watching. Dundee couldn't see that it would benefit his mission any to hang around Runaway. Chances were somebody would just crowd him into smoking up the carbine again. Let John Titus do the shooting, he thought. They were *his* cattle.

So, looking over his shoulder to be sure the only thing behind him was his shadow, he left Runaway. He rode west awhile, then south. Long days stretched into weeks while he prowled the endless hills, leading the packhorse, looking, mapping, noting brands. Sometimes when he found a cabin or a camp, he would sit among the cedars on some high vantage point and watch for hours with that spyglass, until he was sure he knew what brand went with what people, and whether it was a bonafide brand or some optimistic conversion.

Times, he knew he was not only watching but being watched. Times he would look back and see a horseman or two patiently trailing after him, keeping distance. When he stopped, they stopped. When he rode, they rode.

Nobody made a threatening move, but no longer did he enjoy that feeling of obscurity he had had before the trip to Runaway. He was sure the word about him had spread through all these hills. Maybe they didn't know exactly what he was up to, but they knew he was here. He had to watch for more than cattle now. He took to eating his supper before dark, then riding into the darkness before making cold camp in a thicket somewhere. If they caught him in his blankets, they had to be doing a good job of hunting.

The list of blotted brands kept growing in his tallybook. It had worried him at first because he had so few names to go with the brands. He had no one to go to, no one to ask. But in time he quit stewing about it. He knew the greasy-sack spreads where these brands were claimed. He knew many of the men by appearance, even if he didn't know their names. Besides, most of them probably weren't using the names their mothers had given them anyway. A cowthief by any name was still a cowthief.

There came a point, south, where Dundee found no more T Bar cattle. He came across other fresh brands on grown cattle, and he didn't doubt they'd originally been something else, but not the T Bar. These likely had been rustled in the south and brought north, just as Titus cattle had been stolen in the north and brought south. The way Dundee pictured it, these Llano hills were kind of a crossroads for livestock that had made a nocturnal change in ownership. Some of the cattle he saw here bore all the trademarks of Mexico. They had, no doubt, crossed the Rio Grande in a right smart of a rush.

Well, they were a problem for *somebody,* but not for Dundee. His wages were being paid by John Titus. He began bearing east again, and some to the north. Slowly he was completing a wide circle, and with it, his map. The circle would be closed when he returned to the part of the country where he had started, the Rocker M.

That ranch had been stirring in his mind like a restless squirrel worrying a pile of leaves. Every time he came across a valley which in any way resembled the McCown country, he remembered the young woman standing in the dog-run between the two sections of the sturdy log cabin, her long brown hair floating gently in the wind. He remembered the slenderness of her, the voice, the eyes, the soft woman smell.

She came to him in the golden sunlight of morning, and in the dark of night. She came like a song that has been once heard, and not clearly, but which echoes on and on in memory.

Sometimes, staring at the darkness in a live oak motte or cedar thicket, he would rub his scratchy beard, smell the dry dust and the smoke that had sifted into the fiber of all his clothes and clung there. He was glad she could not see him this way. He would try to be sure that she never saw him like that again.

He was carrying close to two hundred dollars now, about as much money as he had ever owned at one time in his life. That wasn't much prospect to offer a woman. Times, when he thought of her, he also thought of the free-wheeling, easy-drifting life he'd led, and wondered if he was really ready to change. Damn, but it had been fun. Hard, hungry, stifling hot or freezing cold . . . but fun, just the same. A restlessness still stirred in him, a prickly feeling that came over him every so often and set him to moving without direction, without any purpose except simply to *go*. It wasn't much recommendation to present to a woman. Not *that* kind of woman.

Times, too, he got to wondering if word had drifted back to her about the shooting in Runaway. It probably had. When she next looked at him, would she see Dundee, or would she just see the blood on his hands?

This was mostly a cattle country, but now and again he would run across a band of sheep, usually but not always herded by a Mexican.

One sheep outfit he watched was made up of three bands, each band totaling twelve or fifteen hundred sheep.

These, Dundee figured, he didn't have to worry about. A man with a flock of sheep on his hands was too busy to be stealing cows. Maybe more sheep was what it would take to civilize this country.

He was nearing the close-up point on his circle when the heavy rain came. It poured bountifully from a leaden sky, the thunder rolling, the water singing as it filtered down through the hillside grass in a growing flood. Dundee had no idea where to find a ranchhouse. He searched for an overhang he could squeeze under, but he couldn't find one. He huddled beneath the live oaks until the rain trickled down through the leaves and reached him. The horses hung their heads and took it, for they had never known a roof. But Dundee was soaked to the skin and shivering, his shoulders hunched and his teeth clicking. He decided he had as well be miserable on the move as miserable hunkered on the ground beneath these leaky trees.

At length he came down off of a hill and saw a picket shack. It was a miserable hovel, and any other time he wouldn't have given it a second glance. But now with the rain and the wind chilling him to the bone, it looked as pretty as a marble church. In a set of brush pens he saw goats hunched against the cold. They weren't leggy and spotted and made up of all colors like the Mexican goats he had often seen. These were Angoras, carrying fine, long white mohair which tended to curl into ringlets, even wet. But he was too cold to wonder much or pause to admire a penful of drenched goats. He shouted, "Hello the house!"

A slump-shouldered old man stood in the open door, the wind whipping his snowy beard as he squinted through the rain. He pointed a long, bony finger. "Shed's yonderway. Put your horses up and git yourself back here to the dry."

The shed was mostly just an arbor closed on three sides and

given a liberal cover of sod and brush on top to turn the water. He took off saddle and pack and turned the horses loose. He stood a moment under the shed, the first time in hours the rain hadn't been beating down on his back. It felt good here. But the shack would feel even better, for he could see smoke curling up from a stone chimney.

He stopped abruptly as he saw a cowhide stretched across the top of a fence. It was fresh, maybe two or three days old. He started to pass it by, but curiosity was stronger than the cold. The flesh side was turned up, the brand easily visible through it.

The T Bar.

Hell of a country, he thought, where even a goatherder steals cattle.

He dug the pistol out of his saddlebag and strapped it around his waist, beneath his yellow slicker. He stalked across the yard and into the cabin. The old man stared at him with pale gray eyes that were almost lost beneath bushy gray brows. A Mexican boy of eighteen or so sat on a wooden-framed goathide cot in a corner, rolling a brown-paper cigarette.

Dundee was too cold to play games. He flung the challenge. "You got a cowhide out yonder with a T Bar on it!"

The old man nodded as if it wasn't any news to him. "I bet you're that feller I been hearing about. Ain't your name *Dandy?*"

"It's *Dun*dee. And I asked you about that hide."

The old man looked sympathetic. "You're cold. And I bet you ain't yet et."

"I'm asking you for an answer."

"I bet you're hungry. Well, you peel some of them wet clothes off and we'll have dinner here directly. You'll feel like a new man when you've surrounded some of this fresh beef."

"About that hide . . ."

"Let's don't talk business right now. You're cold and hungry, and

I never did like to argue with a hungry man. A man just ain't reasonable. You git your belly filled, then we'll talk."

A Dutch oven sat astraddle some blazing oakwood in the open
fireplace, steak sizzling. Dundee pointed his chin. "That steak yonder, I reckon it came out from under that hide?"

The old fellow nodded.

Dundee exclaimed: "That's T Bar beef. You expect me to eat it?"

"Why not? You work for old Titus, don't you? And if you was
on the home ranch you'd be eating Titus beef, wouldn't you? So
what's the difference if you eat it *here*? Who's better entitled to it?"

The off-center logic went by Dundee so fast he couldn't argue
with it. The steak smelled good. And the old man had called the
tune: Dundee was hungry as a she-wolf with six pups.

The Mexican wasn't saying anything. Dundee didn't know if he
understood English, even. But the herder sat like a suspicious watch-
dog, glancing protectively at the old man, most of the time keeping
his narrowed eyes fastened on Dundee. Dundee had a cold feeling
that if he made any manacing move toward the old goat man, he'd
have to beat that young Mexican to the floor or be crushed himself.
In addition, there was a black and white dog of a breed or mixture
that Dundee didn't know. It sat under the Mexican's feet, gaze never
wavering from the stranger. Dundee might have to fight *him,* too.

Coffee boiled in a pot in the corner of the fireplace. The old
man poured a cup of cold water in to settle the grounds and brought
the pot up to set it on the rough table. It left black ash marks, but
they were hardly noticeable; the table was already as discolored as it
could get. "Steak's done. Got a pot of beans, too. Hope you don't
mind cold bread."

The tinware was battered and tarnished, but that was of no matter. The food was good. Dundee's eyebrows went up when the old
man lifted one piece of steak out of the popping grease and dropped

it into an old tin plate on the dirt floor, for the dog. The dog sniffed it eagerly but knew enough to wait for it to cool. The old man dropped him a couple of cold biscuits to keep him busy. "Man's got a good working dog, he's got to take care of him," he said.

Dundee wondered how John Titus would appreciate it, seeing his beef fed to a goatherder's dog.

The meal over, Dundee leaned back and rubbed his stomach. "That was sure fine."

The old man took the compliment with grace. "No trick to it if you got good beef."

"Such as Titus beef?"

"I tried not to notice the brand." The old man smiled gently. "While ago I said you'd be eating T Bar beef if you was on the home ranch. Fact is, I bet you'd be eating some neighbor's. John Titus kills strays, just like everybody else. A man's own beef don't ever taste as good."

"Titus might not see it your way."

"The fact is, Dandy, I kept that steer from being stole."

"What do you mean?"

"Some fellers brought a herd of cattle through here three . . . four days ago, heading south. They scattered my goats by accident, so to make it right they offered me this steer. He was lame and couldn't keep up anyway."

"The rest of the cattle . . . they carry a T Bar brand?"

"Like I said, in this country I don't ever see no brands."

"The men driving those cattle . . . who were they?"

The oldtimer smiled thinly. "Now, Dandy, the way I lived to get so old was by not seeing anything that wasn't my business, and not saying nothing about what I didn't see."

"I could tell John Titus you been eating his beef."

"If you think it'll make things right, I'll swap you for that steer.

He was lame and not worth much. I'll pick out two of my top goats, and you can take them along."

"What would I do with two goats?"

"That'd be up to you. All I want is to pay a debt if I got one. And I ain't sure as I do. After all, I *did* save that steer from being stole."

Dundee shrugged. He didn't figure John Titus would be very hard on a man who just butchered a steer once in a while to eat. Especially if Dundee never told him. Dundee changed the subject. "Them are unusual-looking goats you got. They work good in this country?"

"Them is Angorys . . . *hair*-goats. You shear mohair off of them, like you shear wool off of a sheep. They're the coming thing for this part of the country, once the cowthieves leave. They eat brush and stuff like that. If he has to, a goat can live on next to nothing. And a man can live on goat. Hard to starve a goat man to death."

The old man stared through the door at the rain still pelting down. "Looks like it's liable to hang on awhile. You're welcome to stay here, Dandy."

"Much obliged."

"Where you headed when it's over with? You figuring on trying to trail them cattle?"

Dundee shook his head. "Won't be no tracks left after this rain. No, I reckon I'll go see some folks. Then I'll head back to the T Bar."

"This is a good country down here. You could do worse than stay."

"What for? I got no cattle, and I don't aim to steal any."

"You could start small and build as the country builds."

"This is nothing but an outlaw country."

"The outlaws won't last. They're just part of a country's growing up, like a kid has to put up with measles and chickenpox. One day they'll all be gone, but the country'll be here. All we need in these hills is some good people . . . and a little more rain."

"That," said Dundee, "is all *hell* needs."

VI

D undee had jogged along in a deliberate trot all day, keeping a checkrein on his patience. Now the double log cabin lay ahead of him, and patience evaporated like a summer mist. He touched spurs to the bay, picking up into an easy lope.

All morning he had watched for signs of Warren McCown or Uncle Ollie. He thought they might be riding these hills and the long valleys to check their cattle after the rains. Now, approaching the homeplace spring and the corrals, he looked for the men again. He still didn't see them. A single horse stood in the pen, near the saddleshed. Unsaddling his bay and dropping the pack, Dundee noticed that Uncle Ollie's saddle hung on its rack, but Warren's was gone.

The lazy old whelp probably waited till Warren was out of sight, then snuck back to loaf, Dundee thought. He spread dry mesquite beans for the horses, then set out afoot toward the cabin.

Millie stood in the dog-run, smiling, her long hair adrift in the south wind which had come up strong now that the rains were over and the clouds broken away. He walked briskly toward her. She didn't wait; she hurried to meet him halfway. She stopped when they were three paces apart, her eyes ashine. She made an instinctive gesture of opening her arms to receive him, realized what she had done and brought her hands together.

Dundee stopped. He fought a compelling urge to scoop her into his arms. A man didn't do that . . . not to a woman like this. He swallowed and remembered his place. He had no right.

He crushed his hat in his hands the way he wanted to crush *her.*

"Dundee! I don't know when I've ever been so glad to see somebody."

"Been a while, ain't it?" He rubbed his face and managed a nervous smile. "This time I shaved *before* I got here." He had washed out his clothes, too, though they had dried with the wrinkles of wadded-up paper.

"You didn't have to," she said.

"Yes, I had to."

She smiled, and watching her warmed him like a long drink of whisky. He'd never seen a woman before that a man could get drunk just looking at.

She said, "Dundee, I hope you can stay."

"Well. . . ."

"Warren's not here, and Uncle Ollie's had a fall."

"Bad hurt?"

"Doesn't seem like he's got any bones broken. But he's sore and stiff, and it pains him to move. I need help with him till Warren gets back."

He wondered suspiciously whether the old man was really lame or just lazy. "Where did Warren go?"

"Went south to buy cattle."

Dundee stopped walking. "South, you say? Why south?"

She saw the look on his face and stared in puzzlement. "North of us there's nothing much but T Bar. There are already too many T Bar cattle running around here with somebody else's brand on them. Warren didn't want any, not even *with* a bill of sale."

Remembering what the old goat man had told him, Dundee counted back. "How many days since Warren left?"

"Six. Six days and seven hours." There was sadness in the way she said it.

Six. He frowned, counting on his fingers, finally shaking his head. *Not Warren. Surely not Warren.*

"Come on," Millie said, "let me take you to Uncle Ollie. He'll be real tickled to see a friendly face."

If I find the old codger faking, it ain't going to be none too friendly.

Uncle Ollie lay on his cot, atop the old woolen blankets. He had his britches on for propriety, a concession to Millie, Dundee guessed. But his faded red underwear was his cover from the waist up. It bore patches that must have been stitched there by Millie McCown's patient fingers. Ollie raised himself up on his left elbow and stuck out his right hand, wincing as if it caused him great pain. "Howdy, Dundee. Millie said she seen you ride in, but I didn't hear you. Used to could hear a grasshopper spit from a hundred yards. Used to do a heap of things I can't do no more."

Dundee asked with suspicion, "Horse throw you off?"

Sheepishly the old man said: "Wisht one had. There's a little bit of glory in that. Truth is, I was fishing and fell off of the bank."

Dundee nodded. It was in character, all right. The old man was probably spreading it on thicker than it really was, but he was likely telling the truth in the main.

Millie said: "Just the same, we'll tell Warren it was a horse."

Dundee shrugged. "I reckon a little lie once in a while don't hurt nothing, long's it's for a good cause."

Ollie smiled thinly. "Glad you see it my way, Dundee. Wisht Warren did."

I expect he sees more than you think he does, Dundee said to himself.

Ollie complained: "Way he goes all the time, he'll be old before long hisself. Then maybe he'll know. Only it'll be too late then for me. I'll be dead and in the grave." He sat up and dropped his legs off the cot, wincing and groaning. Millie had moved across the room to the cabinet, where she had some biscuit dough working. Ollie whispered, "Help me outside, will you?"

Dundee took a thin arm around his shoulder and assisted the old man to his feet. Ollie moved slowly, sucking breath between his teeth. Outside, he waved for a pause to rest. "Much obliged. Some things a man can't have a woman help him do. Been having to make this trip all by myself, an it's been pure hell."

"Ollie, when did you take this fall?"

"Why, it was the day Warren left. The very same day. How come you to ask?"

"Just curious." Dundee glanced toward the woodpile, knowing Millie had done most of the chopping herself, unless Warren had left her a supply. Likely he hadn't. That's what Ollie was supposed to be for.

Back in the cabin, Ollie stretched on the cot and began to talk about the old days, when the world had been freer and fresher and the air keener and men more honest and life had been a joy to live. Dundee only half listened, nodding when he thought he ought to, agreeing now and again with a quiet "Unh-hunh." Mostly he watched Millie McCown kneading dough for supper biscuits, cutting the dough and putting it out in a flat pan. He watched her roll steak in flour and never even wondered what brand was on the hide it came from under.

Uncle Ollie came completely unwound at the supper table, and Dundee noticed that even though the old man's legs were stiff and sore, his jaw swiveled quite easily, both for eating and for talking. Ollie had known every famous cowman from the Rio Grande to the Canadian River, seemed like. He had known every gunfighter and had personally witnessed every gunfight of any notoriety since the fall of the Alamo, and Dundee wondered how come he had missed that one.

Millie finished washing the dishes, put away the wet drying towel, looked at Dundee a moment, then walked to the door. "It's nice out tonight. I think I'll get some air," she said.

Ollie leaned on his elbow, nursing his pipe, eyes focused on something far beyond the room, far back in time. "Them was the days, Dundee. I tell you, it ain't nothing like that no more. People don't enjoy theirselves the way they used to."

Dundee looked outside at Millie. "Maybe they do. Maybe it's just a new bunch doing it now."

Ollie clicked his pipe against his teeth, listening to no one but himself. "No, sir, it ain't the same. I mind the time—before the war, it was—me and my brother was out on the Keechi . . ." The old man talked on, immersed in his storytelling, his mind lost in ancient memories . . . or maybe it was ancient dreams . . . it would be hard to separate one from the other. Dundee eased out the door and left him there, still talking to himself.

Millie leaned against one of the heavy cedar posts that held up the brush arbor. She stared down the valley into the gathering dusk. Dundee knew she heard him, but she didn't look around. She said: "Expecting Warren back any day now. He's been gone an awfully long time."

"Just six days, you said. Give him time. Cattle move slow."

"So do the hours, when you're out here so far from anybody, just by yourself. Oh, I don't mean that Warren and Uncle Ollie aren't good company. But I mean, you go so terribly long here sometimes and never see a soul except family. Then, when even one of the family leaves for awhile, it's like somebody had died."

"This isn't good for a woman. You shouldn't be out here."

"I belong. It's the only real home I ever had. When Dad was living, we just drifted around from ranch to ranch. Never owned anything, never stayed anywhere long enough to gather from the gardens we planted, even. Warren said we were gypsies, always on the move, never leaving anything behind us but wagon tracks. He said someday he was going to find him a place and put down roots so deep they couldn't be pulled up by anything or anybody. And I guess this is the place."

"For a woman, it ain't much."

"It's home. When you've wandered most of your life, it means something to stand on a piece of ground and call it your own. It gives you a feeling . . . I couldn't tell you what it's like . . . to look across that valley yonder and know it's yours . . . to know that come tomorrow you'll still be here . . . and next month . . . and next year."

"It's lonesome, just the same."

"Nothing is ever perfect. This is a lot better than we *used* to have. And it'll be even better yet. Warren will see to that."

Warren. Dundee realized that her brother had taken on the aspect of a father to her. The sun rose and set with Warren McCown, and would, until some other man came along to establish a new and different relationship that would displace him.

He said: "You won't always depend on Warren. One of these days some cowboy will take a good look at you and carry you off."

She turned, and he saw in her eyes a want so deep that it startled him. She said: "He wouldn't have to go anywhere. He could stay right here."

Dundee looked away, somehow off balance. "Maybe, if he was thataway inclined."

"This is a good place. A man could be happy here."

"If he was the right kind of a man for it . . . if his feet didn't keep getting the itch to move on."

"If a man found what he was looking for, he wouldn't *want* to move anymore, would he?"

"Some of us never know what we're looking for. We're just looking."

"When you do find it, do you think you'll know?"

"I couldn't rightly say. I ain't found it so far."

She took in a slow breath. "You could have, without realizing."

Dundee looked away, fishing a small sack out of his pocket and rolling himself a cigarette, spilling most of the tobacco. He stole a glance and found her frowning in thought. Finally she asked: "Why do you work for John Titus?"

"For money, I guess."

"You could as easy work for somebody else."

"He's paid me good, and there's more coming. For once in my life I'm going to have me a stake to show for my time."

"And when you get that money, what'll you do with it?"

"Been studying about that a right smart. I'd like to have more to show for the next thirty years than I've had for the last thirty. Been thinking I might set me up a business."

"Like what?"

"Oh, like maybe a saloon. An honest one, of course."

Her eyes disapproved. "A saloon?"

"Beats cowboying. One time I spent three hard months on a ranch. Never saw the bunkhouse in daylight the whole time. Worked till I didn't even sweat anymore; just oozed blood. Went to town finally, and in three days I spent every cent I'd made in three months. *He* didn't sweat. Heaviest thing he lifted in the whole three days was my money as he toted it to the bank."

"Dundee, don't you want something better in life than a saloon?"

"It's a good investment. When times are easy, everybody spends free. Times get hard, they drink to forget their troubles. Either way, the saloonkeeper walks a-jingling."

"There's more to life than money."

"That's what they say, but I never seen much evidence of it."

"There's more to you than you let on, Dundee. You could set your sights higher than that . . . a lot higher."

"What do you figure I ought to aim at?"

"You could take your money and buy cattle with it. Maybe there wouldn't be many at first, but they'd be *yours*. You could take that little start and build, the way Warren does. You wouldn't have to work for other people. You'd have cattle of your own, something that belonged to you and you could be proud of."

"It's hard work punching cows. I *know*."

"When the cows belong to you, it's not like working for the other man."

Dundee figured he was listening to a lecture from Warren McCown, second-handed. "Sure, I've thought about that. But there's something always worried me. What if I got myself all set on a place and had my roots down too deep to pull them up, and then my feet commenced itching again? What if I came to hate the sight of the place? What if it turned out to be more of a jail than a promised land?"

She touched his hand. Her fingertips were warm and startling. It was as if he had brushed his hand against a wire fence in a lightning storm. She said, "Maybe you wouldn't ever get to feeling that way . . . if you had somebody with you. . . ."

He found his lips dry. He licked them with a quick, furtive touch of his tongue. "Millie, I might even get tired of her, too. Then she'd be miserable, and so would I." Her fingers tightened on his hand. He felt heat rising in his blood, and he drew his hand away. "Millie, some men it's best to leave alone. There's a right smart you don't know."

"But there's a lot I *do* know. You're a brave man, and you're kind."

"Kind? Maybe you ain't heard. I shot a man in Runaway."

Her lips tightened. "I heard. Somebody told Warren."

"That ought to be enough to change your mind about me."

"You didn't *want* to shoot him, did you?"

He shook his head. "But I did do it, and that's what counts."

"It doesn't count. You just did what came necessary. I don't imagine it's an easy thing to live with." Her eyes softened in sympathy. "I've heard that when a man has to kill, it haunts him, that the dead man won't let him rest."

"I've lost some sleep, all right, but it's been mostly from worrying about his live friends."

Millie laced her fingers together and squeezed them. She tried to look at him but cut her glance away when their gaze met. Dundee stared at her with hungry eyes, his pulse quickening, his hands shaking a little. He could sense a silent call reaching out to him, a cry of loneliness she didn't know how to express.

And there was a want in *him,* too, deep as a canyon. It was that want which had brought him back here.

Hoarsely she said, "Dundee, I don't think I ever knew a man quite like you."

He had been about to reach for her, to grasp her arms and pull her to him. Now her words fell on him like a sudden dash of cold water. She'd never really known *any* man, he was sure. She waited, trembling in expectation of something she didn't even understand. She was untouched, unprepared.

Times, he'd thought how pleasant it would be to walk into a situation like this, like stumbling across an unclaimed gold mine where all you had to do was reach and take.

Now he drew away, suddenly grave. "Millie, go in the house."

"What . . . ?"

Sternly he said: "You better go see after Uncle Ollie. He may be needing something."

He sensed the disappointment that folded in around her like a dark cloud. "Did I do something wrong?"

"No, but if you stay out here, *I* might."

Face coloring, she spoke almost in a whisper: "I don't guess you'd do anything I didn't want you to."

"There'd come a time you'd wish I hadn't. You'd hate me then, and likely I'd have a contempt for myself. You got a lot to learn yet, Millie. I don't want it on my conscience that I was the one taught you."

VII

Although Uncle Ollie lapped up sympathy like an old dog takes to gravy, Dundee decided it wasn't all put-on with him. The fall had really hurt the old man, and at his age repairs came slow and painfully. Dundee wanted to stay, and warm himself in the glow that came upon him whenever Millie was close. But times, the temptation to reach out and take her was almost more than he could push aside. He found that he feared himself more than he had ever feared any man.

He would have left had it not been for Uncle Ollie. The old man would be a burden to the girl if she had to take care of him alone. Dundee chewed and fretted. Once he made up his mind to leave and went so far as to catch his horses. Then he went in from the woodpile with a fresh-cut armload of stovewood and saw Millie struggling to help her hungry uncle to the table. Dundee knew he had to stay till Warren got home. But he wouldn't stay an hour longer than that. Millie being the way she was, it was just too damned dangerous.

He purposely spent most of his time away from the house, chopping enough wood to carry halfway through next winter, stacking rocks for Warren's stone corrals, hoeing weeds out of the garden patch, anything to keep him mind-changing distance from temptation. Being close to her all the time—studying about her so much—kept him fighting against himself.

Maybe what he ought to do was slip off for a quick, quiet little ride into Runaway, where he might find a bit of diversion down toward the end of the street.

Uncle Ollie was aware, too. Once when Dundee helped him take a walk out back, Ollie said, "Millie's kind of hit you between the eyes, ain't she?"

"What do you mean by that?"

"I been noticing the way you watch her. If I was of a violent nature, being her uncle and all, I could shoot you for the things you been thinking."

Dundee's face went warm. "You got an awful imagination."

"I see what I see." Ollie's eyes narrowed with a hint of craftiness. "You know, Dundee, half of everything here belongs to her. If you was to marry her, you'd have as much to say around here as Warren does."

Dundee held his silence, knowing Ollie was fishing.

Ollie continued: "Warren expects too much out of an old man. He's working me into my grave, I tell you. But you, Dundee, you could put a stop to that. You got a feeling for an old man."

"You're a dirty-minded, shameless schemer."

"An old man has got to scheme. He can't fight."

Dundee was wondering how much longer he would be able to stand it here when he saw the spring wagon laboring its way up the valley, the team straining in the afternoon sun, bouncing the wagon across the ford and up out of the streambed. Dundee dropped a heavy rock he had been about to place on the fence. He straightened his aching shoulders and squinted. Warren? *He* was supposed to come in with a herd of cattle. In any case, Warren hadn't taken the McCown wagon with him. It stood by the saddleshed. Dundee dusted his hands on his trousers, wiped sweat from his face onto his sleeve and started toward the house, watching the wagon.

He could make out two horses being led behind it, and two people sitting on the seat. One was a woman.

"Millie," he called, "you got company coming."

Millie stepped out of the house, wiping flour from her hands onto an apron, lifting one hand to shade her eyes. "I can't make them out."

Dundee stepped into the house and came back with a pistol strapped on his hip. He said, "The man is Roan Hardesty."

Blue Roan slouched on the wagonseat like a huge sack of oats, the reins in his big hands. Beside him, the saloon woman Katy Long sat with her back straight as a ramrod. If he hadn't known better, Dundee might have mistaken her for a schoolteacher.

Bet she could teach me some things, though, he thought. *Katy Long. Bet that ain't her real name. Bet she ain't used her right name in so long she'd have to study to remember what it is.*

Roan wheeled the wagon into the yard. Dundee saw two men in the back of it, one sitting up, one lying atop a stack of blankets. His gaze fell first upon the bandage. He remembered John Titus' contrary boy, the one he'd had that scrap with in Titusville.

This was Son Titus!

The old renegade reined the team to a stop. He took a careful look around, like a coyote surveying a chickenhouse, then tipped his shapeless hat to the girl by the arbor. "Evening, Miss Warren." He shifted his gaze to Dundee, and his eyes seemed to laugh. "Howdy, Dundee. Figured this was where I'd find you at. I got me a couple of problems here I want to dump in your lap."

Dundee glanced at the woman. Katy Long wasn't looking at him; she was staring at Millie McCown.

Dundee walked up to the wagonbed and peered into one defiant eye of the Titus heir. The other eye was swollen shut. "Son Titus, what the hell do you think you're doing here?" Dundee said.

"I come a-hunting cowthieves. I come to do the job *you* was hired for."

Roan Hardesty shifted his great bulk in the wagonseat to look back. "He's the old bear's cub, all right; ain't no doubt about that. Got the looks of old John, and the temper. I *would* say he lacks the brains. Must've took after some other branch of the family."

A bunch of questions were rattling around in Dundee's head, but he figured he'd get them all answered in due course if he would keep his mouth shut.

Roan said: "He come into Runaway proud and loud. Except for a couple of saloon girls, he didn't make no friends."

Dundee asked, "What did you do, run a bunch of horses over him?"

The old thief shook his head. "Soon's I got the word who he was, I give an order: nobody was to kill him. Guess I ought to've said nobody was supposed to *hurt* him, because they tried to see how far they could go *without* killing him." He glanced down at the sullen Son Titus. "He asked for it. Felt kind of like stomping him a little myself, but I always been too good-natured for that kind of thing."

Dundee snorted to himself. *I'll bet.* He looked at the cowboy who lay on the blankets. "Who is this?"

Roan replied regretfully: "Compadre of young Titus. He done what he could to get the boy out of trouble. He's got a bullet in his shoulder. Or *did* have. Katy took it out."

Dundee glanced at the saloon woman. "Playing nurse again. Maybe you missed your calling."

Her eyes flashed. "What makes you think you know what my calling *is*?"

Old Roan growled: "Now look, I already seen enough fighting to do me awhile. I'm turning these two boys over to you, Dundee."

"Why me?"

"They're T Bar property. I want you to get them back to old John. One more thing: make damn sure this cub don't turn up in Runaway again. Next time I might not be there to protect him. Somebody might put a permanent part in his hair."

Dundee said, "Come on, Son Titus, I'll help you out of the wagon."

Young Titus snapped: "I can get out by myself. Just you move aside and don't get in my way." He scooted his rump down the wagonbed and gingerly eased to the ground, favoring sore muscles and miscellaneous lacerations. "If you want to, though, you can help my friend Tobe. He's not in no shape to help himself."

Dundee climbed up. Carefully he lifted the cowboy, who sucked air between his teeth but didn't cry out. Katy Long quickly left the wagonseat. "Take it easy with him," she spoke sharply. "He's not a beef to be jerked around."

"I'm handling him gentle as I know how."

"Then you don't know very much." She stood at the rear of the wagon, ready to help bring the cowboy down. Son Titus waited there too, though Dundee figured he would be as much help as a split slicker in a rainstorm. Millie McCown came to stand beside Katy Long. Dundee got one arm under the cowboy's back, the other under his legs, then eased him down to the women. Sensibly, they shouldered Son Titus aside. Dundee said, "Just hold him now till I can get down out of the wagon." He glanced at Millie. "Looks like you got you another invalid."

"It's all right." She had a lot of patience, he thought.

On the ground, Dundee got the cowboy's good arm around his shoulder. Tobe had just enough strength to keep from wilting completely. "Hang on, pardner," Dundee gritted. "We'll get you inside in a minute."

"It's all right," the cowboy rasped.

Old Blue Roan had silently watched from the wagonseat. Now he laboriously climbed off, his weight pulling the wagon down heavily on one side, even turning the wheel a little as he put a foot on a spoke and shifted his bulk to it.

Dundee said, "I'm curious how you knew I'd be here."

Roan smiled. "I got eyes all over these hills. I've knowed pretty much where you been from one day to the next, ever since you rode out of Runaway. I figured once you got *here,* you'd stay awhile. *I* would, was I a mite younger."

Dundee glanced at Millie. She showed no sign that she caught Roan's implication. Katy Long did, though. She gave Dundee a glare that would kill mesquite.

Lying on his cot, Ollie McCown stared in amazement as they brought the cowboy into the room. "What the hell?" He saw Blue Roan then, and he cringed, dread clouding his eyes.

Roan said: "Lay easy, friend. I come here in a flush of generosity."

Millie pointed toward Warren's unused cot. "Put him there. If Warren comes home, he can sleep outside under the arbor, like Dundee."

Roan looked disappointed.

Katy Long stared gravely at the wounded cowboy, then at Millie. "We shouldn't have moved him this far, but Roan was afraid he'd come to harm in town. He needs to heal awhile before he's moved again."

Roan said: "I feel kind of responsible, seeing as some of my boys done this to him. I don't expect you got any too much vittles in the house. I fetched some extra."

Millie straightened in a flash of pride that reminded Dundee of Warren McCown. "We're not hungry. We can afford to feed an extra one or two."

"No offense. Dundee, you want to help me fetch them vittles in?"

He phrased it like an order rather than a question. Heading for the door, Dundee heard Katy ask Millie, "You ever dressed a bullet wound before?" Millie hadn't. Katy said, "He needs fresh bandaging now, so I'll show you."

Roan had brought the goods in a couple of canvas sacks. In one were dried beans and fruit and some flour and coffee. In the other, canned goods clanked together as Dundee hoisted the heavy sack to his shoulder. He glanced suspiciously at the old brandburner. "This don't sound like what I've heard about you."

"Them stories was mostly lies."

"Maybe not. I seen you awhile back, trying to run a bluff on the McCowns here."

"It wasn't no bluff."

"Then how come you to bring these groceries?"

The old man scowled. "Not for the McCowns. Not Warren McCown, anyway." He paused, face softening. "I reckon I owe John Titus a little something for old times . . . and for all the T Bar cows that have went into my pockets. I figure it's going to be some days before you can haul that cowboy home. I want to send John his son back well-fed and in one piece . . . give or take a couple of teeth."

Dundee waited a moment to see if Roan was going to carry the other sack, but it was obvious Roan hadn't really meant for Dundee to *help* him; he had meant for Dundee to tote them all. Dundee carried the groceries in, dropped the sack on the floor and came back for the other. Roan reached under the wagonseat and brought out a couple of six-shooters with the gunbelts wrapped around them.

"Better drop these into that sack. They belong to young Titus and that cowboy. Was I you, I'd keep them hid till you get them boys back to John Titus." The blue spots on his face seemed to darken. "One thing for damn sure: don't you let that Titus button go back to Runaway. Sit on him if you have to, or tie him to a cedar tree. I can't watch all the time."

"He must've ripped things up a little."

"He's a brassy little devil; I'll give him that. Rode into town like he was somebody come. Scattered the news that he was thief-hunting, and he wasn't leaving without some scalps. I told the boys to let him alone, so they all just turned their backs on him. Then's when he found the women. I tell you, between loud talk and raw whisky and warm women, he was having hisself a high old time. That cowboy, he done his best to get him out of there, but I reckon young Titus had saved up too much of an appetite. I swear, Dundee, it's a mortal shame how that boy has been deprived.

"He tried to provoke them boys of mine by calling them cowthieves, but they all knew they was anyway, and they had my orders. When the fight finally *did* start, it was over one of the girls. Son got to poaching on private territory. If it hadn't been for the cowboy, Titus would've got killed. The cowboy took the bullet for him. Next time, it might be different. Watch him."

"I will."

"And maybe if you're busy watching *him,* you won't be coming back to Runaway yourself, either. You didn't leave no friends there that I noticed."

"I expect I'll be back."

"It'd be a pity. I can't help but like a man a little bit when I respect him. I'd hate to shovel dirt in your face."

Through the open door they could see Katy Long gesturing, telling Millie how to take care of the cowboy's wounds. The old outlaw watched, a gleam in his eyes. "I swear, Dundee, that's a good-looking filly, that McCown girl. And unbroke; a man could train her to suit hisself. Was I you, I'd a whole lot rather spend my time playing games with her than stirring up dust over in Runaway."

Dundee frowned but made no reply. Hardesty went on: "An old man ought not to have to give advice to a young man in matters like this, but I will. Opportunity don't knock often in this life. When it does, you better grab."

"You don't know a good woman when you see one."

"A *good* woman is just one that ain't been given the right opportunities."

Katy Long came outside and beckoned silently with a quick jerk of her chin. Her eyes were sharp, her words clipped. "Dundee, I've told the girl what to do, but she's never had any experience with this kind of thing. You may have to help her."

Sensing her distaste, Dundee stiffened in resentment. "I will."

"There's something else you could do to help her, too. You could leave her alone."

"What do you mean by that?"

"I mean the girl is young, and she's green. She's like a wild flower way out on the prairie. She's never met your kind of man before, and she doesn't know how to defend herself."

"Who told you she's had to?"

"I saw the way she looked at you. You've got her eating out of your hand."

Heat rose in Dundee's face. It was bad enough having to answer for the things he *did* do.

She said: "I'm used to gunfighters. I've even gotten accustomed to thieves. But I'll be damned if I can find any excuse for a man who would take advantage of innocence."

"What would *you* know about innocence?"

Her eyes flashed like lightning against a dark sky. "Enough that I respect it when I see it. It's a sad thing when you lose it; I can remember."

In spite of his resentment, Dundee sensed sincerity in this woman. "If it's any satisfaction to you, I ain't touched her."

She stared hard, and he knew it would be difficult to hide a lie from those sharp eyes. Her gaze lost its edge. "I'd like to believe that."

"Take it or leave it. It's the truth."

Her back lost its rigidity. "Don't tell me you haven't been tempted."

"Hell yes, I been tempted. You think I'm made out of wood?"

For a moment he thought she came close to a relieved smile. "Well then, remember this: the test of a man isn't whether he's ever tempted or not. It's whether he resists temptation."

He glanced at the wagon. "It'll be easier now. You've brought two extra pairs of eyes to watch me."

Now she *did* smile, though it was a fleeting thing and touched with malice. "If the temptation gets too strong, there are women in Runaway."

"Including you?"

"*My* business is whisky."

Roan hollered: "Come on, Katy. It's a long ways back to town."

Dundee suggested to Katy, "If you're worried about Millie, you could stay here and protect her."

Katy shook her head. "I might have to protect myself."

Dundee watched the wagon slowly drop down into the ford and climb out on the far side of the stream. He turned then toward the cabin, bracing himself a little. His eyes found Son Titus as he walked through the door. "You damnfool button, what do you think you was doing in Runaway?"

Defiantly Titus said, "You'd know, if you'd been doing the job my dad hired you for, instead of laying up here passing the time with some nester girl."

Dundee glanced at Millie and saw the color rise. He clenched his fist. "Watch out what you say, boy."

"If you'd been out doing what you was supposed to, you'd of knowed they made a big raid on the T Bar and run off enough cattle to make a whole herd for some greasy-sack outfit like *this* one."

"So you decided to try to make the old man see you've growed up. You decided to go and wipe out the cowthieves all by yourself."

"I ain't finished yet."

"Yes, you are. You've all but got your friend here killed. If it wasn't for old Roan, you'd be laying out yonder someplace now, feeding buzzards."

Son Titus' right eye was dark and swollen, but his left one shone with anger. "You act mighty thick with that splotchy-faced old scoundrel. I've had a notion all along you'd fall in cahoots with that wild bunch."

It was on Dundee's tongue to tell Son Titus that Roan had once been a friend of his father. But anger had a tendency to make words come hard for him. It was easier to ball up a fist and hit something. "Son Titus, if a man just worked at it a little bit, he could get to where he didn't like you atall."

"I got friends enough. I don't need *you.*"

Dundee pointed his chin at the cowboy who lay in silence on Warren McCown's cot. "You like to've lost one of them. Till he gets in shape to move, you'll stay here and behave yourself. I'm not going to take any foolishness off of you, Son Titus. Cross me and I'll slap you down."

Titus' open eye glowered. "You're forgetting, Dundee; I don't take orders off of you. You're working for us."

Dundee corrected him. "I'm working for your old daddy. And you *will* take orders or I'll pack you home tied up like a long-eared maverick."

Son's swollen eye and his stiff joints hadn't left him unable to walk. He limped painfully out of the cabin, trying to stomp but hurting too badly to make it effective.

I'll likely have to clean his plow again before he makes up his mind to wear the bridle, Dundee thought. *And I believe I could do it smiling.*

Dundee turned toward the cot where the cowboy lay. "What did they say his name was?"

Millie's hands were clasped nervously, as if she had expected a fight. "Tobe, I think they said."

The cowboy spoke, barely above a whisper. "Yes, it's Tobe. Tobe Crane."

Surprised, Dundee said: "I thought you was out like a dry lamp. By rights you could just as well've been dead. Didn't you have better sense?"

"Son was bound and bedamned. I had to try and help him."

Dundee frowned. "How old are you?"

"Twenty-one."

"If you want to reach twenty-two, you got some things to learn. One of them is to pick better friends. I'd as soon carry dynamite in my hip pocket as to ride with Son Titus."

"Son's all right. He's just trying to show his old daddy . . . to be the old man all over again . . . and he don't know how."

"I hope he lives long enough to learn." Dundee's forehead furrowed. Underneath those bandages and that bruised skin, he thought there was something familiar about the face. "Wasn't you trying to help Son Titus bob my horse's tail in Titusville?"

"We didn't mean you no harm. I'm glad we didn't finish the job."

Dundee turned as if to go. The cowboy weakly lifted his hand. "Dundee, Son has got his faults, but he's got the makings. The old man knows it, but he don't know how to show it. He's afraid of making Son's head swell, I reckon. So he treats Son like a little boy, and Son keeps on trying to prove he's not. That's all that's the matter with him. You got to understand that about Son."

"Does the old man know Son went to Runaway?"

"No. He give Son orders to go north after a string of horses. Far as old John knows, there's where he went."

Dundee glanced at the girl, whose eyes warmed with sympathy as she looked down on the cowboy. "Millie'll take good care of you. Soon's you can stand the trip, I'll take you and Son home."

"That's decent of you, Dundee."

"I'm being paid for it."

Outdoors, he found Son Titus slumped in a rawhide chair beneath the brush arbor. Son gave Dundee a quick look with his good eye and cut his face away. "I ain't in no shape to fight you right now, Dundee. But I'll heal," he said.

VIII

The distant bawling of cattle drifted across the long valley and fell on Dundee's ears as welcome as the jingle of coin to a broke cowpuncher. Warren McCown was back. Dundee saddled his horse and rode south toward the sound, whistling.

Tobe Crane wasn't ready to be moved yet, but Dundee seriously considered taking Son Titus home anyway. He could come back for Tobe later, or send after him. The days of sitting here waiting had not improved Son's disposition much; he still prowled suspiciously, growled when spoken to and walked around like a crown prince waiting for the coronation.

It'll be worth half my wages to dump him in the old man's lap and then kiss him good-bye with the toe of my boot, Dundee thought.

He could see two riders slowly stringing the cattle along the creek. He could pick out Warren McCown by the way he sat his horse. The other man was a stranger, evidently a cowboy Warren had picked up to help him drive the herd. Dundee splashed the horse across the creek and rode up to Warren, his hand raised in the peace sign.

The bearded Warren nodded, eyes friendly. "Howdy, Dundee. If you want to check the brands, just help yourself."

"I don't reckon that'll be necessary."

"Do it anyway. Then you can tell old John Titus that I got none of his cattle here, and you can vouch for me."

Dundee rough-counted about a hundred mother cows. They carried two brands he had never seen before.

Warren said, "I can show you the bills of sale."

"You don't have to."

"I will anyway." Warren pulled them out of his pocket and extended them at arm's length. "Just in case anybody asks you."

Dundee nodded. Then he shoved his hand forward. "Pleased to see you back, Warren."

Suspicion crept into Warren's eyes. "How come you to know I'd been gone?"

"I been at your place several days."

Warren tried not to show it, but Dundee could see the sudden worry. "How's Millie?" Dundee could tell there was more Warren wanted to ask, but he wouldn't do it, not in words.

"She's fine."

"I don't like to go off and leave her there, just her and Uncle Ollie."

"Nobody's bothered her, Warren. I'll vouch for that."

Dundee could feel the keen probing of Warren's eyes, until Warren at last appeared satisfied. Dundee said: "I found her needing help, so I stayed. Uncle Ollie got himself hurt." He remembered the story the girl and the old man had made up for Warren. "Fell off of a horse. Was too shook up to do much for himself. He's better now, though."

Warren's eyes narrowed. "More than likely fell out of a rocking chair, if the truth was known. He's like my old daddy used to be, a gypsy. He'd starve to death if he didn't have somebody to lean on." Warren paused, embarrassed. "Sorry, Dundee. I know you got no interest in our family problems. I think the world of Uncle Ollie, but I know where his weakness is. I been fighting it all my life, in him, in my old daddy . . . even in myself."

Dundee shrugged. "Anyway, I can afford to leave now that you're home."

Warren stared at him a minute, silent. "Thanks for helping Millie. You didn't have to do it."

"I couldn't of left."

Warren frowned. "And I expect I know why. I could see it, the way you looked at her, the way she looked back at you. You're not for her, Dundee. She needs a man, and she'll get herself one. But you're not the kind, and I think you know it."

"You figure I got some gypsy in me, too?"

"You're not lazy, the way Uncle Ollie is. But you got a restlessness about you. You'll never stay put. Millie needs a man who'll make a home for her and stay there."

"I been wondering if maybe I could change."

"A colt may change color, but a grown horse never does."

They loose-herded the cattle along the creek awhile until the animals settled down and began to graze. Finally satisfied they would stay, Warren signaled the cowboy and pointed toward the house. The rider crossed the creek and waited on the other side. Warren introduced Dundee to him. "We'll treat him to a woman-cooked meal before he heads for home. He's been a lot of help."

The cowboy had nothing much to say. Dundee measured him with his eyes and decided the cowboy would probably take his wages and head for the nearest town to blow them in. That, in all likelihood, would be Runaway. He would ride out of there broke, sadder, but probably not wiser. Dundee knew. *He* had done the same thing more times than he cared to remember.

On the way in, Dundee recounted old Roan's bringing Son Titus.

Warren jerked his head around in surprise. "Son Titus, in *my* house?"

"I hope you don't mind."

Warren frowned deeply. "He's there, so I guess it don't make any difference. But old John Titus looks on all of us as cowthieves. I sure never expected to see any of his kin staying in my house."

"I'm figuring on getting him out pretty quick." Dundee paused. "I better warn you: he ain't the most likable sort you ever met. Chances are he'll insult you before you get out of the saddle."

"Then I'll probably hit him."

"Probably. I want you to know there won't be no hard feelings on my part."

"Wouldn't change things none if there was."

Dundee guessed that was why he had come to like Warren Mc-Cown. Warren had a way of saying what he thought, whether it crawled under your hide or not. Maybe sometime Dundee could bring John Titus around to meet him. The old ranchman appreciated a man who could stand flat-footed and tell him to go to hell.

Millie McCown threw her arms around her brother, paying no attention to two weeks' ragged growth of beard. Warren tolerated her tears for a smiling moment, then reminded her how hungry he and the cowboy were. She begged him to tell her about his trip.

"Nothing to tell," he said. "We come a long ways. No excitement. Now we're mighty lank and looking for something to eat."

Son Titus had been poking around somewhere back of the house. He came up now as if the place belonged to him. He stopped at the corner and stared distrustfully at Warren McCown and the cowboy.

Warren's eyes narrowed a little. "Hello, Son Titus."

Son appeared puzzled. "I don't know you. How come you know me?"

"It don't matter. I know you."

Neither made a move to shake hands. Dundee said, "Son, this is Warren McCown."

Son said: "I figured that. He's got a little the same looks as the girl, only not a bit pretty. Did you get a good look at the brands on them cattle?"

Warren answered for Dundee, his voice tight. "He did. And I also showed him the bills of sale. You want to see them too, Son? If you do, all you got to do is come and take them away from me."

Dundee guessed he ought to stop this before it went any farther, but he didn't make a move. It would be pleasureful to see Son Titus take a stomping.

Millie was the one who headed it off. "Warren, there's hot coffee on the stove. I expect it'd taste pretty good while you wait for me to cook some dinner."

Warren gave Son Titus a hard glance. "All right, Millie. I expect it would." He walked on into the cabin, the cowboy following. Dundee strode angrily toward Son Titus.

"Son, I wisht I knew what it is that ails you. That's a hell of a way to talk to a man after you've enjoyed the hospitality of his house."

"I ain't enjoyed it very much. You're keeping me prisoner."

"You're not a prisoner. You were wondering about them cattle. Why don't you saddle up and go look at them for yourself? You're free to ride."

"You're a slick one, ain't you? You know I ain't fixing to ride very far from here without a gun, and I know you got mine hid someplace."

"You'll get it back when I turn you over to your old daddy."

"I want it now."

"Fiddle with me very much and I'll give you something you *don't* want."

"You'll have to have a heap of help." Son turned on his heel and stalked toward the saddleshed. After several paces he stopped and looked back over his shoulder. "I *will* go see them cattle. Don't hold your breath waiting for me to come back. I'll be awhile."

"Take all the time you want to." The longer he was gone, Dundee figured, the quieter it would be around here.

Son didn't come in for dinner. Warren's cowboy collected his pay, burped happily and left in the general direction of Runaway, as Dundee had expected. A good deal later Son Titus came in. Dundee should have been warned by the triumph in his eyes. But Dundee was enjoying a minor triumph of his own. "You see them cattle all right?"

"I seen them."

"Satisfied they ain't from the T Bar?"

"I reckon."

"Next time maybe you won't be so hell-bent to accuse every-body."

"Maybe not."

Dundee stared in puzzlement as Son walked on by him toward the kitchen. It had been too easy. Up to now Dundee hadn't really won a single argument with Son, except that one in Titusville, and even there it had been a victory of muscle rather than will. In the days they had been here at the McCown place, Son had contested Dundee on almost everything he talked about except the weather. The only thing that had held Son here had been the knowledge that Dundee could clean his plow. As it was, Son stayed around on the edge of things, watching suspiciously from afar, coming in to eat or visit a little with the recuperating Tobe Crane, then drifting off by himself to simmer like a pot of beans at the back of the stove. He even kept his blankets out at the saddleshed and slept apart from the others.

Mostly Dundee had watched his eyes.

The whole time we been here, he's been dreaming up ways to even the score with me, Dundee thought. *Maybe now he thinks he's got something that'll work. He'll bear watching.*

And Dundee watched him, till at dusk Son strayed off toward the corrals as he always did, to sleep alone. To reassure himself, Dundee dug down through the wood in the big box behind the stove, till he found the six-shooters where he had put them. That eased his mind somewhat, for he had begun to suspect that Son might have found his gun.

Next morning Son didn't come in for breakfast. Dundee walked out to the corrals to fetch him and came hurrying back, breath short from running. "Anybody hear a horse leave last night?"

Warren McCown shook his head. "Son Titus run out on you, Dundee?"

"He's gone . . . horse, saddle and all."

McCown smiled thinly. "Can't say it grieves me much."

"It grieves the hell out of *me*. I can't figure him going off without a gun. . . ." A sudden thought struck him like he had been kicked by a yearling. "Warren, that cowboy with you yesterday . . . he was wearing a gun. . . ."

McCown nodded. "A .45, I think it was."

"Son didn't come in till an hour or so after your cowboy left here. I bet he waited out yonder someplace, stopped that feller and bought the gun off of him." Dundee choked down some words he thought Millie was too young to hear.

"Whichaway do you reckon he went?"

"I'll hunt for his tracks, but I think I already know."

He didn't bother trying to follow the trail. The destination was plain enough: Runaway. Dundee put the bay horse into a steady trot, his mind running wild with all manner of notions about the trouble Son Titus could have gotten himself into by now. He saw him being shot, knifed, stomped, clubbed and dragged at the end of a rope. It wouldn't displease Dundee to see any of these things happen to the fool kid, except that most of them were inclined to be so damned permanent.

He stopped at the crest of the hill and looked down over the motley stretch of the town, wondering which picket shack or rock saloon he would find Son Titus in . . . if any of them. By now the button might be lying dead on that riverbank someplace, cast out there like the empty bottles and rusting cans and bleaching cartridge boxes which littered the place, giving mute testimony to many a day and night of revelry and devilment in times past. Though he didn't want to, Dundee gazed a moment at the mercantile across from the Llano River Saloon, coldness touching him as he remembered Bunch Karnes slumping in a lifeless heap on the dirt street in front of it.

He reined up at the wagonyard, stood in his stirrups and peered over the picket fence, studying the horses penned there. He picked out the sorrel that Son Titus had ridden. Son was still here, then. At least, he hadn't left here on horseback.

The liveryman was forking hay into a bunk made of cedar pickets. He stood the fork against a fence and came walking, taking his time. "Howdy." From the man's eyes Dundee knew he was recognized. "Something I can do for you, friend?"

Dundee pointed with his chin. "That sorrel yonder . . . what do you know about him?"

"Just that he's a horse." The man shrugged. "He's got a T Bar brand on him. Boy come in here last night, said he was old John Titus' son. I figured if he was telling the truth, fine. If he wasn't, stolen horses ain't no lookout of mine. Either way, *my* nose don't get skinned."

"You seen that boy this morning?"

"Nope."

"You know where he went?"

"I keep horses, that's all."

Dundee frowned. "Did you hear any shooting last night?"

"There's shooting most *every* night. Most times it's just in fun. Long's it don't hurt me none, I don't pay it any mind."

Dryly Dundee said, "Thanks, friend, you been real helpful." He headed the bay down the crooked street in a walk, gazing suspiciously at every shack as he passed it. He didn't know just what he was looking for. Whatever it was, he didn't find it. When he reached the far end of town he had seen nothing that would help him locate Son Titus. He started back.

His gaze fell upon Katy Long's Llano River Saloon and, inevitably, upon the place in the dirt where Bunch Karnes had fallen. A dun horse had stood hitched there quite a while, evidently, and he had left the sign of time's slow passage on the spot where Karnes' blood had soaked into the earth.

They don't honor death here much more than they honor life, Dundee thought.

He dismounted at the saloon and looked around a moment, warily gauging the prospect of a reception. There was none that he could see. But a tingling along his spine told him he wasn't being overlooked. He stretched to get the saddle-stiffness out of his muscles, then stepped into the saloon.

Katy Long sat at a table riffling a deck of cards. She gazed up at Dundee with the faintest suggestion of a smile. He would swear she was laughing at him. "What kept you?" she asked. "Son Titus got to town before midnight."

"I sleep late." He looked beyond her to the hallway. "I don't reckon he'd be in here someplace?"

She shook her head. "How'd he get out of his cage?"

"I forgot the lock. If he's not in here, where you reckon he's at?"

She continued to smile. "You were his age once. Where would you have gone?" When he didn't answer, she added, "You'll find them down the street, *way* down the street."

"How'll I know them?"

"You're old enough. You'll know them."

Dundee stared at this woman who seemed to enjoy sticking needles in him. "Last time I implied some things about *you,* you got awful mad," he said.

"I got mad because they weren't true. But you're not mad; you're smiling."

Dundee realized that he was, and he tried to put a stop to it. "You've made a big point about how all you sell is whisky. Will you sell me a drink?"

She said: "I sure hadn't figured on *giving* you one. Cricket, fetch Dundee some of our best. I figure he can afford it."

Dundee said: "I'll drink whatever old Roan Hardesty does. He ought to know his liquor."

She shook her head. "Don't take him for a model. He'll drink anything but coal oil. Sit down, Dundee."

"I figured one drink, then I'd go hunt for Son Titus."

"He's all right. If anything had happened to him, I'd have heard. You can take time to sit down and enjoy the whisky."

Dundee looked at the layout of the windows and moved to the other side of the table where the bar and a solid wall would be to his back.

Katy Long's smile faded. "You act like you've been in towns like this before."

"Not many, I'm glad to say. Mostly I've just cowboyed. It don't pay too good, but a man's back is safe." He seated himself, took the drink the bartender had put on the table in front of him and downed it. He frowned darkly. "If this is your good whisky, I'm glad I didn't ask for nothing cheap."

"We don't get a very choosy clientele here."

"Maybe you would, if you'd handle a better line of goods."

"You want to try it? I'd sell you the place cheap."

"It wouldn't be a good long-range investment, not here in Runaway."

"You don't think Runaway has a bright future?"

"And not very *long,* either. I figure old John Titus has got some plans for Runaway, and they ain't likely to be good for the whisky business. If somebody comes along and wants to buy this place, you sell it to him."

Her eyebrows went up a little. "How come you interested in my welfare, Dundee?"

He shrugged. "It don't put no burrs under my blanket, either way. But seeing how you patched up that Crane boy and Son Titus, I don't see no harm in trying to help you out of the gully before the flood comes down."

"You know how hard it is to kill a snake. Runaway won't die easy."

"John Titus has got it wrote down at the top of his list."

She was silent a time. "Well, I came by the place awfully cheap. I don't have a lot to lose." Her eyes narrowed. "Besides, John Titus may not be as tough as you think he is."

"Don't bet on it. If you get yourself an offer, sell." He pushed his chair back. "Enjoyed the hospitality, Miss Long." He realized it was the first time he had called her that—or anything, really—in a respectful manner. "I'd best go find the cub and fetch him home."

"You be careful, Dundee. There's people here who would be tickled to death to pitch in and help pay for your funeral."

"I'll try to save them their money."

He stopped outside the door and took a long look up the street, then down. Again, he wasn't quite sure what he was looking for, but he figured he'd know when he saw it. The death of Bunch Karnes across the street was still on his mind, and he knew it hadn't been forgotten by the people around here, either. He swung into the saddle and started back down the street. He tried not to give the appearance of looking for trouble, but his eyes kept moving. He didn't intend to miss anything.

Down at the far end of town he'd seen a couple of long, narrow frame buildings that had not known the luxury of paint, though he'd seen a woman staring out a window who *had*. He could remember when such a place would have held fascination for him, and he reasoned it might be so for Son Titus. He swung down at the first house, tied the horse and walked in. The odor of cheap perfume and whisky and greasy cooking struck him across the face like a wet saddle-blanket. A woman stood at an ironing board, pressing a dress with a heated flatiron. She was perhaps thirty or so, dressed in nothing but a shift, sweat trickling down her surprised face, her blondish hair hanging in untended strings. Plainly, this wasn't during business hours.

"Mister," she said irritably, "don't you know what time it is? It's the middle of the day."

"I'm looking for a man."

"Most people come in here, they ain't looking for no *man*. There's none here."

Dundee looked past her at a long hallway that had small rooms leading off to one side. "I think I'll go and see for myself."

Face clouding, the woman raised her hand. "Not unless you want a faceful of hot iron, you don't."

She had *somebody* back there she didn't want seen, he figured. "You put that iron down or I'm liable to lay it against your broad rump and brand you like a white-faced heifer!"

She placed the iron back on the board. He started down the hall, opening doors, the woman following along cursing him. There were four doors, altogether. Inside the last room he found a man, but not Son Titus. Old Roan Hardesty was caught with his dignity down. He bawled, "Dammit, Dundee, didn't nobody ever teach you how to knock on a door?"

Dundee said, "Didn't go to bother you."

The woman was still cursing when he walked back to the front room. Dundee laid a few pieces of silver on the ironing board. "Buy yourself a bottle."

He was glad to get into fresh air again, but he knew the next house wouldn't be any better than this one. He stopped at the front door a moment, wishing he had another drink to fortify himself. These places were hell in the daylight.

Son Titus sat in the small parlor in a settee, his bare feet propped up on a soft chair, a bottle in his right hand, his left arm hugging a small blond girl tightly against him. Son grinned with triumph. "Come in this house, Dundee. You're later than I figured you'd be. Old age must be slowing you down."

"I'm not too old, button."

"Well, then, I bet Lutie here can find you a friend."

"All I came for was *you,* and I ain't calling you friend."

"You sound mad, Dundee. You'd of done the same in my place."

"Get up and put your boots on, Son Titus. I'm taking you back."

Son Titus squeezed the girl. "I ain't going back. I like it fine right here with Lutie." The girl smiled at Son and pouted at Dundee. He could tell she had looked into that bottle a good many times.

Dundee pointed down the hall. He noticed this house was built just like the other one. "Girl, you go back yonder and find yourself something to do. I got business with Son."

Son Titus said: "I got no business with you, Dundee. I like it fine, right where I'm at."

Dundee spoke severely to the blonde, "I told you once already, get yourself out of here!"

Eyes wide, the girl got up, tightened her wrapper and weaved down the hall, anxiously looking backward, bumping her shoulder.

Son Titus brought his bare feet to the hooked rug. "Dundee, I'm getting awful tired of you."

"I ain't having much fun with you, either. Put your boots on."

Glaring, Son Titus set the nearly empty bottle on a small table. His fists knotted. "What if I don't?"

"Then you'll go barefooted."

"I mean, what if I tell you I ain't going atall?"

Dundee took a long breath and let it out slowly in exasperation. "Son, you're too drunk to put up a good fight. But I will fight you if I have to. I'll whip you like I whipped you that night in Titusville, and I'll enjoy myself every minute of it."

Son pushed to his feet. "You want to start now?"

The blonde girl hurried back down the hall, bringing with her a large, raw-boned woman with red hair who looked like a sister of the woman in the other house. The woman shouted: "No you don't! I ain't putting up with no fighting in my house. It cost me a wagonload of money for the furniture in here, and I won't allow no brawling drunks to go busting it up."

Must have been an awful little wagon, Dundee thought, looking at the old settee, the old painted table, the kerosene lamps.

Dundee nodded. "All right, Son, if you got to have it, we'll go outside and settle things."

Son's boots lay where he had kicked them off, in a corner. To put them on without sitting down, he had to stand on first one leg, then the other. Watching him, Dundee decided the button wasn't really very drunk, for he managed the job handily.

Dundee had known the time when he enjoyed a fistfight; it limbered him up, roused his blood into good circulation, quickened his heart like a big shot of whisky. Now he felt no relish for it. Not even getting to whip Son Titus seemed worth the effort. But if the job was to be done, he'd best be getting on with it, so he could put this infernal town behind him. He walked out the door and into the street. He glanced at his horse and moved well away from the bay. A horse could be a fool over something like a fistfight. Dundee chose a place and stood waiting for Son Titus to come out.

Son took his time. When he moved through the door, his step was steady, his eyes alert. Dundee wondered if he'd been drinking anything out of that bottle or if he'd just pretended and had been trying only to get the girl drunk.

Maybe he's shrewder than I figured him out to be.

Son's gaze touched Dundee, then darted away. He was reaching for his pistol as he shouted, "Look out, Dundee!"

Instinctively Dundee jumped aside, not sure whether Son Titus was about to shoot him or was going for someone else. A bullet smashed into the frame house even as he heard the crash of a rifle behind him. Dundee whirled, hand darting down and coming up with his six-shooter. Son Titus fired at someone across the street before Dundee got turned. Dundee caught a glimpse of a man at the corner of a picket-and-sod shack, feverishly levering another cartridge into the breech of his smoking rifle. Dundee fired once, knowing he was moving too fast and the distance was too much. He saw the slug kick dust from the shack's wall. Son Titus fired again, chipping wood from a picket just over the man's head. The bushwhacker brought the rifle up again, but he was flustered now with two men shooting at him. Dundee ran, zigzagging. The rifle flashed, but the bullet missed. The man turned and fled, limping badly.

Son Titus hollered, "Let's get him, Dundee!"

Dundee shouted back: "You stay right where you're at! I ain't packing you home dead!"

Dundee raced toward the shack. He could see the man ahead of him, running stiff-legged toward a horse, a little too far for Dundee to hit him. The man swung into the saddle and spurred hard, the rifle still in his hand. Dundee took one more shot at him, knowing he was throwing lead away but figuring he would feel better about it if he at least made the try.

He stopped then to catch his breath, letting the smoking pistol hang at arm's length. He cursed a little because he was angrier than he was scared. He knew who had shot at him: Jason Karnes, brother of Bunch Karnes; Jason Karnes, who had caught Dundee's bullet in his leg in a cowthief camp.

Looks like I'll be forced to put another bullet in him before this is over with, Dundee told himself regretfully. *I'll have to place that next one a mite higher up.*

Son Titus said proudly, "Well, we run him off, didn't we, Dundee?"

Dundee nodded, sober. "I reckon we did. Thanks, Son. If you hadn't hollered, he'd of probably taken me with that first shot."

Son said, "Then I reckon you owe me something."

"I reckon. What?"

"Go off and leave me alone. I ain't finished all my business with Lutie, and you're sure putting a crimp in things."

Dundee frowned. "Son, I'd do anything I rightly could to pay you back. But if I was to leave you here, I wouldn't be doing you no favor. No sir, you're coming on with me the way we started."

Son's voice flattened. "You mean after what I done for you . . ."

"After what you done for me, you're still going back to your old daddy. Now get your horse."

"Like hell I will!"

He stood there within easy reach, and Dundee didn't feel like a prolonged argument. He put his pistol back into the holster, balled his right hand into a fist and brought it up with all his strength behind it. It caught Son flat-footed, but it didn't leave him that way. He lay on his back in the street, shaking his head and blinking.

Son rubbed his jaw, flinching from the unexpected pain. "I swear, Dundee, you sure hit a man hard."

"It helps shorten an argument."

Son's eyes were glazed a little. "If I hadn't saved your life, you'd of been mad at me. I *did* save it, and you won't do me a favor."

"I *am* doing you a favor. I'm getting you out of Runaway while your health is good."

IX

As they topped the hill, son Titus looked back over his shoulder at Runaway below. "I wasn't finished down there."

"Yes, you was," Dundee said.

That was the last Son Titus spoke for many miles. He rode along with his head down, sleeping on horseback. It suited Dundee all right, for so long as Son was asleep he wasn't belly-aching.

I ought to charge old John Titus double for this job, he thought. *Hunting cowthieves is what I hired for. I didn't come here to wetnurse a chuckle-headed button.*

But now and again he would glance at the relaxed face of Son Titus and feel something vaguely akin to liking. Son could have stood there and let Karnes shoot him, but he hadn't. He had pitched in. Maybe it wasn't because he felt any desire to help Dundee; maybe he just wanted the excitement. No matter; if it hadn't been for Son Titus, Dundee knew he'd probably be the cause of somebody having to do a job of digging in the rocky ground that was Runaway's Boothill.

Son Titus stirred finally. He blinked, shut his eyes awhile, blinked some more and came awake. His face twisted as he worked up spittle and tried to clear his mouth of a bad taste. "How far we come?"

"A ways. You ought to swear off of whisky."

"Truth is, *she* done most of the drinking. I didn't really drink much. Just a few little snorts."

Dundee had sort of guessed that.

Son said: "I figured a girl like her would hear lots of things. Figured if she got to drinking it'd loosen her tongue up, and then maybe I'd find out something."

"Did it work thataway?"

"Some. Mostly it made her affectionate. Of course, there wasn't nothing wrong with *that,* neither."

"What did you find out, when she wasn't being affectionate?"

"Found out a little about you, Dundee. Found out they're scared of you in Runaway."

"Did that convince you I ain't no cowthief?"

"Why else you reckon I'd've bothered to holler at you when that feller was fixing to let air through your brisket?"

"I sort of wondered."

"Well, it wasn't on account of your good looks and disposition."

At length they came to a creek, its clear water gurgling over the big polished stones that lay in its shallow bed. Son Titus licked his lips. "Last night I wouldn't of give you a nickel for all the water in Kingdom Come. Now it's worth ten dollars a gallon. I'm going to step down and drink up about a hundred dollars' worth."

Son dropped on his belly and stretched out over the creek's bank, cupping the palm of his right hand to bring water up so he didn't have to dip his face under. He drank long and thirstily, pausing only to catch his breath.

"Ain't you afraid that stuff'll rust your gut?" Dundee asked.

"Not with the coating I put on it last night."

Dundee watered the horses. Son Titus finally seemed satisfied. He pushed to his feet, wiping his sleeve across his mouth. "Nectar of the gods. You ought to try it, Dundee."

Dundee hadn't noticed being thirsty, but he guessed it was the power of suggestion, watching Son Titus, "It's a ways yet to the next water. I reckon maybe I will."

He stretched out on the bank, a little above where Titus had lain. He was drinking when he heard Son's saddle creak and felt the reins jerked from his left hand. He rolled over and jumped to one knee. Son Titus was riding his own horse and leading Dundee's up the creekbank. Out of reach, Son paused to look back. "Go on and drink your fill, Dundee. You got lots of time."

"You bring my horse back here, Son Titus!"

"I hope you're a good walker, Dundee. It's a far piece back to Runaway, or out to McCown's, whichever way you decide to go. Me, *I* could tell you where to go."

"Son Titus . . ."

"Like I said, Dundee, I ain't finished all my business in Runaway yet. That's where you'll find your horse." He swung his sorrel around and led the bay. "Adios, Dundee. Enjoy yourself."

"You crazy button, I'll . . ." Dundee broke off as he watched Son ride away laughing, into the lengthening shadows. He hurled his hat to the ground. He wanted to stomp it, but that wouldn't have been enough. One of these days he'd stomp Son Titus instead. Times, he wished he'd never strayed through Titusville, had never seen old John Titus or Son. He ought to turn his back on the whole damned mess and let them steal the T Bar blind.

But he knew he was in it too far to pull out now. He'd follow on through. But one of these days, when it was over . . .

He clenched his fists and recited Son Titus' ancestry for several generations back.

Dundee was a cowboy, and cowboys seldom walked. It was contrary to their religion. A cowboy would descend into many types of sin before he would risk blisters on his feet. Dundee considered the distance. It might be a little shorter to the McCown place than to Runaway, but not enough to offset the time it would take to get a horse at McCown's and ride all the way back. Another thing, the trail back to Runaway was easier followed in the dark.

Muttering, he climbed the creekbank. He slipped, caught himself, hurled a rock as far as he could throw it and started the long walk.

The night was far gone when he finally got to Runaway. Legs aching, feet blistered and sore, his anger simmering like bitter roots being boiled for backwoods medicine, he dragged himself up to the front gate of the wagonyard. Down the street he could see most of the buildings standing dark. A lantern still flickered in front of the Llano River Saloon, one at another bar farther along. Way down at the end of the street he saw a dim red glow.

The small barn was dark. Well, by George, if *he* was awake, everybody else had just as well be. "Hey!" he shouted. "Where's the man that runs this place?"

He heard a grumbling from a blanket spread on hay in the corner. He struck a match and held it down close. The drunken face he saw there, the eyes blinking in confusion, did not belong to the man he was looking for. "Hey! Stableman, wake up!"

From another corner he heard the squeak of steel cot-springs as a man turned over on his blankets. "You damned drunks . . . you won't let a sober man get no sleep. Go find your own horse and leave me be."

In the reflected moonlight Dundee made out a lantern. He lighted it and turned up the wick. "I ain't drunk."

The yardman swung his bare feet off to the ground. He was wearing long underwear, only half buttoned. He yawned, then peered irritably at Dundee. "Oh, it's you. You'll find your horse in the corral and your saddle on the fence. That button left them here."

"How long ago?"

"I don't know. I been asleep."

"Is his horse here too?"

"He kept his. Just left yours."

"Whichaway did he go this time?"

"Like I told you before, I don't notice nothing that ain't my business. That way my health stays good. Now, take your horse and get out of here so I can go back to bed."

Dundee saddled, swung up and started to ride down the street. The yardman met him, still barefoot and in the long-handles. "Wait, cowboy, you owe me a hay bill."

"How much?"

"Two bits. I ought to charge you extra for waking me up."

Dundee dug for it. A thought struck him. "You heard any shooting in town since that boy came in?"

The stableman held the coin into the moonlight and fingered it suspiciously. "Since you ask me, I heard a couple shots down the street."

"Do you know what happened?"

"Yep. I turned over and went back to sleep."

Dundee rode down the dark street, glad to be off of his sore feet and glad most of the town was asleep. He hoped Jason Karnes was, too. To be on the safe side, he reached down and drew the carbine from its scabbard.

Keeping out of the lantern's glow, he peered inside the Llano River Saloon. He saw the bulky figure of Roan Hardesty hunched over a table studying a hand of cards. Opposite him, Katy Long sat waiting for him to make his play. Best Dundee could tell, most of the chips were on her side.

Dundee rode to the house where he had found Son Titus the last time. He didn't see Son's horse tied anywhere. The house was dark now, except for the glow of a lantern in one of the rooms in the far back. Dundee walked partway back for a look-see, but a curtain was drawn across the window. He returned to the front, pushed the door open and walked in.

"Son Titus! You in here?" No reply. "Son Titus, I come to get you!"

He heard movement down the hall. He brought the carbine up, just in case. A door opened and lamplight came floating toward him, a long shadow preceding a woman. She stopped, the lamp in her hand, her eyes blinking in sleepiness. "What's going on in here? Don't you know what time it is? Decent folks are all asleep."

It was the same red-haired, raw-boned woman he had crossed before. Her stringy hair and the pouches under her eyes didn't help her looks any. Dundee said: "Son Titus came back in here tonight. I want him."

The woman scowled. "He ain't here."

Dundee saw no reason to accept her word. "Where's that girl he was with, the one called Lutie?"

"Lutie's asleep. You ain't going to bother her."

"I asked where she's at." Dundee took two long steps toward the woman. She began to retreat. "Now, mister. . . ."

"I'll find her if I have to tear this place apart. Her and him both. Now, where's she at?"

Grumbling, the woman turned down the hallway, still carrying the lamp. "She's back thisaway. But you ain't going to find out much talking to her."

She opened a door and pointed. The girl lay across a brass bed, her loose gown pulled halfway up her legs, the blanket thrown off.

"Lutie," Dundee demanded, "Where's Son Titus?"

The girl stirred but never opened her eyes. Dundee noticed a bottle lying by the bed. It was empty.

The woman said: "That friend of yours, he brought that bottle with him. Must of let her drink most of it by herself. Time he left here, she was so drunk you'd of thought he'd hit her with a sledge. She won't be worth nothing for two days. It's a sin the way that girl likes whisky. It'll be the ruin of her one of these times."

Dundee grasped the girl's shoulder and shook her. "Lutie, I want to find Son Titus."

The girl moaned, but that was all.

The woman said: "Like I told you, you ain't going to get nothing out of her. She's too drunk."

Dundee stepped back, hand tight on the carbine. Where would he go from here?

"How long's Son been gone?"

"Must've been midnight . . . one o'clock. After he left, I came to see about Lutie. This is the way I found her." She glared. "When you find that Titus, you tell him I don't want him back in here again, ever. He's a bad influence on my girls."

Dundee turned to go. "One more thing. Feller told me he heard some shooting tonight. Was that before Son left, or after?"

The red-haired woman rubbed a hand across her face, trying to remember. "There's always some drunk shooting a pistol around here. I expect it was Titus done it. He left here looking awful satisfied with himself."

Dundee glanced once more at Lutie. *I'll bet.*

Frustrated, uncertain, Dundee walked outside. At the house next door, a woman stepped to the little porch and blew out a red lantern, then retreated inside. That was the house Dundee had searched yesterday, looking for Son Titus. He considered looking again, but he figured Son wouldn't have left Lutie's place to go to another just like it. Dundee looked up the street. The only light he could see now was the single lantern in front of Katy Long's saloon. The rest of the town was in its blankets.

Dundee swung onto the bay and rode back up there. He tied the horse in the darkness and walked around to the rear of the place. He found a rear door and tried it. It was unlocked. He entered the dark hall and carefully made his way along it, guided by the moonlight through the windows. At the door leading into the main room of the saloon, he stopped to look for a moment before stepping into the lamplight. He saw only two people: Katy Long and old Blue Roan.

Roan was gulping a shot of whisky and watching Katy rake in another pile of chips.

Dundee said, "You ought to know better than to gamble with a good-looking woman."

Roan turned quickly, surprised. His hand dropped toward his pistol, then stopped as his blinking eyes recognized Dundee. Katy Long was startled, but she never moved.

Roan recovered his composure. "How come, Dundee? I'd rather play cards with a good-looking woman than with any of the ugly men I've gambled with."

"Hard to keep your mind on the cards."

Katy Long said evenly: "I believe that's the first compliment you've paid me, Dundee. You must want something."

"I want Son Titus. Where's he at?"

She smiled thinly. "You'd make a mighty poor jailer, Dundee. Can't even keep one tight-britches kid under control."

"He was in here, wasn't he?"

She nodded. "Bought another bottle, early in the evening. Said you'd probably come in sometime during the night. Enjoy your walk, Dundee?"

He ignored the barb. "My feet are sore and my patience is run out. I want to know if you saw Son Titus any more after he bought that bottle?"

"Nope. You'll probably find him where you found him yesterday."

"I already looked. He left."

"Then there's not much telling. Maybe he went home."

"Shots were fired somewhere on the street a while ago. What were they?"

Katy glanced at Old Roan, and both of them shrugged. Roan said: "Some drunk, most likely. I didn't hear any more commotion, so I didn't go look." He added ruefully, "I was winning at the time."

Dundee glanced at the pile of chips in front of the woman. "That must've been a *long* while ago."

Katy said seriously: "Dundee, he probably went home. You look like you need sleep. I can fix you up with a cot back yonder. You can go find him in the morning."

"I'll sleep after I've found him. I think I'll tie him to a wagonwheel with wet rawhide and then sleep while the hide dries."

Roan said: "I still got orders out, Dundee. Nobody hurts him."

"Does everybody obey your orders?"

"Not always."

"That's why I got to find him before some of your boys do. If they haven't already."

Dundee turned to go. His tired legs betrayed him, and he almost fell. Roan Hardesty's big mouth turned downward sourly. "He just thinks he's going someplace. You better bed him down, Katy. Next time I'll get them chips on *my* side of the table again."

She smiled. "Glad to give you the chance. Bring lots of money."

"I always do. But I seldom leave here with any." He looked at Dundee. "Wherever that boy's at, he'll keep till daylight. You rest yourself. Where's your horse?"

"Out back."

"I'll drop him off at the wagonyard. Good night, Katy."

"Good night, Roan."

Dundee slumped in a chair and watched Katy Long rake the poker chips into a small leather bag. "You always beat him like that?"

"I let him win now and again, so he doesn't lose hope."

"Crafty, ain't you?"

"I've been taking care of myself in a man's world for a good many years now. I think I know how." She counted and sacked more chips, glancing up occasionally at Dundee. She had poker player's eyes; he couldn't tell what she was thinking. Finally she said: "You're really worried about that thick-headed kid, aren't you?"

"I'm mad enough to chew up nails and spit them in his face."

"But worried, just the same?"

He nodded.

She said: "You know, Dundee, the first time I saw you I figured you were just another tough drifter with a cartridge case where your heart ought to be. But I believe I misjudged you. Times, you're damn near human."

She arose, walked to the front and blew out the lantern that hung on the porch. She shut the door and came back, lighting a lamp that sat on the end of the bar. "Blow out that overhead lamp for me. Then come on back and I'll show you a bed."

He followed her out of the dark saloon and into the hall. She opened the door to the room where she had treated Jason Karnes' wound so many weeks ago. He said: "I'll sleep a while, then slip out. I'll try not to make any fuss when I go."

She stood in the doorway, holding the lamp. Dundee stared at her a moment, a strong urge building in him. He reached up and took her chin and kissed her. She backed off a step, surprised.

"What was that for?"

"I just wanted to do it."

Her eyes studied him unflinchingly. "Comparing me to that country girl?"

"That's not it. . . ."

"Well, do I measure up?"

He shook his head, not knowing what to say. "It's like I told you out yonder that day . . . I haven't touched her. I . . ."

"You've wanted to."

"Sure I've wanted to. I just ain't done it."

"So you come to me, figuring anything you do to me is all right."

Angering, he said: "I didn't mean to get your hackles up. I don't have to sleep here if you don't want me to. I'll just go on like I'd figured to in the first place."

She stared at him awhile longer, and he thought he saw the laughter come back into her eyes. She blew out the lamp and set it on a table. She said: "Empty talk, Dundee. You're not a man to start something and not finish it. You'll stay right here."

X

He was up at daylight, dressing quietly to try to keep from awakening Katy Long. But the tinkle of a spur rowel brought her eyes open. She reached out and caught his hand. Her sleepy eyes smiled. "No good-byes?"

"Hadn't figured on it. I got to find Son Titus."

"You'll be back."

"Better not count on it."

She repeated confidently, "You'll be back."

He walked to the livery barn, where the yardman wanted to charge him another hay bill for the bay horse.

"I paid you once. He ain't been back here long enough to eat any more hay."

"I put it out, and it gets eaten up. I don't know which ones eat it and which ones don't. So they all pay or they don't leave this corral."

"You're a thief."

"Who here ain't? Two bits, friend."

Dundee paid him. The carbine across his lap, he rode down the street for another look by daylight. He saw nothing of Son Titus' sorrel. He rode around back and followed the alleyway, thinking he might find the horse tied somewhere there. That proved to be a waste of time. He scouted the riverbank, but still he found nothing.

Katy and Roan could have been right, he knew. Son could have gotten his fill of town and gone back to the McCown place. It might have been that he wanted to postpone facing up to Dundee for setting him afoot.

Those shots that had been fired during the night still nagged at him a little. True, the chances were it had been some cowboy sharing his celebration with the whole town. But there was always a chance. . . .

Dundee stopped and had breakfast in a saloon that doubled as a restaurant of sorts. He wondered if their whisky was as bad as their cooking and decided it probably was. He rode up the hill looking back over his shoulder, the carbine still across his lap as the sun started to climb. Then he lined out toward the McCown ranch, setting the bay into a steady trot.

It was late morning when he arrived. He rode straight for the saddleshed, looking for sign of Son's sorrel. The horse wasn't there. Well, he thought, maybe Son turned him loose to graze. After all, he'd put in an awful lot of miles. Dundee turned his bay out. He could borrow something from Warren if he had to ride again.

Millie McCown stood in the door, apron tied around her slender waist. Her eyes were wide as she watched him approach, but he could see relief in them. She stepped out to meet him, her hands forward to grasp him. "We were worried about you."

Her fingers were warm, but he pulled his hands away. He tried not to look at her. Remembering Katy Long, he found it hard to meet this girl's eyes. "I'm all right. Did Son Titus come back?"

"You mean you didn't find him?"

"I found him, then I lost him. He hasn't been here?"

She shook her head. "We haven't seen him."

The worry that had nagged him all the way out here descended on him like a dark and gloomy cloud. Of a sudden he was certain something had happened to Son Titus, something a lot worse than Dundee himself had planned to do to him.

In the cabin he found Tobe Crane sitting up on the edge of his cot, his sock feet on a small rug Millie had made. Tobe's arm and shoulder were still tightly bound with clean white cloth. His face was pale, but it seemed to have more color in it than Dundee had seen before. "Dundee, you didn't find Son?"

Briefly Dundee told what had happened, though he left out those parts which might have brought a blush to Millie.

Tobe said: "Could be he was afraid to answer to you, Dundee. Could be he went straight back to his old daddy at the T Bar."

"Do you believe that, Tobe?"

Tobe shook his head. "Nope."

Dundee chewed the inside of his lip, his eyes narrowing. "I got a bad feeling about it. I can't put my finger on it, but I know. Harm's come to him."

Tobe pushed himself to his feet. "I'll help you find him." Tobe swayed, and for a moment it looked as if he would fall. Dundee rushed toward him, but Millie was closer. She grabbed Tobe and eased him back onto the cot, her face drained with sudden anxiety. "Tobe . . ."

Dundee saw how Tobe clung to the girl's hand for a minute after he was on the cot. "You're not ready to go anywhere yet, Tobe."

Across the room, old Ollie McCown stiffly got up from a chair and hobbled a few steps toward Dundee. "I'll go with you. If somebody can help me get *on* a horse, I can ride him."

Dundee watched the old man till he was sure Ollie could do it. "Much obliged, Ollie. I'll be needing help. Where's Warren?"

Millie said: "He went out this morning to check on the new cattle and be sure they're not trying to drift south again. They do that, you know, till they get used to new range."

"You looking for him to come in to dinner?"

She nodded.

Dundee said: "Then we'll wait. Maybe three of us can locate Son."

They split at the creek, the three of them, each to scout a strip of the land that lay between there and Runaway. Dundee himself took the middle one, where the trail ran, for he felt that was the most likely place. Possibly somebody had followed Son Titus out of town and waylaid him. Dundee crisscrossed back and forth, slowly working toward town. In the back of his mind those shots kept ringing, the ones he had heard about in Runaway.

If they'd killed Son, they perhaps had buried him by now. Old John Titus' boy might never be found. But then, there was Son's horse. Somewhere, somebody had to have that sorrel, and it would be a giveaway.

The sun was low when Dundee sat on the hill looking down upon Runaway. He had searched out its streets and alleys this morning, and the riverbank. But he hauled the carbine out of the scabbard and laid it across his lap, knowing he had to look again. He touched spurs to the dun horse he had borrowed from McCown.

Old Roan Hardesty sat on his big gray horse in the middle of the street and watched Dundee ride in. He glanced at the carbine, then shifted his gaze to Dundee's face. "Back again? You been here enough lately that you'd almost qualify to vote."

"I'm still looking for Son Titus. Do you know something you ought to tell me, Roan?"

The old outlaw appeared surprised. "You know as much as I do. I told you I give orders. . . ."

"And you told me not everybody obeys them orders."

"Son Titus ain't in Runaway, Dundee. If he was, I'd know it."

"But he *was* in Runaway, and he ain't showed up anyplace else. Don't that make you wonder, Roan?"

The old man looked genuinely regretful. "I wish I knowed something to tell you." His gaze lifted. Dundee saw the blue spots seem to darken in the aging face as Roan stared past him. Dundee turned in the saddle. His blood went cold.

Two horsemen were coming down the hill, leading a third horse. It was a sorrel. And it had something tied across it.

Dundee turned his dun slowly around, his throat knotting. He didn't have to see any more. He knew.

Warren and Ollie McCown had found Son Titus, and they were bringing him in.

Dundee sat slumped in the saddle, numb, as the two riders came slowly down the street to meet him. At length they reined in, their horses almost touching noses with his dun. Dundee's gaze fastened on the slicker-wrapped bundle tied across the trailing sorrel. He tried to speak, but his throat was too full.

Warren McCown said quietly: "I found him out yonder, a ways from town."

Old Roan Hardesty rode up closer, his face gray in shock, the blue splotches standing out like tar spots. "Dundee, I swear to you. . . ."

Dundee found his voice, and it was bitter. "Any swearing you want to do, Roan, you better do it to old John Titus. I expect you'll get the chance."

He turned his back on the big outlaw. "Warren, it's too far to take him home to his old daddy. I'd like to bury him on your place somewhere. It's sort of friendly ground."

Warren nodded soberly. "It's a long ways. We better get started."

XI

Dundee had seen men die, but old John Titus was the first he ever saw die and yet live. The ranchman scarcely moved as Dundee told him, but the blood slowly drained from his face, leaving it the color of ashes. The bright fire of life seemed to die away and go to nothing more than coals. The strong old hands knotted, the leaders standing out like strands of rope. Dundee thought he heard a single sobbing sound escape from John Titus' throat, but there was no other, and he was never sure. For a long time the old man sat there, blank eyes staring past Dundee into the infinity that only the mind can see.

Dundee wasn't sure the rancher was hearing him, but he went on and told the whole thing from beginning to end—most of it, anyway. At last he brought out the tally book and the map and laid them on the rolltop desk. Quietly he said: "I done what I set out to do, sir. I got it all here on paper, the just and the unjust alike."

The voice that spoke was not the same one which had welcomed Dundee at the door. It was a broken voice now, barely above a whisper. "Would you show me where you buried him, Dundee?"

"I'd want to, sir."

"There'll be more to do after that, Dundee. Will you stay with me?"

"I'd figured on it."

"You done real good." The old man's chin dropped a little. "Who was it you said owned the land you buried him on?"

"McCown, sir. The name's McCown."

"McCown." Titus seemed to test the word like he'd test a pot of beans.

"Maybe you've met them sometime."

"Maybe so." John Titus' eyes closed for a minute. "Dundee, go fetch my foreman, Strother James. We got plans to make."

Millie McCown had fashioned a wooden cross and placed it at the grave. The minister John Titus had brought read words from the Bible. A pale Tobe Crane stood bareheaded in the sun, his good hand clasped with Millie's. Dundee noticed, and regret touched him, but it was covered over by the regret he felt as he watched old John Titus crush his hat in his hands, looking down at the mound of earth which was all he would ever again see of his son.

Around the grave stood some thirty men, each wearing a pistol, each holding a horse that carried a full supply of ammunition in bulging saddlebags. Some wore badges that John Titus had browbeaten the sheriff into passing out as he deputized the lot of them. There hadn't been nearly enough badges to go around. Dundee had not chosen to wear one, for somehow he felt ill at ease that close to a star. The legal authority was vested in the badges. The practical authority they all carried in their holsters, and in the saddle scabbards that bristled with carbines and shotguns.

The minister finished his prayer. The cowboys waited awkwardly for John Titus to put his hat on, then they followed suit, their attention focused on the old man. John Titus shook hands with the minister. "Thanks, preacher. Now I reckon you better be heading back, for the Lord's work here is done. What comes next is the devil's own."

The minister was a thin old man of about Titus' age, badly used up by the rigors of the range country. He said: "I'd rather stand by you, John. I think you'll have need of me before it's done."

But John Titus wouldn't let him.

Tobe Crane took his good hand from Millie's grasp and held it out toward John Titus. "I'll be going with you."

The old man glanced at the bound arm. "Much obliged, boy, but you'd best stay here and mend. I won't forget that you got them wounds helping Son."

"He was my friend. That's why I'm going with you."

Dundee broke in. "You won't be able to keep up, Tobe."

"I'll keep up. You won't have to slow down none for me."

Dundee was about to tell Tobe again that he couldn't go, but John Titus cut him off. "Then, boy, you come on along." The old man turned his attention to the girl. "Much obliged to you and your family, miss, for everything you done. I won't forget it."

Warren McCown stood to one side, watching but not quite a part of it. Titus said to him: "What I told your sister, I meant. If ever there's something I can do for you. . . ."

Warren shook his head. "We'll do all right."

Titus turned to Dundee and his thirty or so men. "Boys, we got us a job to do."

Ahead of them, atop a gentle slope that led down toward a narrow creek, sat a cabin of live oak logs, with a rude lean-to of cedar and a set of brush corrals rambling away lazily toward the hill. Three horses were staked on green grass, their ropes long enough to allow them to go down to the creek for water. In front of the cabin three saddles lay dumped on the ground, blankets flopped across them.

Three saddles, three men, Dundee thought.

When they had left the McCown place, John Titus had said, "Lead out, Dundee." Dundee hadn't realized the old man meant for him to take command. Now as they looked down on the cabin, old Titus said, "What you planning to do, Dundee?"

"I was planning on taking orders."

"I was planning on you giving them."

Dundee's jaw dropped. "I'm no Ranger or general or nothing like that. I been a cowboy all my life."

"You're drawing a right smart more than cowboy pay. I'm counting on you to earn it." With that, the old man just pulled back and checked it to him.

Dundee chewed a little, though there was nothing in his mouth for him to chew on. What smattering of knowledge he had about gunfighting was of a personal nature, man to man. It didn't cover military tactics. What's more, the men with him were cowboys for the most part, not gunhands, though Titus' foreman Strother James had managed to round up a few men who had had experience either packing a star or avoiding one; it would be hard to tell which.

Dundee figured he would have to put most of his hope in those, and in the caprices of Lady Luck, who on occasion had been known to spit in his eye.

He made a sweeping motion with his arm, signaling for a surround. He sat on the bay horse and watched while the men spread out and around the cabin, shutting off any chance for escape by the men inside. Right away he saw his first mistake. The way the posse had tightened the ring, there was no way for anyone to shoot without taking a chance of hitting one of his own men. Dundee signaled for the riders on the opposite side to move up the hill, out of the line of fire.

This was a soldiering job, and for a moment he wished he were old enough to have been in the war, so he would be sure what he was up to. But hell, he would be old and gray now, and fighting off the rheumatism.

The cabin door opened. A bareheaded man stepped out in red underwear, denim britches and long-eared boots. He walked along with head down, whistling. At the woodpile he picked up a chunk of mesquite and placed it across the chopping block. When the ax fell, Dundee started his bay forward, wondering how long it would be before the posse was seen. The woodchopper was so preoccupied, Dundee got close enough that he could chunk a rock at him. These renegades had stolen cattle here so long with absolute impunity there was no reason to suspect the puckerstring was about to draw shut.

The ax stopped its swing above the chopper's head. He gasped at Dundee, then let his gaze drift slowly to the other riders spread out across the flat. He stood that way for long seconds, the ax raised, his mouth and eyes wide. Of a sudden he flung the ax behind him and turned to run for the shack.

"Stop!" Dundee called. The man halted in midstride. Dundee let his voice drop a little. "You'd never make the door. If you don't want some new holes opened up in you, better turn around here and see how high you can raise them hands."

The rustler turned slowly, shaking. Dundee stepped down and handed the reins to the angular old brushpopper Strother James. He slapped the palms of his hands against the outlaw's pockets and down against his boottops.

"No gun. Wouldn't of been no use to you anyway. I take it there's still two men in the shack."

The outlaw swallowed, his stubbled neck quivering. He tried to speak, but nothing came out. He nodded instead, his eyes darting from one rider to another, frightened as a rabbit's. Dundee guessed he was looking at the ropes on their saddles.

"Do what I tell you and maybe you won't have to try one of them on for size," Dundee said. "You call to your friends in there and tell them to come on out. Tell them we got them hemmed in tighter than Maggie's britches."

For a minute he was afraid the outlaw was going to be of no use to him, for the man was so scared that his voice wouldn't function. "Give her another try," Dundee said firmly.

The outlaw cupped his hands around his mouth. "Jake! Hawk! They got us! You better come out!"

Dundee kept the outlaw between him and the cabin. He drew his pistol and stood waiting, his heart quickening. He saw motion at a window. A man stepped out of the door, crouching warily, rifle in his hand. He looked at the ring of horsemen and realized he had made a mistake. "Arnie, what's going on out here?"

Dundee said, "Drop the rifle and walk this way."

The outlaw still crouched, his head turning slowly as he counted the men who waited for his decision.

He made the wrong one. He decided to try for the cabin. Dundee leveled his pistol but never squeezed the trigger. A rifle roared in old John Titus' hands, and half a dozen more shots exploded in the space of a second or two. Dundee could see the puffs of dust as the bullets struck, twisting the outlaw, one way, slamming him another. The rifle flew out of the man's grasp. He fell without a whimper, cut to pieces.

Dundee heard the outlaw in front of him whisper "God!" and sink to his knees. The horses danced in fear at the sudden fusillade, smoke rising from half a dozen guns. He heard excited shouts from men who hadn't been able to see, wanting to know what was going on.

Dundee caught his breath. "You still got one friend in there. If he's any friend atall, you better tell him to come out with his hands up."

Arnie found his voice this time. "Jake, Hawk's dead. They got him. You come on out while you still can."

The door opened cautiously. Dundee saw the barrel of a rifle and leveled his pistol on it. The rifle was thrown onto the ground. The door opened wider and a man swayed out, his arms held straight up. "Don't shoot! Don't nobody shoot!"

Dundee motioned him forward. The men rode in closer, covering the outlaws with their rifles and shotguns and six-shooters. Dundee turned and stared a moment at all the hardware, and he felt almost as nervous as these cowthieves. That much artillery in the hands of a bunch of cowboys was enough to make a man break out into a cold sweat. "You boys be careful with them guns. We want to be damn choosy who we kill."

John Titus edged his horse forward. He leaned on his saddle-horn and stared down at the two cowthieves, his eyes hard as steel. "Dundee, you reckon these two could've done it? You reckon they killed Son?"

Dundee knew he had to be careful how he answered, for the old man's fingers inched down to touch his rope. "These two ain't no more likely than anybody else." Dundee could see the temper in the eyes of the men around him. If old Titus said the word, they'd hang these two from the nearest live oak. Dundee held his breath. That kind of a show wasn't what he had come for.

Titus stared a long time before he said: "Tie them on their horses. We'll take them with us to the next place."

Strother James fingered his gray-laced beard, then pointed to the dead man. "What about him?"

"What *about* him? Leave him there."

Pistol in hand, Dundee approached the shack. He was reasonably sure the three men were all who had been here, but in a situation like this the man who took things for granted might not be around to celebrate next Christmas. He kicked the door open and leaped inside. A quick glance told him he was by himself. He slipped the pistol back into its holster. Seeing a lantern hanging from the ceiling, he took it and emptied the kerosene along the walls. In a corner he found a coal oil can that felt as if it were half full. He poured fuel onto the outside walls, then stepped back and struck a match on the sole of his boot. He flipped it into a patch of dry grass at the base of the wall. The flame grabbed the kerosene and raced up toward the roof, crackling. Dundee heard the horses snort in fear of the fire.

The outlaw named Arnie said plaintively, "I got a little money hid in there."

Dundee watched the flames lick across the wall and find their way into the cabin, the dark smoke aboil. "You *had* a little money in there," he corrected.

They moved fast and struck hard, over the hills, up the valleys, following Dundee's map, picking up one thief's camp and then another, leaving behind them smoke and flame. During that blazing afternoon one more outlaw showed the poor judgment to come out with rifle firing, and he stayed there on the spot where he had fallen, dead before his dropped weapon ever struck the ground.

Through it all, old John Titus never let age cause him to falter or drop behind. He moved in silence, his gaunt face like darkened rawhide dried on a stretching frame. He watched the gradually increasing string of prisoners brought along on their own horses, hands thong-tied to saddlehorns. Titus had nothing to say until after the fourth camp had been taken. He edged his horse against Dundee's.

"These are little fish," he said solemnly. "I want the big one."

"Old Roan? He'll be harder to take. While we're trying, a lot of the others will slip out of the country."

"Let them. It's Roan I want. Wherever we find Roan, we'll likely find the man who killed Son."

Dundee shrugged. He had rather have concentrated on the easy ones, as much to sharpen up this inexperienced posse as anything else. It was one thing to ride into a two-bit rustler camp and flush out one, two or three miserable cowthieves. It might be entirely something else to beard the lion in his own den.

Titus said: "You know where Roan has his headquarters, don't you? You showed it on your map."

"I know where it is. I just wasn't too anxious to see it yet."

"*I'm* anxious."

So they rode. Sundown caught them still many miles from

Runaway, but Dundee figured that might be a good thing. The darkness would help hide their movements.

He didn't know how much surprise there might still be. They had moved swiftly today, and so far as he knew, nobody had gone through the net. But it would be hard to know for sure. Somebody might have come over a hilltop and spotted them without himself being seen. If so, he probably wouldn't let his shirttail touch him till he reached Roan Hardesty.

"Pull them prisoners in tight," he ordered. "We can't let a one of them get away. Tie all their horses onto one rope and lead them."

Far into the night they rode, Dundee always a little ahead, feeling out of the way in the near darkness. There was a trail, but he chose not to follow it. They cut across the hills, climbing wherever he could find a way through, easing down the off slopes, splashing through the moon-trapping creeks that shimmered in the lazy valleys.

He had never been down to Roan Hardesty's headquarters, but he had sat on top of a hill and watched it through the glass most of one afternoon, getting the hang of it. Roan's taste in a ranch layout was much the same as his taste in whisky: rawness was no detriment so long as the thing fitted its purpose. The old reprobate lived in a small log house just far enough up from the creek-bank that he wouldn't have to flee the floodwater. He evidently didn't want to tote water any farther than absolutely necessary. His barn—such as it was—had been built close to the house, too. Sanitation wasn't as much worry to him as the length of the walk from where he had to turn his horse loose.

Roan's men—the ones he kept around him all the time—stayed in a long, low rock structure with a brush-and-mud roof. Far as Dundee had been able to tell, Roan lived in the log house all by himself, though he had had some female company there the afternoon Dundee had spied from afar. Plain house, raw whisky and a painted woman. A man should never get so rich but what he still enjoyed the simple pleasures, Dundee had told himself.

For a while he feared he was lost in the night, but at last he found the hill where he had sat that time before. The men came up around him and let their horses rest. The dim moonlight barely showed the outlines of the buildings down there.

John Titus said, "Is that where he's at?"

"Well, it's where he lives. He spends a lot of time in Runaway. The only light I can see is a lamp in the bunkhouse. Roan's place is dark."

"You reckon he found out about us and ran?"

"Maybe. Or he could be in town playing poker. Or, he could be laying in there asleep. I expect he sleeps a right smart, his age and all." Dundee frowned. "You need some rest yourself, Mister Titus. You been going awful strong."

"I'll rest when the job is done. There won't be much left for me to work for, when this is over. Son is gone."

Dundee didn't know how to answer that, so he didn't try. He had a notion that when the old man's initial grief passed, he'd be back in harness as strong as ever. Work was what kept a man like him going. Dundee said: "We'll *all* get some rest. If they *have* heard we're in the country, they could be waiting there somewhere trying to catch us in the dark. We'd best wait till daylight. But we'll move down closer and put a surround on them. That way there can't nobody slip in, or nobody slip out."

Since he seemed to be the one giving orders, Dundee told the men not to light any cigarettes through the night. That would be a giveaway.

Later a weary Tobe Crane sat beside Dundee where they could look down on the dark shape of the buildings. Crane had kept his word. Weak though he was, he hadn't fallen behind a single time.

Before long Dundee started seeing matches flare in the night, one, two . . . then five and six. He swore. "Looky there. Them matches can be seen for miles. I told them boy . . ."

"A nervous man is bound and bedamned to smoke. And this is a nervous bunch."

Dundee grunted. "Ever so often I think about all them shooting irons in the hands of cowpunchers, and I get a mite nervous myself."

"You got a plan how we're going to take that place?"

"I ain't no general. All I know to do is just ride down there and take over."

"Looks awful risky."

"Everything we've done has been risky."

Dundee didn't intend to, but he dropped off to sleep. The first thing he heard was a rooster crowing somewhere down at the ranch headquarters. He yawned and glanced eastward, where dawn was sending up the first faint promise of color.

Tobe's eyes flickered in surprise when the rooster crowed again. "Is that what it sounds like?"

Dundee nodded. Tobe said: "I wouldn't picture Roan Hardesty as being the type to keep a bunch of chickens around."

Dundee smiled. There *was* something awfully domestic about a set of clucking hens.

Tobe said: "Maybe he enjoys wringing necks."

"More likely he just favors eggs. Old men get contrary about what they eat, and *tough* old men can get *awful* contrary."

Dundee could see the cowboys stirring around, and he knew they hadn't slept much, most of them. From the dark pockets under Tobe's eyes, Dundee could tell *he* hadn't. Tobe said: "I could sure stand a cup of hot coffee."

"We'll cook breakfast on old Roan's stove."

He sent a cowboy to carry word to all the men who encircled Blue Roan's layout: they would move in fifteen minutes. Everybody was to watch Dundee. When he broke into the open, they were all to ride fast and try to get as close as they could. He took out his watch and marked the time. He had gone without a cigarette all night. He had followed his own orders, even if nobody else had. Now in the coming daylight he guessed it wouldn't hurt to light one. He turned his back to the houses, though, and hid the flare with his body till he shook the match out. Most of the fifteen minutes were up when the cowboy came back.

Dundee dropped his cigarette on the ground, saddled his horse and checked his saddlegun. "Everybody here ready?"

Old John Titus sat waiting. Dundee couldn't tell whether he had slept or not; he doubted it. In fact, he doubted that Titus had really known sound sleep since Dundee had brought him word about Son. Dark shadows framed the eyes that seemed drawn back into the stony face. But there was an incandescence to those eyes, a fire that Dundee feared it might take a lot of blood to quench.

"I seen everybody," he said. "They'll be looking for you."

The saddlegun in his hand, ready for use, Dundee swung up. He glanced around to be sure the others were mounted, then said, "Let's go amongst them."

He touched the bay's ribs firmly with the spurs and brought the horse into a long trot down the slope. When he hit the flat terrain, he spurred into a hard lope. Around him he could see the other riders closing in, following his lead. A few shouted like Comanches, and he thought that was a foolish thing to do.

The horse's long stride reached out and gathered in the yards. The outbuildings seemed to rush headlong toward him, and he expected any second the puffs of smoke, the crackle of gunfire.

He could see the windows now, and count the panes; they were getting that close, the horses running full tilt, the hoofs drumming, the dust lifting in plumes as they crossed the grassless roundup grounds near the corrals. *Any second now they'll commence shooting at us.*

He watched the windows, for that was where the firing would come from, most likely.

It didn't start.

Maybe they're waiting for us to get so close they can't miss. They'll wait for us to poke our faces in those windows and then they'll blow our heads off. This is a damnfool way to do it anyhow. A smart man would've sneaked us in there like a bunch of Indians.

He was into the yard now, not a hundred feet from Blue Roan's log house. Dundee realized he was holding his breath, his lungs afire. The last few feet his heart was beating so hard he thought he could hear it, but it was only the hoofs.

Then he was at the house itself. He swung his leg over the bay's hips before the horse slid to a stop. Dundee jumped free and lit running, expecting a blast from the nearest window. He flattened against rough logs, breathing hard. He realized that not a shot had been fired.

He didn't wait to puzzle it out. He ran for the door, kicked it open with one hard thrust of his foot and leaped inside, hands tight on the carbine, ready to fire at the first thing that moved.

Nothing did. Dundee crouched, his chest heaving, his confused gaze sweeping the room.

Not a soul here. Just empty tin cans and dirty dishes, a whisky bottle on the floor; an unmade bed in a corner, a single dark stocking lying on the blankets, the kind the wheeligo girls wore in the saloons. Dundee examined the messed-up plates and found the food had dried. Nobody had eaten here since sometime yesterday.

He whirled at the sound of a footstep on the board floor. He lowered the carbine as he saw Tobe Crane. Crane's voice was heavy with disappointment. "There's nobody here."

"Maybe the bunkhouse."

Tobe shook his head. "Boys already been there. There was a lamp on the table, the coal oil all used up and the chimney burned black as pitch. They fooled us, Dundee. They must of knowed we was coming. Looks like they slipped away and left that lamp to fool us."

Stepping outside, Dundee watched the cowboys search the barn, the corrals. He let his gaze drift to the hill from which they had started.

Tobe Crane was looking the same way. "Maybe it's a good thing there wasn't anybody here. We'd of made perfect targets."

"I never claimed to be no West Point wonder. Leading green cowpunchers into a gunfight ain't my bowl of *chili* in the first place."

Tobe said: "Maybe we ought to've known we couldn't fool an old fox like Roan. He's got eyes in the back of his head, and maybe in his rump." He paused, studying. "Maybe old Roan took to the tulies."

"It'd take more than this bunch of cow nurses to scare Roan Hardesty out of a place like this, and away from a fortune in burnt cattle. I expect he took out for Runaway, where he'd have extra men, and maybe a better place to fight."

Old John Titus silently stared at Dundee, the disappointment keen in his pinched eyes.

Dundee said: "Mister Titus, we better send for more help. If Roan has holed up in Runaway—and I figure he has—there ain't enough of us to root him out. These cowboys of yours have got their hearts in the right place, but very little else."

The old man nodded slowly. "That's already took care of. Before we left, I got word out to other ranches around us . . . told them what we was fixing to do. I told them to send men to Runaway. This is *their* fight, too."

"More cowboys? What we need is Rangers."

"I waited till the very last to send word to the Rangers. I didn't want them getting in our way. They get kind of sticky about rules." The old man made a sweep with his arm. "Let's burn it all. Then we'll get on down to Runaway."

XII

Dundee had been on this hill overlooking Runaway so many times that he had just about all of the town memorized. He thought by now he knew the position of every building, every outdoor convenience, every rainbarrel. Looking down, he decided everything was in its proper place. Nothing moved, not even a jackrabbit.

He sensed Tobe Crane sitting on his horse beside him. Dundee said, "Well, they're down there all right, just waiting for us."

"How do you know? I don't see a thing."

"That's how you can tell."

John Titus halted beside Dundee, taking his first real look at Runaway. Dundee could see the old man's jaw harden. "So that's the place. That's the rattlesnake den that killed my boy."

Dundee nodded. "That's Runaway."

Titus' voice was like two strands of barbed wire rubbed together. "It won't be there when we leave."

"They're ready for us," Dundee said. "We ain't got the manpower just to ride in and take over. They'd cut us down like weeds. Maybe we ought to leave Runaway alone. There's a heap of little rustler camps we could handle instead. With them gone, Runaway would wither anyhow."

"We didn't come to catch a handful of rats. We come to wipe out the nest," Titus said.

Dundee rubbed his jaw. "It's a hell of a big nest."

"We come to take it."

Dundee turned in the saddle and looked back over the cowboys. Thirty of them he had, plus a wounded Tobe Crane and a bitter old man whose hatred was far steadier than his gnarled hand. "It won't come cheap."

"I'll pay the price. You afraid, Dundee?"

Dundee frowned. "It ain't like being in church."

"They can be taken. We got enough men to surround the town and keep anybody from getting out. Sooner or later they'll have to give up."

"They probably got enough food to carry them awhile. I know they got lots of whisky."

"You'll see, Dundee. They'll break down. They'll get nervous waiting, and sooner or later they'll try to bust out. We'll be here, and we'll be ready."

"It'll scatter us pretty thin, trying to surround the whole town."

"When the will is strong enough. . . ."

Dundee would admit that the will of these cowboys was plenty strong. If only they had the aim to go with it. . . . "We'll try it your way, Mister Titus."

"You're damn right you will."

Along the way Dundee had tried to make a study of the men and pick out the best fighting prospects. Two or three of them, he judged, could as well be down there in Runaway as up here waiting to lay siege to it. But so long as they were in on it, he was glad they were on his side instead of against him. He started down off the hill and began a wide circle of the town, dropping off a man here, a man there, at fairly regular intervals where there was cover. About every third or fourth place he dropped one of the men he thought might be better than average with a gun. He placed the men in a wide semicircle, for the bluff itself effectively sealed off that side of the town.

"If they decide to try a break," he told the men, "they'll go for what they figure is the weakest spot in our line. One man won't be much hindrance to them. If you see trouble, burn leather getting there. The man on that spot will need all the help he can get."

He didn't really expect any such break. The outlaws probably felt a strong confidence in their superiority over a little bunch of green cowboys. If they'd wanted to leave Runaway, they would have done it before this posse got here.

The men all placed, he paused at the foot of the hill and looked at the town. Curiosity began to nettle him. How close *could* they get in there? The wagonyard caught his eye. It struck him that if the wind blew hard enough, and if a man could get to that barn and drop a match into dry hay, fire might spread down the street, touching off first one building, then the next. It was a narrow-odds bet, but he'd taken risks ever since he'd left home as a kid, gambling that he wouldn't starve to death. He'd almost lost *that* bet.

He touched a spur to the horse's ribs and decided to see just how far he could get.

He quickly found out. Dundee saw the flash of a rifle and heard a bullet ricochet off the rocks with a vicious whine. He whirled and spurred for the hill. His curiosity was satisfied.

John Titus and Tobe Crane waited on top of the hill. Tobe was not physically able to contribute much; it amazed Dundee that he'd gotten this far without dropping from exhaustion. And he knew he couldn't count on the old man for much action. He said, "Well, sir, I reckon you can see that they've dug into there like lice in a buffalo robe."

Titus' expression never altered. "They can't stay forever."

Presently Dundee's eye was caught by movement in the street, then at the wagonyard. A man rode out of the corral with a rifle in his hand, waving a white cloth tied to the end of it. He moved toward the hill.

John Titus' eyes went wide as spur rowels. "They're giving up."

Dundee said: "Not hardly, not when they got most of the chips on their end of the table. I expect thay want to palaver. I'll go down and see what it's all about."

Tobe Crane warned: "You watch them, Dundee. It'd tickle them to see you dead."

"I'll watch. That idea don't appeal to me."

He took his time, his gaze never straying far from the horseman who held the rifle and the white cloth. It occurred to Dundee that the rifle was probably loaded, just in case. His lips dry, his nerves wound tight as a watchspring, he strongly considered drawing his carbine and making sure it was loaded too. But he resisted.

He recognized Jason Karnes. Now he *knew* that rifle was loaded.

He stopped and let the be-stubbled Karnes travel the last few lengths to meet him. Dundee noticed how the man's leg was held out stiffly away from the saddle. *A little souvenir I gave him.* They stared cold-eyed at each other a minute before Dundee said, "I bet that was *you* who shot at me a little while ago."

Karnes nodded. "It was."

"I'm pleased to find your aim ain't improved much."

"It'll get better. I got me a crippled leg now. They say when a man loses one thing, he gains someplace else. I'm counting on a better shooting eye."

"You ought to've counted on your horse-picking eye and cut you out a fast one to get you away from here. There's an old man up yonder on that hill who's come to see blood."

"He's still on the hill, though. And that's as far as he's going to get. Except under a flag of truce. That's what Roan sent me for. He wants to parley with old man Titus."

"I'll ask him."

"Roan says tell the old man not to bring a gun, and Roan won't bring his either."

Dundee's eyes narrowed. "And maybe ride into a trap? No thanks. The old man may come without a gun, but *I* won't. I'll come along to be sure there don't nothing happen to him."

"Fair enough. And I'll be here to take care of old Roan case one of your bunch gets a foolish notion."

Karnes slowly turned his horse around and started back toward town. He shifted his body in the saddle so he could watch Dundee over his shoulder.

Dundee wasn't even that trustful. He waited until the distance between them had stretched to a good fifty yards before he brought his bay around. He carried the message back up the hill.

John Titus clenched tough fists. "I got nothing to talk to Roan about."

"You say you figure on staying here and starving them out if you have to. Maybe you could convince him of that."

"I won't make him no promises I don't intend to keep. And I know what I plan to do with Roan when I get my hands on him."

So did Dundee. The thought had gnawed on him for a long time. "It won't hurt to go down and talk."

He prevailed on John Titus to leave his pistol and his saddlegun with Tobe at the top of the hill. They started down together. In town, a long way off, Dundee could see two horsemen leave the corral and start toward them. Jason Karnes was still riding the same stocking-legged black he had been on a little while ago. The other figure was the unmistakably blocky one of Roan Hardesty, riding that dappled gray he favored so much.

Dundee asked John Titus, "How long since you've seen Blue Roan?"

Titus thoughtfully shook his head. "Many and many a year."

"You may not know him, then."

"I'll know him. I'd know his hide in a tanyard."

A tiny group of live oaks clustered below the hill. There Dundee and John Titus stopped to wait, for it was about the halfway point. Dundee had brought his saddlegun across his lap now, ready. He noted that Jason Karnes had done the same.

Roan Hardesty didn't rein up until his horse was touching necks with that of John Titus. The blue splotches on his face stood out like the dapple marks on his horse. His eyes were soft with an offering of friendship. "It's been a long time, John." He held out his right hand.

John Titus let his own hands remain at his sides. His eyes were cold as December and seemed to freeze onto Roan Hardesty. He made no effort to reply.

Roan slowly drew back his hand and rubbed it nervously on his huge leg. He looked down a moment, framing his words as if each might fall back and crush him. "John, I felt real bad about your boy. Maybe Dundee has told you: I give orders there wasn't nobody to kill him. I've turned this town upside down, trying to find out who it was went against my orders. Nobody'll own up to it." He paused, waiting for a reaction that didn't come. "I swear to you, John, if I knowed who it was, I'd kill him myself."

John Titus' throat showed a tremor. "I come to see you die, Roan."

The aging outlaw slumped in the saddle. "We was friends for a long time, John. We warred together, remember? We rode the brush together. We seen the elephant and heard the owl hoot."

"I got a boy dead now, Roan."

"John, I've took a lot of your cows; Lord, I wouldn't deny that. But I never took your son. I never had no intention for harm to come to him."

Titus repeated, quieter this time, "I come to see you die."

The silence between them then was long and heavy. They stared at each other, the outlaw's eyes regretful, Titus' eyes cold and grim. It was Roan who finally spoke. "Well, John, I've said all I can. I'm sorry the way it all happened. We was friends a long time. But if this is where friendship has to end, so be it. You can't take our town, not with what you got here. You'd never even get into the street."

"We got you all bottled up. All we got to do now is outlast you. I'll stay all summer if I have to, and into the fall."

Roan Hardesty looked around him, trying to pick out the places where Dundee had stationed the men. "What you got, John? Twenty-five men? Thirty? And just cowboys at that." His eyes narrowed. "I'll tell you something you didn't know. I got friends scattered all over them hills. I sent word last night to the forks of the creek. When they all get here, it'll look like the Confederate army. They'll run over your bunch like wild studs over pet ponies."

Dundee stiffened. He hoped it wouldn't show. This was one thing he hadn't considered, that Hardesty might get reinforcements in substantial numbers.

Titus said tightly: "We'll take care of ourselves, Roan. Tell your men that every time one of them sticks his head out, somebody's going to take a shot at him. They'll get almighty tired of dodging every time they need a bucket of water or a sack of beans."

Roan's splotchy face was clouded now with trouble. "I'll tell them, John." He started to turn away but paused. "There's some women down in town, and a few men that got no part in this. Ain't fair to risk getting them hurt. I'd like to send them out, John."

"Send them, then. We got no war on against women."

Dundee watched John Titus' face as Roan Hardesty slowly rode back toward town. If a momentary softness showed here, it was quickly covered by a steely determination.

Dundee offered: "I think he's telling you the truth, Mister Titus. I don't think he knows who killed Son."

Titus was silent.

In a little while a horseman appeared outside the barn, a white cloth tied to a long stick. He rode into the clear, stopped and waved the cloth from side to side so everyone could see it. Then he turned in the saddle. Out from the corrals came two buckboards and a wagon, trailed by a second horseman. Even at the distance Dundee could see the ribbons and streamers and colored dresses.

"The women," he said. "They're coming out."

Titus' brow furrowed. "No children?"

"This ain't exactly a family town."

The front rider, carrying the white cloth, was the wagon-yard operator. Behind him, in the buckboard, Dundee could recognize Katy Long. Driving was the little bartender Cricket. As they came up even with Dundee, Katy motioned for Cricket to stop. She looked Dundee straight in the eye, and he thought she might be laughing a little. "See, Dundee? I told you you'd be back."

"And I told you to sell that saloon. Did you?"

"Nobody made me an offer."

"A pity."

Any smile she might have had was suddenly gone. "You don't really think you can take that town, do you? With *that* bunch of men?"

"Titus says we'll take it. So, we'll take it."

"Roan Hardesty says you won't. He doesn't make many mistakes."

"He's made one."

The wagonyard operator got as close to Dundee as he could. "Friend, I got a valuable piece of property down there. I've always tried to treat you square."

"Like double-charging me for hay?"

"I'm sorry we had a misunderstanding over that." He reached in his pocket and came up with a silver coin. "Here, I'd like to pay you back."

"Keep it. When this is over, that may be all you got left."

Some of the women were protesting angrily, while others just sat and looked frightened. A couple tried to flirt with Dundee. He waved them on. The horseman who came along behind the wagons was a middle-aged, portly gent Dundee hadn't seen before. "Mister

Dundee, my name is Smith, and I'm a legitimate businessman. I own the mercantile down there." He offered his hand, but Dundee ignored it. Smith went on: "I have a considerable investment. What you're doing here is jeopardizing my property. I'd like to see it stopped, immediately."

"Oh, you would?"

"I would dislike having to protest to the state authorities, but I will if I must. You have no right to stand in the way of an honest businessman and disrupt his trade."

Dundee turned in the saddle and pointed east. "Well, now, you just go right ahead and protest if you want to. About two days' hard ride in that direction will get you to Austin. Three days if that saddle makes your rump sore."

He hoped the women would go on, but they didn't. They moved a little way down the road and proceeded to set up camp. Dundee thought about all those women, and all those cowboys. You couldn't keep up much of a siege when half your men weren't on duty. He said a few choice words under his breath, swung onto the bay and trotted down to where the women were struggling to set up a couple of big tents. He noted that Katy Long was not among them, a point which brought him considerable satisfaction.

"You can just take that thing down and put it back in the wagon," he hollered. "You're not going to use it here."

The big redheaded woman he had had a run-in with before came stalking forward like an angry she-bear, her hands on her hips. Dundee wouldn't have been much surprised if she had breathed fire at him. She didn't, but her breath was bad enough. "Who the hell says so?"

"Me."

She looked back over her shoulder. The women had the tent just about set up. "Now, Mister Tall, Dark and Ugly, what do you intend to do about it? Are you low-down enough to shoot a woman? You'd have to, you know, before we'd take that tent down."

Dundee tried to hold his rising temper. "I'd ask you real polite."

"Well, we won't take it down. So what do you do now?"

Dundee said, "Then *I'll* take it down."

He lifted his hornstring and freed his rope. He shook out a loop and spurred the bay into a brisk trot, nearly bumping the redhead before she could jump aside, cursing. He swung the loop while the women ran screaming. He dropped it over the top of the tent, jerked out the slack, dallied the rope around the horn and squalled a cowboy yell as he spurred the bay into a run. The tent stakes flipped out of the ground, and the tent came sailing after him. The horses took a wild-eyed look at the flying apparition and stampeded. The wagon bounced behind them, scattering clothes and camp goods for two hundred yards up the trail.

Dundee stopped and freed his rope. Recoiling it, he rode back into a circle of shaken, angry women. His gaze fastened on the redhead. "Like I was saying, you ain't stopping here. I'll go fetch your team back, and you'll be going on your way."

He rode up the trail to where the team had finally stopped. At the side of the road, Katy Long had halted her buckboard and had witnessed the excitement from afar. Now she watched grinning as Dundee approached. "You play rough, Dundee."

"Them women got no business here. They'd just be a temptation to the men."

"Am I included?"

"You're not like them others. But you'd be a temptation to *me*."

"Well, thanks for that."

The bartender Cricket helped him take the wagon back. Dundee didn't leave till he saw the women on their way. Even then he knew they wouldn't travel far. He had seen cows that would move only so long as a horseman pushed them. When he stopped pushing, they would stop moving. Dundee knew the women would move on a mile or two, then stop again, confident Roan's bunch would win and they could go back to Runaway.

At least they would be out from underfoot.

At the hill, he watched with John Titus and Tobe Crane as a man started across the street from one saloon toward another. Half a dozen rifles rattled from vantage points around town, including a couple on top of the cliff. Dust kicked up in half a dozen places. The man turned and trotted briskly back where he had come from.

"Not very good shots, are they?" Dundee said.

"They try," Titus replied defensively.

"Trying ain't going to be enough."

In retaliation, rifles set up a racket down in town, Hardesty's men trying to find the places where the cowboys were spotted. So far as Dundee could tell, their aim wasn't a lot better. "Looks to me like a Mexican standoff. We can't go in, and they can't go out."

"We can wait," said Titus. "Time is on our side."

Dundee frowned. "I don't know. I got the feeling old Roan didn't lie about having more men on the way. I tell you, Mister Titus, if there's many of them they can circle our outfit and pick off them boys one at a time. It'd be like shooting ducks in a tank."

"I told you, Dundee, I sent for more help too."

"You didn't get no promises, did you?"

Titus didn't answer.

Through the long afternoon they sat impatiently watching, waiting, Dundee trying a little mumble peg, then whittling sticks down to a pile of white shavings, whistling some half-forgotten tune till it felt as if his lips would crack. The old man huddled most of the time like some wounded eagle, his gaze fastened on the town. Tobe Crane paced till he got tired, sat awhile, arose and paced some more. It finally got on Dundee's nerves.

"You're supposed to be recuperating. Sit down and get still."

"Walking don't bother me."

"It bothers *me*. Sit down."

Tobe Crane did as he was told, but he took his time, as if to show that if the idea didn't suit him he wouldn't have done it. Dundee softened a little. "I didn't much cotton to you coming along in the first place. You don't take care of yourself, Millie's liable to blame me. She's invested a lot of work in getting you on your feet."

Tobe Crane stared at the ground. "Yes, she has."

Dundee studied the cowboy, his eyes narrowed in speculation. "She's a real pretty girl. A man could lose his head over her," he said.

Crane said, "She seemed to think a great deal of you, Dundee."

Dundee winced. From somewhere came a touch of pain. "I'll admit, I've done a heap of thinking . . . wonder if ever I could make myself settle down and try to build a home for a girl like that."

Crane glanced at him a second and looked away. "You still thinking about it?"

"Some."

"Made up your mind?"

"Not yet. I'm afraid I know other people better than I know myself."

"Are you sure you know Millie?"

"I think so."

Tobe Crane pushed to his feet again and stared wistful-eyed down the valley. "I hope you don't figure her wrong."

XIII

They had salvaged a chuckwagon from Roan Hardesty's place before they put it to the torch. Now a couple of the men cooked supper, and the cowboys rode in a few at a time to eat. Dundee tried, but he couldn't stir up much appetite, looking down upon that town. They weren't any closer to it now than they had been this morning. He couldn't help thinking that Roan's reinforcements might show up, and then it would be hell among the yearlings.

The breeze came up with twilight, a breeze out of the south. Dundee got to mulling again the idea that had occurred to him during the day . . . setting fire to the town and forcing the renegades out. He hadn't gotten past the turnrow the first time, but that had been daylight. With luck a man might sneak through in the dark.

He told the old man about the notion, and Titus seemed receptive. He would accept anything right now except retreat. Tobe Crane said, "I'll go down there with you, Dundee."

"You stay here. You ain't got the strength," Dundee said.

"That's what you thought before. I'll go with you."

Dundee didn't argue any further. Tobe Crane was a grown man and able to make his own mind up . . . even if now and then he did seem to have more guts than sense. They circled southward, visiting all the posts to tell the men what they were up to.

"I wouldn't want to get the job done and then be shot by our own bunch," Dundee said. "That'd be a real joke on us."

From the south Dundee remembered a clump of live oaks about halfway between their outposts and the first outbuildings of the town. Saddlegun across his lap, he slow-walked the bay in that direction, hoping to get done before the moon came up. Dundee could sense Tobe Crane's nervousness. Tobe had punched cows all his life. He'd probably never been shot at till the first time he came to Runaway.

"Easy, boy," Dundee whispered. "If they spot us, be ready to leave here like a Jeff Davis cannonball."

They made the trees, somewhat to Dundee's surprise. He tried the bay. "If we get in a jam, Tobe, you run like the devil. Don't wait on me. It's every man for himself."

Dundee moved out from the trees in a crouch, saddlegun cradled in his arm. Because of his wound, Tobe carried only a sixshooter, and Dundee doubted he could hit his own hat with it. But it was reassuring to have company.

The first building they reached was a cowshed, with lots of dry hay in it. That, Dundee figured, would burn easily. The breeze was still out of the south, and it stood a good chance of carrying the fire through the summer-dried grass on into the rest of town. But the closer he could get to start his fire, the better the odds. He decided to try next for an empty-looking log shack. He bent low and sprinted across a short clearing. Flattening himself against the logs, he waited for any sign that he had been seen. When none came, he motioned for Tobe.

They'd made it this far. Maybe they could do even better. The next building was the frame house where he had found Son Titus whiling time away with the girl Lutie. He thought it ought to burn with a jolly blaze. He eased out to make a try for it. He had gone three long strides when a voice came from one of the open windows. "What you doing out there?"

Dundee's heart leaped, but he decided to brazen it on through. "Looking for a bottle. You got an extra one?"

"No. You go find your own."

Dundee let out a long-held breath. Well, he'd found out how far he could go. He retreated to the shack and Tobe Crane. "If we try to go any farther somebody'll chop us off at the knees."

He tested the door and found it open, the shack deserted. "Stay outside and keep your eyes peeled," he said. Finding a kerosene lamp, he spread kerosene on the floor and up the walls. He saved some and spilled it in a line out into the dry grass, as far as it would go. Then he fished in his pocket for the matches. "The boys ain't going to appreciate this much, so get ready to run."

He pulled up a handful of dry grass, twisted it, then used his body to shield it from the breeze until the match's tiny flame took hold and the grass blazed up. He dropped it into the heavy grass around the cowshed. In moments the flames were racing through the grass, found the kerosene, followed it across the clearing and up into the shack.

"It's pretty," Dundee said, "but let's don't wait for the whole show." They struck out in a hard run for the clump of live oaks. A shout went up, and another and another. Dogs barked. In a moment men were running in the street, hollering, everybody trying to give orders. A few wild shots were fired. Dundee mounted the bay. "Let's go back up on the hill where the view is better."

They were halfway there when Tobe Crane said, "Dundee, you notice something?"

"What?"

"The breeze has stopped."

Dundee reined up and looked back. He saw the shack collapse in a shower of sparks, the flames leaping high, then dying down. But Tobe was right. The breeze had quit. There was nothing to carry the flames any farther up the street.

"One cowshed and one flea-ridden shack," Dundee gritted. "But at least we got our exercise."

★　　★　　★

Dundee got more exercise that night, pacing, worrying, thinking about Hardesty's outside men coming to stop the siege, and maybe laying out a bunch of well-intentioned cowboys in the grass to stay. By daylight he was up, sleepy-eyed and irritable. He hadn't slept much. He went down and pulled four men out of the line and put them off on horseback to patrol as outriders, to watch for anyone who might be coming to give aid to the town. One by one he gave the message to the other men: "If trouble comes, the signal will be three shots, fired as quick as a man can pull the trigger. You get on your horse and get there as fast as you can ride. Scattered, we may not put up much fight. Together, we'll give them their money's worth."

Later Dundee sipped coffee and watched John Titus through narrowed eyes. *Crazy old man. Wants revenge worse than he wants to stop the cattle thieving. He could've cleaned this country up, hitting a camp at a time. But he's got to take on the whole town. Crazy old man.*

The mood passed, for Dundee thought he could understand John Titus. Once, the cattle had been important. But that had been while he still had a son.

Dundee turned his attention to Tobe Crane. He thought of Millie McCown. The last thing in his mind as he dozed off to sleep was a mental picture of Tobe holding Millie's hand as they all stood at Son Titus' grave.

Three quick-paced shots brought him out of the nap and onto his feet, grabbing at his carbine. He blinked away the sleep and saw one of the Titus cowboys spurring toward him on the trail that led in from the northeast. The cowboy shouted, "They're coming! They're coming!"

He slid his horse to a stop. Dundee glanced down the hill and saw the scattered Titus cowboys beginning to get into their saddles. It would take a while before they could all get here.

"Who's coming?" he demanded.

"I don't know," the rider blurted, face flushed with excitement. "I didn't let them get close enough to tell. But Dundee . . . Mister Titus . . . there's a hell of a bunch of them. Must be forty . . . maybe fifty."

Dundee swallowed, his fists going tight. This was what he had been afraid of. He glanced back down the hill again, mentally calculating how long it would take all the Titus cowboys to get here.

"How much time we got?"

"They're right on us."

Dundee could see the dust now, and he knew the cowboys wouldn't get here in time, not enough of them. At this moment there were only five: himself, John Titus, Tobe, the outrider and a man who had stayed at the chuckwagon to cook. "Let's get to cover," he shouted. "Maybe we can give them something to chew on till the rest of the boys reach here."

He threw himself down behind a heavy live oak, the saddlegun ready. Old John Titus knelt behind another, rifle resting against the trunk. Tobe Crane lay on his belly, favoring the wounded arm, holding a pistol in his hand.

Dundee took a deep breath, then drew a bead on the lead rider. He would wait until he knew he couldn't miss.

John Titus shouted. Dundee tried not to be distracted, but he lost his head. The old man shouted again. "It's *our* bunch, Dundee! It's ours!"

Dundee lowered the carbine "What'd you say?"

"It's my neighbors, Dundee, the ones I sent for. That's old Charlie Moore there in the lead. I'd know his dun horse anywhere. And that man on the *grulla,* he's Walter Matthews of the Half Circle M. They've come to help us."

Dundee pushed to his feet and took off his hat, wiping cold sweat from his forehead onto his sleeve.

*   *   *

In town, a commotion began in the streets as the new riders showed on the hill. Horses stirred dust. Men ran to and fro. Though the sound didn't carry, there was visible sign of violent argument. Some of the Titus cowboys started dropping slugs down there, adding to the melee. Then there came the muffled rumble of hoofs, the sharp shouts of excited men. Twenty or more horsemen spurred toward the south end of town, toward the river and the span of open country that stretched beyond.

"They're trying a break!" Dundee shouted. "Let's get them!"

He swung onto the bay and took the lead, moving headlong down the hill, angling southwestward, running over brush, scattering rocks. He didn't look back, but he could hear other horses running behind him. Dundee took an oblique course that he hoped would intercept the fleeing outlaws. He could see desperation in the way they spurred, flaying horses with their quirts. Some began snapping wild shots toward the Titus posse. None struck Dundee, and he didn't have time right now to see if they hit anyone else. He just kept spurring.

Now he could begin to make out faces. He looked for the bulky shape of Roan Hardesty but couldn't pick him out from the crowd. It occurred to him that the dappled gray wasn't in the bunch. Roan was still in town.

They've run out on him, he realized. *They seen they was whipped and they run out on him.*

He saw one face he knew too well. Jason Karnes, on the stocking-legged black. Dundee couldn't hear the words, but he could almost read them on the twisting lips of the black-whiskered outlaw. Karnes raised a six-shooter and snapped a shot at Dundee. His horse almost stumbled, and Karnes was busy a few seconds getting his balance. Then the pistol came up again.

Dundee swung his saddlegun into line. It was hard enough, making a shot from a running horse. It was almost impossible, making one to the right. Dundee tried to compensate by twisting his body as far as he could. He squeezed the trigger and knew he had missed. Karnes pulled closer, within pistol range. The pistol cracked again, and Dundee felt a tug at his sleeve, a searing pain as the bullet raked him.

Now the range was almost point blank. Dundee squeezed the trigger again. Karnes jerked backward, slipped over the horse's right hip and tumbled to the ground. Dundee lost sight of him in the dust as horses went over and past him.

Other shots were being fired. He saw the outlaws begin reining to a stop, trying to raise their hands. Some still spurred, attempting to outrun the cowboys.

Dundee's bay was slowing, tiring. Dundee let him bring himself slowly to a stop, for he knew the horse had about done its do. Around him, possemen were gathering in those fugitives who had quit. Others kept up the run.

They'll catch the most of them, he told himself. *I better get down yonder and see about Roan.*

Moving back toward town in a slow trot, he passed the still form of Jason Karnes. One look was enough. He took no pleasure in the sight, no satisfaction from bringing the outlaw down.

That's two I've took out of the family, he thought. *It ain't a thing to make a man proud.*

John Titus angled down to meet him, trailed by Tobe Crane. The old man knew before Dundee told him. "Roan's still in town."

Dundee nodded. "He wasn't with that bunch. They deserted him. Not many of them will get away."

Titus said severely: "I don't care so much about them. I want Roan."

"I'll go down there and see if I can find him."

"Roan's mine. I'm going with you."

Dundee wanted to argue, but he knew it would be useless. He

glanced at the young cowboy. "You coming, Tobe?" When the cowboy answered yes, Dundee said: "Keep a sharp eye out, then. A cornered bear is apt to bite."

They rode slowly up the street, three abreast. Dundee's sweeping gaze probed the open doors, the windows, the alleyways.

Titus called: "Roan! Roan, you come on out here. I want you."

No reply.

Ahead of them lay the Llano River Saloon. Instinctively Dundee felt drawn toward it. He'd seen Roan there before. He pointed and said quietly, "Mister Titus, I think yonder's the place."

He rode as close as he dared, then started to swing out of the saddle. Halfway down, he caught a glimpse of movement, saw the big man step out through the open doors, shot-gun in his huge hands.

"Hold it right where you're at, Dundee! Don't move another inch."

Dundee halted, half in and half out of the saddle, the saddlegun in his right hand but not where he could swing it into play. Tobe Crane held a six-shooter uncertainly. John Titus just sat there staring down into the awesome bore of that shotgun, both hands resting easily on the saddlehorn. If he felt any fear, his face did not betray it.

Roan said in a heavy voice that was a mixture of anger and desperation: "John, I told you not to come down here. I told you I didn't kill that boy."

Titus was steady as an ancient live oak. "If you're figuring on pulling that trigger, Roan, do it now. It's going to be you or me."

"John, we was friends once. I don't want to have to kill you."

"I come to hang you, Roan. I'll do it, unless you shoot me."

It came to Dundee with the force of a mule-kick what John Titus was attempting to do. He was trying to force Roan into shooting him, knowing Roan wouldn't live to get ten steps down the street.

He was willing to throw himself away to see Roan Hardesty brought to the ground. "Mister Titus. . . ."

Titus ignored Dundee. He said: "Go on, Roan. Do it if you're going to. I'm fixing to draw my gun." The old man's hand slowly went down to his hip, closed over the pistol there and came up again. It seemed it took him all day.

Roan Hardesty's face whitened, and the blue blotches seemed to go almost black. For a moment it was in his eyes to pull the trigger. But then his chin fell. Slowly he let the muzzle of the shotgun sink toward the ground. He leaned on a tiepost for strength.

"I couldn't do it, John."

Titus said, "Get him, Dundee."

Dundee hesitated. "What you going to do?"

"Just what I said I was. I'm going to hang him."

"You can't do that. You got to wait for the Rangers."

"My boy'll sleep easy tonight. The man responsible for killing him will be dead."

"Mister Titus. . . ."

"Your work is finished, Dundee. I'm taking over now. We'll wait till the men get back. Then we'll take Roan to a fit place out yonder on the river. Runaway is fixing to die. We'll let him die with it."

Dundee glanced sadly at the aging outlaw, his eyes trying to tell Roan he was sorry now that he hadn't gotten away. Roan seemed to understand. "Don't worry yourself, Dundee. I already lived beyond my time. I wouldn't lie to you; I don't want to die. But I reckon I've had my day."

Dundee walked into the saloon, sick at heart. He rummaged around behind the bar and came up with part of a bottle of whisky. He stood in the door, leaning his shoulder against the jamb, drinking straight out of the bottle and watching the cowboys slowly drift in, bringing their prisoners with them—one here, two there, three in another bunch. Roan Hardesty sat slumped in a chair that had been dragged out into the street, the cowboys ringed around him. John Titus still sat on his horse, his leathery old face dark and grim.

A buckboard came down the street. Leaning out the door, Dundee saw Katy Long, a thin girl riding beside her. The girl was Lutie. The cowboys turned to stare. Katy pulled her team to a halt and took a long, apprehensive look at Roan Hardesty. Then her eyes went to Dundee. She jumped down from the buckboard and motioned for Lutie to follow. The girl moved slowly, reluctantly. Katy rushed to Dundee's side.

"What're they going to do to Roan?"

"John Titus says he's fixing to hang him."

"He can't."

"With all them cowboys? He can do anything he damn pleases."

"It's not right, Dundee. Roan didn't kill Son Titus."

"You know it, and I know it. I think even John Titus knows it. But we can't prove which one of his men did do it, so Roan pays."

Katy's eyes turned blue with regret. "Dundee, I've got something to tell you. I didn't want to, didn't intend to. But now it's the only way. It's got to be done."

"Tell me what?"

"I'll let Lutie." She motioned for the girl. Lutie came to her unwillingly, dragging her feet, looking at the floor. "Lutie, you tell Dundee what you told me."

When Lutie's story was over, Dundee found his left fist clenched so tightly the knuckles were white. He lifted the bottle and took a long, long swallow. He cut his eyes to the girl and demanded threateningly, "You sure you ain't lying to me?"

Frightened, Lutie shook her head. Katy said protectively: "She's telling the truth, Dundee. Added to everything else, it figures."

Dundee turned and hurled the bottle at the saloon wall. It shattered, the whisky spattering and running down to the floor. He rubbed his hand across his face, then stalked out into the street. He strode to where John Titus sat on his horse.

"Mister Titus, you've trusted me for weeks now. Do you still trust me?"

Surprised, the old ranchman said, "Sure, Dundee."

"Then trust me when I tell you old Blue Roan didn't kill your boy. It wasn't Roan, and it wasn't none of Roan's men."

"Then who was it?"

"I can't tell you yet. I know, but it's something I got to handle myself. Trust me."

"Dundee, I got to have more to go on than this. I got to. . . ."

"You got to wait. You got to let Roan live till I get back. Then you'll know the whole thing. Will you do that? Will you trust me?"

The old man stammered. "I ought not to . . . But I will, Dundee. I'll wait."

Dundee turned. "Katy, if I ain't back in a reasonable time, you tell John Titus what you told me."

Katy's voice held a tremor. "Dundee, you better take some help with you."

He shook his head. "This job I got to handle alone." He mounted the bay and rode toward the hill.

XIV

A head of him lay the creek, and beyond that the McCown headquarters. Face rigid, his jaw set square, Dundee rode toward the
spring where Uncle Ollie McCown sat watching him. Ollie had his
fishing pole, the hook sunk into the water below the spring.

"Howdy, Dundee," he called. "You-all do up your business in
Runaway?"

Dundee stared hard at the old man, wondering how much he
knew. "Ollie, I'm looking for Warren."

The tone of his voice betrayed him, for Ollie shrank back.
Dundee could see realization sinking in. "Ollie, I asked you, where's
Warren at?"

Ollie's voice was strained. "Big bunch of men rode by here
some hours ago, on their way to help you-all. I reckon you took
good care of old Roan and his bunch by now, didn't you?"

Now Dundee was convinced: Ollie knew. He might not have
participated, but he knew.

"Ollie, I know the whole thing now. I'll ask you one more time,
where's Warren?"

Ollie looked down at the water. "Dundee, Millie's up at the
house. I bet she'll be real tickled to see you back. She baked up some
cookies. They'd sure go good with a cup of coffee. I bet you and her
could find a right smart to talk about." He paused, trying to gather
strength. "She thinks the world of you, Dundee. If you was to ask
her, she'd marry you in a minute. You could do a lot worse. She's a
good girl."

"Ollie, does she know anything about this?"

Quickly the old man blurted: "She don't know nothing,

Dundee. Warren didn't tell her nothing, and he'd of beat me to death if I'd ever even hinted to her. . . ." He realized he had said too much. He looked down at the fishing line again. Cold sweat broke on his forehead.

Dundee said, "Ollie, I still want to know . . ."

The old man wiped his sleeve over his face. "Sure is hot." His voice was almost gone. He was on the verge of crying. "Seems like it gets hotter every year. Things ain't what they used to be. Things has gone to hell, seems like. Time was when the world was fresh and sweet as dew. Now everything's got a bitter taste, and there's no pleasure left in being alive. It's hell to be an old man, Dundee."

Pitying him, Dundee turned away.

He rode to the house. Millie came out into the doorway, trying to brush back her long hair with her hand. She smiled, and her face was so pretty Dundee could feel his heart tearing in two. The joy that danced in her eyes brought the bite of tears to his own.

"Dundee, is it all over with? Are you all right?"

He clenched his teeth and tried not to look at her. He couldn't help it; he had to look, and he felt his throat tighten. "Millie, I've got to see Warren. Is he here?"

She caught the gravity in his eyes now, and in his voice. Her joy faded, and worry rushed in. "He's up yonder working on his rock corrals. What's the matter, Dundee?"

He looked toward the rock pens that were the symbol of a man's driving ambition, of a poverty-born obsession for acquiring land and cattle, for building a protective wall of stolen wealth around him so that never again could he slide back into the squalor that had scarred his soul.

Millie demanded: "There's something wrong, Dundee. What is it?"

"I'll have to let Warren tell you."

He pulled away from her and rode toward the pens. He didn't

dare look back, but he knew she was standing there watching him, confusion and fear crowding in around her. Though she did not know it yet, her world was about to come tumbling down; her anchor of security was about to be dragged away.

Warren McCown stood behind a half-finished rock fence, sweat soaking his dirt-crusted shirt, rolling down his sun-browned face. Dundee guessed that by his own appearance and manner he was betraying himself, for he could see suspicion in Warren McCown.

"What's the trouble, Dundee?"

"Maybe you ought to tell *me*, Warren. Maybe you ought to tell me what really happened to Son Titus."

Warren tensed. They stared at each other a long time in silence. "You know as much as I do, Dundee."

"Maybe. I think I've figured out some things now. For one thing, I know why you used to have trouble with Roan Hardesty and his men. It wasn't for the reason you said, that they was driving stolen cattle across your land. It was because you was in competition with them. Old Roan wanted to run things in this country, but you was stealing for yourself and wouldn't split anything with him.

"That time you went south to buy cattle . . . you went north first. You stole T Bar cattle from old Titus, drove them south and traded them for cattle that had been stole down on the border. That way you didn't have any T Bar stuff on your country."

"You got an awful imagination, Dundee."

"Not very. That cowboy that helped you . . . first thing he done when he left here was to head for Runaway to fill his belly full of liquor and wrap himself around a soft, warm town girl. He told her things he ought to've kept to himself. Then Son Titus came along, and he found that girl. He got her drunk enough that she told him things *she* ought to've kept quiet. Last time he left Runaway he was coming out here to brace you with the facts. Somewhere out yonder you ran into each other, and you killed him."

Warren McCown rubbed his sweaty hands on the legs of his britches. "What you figure on doing, Dundee?"

"I figure on taking you to the Rangers. If old John Titus gets hold of you, he'll hang you."

Warren's face twisted in bitterness. "Titus. It's always been a Titus. I told you my daddy died on a ranch, didn't I, Dundee? But I didn't tell you which one. It was the Titus ranch. Daddy had dragged us there just the week before, the way he dragged us everywhere, hungry and broke and wearing castoff clothes that nobody else wanted. Old man John Titus was so big he didn't know the names of half his men. I doubt he ever even seen my daddy. Son Titus was just a button then but spoiled rotten as a barrelful of bad apples. He was playing around the herd instead of tending to his job, and he let a big steer get out. Daddy spurred off after him, and his horse fell. Daddy never knew what hit him. They buried him right there on the Titus ranch, gave us kids a couple of months' wages and told us how bad they felt. Well, John Titus has owed us something for that, something a lot more than a little handful of money."

"He didn't owe you his boy's life."

"I didn't want to kill him. He forced it on me. Said he'd take away everything we had and burn our place to the ground. I'd put in too many years of sweat. I couldn't let him wreck us."

"I got to take you in, Warren. Maybe a jury will see your side and go easy."

"And what happens to Millie? What happens to this place? No, Dundee. You're not taking me anywhere."

Dundee reached for his pistol. Warren moved suddenly, crouching behind the rock fence and coming up with a rifle.

Dundee shouted: "Don't be a fool, Warren. Kill me and there'll be others. There'll be no end to it."

But he saw the intention in Warren's eyes as the rifle came up into line. Dundee threw himself off the bay as the first shot ex-

ploded. He went down on his hands and knees. For a couple of seconds he was shielded by the frightened horse. He used that time to
get moving toward another section of rock fence. He vaulted over
and dropped behind it as the rifle cracked again.

At the house he heard Millie screaming. He glanced in that direction and saw Uncle Ollie hobbling up as fast as he could from the
spring. Millie ran toward the corral, crying: "Warren! Dundee!"

Dundee raised up enough to see over the fence. He leveled the
pistol where he thought Warren would come up. He saw the top of
Warren's head, then the rifle. Warren arose, drawing a bead. This
time, Dundee knew with a sickening certainty, Warren wasn't going
to miss. Not if Dundee let him fire.

Dundee squeezed the trigger. He saw Warren lurch back, heard
the rifle clatter against the stone. He jumped up and ran around the
fence. Under his breath he was praying.

He stopped abruptly, his blood cold. He turned then, Millie
came running, crying. "Warren! What did you do to Warren?"

Dundee grabbed her. "Millie, don't go back there!"

She beat at him with her fists. Hysterically she screamed: "Let
me go! Let me go!" She twisted away from him and ran on. At the
fence she stopped, her voice lifting in agony.

The bay had tangled in the reins a little way down toward the
house. Walking in that direction, Dundee met the struggling Ollie
McCown. The old man looked at him, his eyes begging. "God,
Dundee, how am I going to tell her?"

Dundee shook his head, his eyes afire so that he could barely see.
"I don't know, Ollie. I don't know if you ever can."

The ride to town was one of the longest Dundee had ever made,
seemed like. It was full dark long before he got there. He found the
cowboys scattered in the buildings up and down the long, crooked
street. The Rangers had arrived to take charge and collect any pris-

oners on whom they had claims. Katy Long was back in her saloon, serving liquor to John Titus.

The old man looked up as Dundee walked through the door into the lamplight. His eyes seemed to have softened now. Maybe it was Katy's whisky.

"Dundee, where's McCown?"

Tightly Dundee said, "He's dead."

The old man nodded gravely. "This girl here, she told me the whole thing, once you was a long ways down the road. I reckon it was tough on you."

"Life's always been tough on me."

John Titus pushed the bottle at Dundee. Dundee took it, though he absently rolled it in his hands instead of drinking from it. "Where's Tobe Crane?"

Somebody went out and fetched the cowboy. Dundee looked up painfully. "Tobe, Warren McCown is dead. I killed him." He took a long drink then, and followed it with another. "Millie's the one who'll suffer the most. She needs somebody right now. I think she needs *you*."

The cowboy just stood and stared at him.

Impatiently Dundee demanded: "You love her, don't you? You as much as told me so."

"I love her, Dundee."

"Then go to her. She'll never need you more than she needs you now."

Tobe turned to go. Dundee said: "And Tobe . . . you be real good to that girl, you hear me?"

"I will."

Dundee turned back to the bottle. He didn't quit drinking till his head was starting to spin. It occurred to him suddenly that he hadn't seen Roan Hardesty. He half-shouted: "Where's Roan? John Titus, you promised me. . . ."

Titus shook his head. "Don't worry. Roan has took to the tulies." He pointed his stubbled chin toward Katy Long "After this girl here told me what she did, I got to thinking. When the Rangers got here, they'd take old Roan and lock him up, and he'd never see sunlight again the rest of his days. He's an old man, Roan is. He ain't got many years left."

"You mean you just let him go?"

"We was friends once. *He* remembered it. He couldn't bring himself to shoot me. After I found out the truth of what happened to Son, I couldn't bring myself to see him rot away in a cell the few years he's got left. So I told him to head south for Mexico."

"He's liable to take some of your cattle with him as he goes."

Titus looked surprised, as if that thought hadn't occurred to him. Then he shrugged. "You can't expect an old man to go hungry."

Next morning the Rangers had picked out the men they intended to take to jail. The rest of the prisoners were turned loose and advised to see how far they could get without stopping to rest their horses.

Titus' foreman, Strother James, looked down the emptying street. "It'll be a funny-looking town, nobody living in it."

Titus said: "It won't be no town atall. We're going to burn it."

"All of it?"

"Every stick. Get the men started at the job."

They began at the far end, setting the buildings afire one at a time. Some had rock walls that wouldn't burn, but the roofs would go, and the floors if they had any.

Dundee said: "Mister Titus, I got money coming. I'd like to collect it now and be on my way."

Disappointed, Titus said: "We need you here, Dundee. I was hoping you'd stay."

Dundee shook his head. "I studied on it awhile, but I'm afraid this part of the country is spoiled for me now. It's best I go on."

"Any idea where?"

"West someplace. Don't make much difference."

"I ain't got much cash with me. I'll give you all I got and send the rest on to a bank where you can pick it up. How about Pecos City?"

Dundee shrugged. "Pecos City would be all right. I expect it's a good place to get drunk."

Katy Long had her team hitched to the buckboard and was carrying out what belongings she could pack into it. A couple of cowboys were helping her load a trunk. Dundee looked down the street where the plumes of smoke were rising. They'd be to the Llano River Saloon in a few minutes now, sprinkling kerosene, striking matches.

Dundee said, "Too bad about your place here."

She didn't appear upset. "It's worn itself out anyhow. There are other places down the road, fresh places."

"Got any particular one in mind?"

"Nope. Thought I might ride along with you if it's all right. A woman alone . . . no telling what might happen."

He shook his head. "You can take care of yourself; I don't worry none about that. As for me, I got some problems to think out. It's better I ride by myself. *Adios,* Katy. Maybe I'll see you someplace."

He swung up onto his horse, nodded at John Titus and took the trail that led around the bluff and west from Runaway.

John Titus disconsolately watched him go. "Dundee's a good man. I hate to lose him."

Katy said, "*I* don't intend to lose him."

"I'm sending him some money. He's supposed to pick it up in Pecos City," Titus suggested. He looked at the girl, and his eyes came as near smiling as they had in a long time. "Whichaway you headed?"

She arched her wrist as invitation for one of the cowboys to help her into the buckboard. Half a dozen rushed to do it. Seated, she smiled back at the old ranchman.

"I've been thinking I'd try Pecos City."

She flipped the lines, and the team took her west, while the dark smoke that had been Runaway rose into the blue summer skies and slowly dissipated over the rocky Llano River hills.